Tapestry of Life

Tapestry of Life

ALF RATTIGAN

2012

Fastnet Books
227 Donnelly Street
Armidale, New South Wales, 2350
Australia

www.fastnetbooks.net

publishing@fastnetbooks.net

First published 2012

National Library of Australia
Cataloguing-in-Publication entry:

Rattigan, Godfrey Alfred — 1911-2000
Tapestry of Life

ISBN-13: 978-0987171252
ISBN-10: 0987171259

For Win, who heard these stories first hand during almost 60 years of marriage.

CONTENTS

INTRODUCTION

Godfrey Alfred Rattigan was born in 1911 in the remote Western Australian gold-mining town of Kalgoorlie. With the rare exception of the most formal of occasions and documents, throughout his life he was invariably known as 'Alf', a fact that enabled him, when asked why he had declined a knighthood (offered some years before his retirement), to joke that he could not countenance the possibility of being referred to as 'Sir Alf' at his bowling club. He added that his wife, Win, could not imagine being called 'Lady Rattigan'. While this may be seen as evidence of Alf's puckish sense of humour (on display in many of the stories in this collection), it also speaks to Alf's firmly entrenched probity. Given the many battles he had with a number of ministers and senior public servants (details may be found in his factual account of those years, *Industry Assistance: The Inside Story* [Melbourne University Press, 1986]), Alf may well have felt the offer of such a conspicuous 'honour' was far from politically disinterested.

Alf was most prominent publically (and politically) in the years in which he was Chairman of the Tariff Board (1963-1973) and Chairman of the Industries Assistance Commission (1973-1976), years crucial in historical and continuing ways for the Australian economy that, nonetheless, find little or no mention in short stories that follow. Instead, and in the absence of an autobiography, these stories draw on incidents and individuals, places and events that formed part of the 'tapestry' of (mainly) Alf's early life. Do these stories altogether constitute a memoir? Yes and no – as Alf himself explained (in an undated and handwritten note found amongst his papers):

> *I have been connected in one way or another with the events on which each of these stories is based but the 'I' in some instances is not Alf Rattigan. All the details are not necessarily strictly historically correct. (In some cases I have altered them to help the theme of the story.) But I have tried to depict fairly accurately the attitudes of people, living and working conditions at the time in which the events in each story are placed.*

Alf's father, also Godfrey, had been born in County Roscommon, Ireland in 1874 and had migrated to the (then) Colony of Victoria with his parents, grandmother and eleven of his siblings in 1883. (Alf was occasionally described as having an Irish sense of humour and an 'unmistakeably Irish face'. If the latter is so, it must also be observed he did not bear a close physical resemblance to his father. As will be noted, Alf did not know his father well enough to have got his sense of humour from him.) By 1901, Godfrey was living in Perth, Western Australia where he was a fireman at the Metropolitan Fire Station. At the time of his marriage to Jeannie Handford (who was usually known by her step-father's surname of Cole) in 1909, Godfrey was described (on the marriage certificate) as an 'electrical engineer'. Jeannie's family background is less transparent. Her mother, Louisa Bowen, seems to have left Jeannie's father, William Handford, shortly after Jeanne's birth and to have married (possibly bigamously) a William Cole (by whom she had a further five children). At some point, this second family lived in Brisbane, Queensland, which may account for the reference by the first-person narrator in 'A Marvellous Encounter' of his mother coming from Brisbane.

In an obituary that appeared in *The Australian*, written by a close colleague and friend, it was asserted that Alf's motivations and actions as a public servant were driven by 'his determination to overcome the deprivation he experienced early in life'. It is not quite clear what form this deprivation may have taken but two events in his childhood do find reflections in a number of the stories here. The first is the separation of his parents. This seems to have happened when Alf was about ten or eleven years old. An absent father forms the background to two first-person narratives in his stories: 'A Marvellous Encounter' (in which the narrator dates the event to when he was two) and 'A Brown Purse' (where the narrator is even younger when this occurs). The placing of the departure of the father of two (different) narrators at such an early age may simply be a literary convenience to allow the narrator to say little or nothing about him. However, the absence of the father is important in both cases, and arguably in Alf's real history, because of the manner in which this affected the way Alf, his mother and his siblings – these latter vary in the two stories just mentioned – lived from then on. The details of this, such as the wooden packing case furniture, or his mother's employment as a 'temporary' teacher, are substantially the same in both stories, and were clearly such as to impinge strongly on Alf's attitudes and memories and thus to give some credence to any notions of 'deprivation'.

The second, and arguably more important event, followed on from the first. At the age of twelve, he successfully passed the entrance examination for the Royal Australian Naval College and entered the College in 1925. In the same obituary in *The Australian*, the sitting for this examination was described as being at the 'suggestion' of his mother. Anyone who knew Alf's mother would be more likely to accept it would have been at her *insistence*. The way in which the first-person narrator describes this in 'A Marvellous Encounter' is strangely self-pitying, at odds with the usual detached, albeit amused, observational tone of nearly all these stories.

Alf completed his secondary education at the Naval College, graduated as a midshipman, and seemed set for a career as an officer in the Royal Australian Navy. His years at the Naval College and then in the RAN have not provided any characters or incidents for any of these stories, other than to explain how he came to be on the train where the first-person narrator meets another traveller who tells him the tale that is substance of 'A Journey Around the World'. In any case, like most of his generation, Alf was affected by the Depression of the 'thirties and cost-cutting (what would now be called 'down-sizing') in the Navy led to his being discharged in 1930.

For reasons not clear (but presumably bureaucratic procedure), Alf returned to Western Australia – despite, it may be conjectured, the problems of his relationship with his mother. In his own words (in a speech many years later to Probus, a club for 'active retirees'), he 'was offered and accepted a position of base grade clerk in the Commonwealth Public Service'. This was to prove to be significant in personal, professional and historical terms; it was the start of a career that would see Alf become one of Australia's most outstanding and influential public servants.

After a short period at the Australian Taxation Office in Perth, Alf was promoted in 1934, to Assistant Wharf Examining Officer in the Department of Trade and Customs in Fremantle. In 1937, internal promotion took him to Canberra, which, service in World War 2 and overseas appointments notwithstanding, was his home for the rest of his life. He married in 1940. His time in the Customs has provided the substance of a number of stories in these pages: 'The Senior Inspector', 'Christmas Day', 'See 'Um Peter', and 'The Collector and the Gun'.

Alf was recalled to the Royal Australian Navy in 1942. He served most of this time at HMAS *Melville,* the naval base for the RAN in Darwin. This provides the background and some of the details for 'A Nutmeg Pigeon'. Naval service also provides a key event in the story 'A Marvellous Encounter'.

At the end of 1944, Alf was recalled from the RAN to Customs and Trade in Canberra. In 1946, somewhat to his surprise, given most of his public service had been with the Customs side of the Department, he became part of the Australian delegation to a series of overseas conferences on international trade. These occasions provided more grist to his mill and find reflection in incidents and characters in 'Dressing for the Occasion', 'The Irish Connection', and 'The Confession'. Alf was certainly a member of the quite numerous Australian delegation to the Havana Conference in 1947, the location of main incidents in 'Dressing for the Occasion'. He was also a member of an even larger delegation to the trade talks in Geneva that preceded it in the same year and which provided material for 'The Irish Connection'. (It would possible to conjecture which of the other delegates with Irish surnames are those mentioned pseudonymously in this story, but, even at this distance, perhaps not appropriate to do so.)

After his return from overseas duties, which included a time in London (that has not supplied any material for stories), Alf took various important positions within the newly created Department of Trade and Industry. This has provided the material for one story, 'The Copper Problem', in which, for a rare moment, Alf allows his detachment from the less seemly side of politics and bureaucracy to slip.

Alf's post-war star continued in the ascendant: in turn he was appointed First Assistant Secretary in the Department of Trade and Industry, Deputy Secretary, acting Secretary and then in 1960, appointed Comptroller-General of Customs. With the exception of a mention that the narrator of 'The Senior Inspector' occupies that last position and the aforementioned 'The Copper Problem', there is nothing in any of the stories that seems to draw directly or indirectly on these years and these experiences. The same is true of the years in which Alf was chairman of the Tariff Board or the Industries Assistance Commission. This may well be because of normal public service discretion or because he has said all he has to say, of the Tariff Board and the Industries Commission at least, in the nearly three-hundred pages of *Industries Assistance; The Inside Story*. There is one passing exception: 'The 13/16th Buttonhole Attachment for a Singer Sewing Machine' which relates an amusing 'adventure' that arises simply because of a tariff 'issue'. It takes place, according to the precise date given in the story itself, towards the end of Alf's period at the Department of Trade and Industry and, not peripherally, reflects on the activities of that Department.

If some sort of rough chronology is applied to these stories, it may be found that a few take place in the years after Alf's twenty years of the high-ranking public service. 'On Tour with a Garden Club' is specifically dated to take place after Alf's retirement (and is presumably based upon a real-life incident like most of these stories). However, the greater proportion of the stories takes place in the 1930s, 1940s and early 1950s. Even 'On Tour with a Garden Club' is concerned with events which took place (are told to the narrator-interlocutor) around the beginning of the twentieth century. This story is also worth noting for another reason. Its internal narrative is disrupted by 'asides' where the person to whom the main tale is being told (the first-person narrator of the whole story) takes time to describe plants, gardens and the landscape the tour touches upon. An interest in plants, especially native plants, was indeed an interest of Alf's and in several stories – 'A Pruner's Funeral' and 'Aunt Molly Should Have a Turn' (two of the most deliberately humorous in this collection) – plants and gardens have significant roles to play.

Nonetheless, for reasons both as speculated above and possibly personal, these stories are for the most part of events, characters and places that figured (in one way or another) in the first part of Alf's life. Perhaps these incidents were (or seemed) more vivid, more lasting (as effects or as memories).

Given both the muted playfulness and the strong sense of reality with which these stories are told, it is difficult to see within them much of the psychology, indeed, the psyche of Alf Rattigan. Of course, it may well be asked in this regard why then he wrote them down at all. But at least two stories suggest themselves as revealing in a deeper, subconscious way. There is no doubt, as his dealings with often hostile politicians and opponents during the Tariff Board and IAC years showed, Alf was a person of great, even unshakeable personal integrity. (As politicians by definition favour expediency over integrity, such 'clashes' were almost inevitable.) Where did this sense of integrity come from? One story, the only detailed 'reminiscence' of his childhood, is suggestive in this regard. The lessons learned by the (unnamed) boy at the centre of 'A Brown Purse' from his exposure to adult duplicity and prejudice may well be seen to be formative in this regard. One other story invites an allegorical reading: 'A Trip around the World'. This story seems the most 'fictional' of all the stories in the way in which its narrative posits a plot of the continued thwarting of a search for evidence of the truth as well as an exciting climax when all seems lost. But the story is also an allegory of the need for persistence in the face of malevolence, mendacity and prejudice and of the eventual vindication through revelation of the truth.

In the final analysis, despite his prominent public service positions and despite his actions (or those of his Board and Commission) receiving considerable attention (not always positive or flattering) in political, financial and industries circles (including the media), Alf Rattigan was a very private person. No story he wrote seems to draw directly upon or even mention the actual circumstances of his own immediate family. He was married for sixty years and had three children but nothing of this finds reflection in these pages (with perhaps the unique exception of the anonymous wife who instigates the actions of 'The 13/16th Buttonhole Attachment for a Singer Sewing Machine'). Other 'wives', other liaisons are mentioned in some stories – 'The Nutmeg Pigeon' notably – but these are totally fictional.

Alf's 'family', in a broader sense than wife and children, are mentioned (or serve story purposes) but only rarely. Admittedly his mother, as noted previously, did serve as the 'model' for the childhood mother in 'The Brown Purse' and 'A Marvellous Encounter' – the details are identical in both cases and very much correspond to Alf's mother. He does however draw upon members of his family in some other stories. This is particularly true of 'The Cannibal in the Family'. Alf did indeed have an uncle (by marriage) who had been a missionary in New Guinea and who, after retirement to England, did select restaurants on the basis amusingly described in that story. Alf did have an actual Aunt Ruby (again by marriage but not a 'courtesy aunt') but whether she matched the redoubtable figure of 'Aunt Ruby' in 'A Well Trained Executive Takes the Cake' is not known. It is, in fact, more likely some of the behaviour attributed to 'Aunt Ruby' is drawn from Alf's wife, including the garbage bins full of cake-making ingredients. The 'well-trained executive' of this story is possibly loosely based on one of Alf's brothers, who is also quite likely the inspiration for the protagonist of 'The Parcel' (one of the few third-person stories in this collection).

A memoir is usually considered to be 'a record of events or history from personal knowledge or from special sources of information'. Elements of many of the stories collected here suggest, as a whole, this volume may well serve as the memoirs of Alf Rattigan. As noted, Alf claimed that he had 'tried to depict fairly accurately the attitudes of people, living and working conditions at the time in which the events in each story are placed'. As such, and taking this claim at face value, it is possible to argue that these stories do provide (perhaps) small, personal but valuable glimpses of aspects of Australian social history, at life in Australia, at Australians, in the twentieth-century (the second half of which Alf Rattigan affected in fundamental ways not hinted at in this self-effacing 'memoir'). As such, the stories, separately and together, furnish (in an apparent paradox) a written oral history. This notion is enhanced by the fact that these stories in many instances take the form of a story being told to the listening narrator. Even those that do not take this structure have much of the form or feel of a spoken story. This is hardly surprising. As Alf's family and friends could readily testify, long before he wrote them down, Alf had verbally rehearsed his stories – these and others he did not (sadly) write down. Those that he did are reproduced here just as he wrote them.

CUSTOMS DUTY

THE SENIOR INSPECTOR

For about two decades after federation the staff of the Western Australian Branch of the Australian Customs Department was, in many respects, isolated from the rest of the Departmental officers. Senior officials in the head office had met the Collector (who spent a week in Melbourne in 1902) but neither they nor the staff in the branches throughout the eastern states had any opportunity of becoming familiar with the appearance and personality of their other colleagues working beyond the thousand miles of desert that separated Western Australia from the remainder of the Federation.

The second highest officer in Western Australia during most of those two decades was Senior Inspector Gould. Gould, who had risen quickly through the service in pre-federation days (some said because of his family's influence), had reached that position at a relatively early age. He was unusual in both appearance and personality. Very short (well under five feet), rather rotund and a little bow-legged, he had an unsmiling face, a fierce temper, a loud voice and a very authoritative manner.

Because, he claimed, it was necessary for him to keep in touch with the business community, Gould left the Customs House at 4 pm each Wednesday afternoon to join the President of the Shipping Association in a game of golf at a club to which they both belonged. Gould came to work each Wednesday morning dressed in his golfing outfit – very baggy plus fours, a long jacket and a cap with a huge peak, all made from the most gaudy check material ever produced. In this outfit, Gould set off at 4 pm each Wednesday marching – head held up (with face barely visible under the cap), back straight, arms swinging high and rhythmically – through the town towards the office of the President of the Shipping Association. As the awesome figure approached, dogs barked, horses bolted, children cried and women fainted. It must be remembered that this was well before the feminism virus had infected a large part of the female human population, a time when women were women, delightful, pretty, frail, demure creatures likely to faint on the slightest provocation and whose spirits could be restored, not by smelling salts as depicted in novels, but by sweet, comforting words and a little cuddling.

The Senior Inspector's main claim to fame was his ability to identify, track down and take into custody illegal Chinese migrants. He was always on the look-out for the yellow-coloured, slant-eyed defiers of the Immigration

3

law and asserted he could, by close observation, readily distinguish an illegal from a legal Chinese migrant. Although his activities in support of the White Australia Policy pleased the higher authorities, they did not always please his subordinates. One of these, a friend of mine, Bill Frost, claimed his life had been ruined by the Senior Inspector's activities.

Bill, a cheerful, handsome fellow with a very attractive smile, was liked by almost everyone and especially by women. But he was not quick in the uptake and tended to jump to conclusions. His ruination came about through several events in 1921 which he recounted to me at that time. Sixty years later I cannot recall precisely what he told me but this is broadly how he said it all happened.

Upon a windy spring day Bill was sent from the Customs House in Fremantle to Perth to get as quickly as possible a sample of some goods held in a bonded warehouse. As he was walking from the Perth Railway Station towards the warehouse he saw approaching him the most beautiful girl in the world. Suddenly the wind seized the girl's natty little hat and blew it in his direction. Making a great leap Bill grabbed the hat and restored it to the girl. This acrobatic feat led to the girl having a cup of tea with him (quite hurriedly because both of them were on urgent missions) and agreeing to meet him at 7.45 pm on the following Wednesday outside a local cinema.

When the evening came, dressed in his best suit and a new tie especially bought for the occasion, Bill caught the 6.50 pm train from Fremantle to Perth. He was alone in a compartment as far as North Fremantle when a Chinaman got in. At Claremont Senior Inspector Gould became the third passenger in the compartment. As soon as he was seated the Senior Inspector fixed his attention on the Chinaman. Bill had never before seen the Senior Inspector in action deciding by observation whether a Chinaman was a legal or illegal immigrant. He watched the process with great interest, got immersed in it, forgot the Senior Inspector's fearsome reputation and excitedly awaited the outcome. After the oriental gentleman had been under the Senior Inspector's unrelenting gaze for a while he began to look uncomfortable and twist and turn a little. When they were getting close to West Perth he got up and stood near the door. Before the train had completely stopped at the station he opened the door and jumped rather than stepped off. The Senior Inspector turned to Bill and barked 'After him Frost, after him, and tell me in the morning where he went'.

Bill (like the rest of us at that time) was used to obeying orders from senior officers wheresoever and whensoever they were given. He got out of the train in something of a daze, hurried up the platform, left the station, crossed Railway Street and followed the Chinaman up Fitzgerald Street Then he came out of his daze, said to himself 'What the hell am I doing, I've got to meet the girl' and dashed back to the station.

The next train to Perth was due in half an hour. Bill paced up and down the platform biting his nails and cursing the Senior Inspector. When the train did not turn up on time he nearly drove the porter on duty crazy with demands to find out what had happened. The train eventually arrived ten minutes late. Bill did not get to the cinema until 8.30. There was no sign of the girl. Although he waited, fretting, until the end of the show and all the audience had left, she was not to be seen. All he knew about her was her name, Nancy Brown.

Bill realised he had two problems to tackle: how to find Nancy Brown and what to say to the Senior Inspector. The second was the more immediate and it occupied his mind the next morning while dressing, breakfasting and travelling, but by the time he reached the Customs House he had thought of a way of tackling it.

Only a short walk from the West Perth Railway Station, in Roe Street, there was the most famous (or notorious) collection of brothels in the metropolitan area. Bill went to the Senior Inspector's Office and told the fearsome occupant that the Chinaman had disappeared into the second brothel along Roe Street from its junction with Fitzgerald Street.

Bill had worked out that giving a brothel as the man's destination would indicate that the Chinaman was a well-established Australian citizen who had gone to West Perth for an evening's entertainment and that therefore no further action would be taken. How wrong he was! The Senior Inspector exclaimed 'Ah, that's where he's hiding!' and promptly ordered two investigation officers accompanied by Bill to extricate the Chinaman from the brothel and bring him to the Customs House.

The law, which at that time gave Customs Officers the power to search, seize, detain etc. was based on some old British legislation. It gave Customs Officers unlimited authority to enter premises, break down doors or other obstructions, seize vehicles, dig up gardens, chop down trees, search cupboards, desks, containers, safes and people, and detain anyone they didn't like the look of, all in the name of the King – God bless him. Other law enforcement officers in Australia were tied up with red tape. They had to get the approval of a magistrate or some similar authority before doing most of those things.

When Bill and the two investigation officers hammered on the door of the brothel in West Perth, the startled inmates soon found that the visitors were not eager clients demanding prompt attention but Customs Officers searching for some – undisclosed – illegal import. Not finding the Chinaman in the first one, the diligent officers carried on with the good work by thoroughly searching every brothel in Roe Street. They found no sign of the Chinaman.

When they returned to Fremantle and reported to the Senior Inspector, they were loudly upbraided. If he had been there, he shouted, the Chinaman would have been discovered wherever hidden. Of course Bill had a sound reason for doubting that prediction but he didn't mention it.

During the following week-end Bill began his search for Nancy Brown. First he rang up all the Browns in the telephone book – not one of them knew anything about a Nancy. He then asked a friend who worked in the Electoral Office to go through the electoral roll. A few weeks later his friend told him that Nancy lived in Maylands. On the following Saturday, once again dressed in his best suit and new tie, Bill, tremendously excited, made his way to the address in Maylands. He was just about to ring the front door bell when the door was opened by a handsome middle-aged woman obviously dressed to go out. Bill said he had never considered what sort of a mother Nancy might have but was very pleased to see that she had such an attractive-looking one. When he smiled at Mrs Brown she smiled back very pleasantly and asked 'Who are you?'

Bill replied 'I'm Bill Frost and I would like to talk to Nancy Brown'.

'Would you, indeed! I'm just about to go into town. What do you want to say to Nancy Brown?'

'I want to ask her to have lunch with me at a very nice little restaurant just off The Esplanade'.

'You don't beat about the bush, do you? Good heavens! There's the bus! Come on we'll have to run'.

Bill assumed that Nancy was already in the city and ran with Mrs Brown to the bus stop a few metres from the Brown's front gate.

That Saturday was a very important one in Perth – the football grand final day. The bus, the railway station and the train were all packed with boisterous football followers shouting their team's slogan and singing their team's song. Caught up in this hubbub, Bill had considerable difficulty just keeping an eye on Mrs Brown's whereabouts and had no opportunity to talk to her.

They both separately detached themselves from the crowd milling around outside the Perth station by starting to walk across Wellington Street in the direction of Boan's department store. When they got together Mrs Brown said, 'I want to buy a light cardigan; you don't mind if we do that first?'

Very pleased that his meeting with Nancy was close at hand and anxious to get on well with her mother, Bill replied, 'Not at all'.

Mrs Brown's next question surprised him. 'Did you go to the war?'

When he told her was too young she went on to say that she was a war widow, her husband had been killed in the battle of Hargicourt in September 1918 after he had been in France for two years and fought in several important battles which she mentioned. By the time that conversation had finished they had reached the women's garment section of Boan's store.

The purchase of the cardigan was a long drawn-out affair. They walked through practically the whole shopping area in the City of Perth and went into every departmental store and every specialty shop selling women's clothing. Every type of cardigan in every shop was tried on and Bill's opinion asked for on practically every aspect of every garment − did the colour suit her?; was the pattern attractive?; was the cardigan too long or too short?; did the shoulders fit?; would it be too warm?; were the sleeves right? and so on. Bill, even more anxious to establish himself with Mrs Brown now he knew she was Nancy's only parent, racked his brain to offer sensible comment, took in good part the fun she frequently poked at what he said and, with feigned cheerfulness, accepted her coquettish, affected, playful attitude towards him, although embarrassed and disappointed by it.

A cardigan was eventually chosen and while Mrs Brown was paying for it Bill put out of his mind the dreadful shopping expedition and basked in the joy he felt at the prospect of soon being with Nancy.

As they came out of the shop Mrs Brown said, 'Now I'm ready for lunch'.

Bill had by that time accepted that he would have to take Mrs Brown as well as Nancy to lunch but was surprised when Mrs Brown did not mention where they were going to meet Nancy. He asked, 'Where is Nancy?'

'What do you mean "Where's Nancy?"'

Puzzled Bill said, 'Your daughter Nancy, where is she?'

'What on earth are you talking about, I haven't any children'.

Bill stood for a moment completely dumbfounded but then the ridiculous situation he had got himself into became clear. As Mrs Brown was calling him an idiot he said, so loudly that it attracted the attention of people passing by, 'I'm very sorry', dashed away through the town to the railway station and caught a train to Fremantle.

About a month later Bill was able to take a week's leave. Each day he spent walking up and down William Street where he had met Nancy on that wonderful spring morning, he asked people working in shops and offices along the street, even passers-by, he described her a hundred times, but nobody knew Nancy Brown. He returned to work at the end of the week footsore, bitterly disappointed and depressed.

Unable to think of any other line of inquiry, Bill went about his affairs expressing his discontent not only by cursing the Senior Inspector every day but also by having his *bete noir* vilified in a more ceremonial way once a week. After work each Friday Bill went to the Fremantle Hotel for a few drinks with some fellow-workers. As the drinking session was drawing to a close, Bill always offered to shout a drink for anyone who would join him in cursing the Senior Inspector. With great vigour and appropriate gravity all his workmates, without hesitation, joined Bill in the weekly ritual.

•

Although, as one of Bill's workmates, I vilified the Senior Inspector every Friday, I did so with some mental reservation. My association with the Senior Inspector differed greatly from Bill's; he helped me become the first active conservationist, certainly in Australia and probably in the world. To explain how that came about I must first mention my position in the Department. I was the Landing Inspector's Clerk. I worked in his office, at his desk, alongside his 'phone because the Landing Inspector (David Stockham) was busy all day outside the Customs House resolving problems at the wharves and in the cargo sheds.

The door of the Landing Inspector's Office was always open. This enabled members of the staff and the public who wanted to discuss something to look in and decide whether to talk to the clerk – me – or go off and try and find the Inspector. Sitting in the Landing Inspector's chair, I had a clear view of the short passage running at right angles to the office I shared with the Inspector. One side of the passage was the back wall of the

Invoice Room. On the other side there was, first of all, the Senior Inspector's Office, then a toilet, beyond that a kitchenette and finally a room inhabited by two Amazons only slightly disguised as large, middle-aged typistes – their spears and bows and arrows at the ready were not visible to the casual observer but hidden in the cupboard at the back of the room.

Watching the daily movements along the passage of the three members of the Customs staff accommodated in rooms off it was constantly interesting.

It was well known in the Customs House that both the Collector and the Senior Inspector were wont to discuss at length the many fine points which arose day by day in the administration of the complicated Customs legislation. At least three or four times a week I saw the Senior Inspector with furrowed brow leave his office carrying several files and I knew he was on his way to discuss some current problems with the Collector.

After I had been the Landing Inspector's Clerk for several months I could estimate with a reasonable degree of accuracy – from the number and size of the files he carried – how long the Senior Inspector would be away. My ability to make these accurate estimates was of great importance in preventing a waste of the world's resources.

One of the duties of the Amazons was to bring a cup of tea twice a day to each of the inspectors located on the ground floor (except, of course, the Landing Inspector who was only nominally located there). This duty they carried out punctually at 10.30 in the morning and 3.30 in the afternoon and with similar punctuality twenty minutes after delivering the tea they collected the cups and saucers. Several times each week an Amazon carried away from the Senior Inspector's office a cup full of tea which, I soon discovered, was poured down the drain in the kitchenette.

The terrible waste of tea, milk, sugar (the Senior Inspector took at least two teaspoons full), water and electricity (required to heat the water) was placing a strain on the world's resources. It had to be stopped. Whenever I judged that this waste was likely to occur I went into the Senior Inspector's Office and drank his tea. Whilst it was always the right temperature, of the right strength and had the right amount of milk, it was not quite to my taste – a little too sweet – but I bore the blemish manfully.

The work I did week after week to protect the biosphere in this way was not undertaken lightly. It required not only careful observation, good judgement, accurate timing but also great courage. My career would be at risk if the Senior Inspector caught me, my life would be at risk if one of the Amazons caught me.

One day I had come out of the Senior Inspector's office after drinking his tea and was walking down the passage towards 'my' office when the Senior Inspector came round the corner. My heart stopped. However, as soon as he saw me he asked, 'Has Stockham a copy of Siemen's first edition?' (Siemen was a lawyer who during the first decade after Federation wrote about Customs Law).

'Yes'.

'Give it to me'.

He followed me into my office. About five or six minutes remained before one of the Amazons would collect the empty cup. How could I keep him out of his own office for that length of time? I knew Siemen's book was at the right hand end of the upper shelf. I started to look at the left hand end of the lower shelf. I had not got very far before the Senior Inspector asked, 'Is there something wrong with your eyes?', walked along the shelves and pulled the book off the upper shelf.

I hoped he would remain there, open the book and search for whatever he was after. But he didn't. He started to walk towards the door. The only way of stopping him which immediately came to my mind was throwing myself on the floor and pretending I was having an epileptic fit. But I hesitated − uncertain as to whether could carry it off − and the Senior Inspector brushed past me. In a loud voice I asked, 'Is there anything else you want, Sir?'

He paused, turned slightly towards me, said, 'Why are you shouting? I'm not deaf', then, without answering my question, walked out of the office. But instead of going straight on towards his own room, he turned to the right and disappeared in the direction of the Collector's office.

I leaned against the desk and took a deep breath.

My alarming encounter with the Senior Inspector made me consider ceasing my conservational activities. For a week I did not take any action, but then courageously decided that as the welfare of the human race was at stake I should continue to prevent the dreadful waste of resources.

•

My conservation activities ended in 1922. That year the Comptroller-General of Customs apparently decided to bring some of the Western Australian officers over to the Eastern States. I was promoted to a position in the head office in Melbourne and Senior Inspector Gould was promoted to Collector, Tasmania.

About six months after I took up my position, Barry Howe from the Tasmanian branch was brought to the head office to assist me. Finding that I knew Gould, he told me about both the situation in the Tasmanian Branch before Gould took up the position of Collector and what happened on the day that Gould arrived in Hobart.

He said that when in 1921 the Tasmanian Collector died suddenly the Senior Inspector, Ray Conrad, became the Acting Collector. Conrad had joined the Customs Department in Hobart and had remained there, steadily advancing in the service, for nearly forty years. A big, white-haired, handsome man, he knew every member of the staff and of the public who had regular business with the Department. He was very well thought of by both the staff and the public. Everyone expected he would be appointed Collector. Unlike most of the senior officers in the Public Service at that time, Conrad was very approachable. It was typical of him that while Acting Collector he worked with his office door open so that any member of the staff who wanted to talk to him could walk straight in.

Gould's appointment as Collector after Conrad had been acting in the position for nine months came as a great shock to everyone in Tasmania.

The outrageous treatment of one of their own by some bureaucrats in Melbourne was not something Tasmanians were prepared to accept lying down. At a public meeting attended by businessmen, concerned citizens and customs officers, the extraordinary step was taken of sending to the Comptroller-General a letter of protest signed by all present at the meeting except the customs officers. The Comptroller-General replied quite quickly simply saying that he had to take into account the staff available throughout Australia when making appointments.

Gould lost no time in leaving the West to take up his new position. While making his way to Tasmania he bought a 'T' model Ford car in Melbourne; he and it crossed the Bass Straight to Devonport on the same ship. From Devonport Gould drove down to Hobart dressed in his golfing outfit (including the large peaked cap) presumably because he considered it the most comfortable clothing in which to travel.

Apparently his journey across Tasmania was not without incident. A few days after he arrived in Hobart a story reached the city about a very small, rotund man in a flamboyant golfing outfit driving a 'T' model Ford who stopped in Hadspen to buy two meat pies and some petrol. A woman in the baker's shop immediately recognised him as one of the two dwarf clowns she

11

had seen during the previous week-end performing in a circus set up on the outskirts of Launceston. She very quickly spread the news around the town and while the clown was having his car's tank filled at the petrol station the woman and a group of people gathered around him and asked about the funny things he did in the circus ring. He kept the group amused by pretending he was very annoyed, saying he had nothing to do with the circus, that he was the Collector of Customs and if they didn't treat him with more respect he would have every house and business premise in the town thoroughly searched for illicit stills, moonshine liquor, smuggled goods and illegal migrants.

When he reached Hobart Gould was seen to park his car and enter the Customs House through the main door. Inside he accosted an Invoice Officer named Keating who was passing through the entrance hall carrying some documents. In his authoritative manner Gould snapped 'Take me to the Collector's office'.

Strangers did not often come into the Hobart Customs House and Keating, a man of considerable curiosity but few words, was amazed at the sight of this extraordinarily-dressed, little, rotund, bow-legged man with his face barely visible under a huge peaked cap striding into the Customs House and demanding to be taken to the Collector's office. But Keating didn't ask any questions, he told the stranger to follow him and silently walked ahead. When they reached the Collector's office, he said 'Here it is', then remained at the open door to discover the very odd-looking visitor's business with the Collector.

What happened in the next few minutes so surprised Keating that, for a while, he ceased to be very sparing with words and went around the Customs House recounting at length the dramatic event in which he had participated.

He said, after describing how the extraordinary-looking little man accosted him and followed him to the Collector's office, that when the man marched rather than walked into the office Conrad had his head down working at his desk but on hearing someone coming in, looked up. Obviously surprised by what he saw Conrad asked, 'Who are you?'

In a very loud voice the visitor announced, 'The Collector!'

Falling back a bit in his chair Conrad exclaimed 'Good God!! You can't be!'

•

12

Twenty-three years later, after working for a while in another department, I returned to Customs as the permanent head, the Comptroller-General. Immediately after taking up that position I set off to visit all the state branches, starting with the more remote.

I went first to Tasmania. On my second day there I asked the current Collector, Sam Lemon, who had worked in Tasmania throughout his career, how Gould had got on as Collector. Sam told me that although Gould was very knowledgeable about Customs matters and not a bad administrator, his arrogant manner, eccentricities and aloofness put him, right from the beginning, at odds with the staff and some of the business community. Two questions Gould asked at his first meeting with the senior staff greatly surprised everyone. He asked where the Chinese community was located and seemed disappointed when told there was none; the only Chinese in the state had left twenty years earlier when the tin they were mining ran out. Then he asked for the names and positions of important men doing business with the Department who played golf. By following up the answers to the second question, Gould established an arrangement to play golf every Wednesday with the President of the Chamber of Commerce – Bert Kelly – a semi-retired Customs Agent.

Sam then aroused my curiosity by adding that Gould's aloofness had been, however, penetrated by two people; first by a young businessman and later on by a middle-aged woman. Intrigued, I got him to tell me about both these remarkable people.

'The young businessman was Harry Rimmer the manager of the Tasmanian branch of Rimmer Pty Ltd, a Melbourne-based firm (established by Harry's father) which imported, manufactured and distributed haberdashery and women's underwear. Gould met Rimmer through his golf. Kelly, it seems, insisted that the game each Wednesday be a foursome – probably he did not like the prospect of having Gould as his sole companion for three to four hours each week – and Rimmer was one of the four. The other member of the four was a neighbour of mine, Ted Parkinson, an Indent Agent and Importer whose business activities were to some extent in competition with Rimmer's. Both men undoubtedly wanted to have a good relationship with the new Collector. They were, however, quite different; Rimmer young, genial with a lively sense of humour; Parkinson middle-aged, dour, narrow-minded, strict Methodist.

13

'From time to time Parkinson talked to me over the fence about the weekly game of golf. It seemed that from the beginning Rimmer somehow got on well with Gould and his success annoyed Parkinson. Parkinson maintained that Rimmer set out to monopolise the Collector's attention – even playing his shots in a way which enabled him to be close to Gould when the other members of the foursome were not.

'Towards the end of the foursome's first year, Parkinson told me that Rimmer, throughout a round had chatted about women's legs in a distasteful way. When he gave me a detailed account of it I thought Rimmer's 'distasteful chatting' was an interesting portrayal of a dramatic change in women's clothing and, from what happened later on, apparently so did Gould.

'Rimmer said that for as long as anyone could remember – certainly in fashionable circles – women's skirts had reached the ground, but after the war they had begun to get shorter and shorter and reveal more and more the shapeliness of women's legs. With the change in the length of women's skirts he said a change had come in the material used in the manufacture of stockings. In the days when the skirts reached the ground the stockings were made of cotton or woollen material; when skirts became shorter, rayon (or to a limited extent silk) was used to make the part of the stocking visible below the skirt. In Rimmer's opinion the silky look of rayon made women's legs much more alluring and he predicted that soon the whole of the stocking would be made of rayon.

'Several weeks later Parkinson told me that Rimmer had once again referred to women's skirts and stockings; he had asserted that women's skirts were so short that many women were insisting on having stockings made wholly of rayon. Rimmer had then alarmed Parkinson – who imported stockings – by stating that rayon stockings should be produced in Australia, although a substantial Customs duty would be required to ensure that the production was profitable. Parkinson had apparently become even more alarmed when Gould suggested that Rimmer come to his office and discuss the matter. Considerably upset, Parkinson said to me that it was improper for Gould to discuss such a matter with Rimmer'.

Sam went on to say that he was doing a stint as Chief Clerk when the discussions between Rimmer and Gould took place and consequently was aware of the considerable assistance Gould gave Rimmer in preparing, and following up, the request that the level of Customs duty on stockings be referred to the Tariff Board. In Sam's opinion Gould did nothing improper; he simply pointed Rimmer in the right direction to get useful information and he suggested improvements in the wording of the draft request and the 'follow up' letters. Gould was, Sam thought, participating as a friend rather than a government official and, although it might have been better if the discussions had not been held in the Customs House, the ready access to official publications in the Customs House made it a very convenient place to hold them. However when the reference was eventually sent to the Board, Rimmer was recalled to Melbourne to handle the matter from his company's head office and he never returned to Tasmania. Sam was of the opinion that Rimmer's departure was unfortunate for Gould and for everyone associated with the Collector; he considered that if Rimmer's humanising influence had continued it might have changed Gould's disposition.

Having explained Rimmer's association with Gould, Sam looked at me in a questioning sort of way. I told him to go on and tell me about the middle-aged woman.

Sam said that for a very long while after he came to Hobart, Gould did not seem able to find living quarters that suited him. He moved around between three or four hotels and two or three guest houses. It was common talk around the Customs House that Gould was an only child spoilt by his mother who had continued to live in the family home until he came to Tasmania. 'I don't know from where the gossip came', Sam said, 'but probably you know whether it is true'.

I told him I didn't know anything about Gould's private life.

Sam said Gould eventually settled down at a guest house in Battery Point. Eighteen months later he created a great stir in the Customs House (and beyond it) by informing the staff clerk that he was married and that he had moved to a house on the outskirts of the city. Busy-bodies soon discovered that Gould's wife had been, for a long time, the matron of a small country hospital but, after inheriting some money, she had retired from nursing and come to live in Hobart at the guest house where Gould was staying.

Six months after the marriage, to the amazement of us all, Sam said, the couple adopted eight year old twin girls whose parents had been killed in a car crash. The Gould family did not socialise to any great extent with the families of the Customs staff. 'I remember seeing Mrs Gould with the

Collector at a staff dance only once', Sam said, 'but did see the whole family at the children's Christmas party held each year. Mrs Gould seemed an amicable woman who accepted with good humour Gould's eccentricities. At the Christmas parties Gould watched rather than participated in the children's entertainment but Mrs Gould threw herself whole-heartedly into the fun'.

After his marriage Gould obviously attempted to improve his relations with the staff; he used less abrasive language and shouted less but remained very authoritative – an attitude which might have been acceptable in Western Australia but was not acceptable in Tasmania. Sam considered that Gould, throughout his time as Collector, did not mind being unpopular but, certainly during the last few years, did mind being treated as an outsider.

Sam's account was at this point interrupted by his secretary coming into the office with tea. While we were drinking the tea, Sam recalled that during the week-end before Gould retired there had been a heavy fall of snow in Hobart and Gould and his family had made a big snowman on their lawn. A passing journalist had taken a photograph of the snowman and the family which appeared in the local paper the next day. Sam got a copy of the photo out of a drawer and gave it to me.

The photo showed Gould (looking much older than I remembered him), his wife and the two girls standing alongside a snowman about five feet high. On the head of the snowman was what looked like a straw hat, conical in shape, with a shallow crown and a broad brim, secured by two pieces of string tied together under the chin; the sort of hat I had seen many times on the head of a Chinaman working in the market gardens on the outskirts of Perth or driving a cart full of fruit and vegetables through the suburbs.

Looking at the photo I got the impression that Gould, on the eve of his departure from the service, was wistfully recalling for a while the 'good old days' in Western Australia when he was accepted without question by the staff and the public as the very formidable Senior Inspector.

CHRISTMAS DAY

When I reached Beach Street I found that Christmas Day made no difference, Matt was there sitting on the bench under the pine tree smoking the old briar pipe he had told me he was not allowed to light up in his boarding house. After we had exchanged Christmas greetings, Matt said, 'You're looking better everyday and putting on weight now. I suppose you will soon be returning to Merredin'. I nodded agreement.

Neither of us felt any pressing need to make conversation. For a while we were content to watch the waves breaking rhythmically on the sandy shore and the seagulls diving on a school of fish out in the channel. Then I asked Matt whether he could remember any interesting event which had occurred on a Christmas Day. He puffed away on his pipe for several minutes before saying in a questioning sort of way, 'A terrifying misadventure happened over forty years ago, not long after I joined the Customs. It has some moral significance?'

When I said 'That seems appropriate', this is what he told me.

'Before World War Two the Blue Funnel Company ran a weekly shipping service for passengers and cargo between Fremantle and Singapore via Java. During the summer the Blue Funnel ships brought from Java large cargos of bananas. Each cargo was unloaded into the old 'H' shed, and it was in that shed on Christmas Day 1923 that the terrifying misadventure occurred. The shed was a large rectangular building with no internal fittings and having four pairs of big sliding doors opening onto the wharf on its northern side and four pairs of similar doors opening onto a vehicle loading bay on its southern side. The unencumbered space inside the shed was so extensive that when free of cargo it was often used by the stevedores for football practice during their lunch hour.

'The bananas were taken into 'H' shed for sorting under Customs supervision. The sorting allowed the importer to put aside for destruction (also under Customs supervision) any bananas he considered were too ripe to market. He then paid Customs duty on the remainder. The sorters were regularly recruited from the men waiting about the wharf area looking for casual work. Amongst them were ex-sailors who, tired of following the sea, had found Fremantle with its mild climate and small, friendly, rather egalitarian community, a suitable place to drop anchor. One of these, Harry Darrow, had been a shipmate of mine when I first went to sea and on two

18

occasions later. Harry had become an expert splicer of wire and hemp rope. This skill enabled him to occasionally get a job repairing a cargo sling, guide rope or ship's hawser and he always carried, in a leather pouch attached to his belt, the marline-spike required for such jobs. To entertain his friends Harry frequently did juggling tricks with the marline-spike or used it, with great accuracy, as a sort of throwing knife, to hit, point first, any nominated target. If used as a weapon (which it sometimes was in the sleazy neighbourhoods of large European and Asian ports) the marline-spike was much more deadly than a knife because its weight, its tapered, cylindrical shape, highly polished surface and sharp point enabled it to penetrate much deeper into any object it hit.

'But I have digressed from the banana sorting. To comply strictly with the Customs regulations the bananas should have been sorted into two categories – those which would reach the consumers in an edible condition and those which were to be destroyed. However – with the connivance of the Customs' and importers' supervisors – the bananas were divided into three categories, the third consisted of the fruit which would not reach the consumers in an edible condition but which would be very enjoyable to eat at the time of sorting. The bananas in the third category were mostly eaten by the sorters and the supervisors during the ten minute break at the end of each two hour sorting session, but some were taken home in their dilly-bags. This illegal practice resulted in some Australian citizens eating imported bananas on which no Customs duty had been paid.

'One of the Blue Funnel ships which so regularly brought bananas to Fremantle had been christened at its launching *Gorgon* after the mythical snaked-haired female monster with an aspect so terrible that the sight of her turned her beholder into stone. It was on this ship as second mate that I spent my last two years at sea. Like every ship she had her own distinctive character, and in her case it was malevolent. She resented male domination and constantly created problems for the men who stoked her boilers, operated her engines, washed her decks, and attended to her passengers, but most of all for the men who controlled her movements.

'Those of us who knew her well expected that the *Gorgon* would one day break out of her male imposed bonds and use her formidable female powers for some purpose fraught with wanton wickedness.

'The malevolent atmosphere which pervaded the *Gorgon* reached to her cargo. From time to time quite peculiar and serious accidents occurred when freight she had carried was being handled by the stevedores on the wharf or in one of the sheds.

'In December 1923, when the *Gorgon* with a large shipment of bananas on board was steaming down the north-west coast, her captain received instructions to put into Broome to pick up a prize bull. This diversion delayed the ship's arrival at Fremantle from her scheduled time of 7 am to nearly midnight on Christmas Eve.

'I had joined the Customs Service in January 1922 and was the Customs Officer who boarded the *Gorgon* when she arrived off the entrance to Fremantle harbour on that Christmas Eve. She had hove to about a mile off the North Mole and boarding her was difficult in the very choppy sea.

'It was a wild night. A fierce north-west wind was picking up clouds of sand from the northern beaches, driving them across the breakwater, swirling them around the port area and hurtling them against the buildings in the town. There was no moon; the clouds of sand frequently blotted out both the stars and the lights along the break water and the wharf apron. For most of the time the ship moved along in pitch blackness. The passage down the harbour in these very unpleasant and dangerous conditions must have given the captain, who had permission to bring his ship in and out of harbour without a pilot, many anxious moments. When she lost steerage way as she slowed down the *Gorgon* broke away from the tug trying to keep her bow pointed east, and, driven by the north-westerly wind, came racing towards the *Swan* berthed at 'G' station. A tug making her way westward to pick up another ship at the entrance to the harbour managed to divert the *Gorgon* but she crashed alongside the wharf at 'H' station so hard that some passengers, fed up with the delay, who had gathered at the gangway hoping to disembark quickly, were flung onto the deck and two seamen who were handling a hawser required to secure the ship were thrown so heavily against the guard rail that they dropped the end of the hawser and it became jammed between the wharf and the ship. The *Gorgon* was held in position with some difficulty by two tugs while the end of the hawser was recovered. After that had been done the ship was finally secured to the wharf – much to the relief of all concerned.

'Before the *Gorgon* had reached Fremantle a decision had been taken which made a misadventure on Christmas Day while freight from the ill-omened ship was being handled on the wharf or in the shed, a possibility. The Customs authorities generally prohibited ships being 'worked' in

Australian ports on Good Friday or Christmas Day but on this occasion the Collector of Customs in Western Australia gave permission for the bananas to be unloaded and the bull to be taken off the *Gorgon* on Christmas Day.

'The two Customs Officers who volunteered to oversee the sorting of the *Gorgon*'s cargo of bananas were as different physically and in character as probably any two middle-aged men could be. Peter Pierce, a very tall, thin, bony man, was an occasional lay preacher in the Baptist church, a teetotaller and non-smoker and opposed to gambling and dancing. Lindsay Smith was a man of average height whose good figure and handsome face had been only slightly spoilt by some years of intemperate living. He had a well-earned reputation as a philanderer, narrator of bawdy stories, gambler and an occasional heavy drinker and customer of the local brothels. Both men were fond of bananas.

'But it was not only fondness for bananas which induced them to volunteer to supervise the sorting on that Christmas Day. Customs Officers were paid triple the normal rate when working on public holidays. That enabled the root of all evil, money, to play its part. Lindsay was always in need of money for his pleasures. Peter had six children and a nagging wife who did not consider her husband's religious scruples should prevent the family getting a useful sum of money and a supply of nice bananas from work done on Christmas Day, especially when Peter could attend an early morning service.

'Both Lindsay and Peter accepted the long standing practice of allowing the bananas to be sorted into three categories. We all accepted it without question at that time. Later on, after the terrible misadventure and its sequel, I found it difficult to understand why a very straight-laced man like Peter participated in the illegal practice and I wondered how much his wife was to blame and whether his attitude would have been different if he had been, like me, a bachelor. By mutual consent Lindsay took the first period from 8 am to noon and Peter from noon to the end of the sorting.

'The strong wind had ceased with the dawn and it was a still, hot morning when Peter set off at 11.45 to walk from the railway station to 'H' shed. As he approached he was astonished to see that all the big double doors had been pulled nearly closed and that the sorters, clustered in groups outside the shed, were peering in through cracks between each pair of doors.

'Peter hurried forward and when he reached the first set of doors was able to look over the heads of the sorters and get a good view of what was holding their attention. He saw hundreds of bananas, parts of trestle tables and broken crates scattered about a section of the floor. Glancing to his left he saw Lindsay crouched under a narrow jarrah table (generally used to hold shipping papers) which stood against the eastern wall of the shed. Lindsay's face was unusually pale and his gaze was riveted on something towards the other end of the shed and there Peter could see a big brown bull. With its head down it was staring at Lindsay with bloodshot eyes, and restlessly striking the floor with its forefoot.

'The men at the door told Peter that the owner of the bull had been badly gored and that his assistant had taken the injured man to the hospital in the van brought to the wharf to carry away the bull. Immediately after attacking its owner the ferocious animal had charged into the shed. Everyone had escaped except Lindsay and now it seemed likely that the bull intended to take out on Lindsay its rage and fright brought on by its very unpleasant sea voyage and its removal from the ship by a crane.

'The account of the exciting events was given Peter in hushed voices as if all the speakers thought any loud conversation might further enrage the bull.

'The bull stopped pawing the floor and, with its gaze still fixed on Lindsay, began to move forward. As it did so Lindsay rocked back on his haunches into a squat and became so perfectly still, so rigid, and so pale that he looked more like a wax model from Madame Tussaud's than a real, live Customs Officer. Peter in his powerful voice called upon the Good Lord to deliver Lindsay from the bull and then – perhaps in case his first request was not granted – quickly called upon the sorters to join him in praying that Lindsay's soul might be saved from damnation. Although the sorters were not, by and large, church goers, they nevertheless thought that sinners went to hell and many joined Peter in his solemn petition.

'The bull suddenly accelerated and immediately, almost as if its acceleration had been a signal for which the onlookers had been waiting, the doors nearest to the table were pulled apart and Harry Darrow sprang in with his marline-spike in his hand – a remarkable sight, Harry had never been noted for his courage. He quickly, but warily, moved towards the table unnoticed (or ignored) by the bull as it tore along at a furious pace.

'Harry stopped, took aim and sent his marline-spike flying at the charging bull. Then, without waiting to see the result, he turned and rushed back towards the safety of the shed doors.

'The bull was only two or three yards away from the table when the marline-spike hit and remained embedded in its head. The wounded animal let out a frightful bellow of pain and flung up its head. Its left horn struck the top of the table, its body twisted and falling, slid, back first, under the table up against Lindsay's knees.

'For some moments, the bull, Lindsay and the spectators were perfectly still and silent then from every door a flood of advice was shouted: 'Get out', 'Wait', 'Run for it', 'Don't move', 'Now's your chance', 'Don't wait'.

'Neither Lindsay nor the bull moved. Lindsay seemed to be in a trance. The bull seemed to have lost consciousness.

'After some agitated discussion Peter and a burly sorter, who had several of the physical characteristics of a heavy drinker but said he had had experience as a stockman, decided to go to Lindsay's aid. They cautiously made their way through the upset trestles and broken crates towards the table. Before they had gone far the bull was seen to move and more advice came from the onlookers. 'It's getting up' 'Look out' 'Run for it'.

'The rescue party halted. Each of them rose up a little on to his toes as he anxiously stared at the bull. The animal's movements seemed to be confined to some convulsive contractions. Lindsay remained perfectly still looking with fixed and wide open eyes at the bull lying in front of him.

'A little hesitantly the two men resumed their journey. When they reached the table they could see that the marline-spike had struck the unfortunate animal in the eye and driven deeply into its head. The ex-stockman knelt down to look closely at the bull while Peter grabbed hold of Lindsay.

'After a very quick examination the ex-stockman announced, 'It's dead'.

'Getting Lindsay out from under the table and across the bull's body took more time and when that had been done, to everyone's amazement Lindsay fell on the floor in a faint.

'Tempted by the prospect of easy money and a feast of delicious bananas I had volunteered to supervise the destruction of the over-ripe fruit. When I arrived at 'H' shed late in the afternoon Lindsay had been escorted home, the bull's body had been removed and order restored in the sorting area. As I ate my share of bananas I listened to several vivid accounts of the dramatic events which had interrupted the sorting earlier in the day'.

Matt stopped speaking and knocked out his pipe. For a minute or so both of us remained silent. Then Matt said, 'Lindsay's encounter with the bull occurred exactly a month after his forty-fifth birthday which he had celebrated with a long remembered, very boisterous, party. He died only a year ago at the ripe old age of eighty-five. But his frightening experience on Christmas Day 1923 had a lasting effect on him. During the second half of his long working life Lindsay never supervised any sorting or destruction of bananas.

'However, neither the momentous event on Christmas Day 1923, nor his colleague's subsequent abstention from the supervision of the sorting and the destruction of bananas had any noticeable effect on Peter and Peter's apparent indifference to those portents had no significance for me until he died suddenly on a Christmas Day at a relatively early age – he was only sixty-nine, no older than I am now. Peter's death in such circumstances seemed to be something I could not ignore. For a while I did not volunteer to supervise the sorting or destruction of bananas. But the lure of easy money and a feast of bananas proved too strong and I once again became supervisor at weekends and on public holidays'.

He paused then added, 'What a senseless thing to do! I was not in need of money and could have bought in the normal way all the bananas I desired'.

Matt looked at his watch and as he stood up said 'I must be off. They'll soon be having Christmas dinner'.

•

On each of the next four days I walked to Beach Street in the morning and sat on the bench for an hour or so, but did not see Matt. Concerned about his non-appearance and wanting to say good-bye before I left Perth, I went, on the Sunday, in search of Matt's boarding house. When eventually I found it, and asked about him, the landlady told me that he had died suddenly on Christmas Day.

SEE 'UM PETER

When I left school in 1924 at the age of fourteen I got a job as a telegraph messenger at the Perth post office. Two years later I was promoted to senior messenger in the Customs Department at Fremantle. As the senior messenger I did the outside work. I took papers to and from the wharf stations, shipping offices and bond stores, and consequently went in and out of the Customs House at regular intervals throughout the day with the official messenger's bag slung across my shoulder.

At about four in the afternoon on the second day in my new job as I strode along Phillimore Street I saw an aboriginal, barefooted, dressed in faded dungarees and a badly worn football guernsey, standing patiently at the foot of the steps leading up to the main door of the Customs House. When I drew abreast of him he stepped towards me and said in the form of a question 'See 'um Peter?' I was taken by surprise. I had never seen an aboriginal before let alone spoken to one. I didn't understand the question. The aboriginal repeated it, and looking at me with his black appealing eyes pointed in the direction of the Customs House. I still did not understand. When I mentioned the matter to the girl at the inquiry desk in the main hall she said 'Oh yes, he wants to speak to Peter Derham, the man with the beard in the far corner of the invoice room'.

I found Peter leaning over his desk working on some papers. I could only see the longish brown curly hair on the back of his head and some of the gingerish curly beard on his face. When I gave him the message he said nothing, just stood up and strode towards the front door; a big man dressed in an old sports coat and baggy grey pants, walking with a springy step.

About once a week an aboriginal stopped me on the front steps to the Customs House and said 'See 'um Peter?' in the same questioning way. Sometimes one of them would touch me lightly on the arm and say 'Me Billie', 'Me Hoppy' or 'Me Darkie' before asking the question. He seemed to preface the question with his name in the hope that this might influence the decision as to whether he would be able to see Peter. The way the aboriginals looked, the way they asked the question, the way they touched my arm conveyed the impression that they thought a meeting with Peter could not be taken for granted. Yet every time I told Peter that an aboriginal was waiting to see him, he got up and went outside without the slightest delay. Whenever I said to him 'There's an abo outside, Mr. Derham, he always got out of his chair and walked out of the room; he never acknowledged the message, or thanked me, or even looked at me.

Peter Derham, so friendly with the aboriginals, and, as I soon discovered, so estranged from his fellow workers, aroused my curiosity. At every opportunity I asked questions about him from people working in and around the Customs House. Most of the replies I got were not very helpful 'mad as a hatter', 'crazy about boongs', 'a bloody outsider'. One of the invoice examiners said Peter did not care for anything but blacks and pigeons. 'Pigeons?' I asked. 'Yes' said the invoice examiner, but then added 'Perhaps he really doesn't care for the pigeons. His uncle died and left him a small house in East Fremantle with a pigeon loft containing thirty or forty homing pigeons. Every Saturday morning he goes with old Joe Robinson in the mail cart to the black's camp about five miles down the Rockingham road and takes a basket of pigeons. Joe says Peter lets the pigeons out of the basket one or two at a time while the abo's sit around and laugh and shout. As far as I know he never races pigeons or enters them in any sort of competition'.

'How does he get the Saturdays off?' I said (for in those days we worked on Saturday mornings). 'Well' said the invoice examiner, 'he takes all his recreation leave each year in the form of half days on Saturdays and he works quite a lot of overtime and takes time off on Saturdays in lieu of payment'.

After several weeks of asking questions I seemed to have exhausted all the sources of information available to me, other matters engaged my attention and my strong desire to know more about Peter and the aboriginals lay dormant for a while. It was aroused at the Customs Social Club's Christmas party by a retired officer named Bill Watts.

The party had been in progress for about an hour when a baldheaded, thick set man with a protruding stomach came up to the group with whom I was standing. As he was greeted with remarks such as 'What's it like in the bush?' and 'Where's the cork hat?' I gathered that the newcomer lived beyond the town limits. After I was introduced to him, Bill Watts joined in the conversation about horse racing for a while; he then said 'How is Peter Derham making out these days?'

'Same as usual'.

'Still a nut'.

'Ah well', said Bill 'that's a pity! He worked with me for several years you know – before he went up north – I thought he would go far in the service'.

I said, 'What changed him? How did he get to know the Abos'? Bill turned towards me with a look of surprise. 'You interested in him'? I nodded. He said 'Ah well! If you want to know about him you've come to the right man. I'll fill up my mug and we'll find a quiet corner – if that's possible in all this tumult'. We found some unoccupied chairs in an alcove off the main hall and Bill began by saying 'Ah well! Peter ran into trouble at Roebuck. You've heard of Roebuck I suppose; it's up in the northwest, a little one-man Customs outpost'? He paused. After I said I had heard of Roebuck he launched into his story.

I can recall most of what Bill told me but not some of the unusual phrases he used. In recounting the story I will make do with my own words for a great deal of his narrative.

'Ah well! Peter was my assistant when I was in charge of the Customs work at 'A' shed here in Fremantle. He was a very good, intelligent worker; a bit on the quiet side, but occasionally he would have a drink with the boys; he didn't play football or cricket but belonged to a bush-walking club. Some members of the club were naturalists and Peter not only got a lot of exercise on these walks but also learnt a lot about native plants and animals. As far as I know there weren't any girls on the walks, just men.

'Peter told me that he was an only child and had lived in Kalgoorlie all his life before coming to work in Fremantle. His father, a prospector, died when Peter was twelve years old and his mother died not long after he commenced work. The only other relative he ever met was an uncle who was also a prospector. Soon after I joined the Department, I worked in the Excise Branch in Kalgoorlie and occasionally came in contact with a prospector drinking alone in a pub when he was in town to get stores or one camping alone in the bush when I was investigating reports of illicit stills in the hills. They were not very sociable people. Perhaps the characteristics which Peter inherited from his father have made him somewhat indifferent to companionship, at least with white people.

'Because I finished a spell as Sub-Collector at Roebuck a few years before Peter went to the outport, I know a lot about the place and the people. From time to time after I returned to Fremantle, Roebuck people down here on holidays came and had a chat to me so I have a pretty clear picture of what happened there'. 'When did he go to Roebuck?' I asked. Bill Watts thought for a moment and then said 'It was early in 1913, about a year or so before the war.

'The town is about five miles from the mouth of the river. At the mouth there is only the Customs house with a small Customs bond attached. About once a month the *Kybra*, belonging to the State Shipping Line, called there. It anchored off the shore and the goods and passengers were taken on board and discharged by means of the ship's boats. The ship was specially equipped to handle cargo in that way.

'Peter at first lived in a hotel in the town, mixed a bit with the locals, and had an occasional drink. Often after he finished work for the day at the Customs House, and there wasn't a great deal of work to do, he went for a walk along the beach or in the hills behind the sand dunes. On some of these walks he must have passed close by the aboriginals' camp about two miles south of the Customs House near a soak in the hills.

'One Friday afternoon at the commencement of a long holiday weekend, Peter took a rucksack with some food in it and set off to explore a patch of rugged hills not far from the aboriginals' camp. The next morning he badly sprained an ankle. Two aboriginal youths found him hobbling around and helped him get to the camp. He remained there for several days with a soft earth poultice applied to his ankle. The indigenous treatment relieved the pain and cured his disability.

'Soon after spending the long weekend at the aboriginals' camp Peter began having stores regularly delivered to the Customs House – corned beef, flour, sugar, tea and those sort of things. These he gave to the blacks in the camp. He maintained constant contact with the aboriginals, learnt something of their lore and occasionally went on hunting and gathering expeditions with them. At first he was quite open about his relations with the aboriginals and eager to talk about them to anyone who would listen, but it was not a popular topic of conversation. He was often rebuffed and began to withdraw from normal social intercourse with people in the town.

'As his association with the townspeople contracted Peter spent more and more time with the aboriginals. Late in 1914 he gave up his room at the hotel and made one of the two rooms in the Customs House his living quarters. By that time it was common knowledge that most of his wages were being used to pay for stores for the aborigines. As various items of Peter's clothing wore out they were not replaced. The usual attire in the north-west was (and probably still is) a shirt and shorts in the day time and a shirt and long pants at night. Customs officers in those days did not wear a uniform but had to wear a Customs cap when on duty. By 1915 the only clothing suitable for tropical conditions that Peter had were a few rather tattered pairs of shorts. He wore one of these and a Customs cap when on duty; no shirt, no shoes, no socks. He was acting strictly within the regulation; they provided that an officer on duty must wear an official cap, they did not state that he had to wear anything else'.

We were interrupted by an announcement that supper was being served and several of our colleagues breaking up our *tête a tête* to ensure we did not ignore the call. After supper I was pleased to find Bill wanted to finish his story. We went back to the alcove at the far end of the hall and he bagan again by saying 'Ah well! Peter became increasingly unpopular in Roebuck for a number of reasons. The aboriginals in the camp had been for many years a convenient pool of casual labour for the townspeople. In return for their work the aboriginals received tobacco, food and second–hand clothing. The receipt of food from Peter made them far less willing to work for the townspeople.

'Apart from the problem he created in connection with the workforce Peter became increasingly unpopular because he did not conform. He no longer drank alcohol and drinking alcohol was widely accepted as a sign of manliness. He lived apart and preferred the company of aboriginals to that of white people. Although an important government official he wore nothing but a cap and tattered shorts both on and off duty. The townspeople had plenty of experience of men who drank too much, were dishonest, cruel, vulgar or lazy but none of an honest person who did his job very competently and courteously but blatantly ignored their social conventions'.

The Australian government's declaration of war against Germany in 1914 was greeted with great patriotic fervour in Roebuck and most of the young men in the district rushed off to enlist. Peter was young and healthy and the fact that he had no interest in the war, expressed no patriotism and obviously had no intention of enlisting became an additional cause of resentment.

'News of Peter Derham's behaviour reached the Collector of Customs at Fremantle. The question of whether he should be recalled was discussed on one or two occasions but, as a result of the enlistments in the armed services, there was a shortage of suitable officers and no action was taken. Peter remained in Roebuck until 1917. By then his behaviour had become too serious an embarrassment to the Department for it to be ignored and he was brought back to a job in the Customs House in Fremantle'.

At this point Bill said, 'This is pretty thirsty work, do you want a drink?' I said 'No!' Bill got up and walking with quick, short steps and a swaying motion of his body he made his way through the crowd in the main part of the hall. I sat thinking about Peter's life in Roebuck. When Bill returned, he picked up the thread of his story by saying 'Ah well! I was the sub-collector at Albany when Peter arrived in Fremantle so I have only second-hand knowledge of what happened. He apparently came back from Roebuck wearing the sports coat and pants he had worn when he went up there four years earlier. His eccentric conduct in Roebuck was well known and made him the butt for jokes. Also the war loomed large in the lives of people working in the Customs House; almost everyone had relations or friends killed or wounded; a number of badly wounded returned soldiers were back in the House and a Government sponsored campaign was in full swing to get young men to enlist so that they could help their 'hard pressed mates over there'. Peter, fit and in his early thirties, had no interest in any aspect of the war and this increased his unpopularity. Peter did not respond at all to any criticism, laughter or goading; he ignored everyone. He did his work as an invoice examiner with his usual efficiency and gradually those people who knew him realized that he did not regard his unpopularity and isolation as any burden.

'Peter must have made contact with the aboriginals in the camp south of Fremantle soon after his return, slowly gained their confidence and before long once again started supplying the aboriginals with stores and a few other necessities. In doing so he did not run counter to the vested interests of most of the local inhabitants as he had in Roebuck. Only a few people around South Fremantle who used the aboriginals as casual labourers were directly affected to any extent. But Peter's close association with the aboriginals combined with his refusal to slavishly observe the customs of our society made him very unpopular. It still does. Perhaps his concern for the aboriginals leaves the rest of us with a faint pang of conscience, although personally I don't think it's worthwhile trying to do anything for the abos; they are just naturally lazy, dirty and unreliable. He does serve as some sort of liaison occasionally between the aboriginals and authorities such as the police, council, hospital etc., but I understand he does not take kindly to that function and refuses to co-operate in a lot of cases'.

That was all Bill Watts could tell me, but by watching Peter and the aboriginals and occasionally asking questions of others I gradually learnt more.

Although I frequently saw groups of aboriginals in other parts of the town there was never more than one aboriginal on the Customs House steps waiting to see Peter and he was always a man and never young. I asked several people about this but did not get a helpful answer until I mentioned it to Tom Dougherty. Tom was the oldest Customs Agent in Fremantle. He was a very polite, affable man, always well dressed in a slightly old fashioned manner. He never passed me in the Customs House or in the street without a word or two of greeting. He moved around Customs House and between it and his office and the wharves, bonds and importers' warehouses at a measured, leisurely pace; it was difficult to understand how he made a comfortable living in competition with his busy, bustling, professional brethren.

One day in March 1927 I saw Tom standing in the entrance hall of the Customs House filling his pipe with tobacco. I went up to him and asked if he could explain why there was always only one elderly aboriginal man at the foot of the Customs House steps asking to see Peter when in other parts of the town the aboriginals were generally in groups. Tom showed no surprise at being asked such a question, he pushed the last few threads of tobacco into his pipe and then said 'When, a year or so after he returned from the Northwest, Peter established close contact with the aboriginals, groups of them occasionally came to the Customs House and asked to see Peter. The Collector did not like aboriginals congregating in the vicinity of the Customs House and the police arrived and moved them on. After that happened two or three times the aboriginals got the message and since then they have sent one man as a sort of emissary'. He paused, took a box of matches out of his pocket and lit his pipe. When the pipe was drawing satisfactorily, he added, 'I suppose it is their custom, if they can't all participate, to have an elderly man as their go-between'.

As time went on I wondered what sort of matters the aboriginals raised with Peter on the Customs House steps. Usually he only remained outside for five or six minutes and then returned to his work but there were times when he went off with an aboriginal and stayed away for an hour or so. It seemed to be generally accepted that the aboriginals didn't seek, or get, money at the interviews on the Customs House steps. I was told that nearly all Peter's money went in meeting accounts that the aboriginals ran up at a store in South Fremantle from which they purchased most of the food and the few other necessities they needed or could afford. When I walked past

Peter and an aboriginal together at the foot of the steps, Peter always seemed to be standing with his head bent listening intently to some explanation which the aboriginal was making in a soft musical voice.

At 8.30 each morning Peter arrived at the office carrying a battered old gladstone bag. He started work immediately. At lunch time he ate a frugal meal and then usually returned to his work but sometimes he darned a sock before doing that. The socks were heavy woollen ones repaired with a strange mixture of colours. It was said that Peter knitted his own socks but if this was so I never saw him doing it. One other story told about Peter and his socks was that he had three of them and followed the routine of wearing each sock for one day on the left foot, one day on the right foot and then washing it. If that was true I don't know how he fitted in the darning.

Peter left the office at 5.30 pm. This meant he worked about an hour and a half more than the official working period each day. Even though there had to be offset against this that part of his time-off on Saturday mornings which could not be allocated to his recreation leave entitlement and the interruptions to his work while he attended to the affairs of aboriginals, undoubtedly he worked a considerable amount in excess of the official working hours each year. He refused to seek payment for the overtime although pressed to do so by the Public Service Union representatives who regarded his failure to seek payment as a breach of union policy. He also refused to work overtime outside his set hours of 8.30 am to 5.30 pm. His attitude towards overtime and payment for it puzzled me. I could only speculate about his objectives but eventually concluded that he had two. First, he did not want to leave any doubt that he more than made up the working time lost while he attended to aboriginal matters, and, secondly, he regarded the amount of work he did as necessary to enable him to live and make some contribution to the welfare of the aboriginals but he did not consider spending any additional time in that way was warranted. I also found the freedom Peter was given to largely determine his own working hours perplexing. He was regarded as the most efficient examiner in the invoice room, very knowledgeable in Customs matters and always thorough and intuitive. Very rarely indeed did he order packing cases to be opened, the contents checked against the documents lodged with the Customs entry or samples of the goods sent to him, without some error in the Customs entry being discovered. But it seemed unlikely that the excellence of his work by itself, could account for the latitude he was given. I was told that an inspector from the Eastern States who had charge of the Invoice Room for six months while the permanent occupant of the position was on long service leave attempted to stop Peter walking out of the invoice room whenever an aboriginal indicated he needed his help. The Collector overruled the inspector. The Collector prided himself on being civic-minded – he was a member of a service club and of the Fremantle Council. Perhaps he thought Peter made a contribution to civic affairs. From a management point of view Peter's way of operating had obvious disadvantages. If other invoice examining officers decided to look after the affairs of widows, orphans, indigent sailors or lost dogs and walk out whenever the needs of these worthy people or animals required it, the work in the Invoice Room would be in chaos. However, the Collector may have had a good look at the men in the Invoice Room and decided there was little risk of that situation developing.

Late one afternoon in spring, I remember it was the day after my birthday, and I had turned seventeen, I went out of the Customs House to take some papers to a wharf station, and as I left the building I saw Peter going off with an aboriginal. I returned at 5.15 pm and went into the Invoice Room. All the invoice examiners had gone but I noticed Peter's old gladstone bag was on the floor near his table. I decided to sit down and wait. I thought that if no one else was there when Peter returned he might talk to me. I waited until 6.30 pm but he didn't come. I picked up his gladstone bag, went out and caught a tram to East Fremantle.

I found Peter's house. It was set back only a little way from the footpath and in the partial darkness of the evening I could make out a small brick dwelling with a narrow wooden verandah along its front wall and a diminutive garden consisting of patches of lawn on either side of a gravel path leading up to the verandah.

By the time I got to the house I had considerable misgivings about my errand, but nevertheless went up to the front door and knocked firmly on it with the iron knocker hanging there. A light came on over my head and Peter opened the door. I held out the bag and said rather hurriedly 'I saw your bag in the invoice room and I thought you might want it tomorrow'. For the first time Peter looked at me. He had blue eyes which were so bright and lively as to seem diametrically opposed to his habitual taciturnity. As he took the bag he said 'Thank you, it's very kind of you' and smiled as he said it.

He stood at the door while I walked back up the path and waved to me as I closed the gate. Whilst I retraced my steps and travelled in the tram back to Fremantle I wondered why Peter's workmates had remained for so long unaware, or so heedless, of the warm friendliness so apparent in his eyes.

A few days later I look my annual leave to get in some intensive study for a Public Service examination which was being held in October. The examination was very important to me. With little more than a mediocre primary school education I had entered the public service in the lowest category of workers, the fourth division. People in that division were relatively poorly paid and performed only a limited range of routine tasks. Entry into a higher division was restricted to young men who, at the end of their secondary school education, had obtained a good pass in the university matriculation examination, or men in the fourth division who passed an examination, at roughly the matriculation level, held by the Public Service Board every two to three years. To prepare for the Public Service Board examination I had devoted all my spare time to study for the last two and a half years. The examination was immediately following my leave; consequently I was away from the Customs department for over three weeks. The first morning after I returned to work was a particularly busy one; I was only in the Customs House for two or three very short periods. At 1.00 pm I joined five other young fellows for lunch in a sunny nook at the back of the building. I had nearly finished my lunch when one of the boys said to me 'You know old Peter Derham died about ten days ago'. It was said so casually that at first I could not accept it. But while I sat stunned, remarks were made by those around me that left no room for doubt.

'He fell out of his chair on to the floor, dead as a dodo'.

'No relatives or money could be found so the social club arranged the funeral. They didn't know what religion he belonged to but the committee decided on a Church of England funeral'.

'Never seen so many boongs as there were at the cemetery – must have been a hundred of them'.

'The boongs kept well back from the grave; they squatted or stood at least fifty yards away and didn't take any part in the ceremony. Perhaps they held a corroboree round the grave after we left'.

'There were no boongs at the church'.

During the afternoon I went into the invoice room. Tom Hammond, a wharf examining officer, sat at Peter's table. Everything else seemed the same; everyone was working just as though nothing had happened.

On the following Sunday I caught the first train out to Karrakatta and went to the Church of England section of the cemetery. But I could not identify Peter's grave and had to return to the cemetery office near the gate. Here I not only found the location of the grave but also learnt that Peter was only 43 years of age when he died.

Peter's grave consisted of a mound of earth with one wreath on it. The rain had washed away a corner of the mound and I scraped up the earth and squared it off again. Sitting on a seat across the road from the grave I recalled all the contacts I had had with Peter and tried to picture his death, funeral and burial. I had never been to a funeral and at first I thought I had never seen a dead person, but I suddenly remembered an incident which occurred when I was about six years old.

My mother, elder brother and I lived in the boarding house for some time, probably 18 months or two years. During this time a woman who was also a boarder in the house died. A day or so later my brother and I were dressed in our Sunday clothes and told that we were to pay 'our last respects' to Mrs—. First my brother was taken into the parlour, then, after he came out, I was led in by my mother. A coffin rested on two trestles; several people sat silently watching my mother and me. When my mother lifted me up I did not see Mrs—. I had my eyes open because I thought if I shut them I might be held there until I opened them, but I had closed my mind and saw nothing. I recalled now that my brother had never referred to this incident although we were very close and had seemed to discuss everything that happened to us. Did he close his mind and not see the dead body either, or did he know I didn't want to talk about it?

As the morning wore on, people, mainly in ones and twos, came and stood near particular graves; some left flowers, others stood quietly looking at a grave. An elderly lady crouched down and removed some small weeds from a very neat well-established grave. I got up and made my way out of the cemetery and back to Fremantle.

During the week I discovered where Joe Robinson lived and went out to his house. When I asked if I could go to Rockingham and back with him on the following Saturday, he simply said 'It'll cost you a bob'. The next day I asked the Chief Clerk for leave without pay on the Saturday morning. I told him I had some urgent personal business which could only be attended to at that particular time.

When I arrived at the Fremantle Post Office on Saturday, Joe was sorting out the mail which he had to deliver en route to Rockingham. In reply to my 'good morning', he said 'Hop up in the trap' and a few minutes later we set off; the horse trotted smartly for the first two hundred yards then settled down to little more than a walking pace. After we left the suburb of South Fremantle, the white limestone road wound through low hills covered with banksia and wattle scrub. The soil was obviously poor but in the three or four places where we dropped mail in roadside boxes there were small farmlets with one or two cows, some fowls and a few pigs. When we reached the aboriginals' camp, I found it was back a little from the road and consisted of humpies made of kerosene tins, hessian, old galvanised iron and the remains of wooden packing cases. Some of these ugly ramshackle buildings stood on a piece of flat stony ground and others on the sides of two small hills. A few stunted trees eked out a struggling existence near the humpies and smoke rose in a tired listless manner from rough open fireplaces scattered amongst the trees and the miserable looking dwellings.

I waited until we had gone about three miles past the camp then I asked Joe to set me down and said I had decided to have a swim and eat my lunch on the beach nearby and not go on to Rockingham. He growled that he would not wait if I was not on the road ready for him at about five o'clock. 'You better be here by 4.30 pm to make sure I don't miss you' he shouted at me as the trap moved off.

I walked slowly back along the road. When I turned off the road towards the aboriginal camp, the children stopped playing and shouting, the women stopped cooking at the open-air fireplaces and the men stopped talking. At first everyone seemed frozen in the position in which they first saw me. Then the children and women nearest to me moved silently back; the men remained. I continued walking steadily forward. A rather elderly man in patched cotton pants and an old woollen pullover who had been squatting down in a group stood up. I said 'I am a friend of Peter's – Peter Derham'. The elderly man said 'Bad man! Go away'. I repeated 'I am a friend of Peter Derham'. About seven or eight men stood up and formed a semi-circle facing me. I could not think of anything to say but 'I am a friend of Peter's'. I wondered if I should have brought something. The elderly man said once again 'Bad man! Go away'. The group looked menacing. I turned and walked away, across the road, through the sandhills and out on to the beach.

I changed into my swimming togs and swam for a while to let the chill of the water jar some of the nervous tension out of me. Afterwards I sat on a sand dune, ate my lunch, stretched out in the sun and fell asleep.

I awoke and lay lazily in the warm sand until my attention was attracted by some movement away to my left. Looking across I saw that four aboriginals were squatting under a banksia tree watching me. I waved to them but they did not respond. I considered going over and trying to talk to them but I lacked the courage and instead picked up my clothes and walked along the beach towards Rockingham.

When I judged I had walked about three miles, I went into the sand dunes, got dressed, made my way inland to the Rockingham Road and waited until the trap appeared. When I took my seat alongside him I found that Joe's breath smelt strongly of whisky and from time to time he sang a verse or two of some unmelodious song. We passed the aboriginal camp and he stopped singing and began to talk about Peter in a disparaging way. 'He was always fooling around with them abos'. 'Paying their bills and things'. 'No sense in it. Only made 'em lazy. They'd spend any money they get on metho, get drunk and then all hell was let loose in the camp, fighting, yelling and breaking up humpies'.

He sat in silence for a while then said 'And every Saturday he'd bring them damned fool pigeons and when we got to the camp the abos would come out to meet him; kids laughing and shouting, gins grinning from ear to ear, bucks waving and talking. The fuss they made you'd reckon that the Mills Bros. Circus and Houdini were all arriving at once – it was nothing but Peter and a dozen damned fool pigeons.

'And when I picked him up in the evening they'd see him off as though he was going to England or something. All of them standing there on the road shouting and waving until we went round the corner. It was just like blokes seeing their friends off to Europe in the mail boat with streamers and a brass band. If them abos had had a brass band they'd a played it every Saturday, and if they'd had streamers they'd thrown them every Saturday too. You'd reckon he'd be away for years, or never coming back, instead of being gone for just a few days.

'Why the hell did Peter waste all his money on them damned abos? It only made them lazier and more impudent. Gave 'em more time to breed instead of working. All the gins got dozens of kids and most of 'em bastards too'.

Joe went on muttering about Peter. He obviously thought that Peter's treatment of the abos had resulted in all white people in the area bearing a cross of some sort but he had been forced, by his need of an extra shilling to spend on whisky, to bear a much heavier cross than the others; he had been made to see the joy with which Peter was welcomed every Saturday morning and the ceremony, and underlying sadness, with which Peter was farewelled every Saturday evening.

For some time after my trip with Joe I lived with a nagging sense of failure. Then I bought a hammer and a tomahawk. This might not seem very much but it strained my financial position to the limit – in fact, I had to borrow six shillings which I repaid in two installments over the following two pays. I had spent some time worrying about what I should buy but had finally thought that these two tools would be as useful as anything I could afford to get.

A few weeks later I set off again from the Fremantle post office in the 'Rockingham mail'. Joe kept looking at the parcel containing the hammer and tomahawk and, as we were leaving South Fremantle, he said 'The abos don't like white men hanging around the camp; they think they're after the young gins; any white man beaten up by the abos at the camp gets little sympathy from the police or anyone else for that matter'.

The fact that Joe knew I'd been to the aboriginals' camp on the last trip unsettled me and I stayed with him all the way to Rockingham.

I declined Joe's invitation to have a drink with him at the Rockingham Hotel and wandered round the town. It was a holiday resort for the well to do. In the 1920s in Western Australia only the privileged few owned motor cars and, as Rockingham was not connected by train to Perth or Fremantle, there was no method of reaching the village except by road. Scattered along the beach-front and amongst the banksia, wattle and eucalypt trees behind it were about fifty beach homes, some guest houses, a store–cum–post office, and, of course, the hotel. I could not find any changing sheds and finally got into my swimming togs in the bushes just beyond the limits of the town. I swam near the old wooden pier. After I had been in the water for a while a group of boys and girls of about my own age came down and swam and played with a beach ball nearby. At one stage the ball hit me on the head and a pretty blonde girl sang out to me 'I'm so sorry' as I picked up the ball and threw it back to the group.

After my swim I lay in the sun not far from where the boys and girls had joined their parents who were also lying in the sun. I enjoyed watching the group as they mixed laughter and horseplay with their sunbaking. After about half an hour a strong south-west wind began to blow and the party broke up. Family groups picked up their towels and beach gear and walked off towards the cottages. The last to leave was the pretty blonde girl and her parents. As they stood up, the wind caught a beach hat her mother was wearing, and it blew along the beach past me with the girl in hot pursuit. I joined in the chase and caught the hat.

The girl and I started walking back. 'I'm so glad you caught the hat; Mother's very fond of it', she said. Then she bent down, picked up a shell and said as she straightened up and held it out towards me, 'Aren't the colours lovely!'

I took the shell out of her hand. Not because I wanted to look closely at the shell but because it gave me an excuse to touch her skin. Her mother sang out in a high-pitched musical voice 'Mary, it's lunch-time'. 'Coming mother', Mary replied.

She walked a few paces then turned and still moving towards her parents but walking slowly backwards said 'Where are you staying?'

I was unprepared for such a question and it was a few seconds before I blurted out I'm leaving today'. Mary continued to walk backwards looking at me, then she said, 'Bye bye and thanks for helping with the hat'. She turned and ran towards her parents. I stood and watched her. Perhaps she knew I was watching her because when she reached her parents she looked in my direction, waved and smiled at me.

I made my way back to where I had left my things, and ate my lunch. Although I stayed on the beach until I had to join Joe outside the hotel at 3 o'clock, I did not see Mary again. At the hotel there was half an hour's delay while Joe waited for a small parcel to be urgently delivered in Fremantle. Joe filled in the waiting time drinking the extra whisky which the shilling for the special delivery enabled him to buy.

As we moved slowly along the road away from Rockingham I tried to find out from Joe how long he had been making the mail run and whether Rockingham had changed in that time. However, he greeted all my attempts at starting a conversation with 'Watch the horse'. This did not seem to be a very fruitful occupation. The horse wanted to get back to Fremantle and was not likely to go off the road, so there was no point in watching him for that

40

purpose. He was a large, ugly looking brute with an awkward gait and watching him was not likely to give any aesthetic pleasure.

Joe fell asleep and I fell to contemplating the parcel containing the hammer and tomahawk and wondering at my timidity.

When we reached the aboriginals' camp I pulled the reins and shouted 'Whoa!' The horse stopped and Joe woke up and sang out 'What the hell you doing?' I jumped down and ran into the camp. When I got near a group of men I put the parcel down on the ground, said 'For you', turned, and ran back to the trap.

The trap moved off and Joe fell asleep again. I thought about the aboriginals in the camp and about Peter. Why had I found it so difficult to communicate with the aboriginals? Could I only make some real contact with them if I gave up all the pleasant things which life now seemed to promise me?

Before long we turned on to the beach road at South Fremantle. The wind had ceased to blow and it was a lovely, still summer's evening with the full moon standing high in the eastern sky waiting patiently to replace with its pale white light the pinkish glow left by the setting sun. I wondered what Mary was doing.

When we got about two hundred yards from the Fremantle post office, the horse broke into a trot. He always started and finished the journey by trotting this two hundred yards. Perhaps he wanted to impress the post office staff with the speed at which His Majesty's mail was carried.

I continued to see some aboriginals in the streets each day as I went to and from the Customs House. They were generally in the vicinity of the fish market where a few obtained casual work. They were prohibited by law from buying alcoholic beverages but some bought and drank alcohol in forms such as methylated spirits. Most of the drinking was done at their camp but occasionally I would see a drunken aboriginal weaving his way along a Fremantle street.

Amongst the groups of aboriginals I saw near the fish market and elsewhere in the town I could recognise two or three who used to call and see Peter. The most conspicuous was 'Hoppy'. He usually wore some tattered shorts. He only had one leg and used two homemade crutches to get around. Each crutch consisted of a strong sapling cut to the right length with, at the top of it, a smaller piece of sapling padded with rags and sacking and about two feet below the top another piece of sapling worn smooth by the grip of Hoppy's hand. Hoppy's leg was a little bent and thin so that it tended to match the saplings. When he was standing some distance away it was hard to tell which was the leg and which were the saplings. When he wanted to Hoppy could move with surprising speed on his home-made equipment. He was a very cheerful fellow who smiled and nodded his head a lot when talking.

In January I received a letter advising me that I had passed the Public Service examination. I was elated because it was now possible for me to reach the top echelons of the public service if I had the ability and worked hard enough. Two weeks later I was advised by the Public Service Inspector that I had been appointed to a position in the Department of Commerce and Agriculture in Perth.

As I was returning to the Customs House just before 5 pm on my last day as the senior messenger I saw Hoppy standing at the bottom of the steps. When I came up to him he asked in the soft appealing way I had heard so often 'See 'um Peter?' A whiff of methylated spirits accompanied his words. I said 'Peter's not here anymore; he's dead'. Hoppy repeated his request and reinforced it by adding 'me Hoppy' and touching my arm. I said 'Peter's not here Hoppy; he's dead'. Hoppy swung around and moved off down the footpath.

I walked slowly up the steps thinking about Peter and wondering what Hoppy wanted to talk to him about. When I reached the top of the steps I stopped and looked back. Hoppy was standing at the edge of the gutter leaning on his crutches looking up at me.

43

THE COLLECTOR AND THE GUN

Although I had met Andy Watson on several occasions at cocktail parties in Canberra hosted by embassies and business organisations, I knew little about him except that he was a senior officer in the Customs Department and had a reputation for telling anecdotes – whether or not you wanted to hear them. In May 1972 we were both at the Ansett departure counter in the Melbourne Airport being allocated seats on a plane to Canberra when an announcement was made that the air traffic controllers had called a lightning strike and all departures would be delayed.

The booking clerk said there might not be a long delay and asked us not to leave the airport. Andy and I decided to fill in the time by going to the café for some coffee.

On my way to the airport I had read an article in the afternoon paper reporting the death of a youth while he was playing around with a rifle. When I referred to this as we sat down, Andy said that any mention of playing around with a gun reminded him of a disturbing episode involving a collector of Customs and a hand gun. He seemed eager to talk about the episode and I had the time to fill in.

Between sips of his coffee Andy said, 'I joined the Customs as soon as I left high school. The Collector in Sydney was Arthur Bennet, a Victorian officer who had been promoted to the position three years earlier. He was the first officer from outside the state to be promoted to a senior position in the NSW part of Customs. By the time I joined the Department he had a well-established reputation amongst his staff as a parsimonious tyrant.

'Because the economy was buoyant in the first three years of Bennet's Collectorship, the Customs work increased considerably. But I heard Bennet was not concerned about the effect of this and knocked back all requests from branch heads for additional staff. The resultant pressure of extra work on everybody was one of the many changes brought about by Bennet that destroyed the relaxed, easy going attitude of officers which, I was told, had been for many years a pleasant feature of the work in the NSW part of the Department – of course, the easy going attitude of officers may have brought about some slack working practices which Bennet wanted to eliminate.

'However Bennet not only economised by keeping the staff to the absolute minimum, he reduced the funds available for practically every other purpose.

'He greatly lowered the standard of furniture in the Customs House as a whole, but particularly in the offices of the executives and in his own office. Comfortable chairs for visitors were sent off to be auctioned at Commonwealth Disposals, being replaced by wooden kitchen chairs. Bennet said that offices in the Customs House were for the conduct of Customs business, not for people to loll about in lounge chairs gossiping. He insisted that floor boards should be covered only with polish, not carpets or linoleum, and that windows should not be decorated with curtains or walls with pictures and that desks be of simple construction and the number of drawers in them kept to a minimum.

'Some of the measures he took were extraordinary. The envelopes in which the mail came to the Department had to be opened right out and used as note paper by the staff – Bennet himself used opened-out envelopes for that purpose. He kept a close watch on the use of electricity. Generally the last to leave the Customs House each evening, he walked right through the building; if any officer had not turned off the light in his room before leaving, the offending officer, or in a room occupied by several officers, the senior officer, would be taken to task the next morning. He arbitrarily cut the expenditure on pens, pencils, chalk etc. by ten per cent, saying that officers were throwing away these consumables before they were unusable. He considered some of the desks provided for junior officers were too big and he ordered two junior officers to work at each of them.

'From the way he controlled the departmental expenditure you would have thought every penny of it was coming out of his own pocket.

'Bennet also brought a lot of pressure on officers by checking their work in a way which no Collector before him had ever done. For instance from time to time he had brought to his room the entries and all the documents relating to some shipments which had been cleared through the Long Room and were ready to go down to the wharves for release of the goods. He went through the documents quite quickly and in a way that revealed he had a tremendous knowledge of Customs work, a good memory and an intuition which frequently enabled him to sense something wrong, even when the documentation was in perfect order, the entry correct in every detail and when there was nothing in the Department's confidential reports that suggested anyone associated with the export or the import of the goods might be involved in illegal practices.

'On several occasions when he held up the release of goods in what appeared to be a flawless importation and had packing cases opened and goods checked against the documents, something was indeed found to be wrong. With such a check by the Collector always a possibility, the Invoice Examining Officers and tariff Officers in the Long Room had to be very careful in dealing with every entry.

'Bennet checked the work of officers in the other branches from time to time in much the same way as he checked the work of the officers in the long room.

'Another of Bennet's checks considerably irritated many officers. At all hours of the day and night he stalked through the cargo sheds, the ships alongside, the bonded warehouses, the excise stations and the Customs House, keenly watching every officer – it was as though he had no private life and little to do in his own office. Woe betide any officer he found not at his post working flat out. With the Collector likely to be on the prowl at any time, no officer could risk, even in the early hours of the morning, finding a quiet corner to put his feet up for a while.

'Bennet did not seem to hold any of the senior officers under his control in high regard, but insisted on all of them being at his beck and call. So in every senior officer's room, he had installed a buzzer connected to a little switch board on the Collector's desk. When Bennet buzzed he expected his senior officer to appear not only quickly but to be – properly dressed. I can remember several times seeing a senior officer struggling into his coat as he raced down a passage or charged up the stairs towards the Collector's office. I was in the air force in England during the war and I can assure you that none of the fighter pilots responded to the scramble hooter faster than did the senior officers in the Customs House to the Collector's buzzer'.

Watson paused for a moment, laughed and said, 'I suppose you think I am never going to get to the incident with the gun, but it is important that you know what Collector Bennet was like if you are to understand what happened'.

He stopped, again and seemed to expect me to say something, so I asked, 'Did you have any personal contact with Bennet?'

'I saw him frequently walking around the Customs House', Watson said, 'but I had a conversation with him only once – on my first day in the Customs Department. The Chief Clerk introduced all new appointees to the Collector. When I was taken in to his office I was impressed with both the

Collector and the office. Bennet was a well-dressed man of average height with a firm handshake, grey hair neatly parted, a big nose, thin lips and piercing blue eyes. The office was large with two big windows overlooking the busy Circular Quay and the beautiful harbour beyond. I did not know then that the office was very sparsely furnished by the standards set by Bennet's predecessors and successors. On that first day I sat on a rather uncomfortable chair in front of the Collector's desk while he asked me questions about my background and schooling. He told me that I would have a good career in Customs if I worked hard at every job I was given and devoted as much time as I could to studying the Customs Act and Regulations, Tariff Guide, Confidential Instructions etc. Dignified in his bearing, probing in his enquiries, seated in a large office with a lovely view, at a desk equipped with two phones and a small switchboard, Bennet seemed to me, only seventeen and fresh from school, an impressive person.

'Later I learned that all that was known in the Department about Bennet's private life was that he was a bachelor who lived in a flat at Potts Point and owned a large German Shepherd dog which he took for walks in Rushcutters Bay Park'.

Watson paused again, then said, 'I think that's all I can tell you about Bennet. I'd better get on with the gun episode.

'Every day the money received by the cashiers in the Customs House was placed in a specially constructed suitcase and, at 4.15 pm, taken to the Commonwealth Bank in Martin Place. The case was carried by a base grade clerk and another base grade clerk went with him as guard. The guard was armed with a hand gun carried in a holster worn under his coat. In turn, each of the base grade clerks in the Customs House undertook a three month spell as carrier or guard.

'Near the end of my first year in Customs I was given the job of carrier and David Jones, the job of guard. David and I were close friends though our family backgrounds were very different. We had gone through the Sydney High School together, joined Customs at the same time and were both studying part-time at the Sydney University. David was a good-looking, well-built fellow and he had 'a way' with the girls. He was much more sophisticated than I was and knew a lot of what went on in the city, such as how the police controlled the brothels, gambling dens and starting price bookmakers. He said that all the police were 'on the make' in one way or another and so were many of the politicians. I was fascinated by what he told me about shady deals carried out by both police and politicians.

47

'Because David and I were studying, the Chief Clerk arranged for the two of us to perform the cash carrying duties during the university long vacation. As we knew by the time we took up the duties that we had both passed our first year subjects at the University, we were feeling very pleased with ourselves and looking for opportunities to have some fun.

'The previous guard, and a number of other people in the Customs House, warned us that the gun was dangerous. They said that the safety catch was useless and the gun was likely to go off if the guard took a deep breath. One of the ex-guards who had experienced an unintended firing of the gun said, "If it goes off it'll scare the wits out of you. The ancient blunderbuss makes a hell of a lot more noise than any modern gun." The Collector was blamed for the dangerous gun. Apparently soon after Bennet arrived, the Chief Clerk told him that the gun was in poor condition and should be replaced. "Can it fire a bullet?" asked the Collector. When told it could, he dismissed the matter; "That's all it's required to do," he said'.

I interrupted Andy to ask him whether the guards were given any training in the handling and firing of the gun.

'No! Strange as it may seem now it was apparently assumed then (obviously wrongly) that everyone knew how to load, cock and fire a gun safely and with reasonable accuracy', Andy said.

After waiting a moment or two to see if I wanted to ask any more questions he went on with his story.

'The Collector was also held responsible for several aspects of the money-carrying task, other than the dangerous gun, regarded as unsatisfactory by the staff. The carrier and the guard travelled to and from Martin Place by tram. As the amount of money carried was increasing steadily during Bennet's Collectorship, the Chief Clerk suggested it would be safer for the officers to go by taxi to the bank; and they could return by tram. But Bennet said, "A waste of money!"

'The non-payment of overtime was another cause of dissatisfaction. It was impossible for the two officers to take the money to the bank, wait while it was counted and return to the Customs House by 5 pm. With more money in the suitcase the time taken became longer. The Chief Clerk suggested that the officers be paid overtime if they returned after 5 pm. "Paying overtime would only encourage them to dally", said the Collector.

'David and I were not concerned about the gun being dangerous, riding in a tram and not in a taxi, or not being paid overtime. We considered the money carrying job was a lark; we were determined to enjoy it.

'As soon as we had deposited the money in the bank on our first day, we looked around for a café where we might have a drink and find some attractive girls. It meant we would be very late in returning to the Customs House, but as we were not being paid overtime, we thought nobody would be concerned.

'After investigating several cafes, we found one not far from the bank where there were two good-looking waitresses. We went there each afternoon. One of the girls was strikingly beautiful, having what might be described as classical features. She served our table. The other girl, serving tables nearby, was pretty rather than beautiful, but had a lovely smile. We chatted to her as we passed by on our way in and out. We soon learned the names of both girls. Mary had the classical features and Jane the pleasant smile. From the exchanges we had with Mary as she served us, I thought she took herself very seriously and on about our fourth visit after she had gone to get our coffee, I told David that she seemed to me to be rather prim. "I'll shake the primness out of her", said David.

'When she returned to the table with the drinks, David whispered to her "We are two secret service men." Opening his coat he showed her the gun in its holster. The girl was certainly surprised! She stood for a moment looking aghast, then hurried away without a word.

'Just as we were finishing our coffee, two large men in business suits strode up to us. One of them pulled out a gun and said: "We're police – put your hands up and stand up!" Astonished and unnerved we stood up and were frisked by the other man. He pulled David's gun out of its holster and handed it to his companion who, as he put it down on the table, said, somewhat menacingly, "Right, sit down!" The two policemen also sat down over from us and "the boss" demanded "Who are you?"

'After we had explained who we were, "the boss" said "I think had better talk to the Collector about this prank."

'David, who had recovered his composure quite quickly, said "We are sorry to have caused you all this trouble inspector" – the policeman interrupted "Sergeant," he said. After a pause David went on, "It has taken you away from your work ... perhaps you might like to have a drink on us." He produced a pound note from his wallet and slipped it to him. The other policeman looked hard at me so I passed to him the only pound note I had.

'As he stood up the sergeant said, "If we have any more of these pranks, you'll not only be up before the Collector, but also before the Bench on a charge of creating a public nuisance".

'The policemen strolled out and we left soon afterwards. We felt everyone in the café was watching us.

'Embarrassed by the public confrontation with the police, we decided to find another café and eventually found one not too far from the bank. The two girls we made up to were not as handsome as the two in the first café, but attractive enough. We were soon able to take them to the cinema on a Saturday night and then on several Saturday nights to dance at the Trocadero. But we found eventually that the best thing we could say about the girls was that they danced well. David wanted to have another try at getting to know Mary, and so after over six weeks' absence we went back to our first café.

'The girls did not greet us enthusiastically – and it became clear, after a couple of days, that they were unlikely to accept any invitation to go out with us. On the third of our return visits, we left the café to board the tram as usual at the corner of Martin Place and Castlereagh Street. There was a big crowd of people waiting. Soon after we had sat down, a very beautiful young woman climbed into our toast rack section. There were no vacant seats. David stood up, took off his hat, made as low a sweeping bow as room permitted and said "Please have my seat."

'As he straightened up the gun fell out of the holster, hit the floor and went off. God what a nerve shattering noise it made!

'In Sydney at that particular time, disagreements between criminal gangs had led to several brief, but deadly, gun fights in the city. Probably the accounts of the gun fights increased the tram passengers' alarm and panic when the shot rang out. The beautiful woman screamed, the other passengers in our section of the tram leaped to their feet, many shouting curses and profanities. All of them and the people in the sections on either side of us began to scramble off the tram.

'As far as I could see nobody had been hit by the bullet; there was no indication of where it had gone. David picked up the gun and bellowed in my ear above the shouting and screaming "We'd better get out of this before the police arrive." As we struggled to get off the tram stop the conductor, standing amongst the disembarked passengers, demanded "Who fired the shot?" and one of the milling passengers pointing at David said "He did."

'David and I ran off and at great risk to life and limb, wove our way through the Castlereagh Street traffic and when we reached the footpath, hurried up to the Martin Place corner. Just after entering Martin Place we saw to our great relief a vacant taxi. We told the driver to take us to Circular Quay via George Street

'We thought it would be unwise to get out of the taxi anywhere near the Customs House and so we got the driver to put us down at the corner of George Street and Circular Quay.

'As we walked to the Customs House, pleased at having got well away from the tram stop, I suggested to David that he shouldn't make any more bold, romantic gestures while wearing the gun; they were too costly. We couldn't afford any more bribes for policemen or fares for taxis.

'At the Customs House, instead of just putting the gun and holster into the steel cupboard where they (and some ammunition) were kept when not in use, David started to put another bullet into the gun. I stopped him and suggested that he not replace the fired bullet and line up the empty chamber of the magazine with the barrel of the gun to reduce the chance of another shot being fired unintentionally. David disagreed – I found he took his role of guard more seriously than I did – and said 'If I do that my effectiveness as a guard will be greatly reduced; also someone might inspect the gun and inquire as to why the magazine was not fully loaded – the Collector is certain to have a key to the cupboard and he looks at everything.'

'Not adopting my suggestion unfortunately led to another unintentional firing of the gun with quite serious consequences.

'The ruckus with the gun at the tram stop got some publicity. A news item in the Sydney Morning Herald the next day stated that a shot had been fired in a tram in the city and the man who fired the shot and his companion were seen running towards Martin Place; the police, who were quickly at the scene, believed it likely that the men were on their way to commit a crime and the shot, which apparently had been fired accidentally, had diverted them, at least temporarily. The news report had a sobering effect on David. He thought we should adopt "a very low profile" during our remaining three weeks on the money moving job and not visit any cafes and walk back from the bank to the Customs House instead of going by tram. The three weeks of carefully restricted activity passed uneventfully.

'I handed the money-carrying task over to Ron Campbell who, though a returned soldier from World War I in his late thirties who had joined Customs soon after the war, was still a base grade clerk. David and I then went to hand the gun carrying over to Pat O'Shea, a man of our own age, cheerful, pleasant but a bit of a "show-off." I knew him well because we not only worked in the same branch, the Jerquer's Branch, but at the same desk.

'When we arrived Pat stood up and took the gun from David. Then, without even looking closely at it, he amazed us by jumping acrobatically onto the desk, shouting "Where are the Indians?" and waving the gun above his head.

'It went off.

'The noise from the explosion in the rather crowded Jerquer's room was terrific. Everyone jumped out of their chair, the Jerquer dashed out of his small, glass-partitioned section of the office, men in the rooms on either side of the Jerquer's room came running in. The Assistant Collector, whose office was further down the passage, rushed in shouting "What's happening? What's happening?"

'The bullet had passed through the ceiling right above our desk; the hole it made clearly visible. The excitement in the room increased when we recollected that the Collector's office was immediately above the Jerquer's room. The Assistant Collector sent the Jerquer racing up to see what had happened in the Collector's office.

'Meanwhile, after having sent off to the shipping branch (where he worked) David, who was looking a bit shocked and no doubt regretting not accepting my suggestion about loading the gun, the Assistant Collector went into the Jerquer's partitioned section and got on the phone to somebody. The rest of us hung about, all like me, I suppose, very excited and somewhat concerned.

'The Jerquer took longer than expected. When he returned he looked quite shaken, which added to our apprehension. However, he told us that the Collector was not in his office and obviously had not been there when the shot was fired. Now we felt somewhat let down. But the Jerquer went on to say that he had hunted around the office to see where the bullet had gone. He found it had passed right through the seat of the Collector's chair, finishing up in the ceiling. "If the Collector had been in his chair," he said sombrely, "it would have gone right through him."

'The Jerquer's report galvanised the Assistant Collector into action — perhaps he was anxious to impress the Collector on his return with his promptness and the severity with which he had dealt with Pat's tomfoolery. He told Pat to report to him in his office and told me to tell the staff clerk to come to his office immediately.

'It was about ten minutes before Pat reappeared in the Jerquer's room. He was obviously feeling very dejected and hard-done-by. He told me he had been given a dressing down, fined two pounds and had a reprimand for unsatisfactory behaviour recorded in his personal file. I could see he was wondering what effect it would have on his Customs career.

'For a few minutes after he had told me about the severity of his punishment, Pat sat just staring gloomily at the gun which lay on the desk where he had put it – carefully – after the shot was fired.

'The telephone rang. He despondently picked up the ear piece. Just as he was putting it to his ear I heard a man shouting through the phone "Quick! he's in his chair now."

'Pat dropped the ear piece; fortunately it missed the gun'.

•

Andy and I decided to get another cup of coffee but before we could place the order an announcement came over the loud speaker system. 'Attention please! All passengers on Ansett Flight 252 to Canberra and Sydney please go immediately to departure gate five'.

The frustrating delay was over. It had passed quite pleasantly.

GROWING UP

THE BROWN PURSE

I had an evening meal on the express from Kings Cross and arrived home just before eight. Marjorie, who was ready to go to the monthly meeting of the Women's Institute, said 'There's some coffee in the kitchen. Oh! Robin found in the forest a very unusual-looking purse – there was nothing in it – it's on the dining room table'.

After getting a cup of coffee I went to look at the purse. What a shock I got! It was a replica – same size, same thick, brown leather, same solid brass fastener shaped like a ship – of the purse that brought to an unseemly end the only close friendship I enjoyed during five years of primary schooling.

Sitting at the dining room table sipping my coffee, looking at the purse, my mind harked back to the year so long ago when Tommy and I lived in the same street in Perth, Western Australia.

I recalled my mother saying, 'At last we have a house of our own'.

It was January 1923 and she had bought a house, a very small house – smaller than any of the many houses she had rented year after year for as long as I could remember – it had no hall or passage, just four rooms and a back verandah. The living room (into which the front door opened) and Mother's bedroom faced the street. Behind them were the kitchen and my sisters' bedroom. The back verandah had a bathroom at one end and a laundry at the other. The space between these two hygiene facilities was my bedroom, open on one side to the elements, and furnished with a canvas folding stretcher and a cupboard made of six packing cases stacked sideways on one another. The packing cases! How well I remember them! Besides serving as my wardrobe, they were used to carry the girls' and my clothing every year when in December we moved to a house near the school at which Mother would be teaching in the following year.

My sisters were older than me. When we moved into our own house Dot was sixteen and Liz fourteen and I was only nine. Dot was a great source of information for me. She always knew what was going on around us. However sometimes she wouldn't answer my questions. I couldn't get much information from her about our father. She would only say he had 'nicked off' shortly after we moved from Melbourne to Perth and I was only one year old. She wouldn't tell me why he 'nicked off' or where he went. Several times I tried to find out from Mother but she was always too busy, too tired, or too angry to talk about such an apparently irrelevant matter as my father.

The 'house of our own' was on a small, narrow block of land in Wattle Street, West Subiaco. Most of the houses in the street were similar to ours but there were two bigger houses with much larger grounds. One of these, a rather dilapidated-looking building surrounded by an overgrown garden, was on the western side of our block. In it lived a very old man whom I occasionally saw in the street walking slowly with the aid of a stick. Each evening the old man played a violin. Mother said he played it poorly but I liked to hear his music – some plaintive but a lot stirring and joyful – as I lay on my stretcher drifting off to sleep.

Our neighbour on the eastern side was Miss Denning. Her house was very similar to ours. Hanging conspicuously in her living room was a Bachelor of Arts certificate awarded by the University of Birmingham to Mary Denning. Miss Denning told Mother that she had been a teacher at a well-known private school in England but had to give up teaching and come to Australia because she had severe bronchitis and a weak heart. She said her doctors had instructed her not to do anything strenuous or get upset in any way.

Mother made quite a fuss of Miss Denning; Dot said it must have been because of the Bachelor of Arts certificate. Mother was a primary school teacher with no academic qualifications who had become a teacher by training on the job as a monitor. She had scant regard for teachers with a diploma of education but was in awe of those with a university degree. To, in Dot's words, 'suck up to Miss Denning' Mother said 'the children would help her in every possible way'.

The task of helping Miss Denning 'in every possible way' became mine. My sisters were busy doing the housework and cooking the meals in our place, Mother was not at home very much and when at home spent a lot of time marking tests and preparing for sessions with pupils she coached privately in their own homes on two or three nights each week and during weekends and school holidays.

Miss Denning was abominable. She treated me like a slave. I had to wash and dry the pots and pans, crockery and cutlery, sweep the floors, cut the lawn with a worn out hand mower and run her messages. She gave me orders snappishly and continually criticised me. Admittedly I was rather small for my age, wore glasses and was a little clumsy.

The move to West Subiaco brought a change of school for me – the fourth change in four years. I was put in Grade 6, a grade higher than most other boys of my age. I did very well at school work – which I liked – and was pushed along by mother. On my second day at the West Subiaco school, I answered practically every question the teacher asked the class. When I was about to leave the school grounds three boys, each bigger than me, stopped me. Two of them grabbed my arms and the other one said, right in my face, 'We don't like little, four-eyed, smart bums and we're going to kick your bum so hard you won't be able to sit down for a week. Turn him around'.

They were twisting me around when one of them shouted 'Christ! Tommy!'

Running towards us was a boy in our class who was bigger than any other boy in the school. (I found out later he was older than the rest and lagged scholastically, not because he was less intelligent but because he had been living in the bush and not able to attend school until he was eight years old.) My attackers started to run off but Tommy grabbed the leader and said 'If you touch him again I'll give yer a bloody good hiding'.

He then turned to me, 'I'll walk home with yer', he said.

On the way home he told me that he lived in Wattle Street six houses away from my home and he had seen me walking to and from school ahead of him. From that day until the end of November when the trouble with the purse occurred, Tommy and I always walked to and from school together.

Tommy was a little darker skinned than the rest of the boys and had a slightly broader nose but I hadn't noticed those features until after Mother saw the two of us talking outside our house one evening. She called me in and then said 'I don't want to see you talking to that boy, he has bad blood in him'.

Mother was so angry that I didn't ask her what was wrong with Tommy's blood. When I asked Dot she said, 'Don't be stupid, there's nothing wrong with his blood. His mother, who's dead, was an abo and his father is a drunkard'.

Mother always went off to her school before I did, came home later and was away a lot on her coaching work so I not only continued to go to and from school with Tommy but also spent some other time with him nearly every day. At first we were both rather cautious in our approach to each other but before long we were trying to outdo one another in describing boys in our class and our teachers in absurd terms and in devising new ways of mucking about when we were playing together.

Although I didn't mention mother's disapproval of him, Tommy somehow seemed to be aware of it because, without any effort on my part, we never again dawdled near my home. I never visited his home (until the trouble with the purse) and he never visited mine but that was not of any importance to me or, apparently, to Tommy.

I had to go into Miss Denning's house as soon as I had dropped my school things at home. The first task Miss Denning gave me was often to post a letter or purchase some things from the grocer or chemist. When Tommy reached his home he would wait for a while by the front gate and, if I came along, join me on the errand. Unlike me, Tommy never seemed to have chores to do as soon as he came home.

For an errand to the grocer or chemist Miss Denning gave me a brown, leather purse with a brass fastener shaped like a ship. In the purse she said was a list of the goods she wanted and the money to pay for them. She told me to give the purse straight to the grocer or chemist. At no time did she send me to both the chemist and the grocer as part of the same errand. It must have been on the third or fourth errand that Tommy and I began to throw the purse to each other as we walked or trotted along. Soon afterwards we made the game more vigorous by also throwing between us a tennis ball we found in the gutter.

After I had been on the errands for several weeks and the grocer (Mr Barton) and the chemist (Mr Drew) had got to know me, I caught their attention when we entered the shop, put the purse on the counter then Tommy and I went outside to 'muck about' with the tennis ball. When the order was ready Mr Barton or Mr Drew called out and we went back into the shop and got the goods and the purse. The first time I was on an errand to his shop Mr Barton said, as he gave me back the purse. 'I have marked the price against each item and put the change in the purse'. I assumed that Mr Drew did the same. On the way back to Miss Denning's Tommy always helped me carry the goods as far as his front gate.

At pre-arranged times every weekend, and on a number of days during the school holidays, Tommy and I got together for a couple of hours, mostly in King's Park, the 1,000 acres of bushland only two blocks away from Wattle Street.

There were a few narrow, winding paths in the park made by people walking to the city from its western suburbs. Sometimes Tommy and I stalked an individual or a group of walkers, moving stealthily through the trees and bushes unseen by our prey but always (we hoped) within easy reach of them. Although Tommy seemed instinctively adept, our stalking was not always successful – we sometimes found our way blocked by dense shrubs, or unexpectedly came out right onto the pedestrians.

The high branches of a tall tree near the junction of two paths became our haunt. At first I could only climb there with Tommy's help but before long climbed unaided. With 'Cooees' from our haunt we frequently startled passing pedestrians who stopped and looked around puzzled to ascertain where the 'Cooees' were coming from.

Often during that winter while we were perched in our tree, shafts of light from the setting sun came through gaps in the foliage and lit up us and the twisted, gnarled branches around us with an eerie radiance that turned the haunt into our dreamland and each of us told little stories about the weird people and animals living there. My weirdos always did my bidding but Tommy's were beyond his control and just as likely to perform nasty as helpful deeds.

With the spring came the flowers. Not large flamboyant blossoms standing out boldly on strong stalks from bright, green foliage like those in Liz's garden but small, delicately coloured blossoms appearing quite suddenly amongst the weathered grey and brown leaves of the shrubs and the ground cover. It was Tommy who made me notice them. I was then quite uninformed about native flowers.

Tommy's father – who Tommy said had been wounded twice during the war and continued to suffer a lot of pain from his wounds – had taught Tommy songs popular with Australians fighting in France. Tommy taught me the songs and when we were not stalking pedestrians or climbing our tree, we often marched along one of the paths singing the soldiers' songs.

What a wonderful place was Kings Park and what a wonderful companion was Tommy. For the first time in my life I felt independent, no longer a small, timid, very regimented adjunct to a predominantly female family but a very special, adventurous, companionable person.

One day in November Tommy asked me to go 'crabbing' with him. He said he used to go with his father but during the last year his father had become too sick. I was thrilled at the prospect. Tommy said we would have to go through the park to the river getting there about an hour before sunset. He thought I would be away from home for a little more than three hours all told.

At that time Mother was coaching every Saturday afternoon a girl with the rather peculiar name of Eve Ely who lived in Mt Lawley. To get there Mother had to take a long journey by train and tram. After the coaching was finished, the girl's parents always asked Mother to take an evening meal with them. I was confident that I could go crabbing without Mother finding out.

When Tommy met me just inside Kings Park on the following Saturday, he looked like an itinerant tinker. He was carrying a kerosene tin bucket, a large billy, a hand net with a long handle, two balls of string, a big pocket knife, meat, bread, newspaper and a box of matches. After we had shared the crabbing gear we walked through the park along a track which was barely visible to me – but which Tommy said he knew well – singing the soldiers' songs at the top of our voices.

When we reached the river we first of all gathered some stones, drift wood, branches and twigs, built a small fireplace and set out in it everything ready to light. Then we went to the far end of an old, dilapidated jetty. There Tommy securely tied a piece of meat to one end of each ball of string and flung the meat into the river. The other end of each ball of string he tied onto the jetty, leaving a little bit of slack in each line. Tommy told me that when the slack was taken up I had to pull in the string very slowly and steadily. It took me a while to get the hang of it but when I did I brought close to the jetty the piece of meat with a large blue coloured crab holding on to it with his claws.

Tommy, hanging precariously by one hand from the end of the jetty, first carefully slid the hand net under the meat and the crab and then, with a quick upward motion, swung the crab and the meat out of the water. Several times a crab eluded us, breaking his hold on the meat and racing off sideways before the net reached him.

Just after the sun set we left the jetty and lit the fire. The crabs, which had been kept in the kerosene tin bucket, were cooked one by one in river water boiled in the billy. I will never forget that evening meal, both the setting and the food delighted me. The night was dark, no moon, some clouds passing overhead, a breeze blowing across the river, nobody else around, just Tommy and I tending the fire, cooking the crabs, breaking open the hard shells and making succulent sandwiches with slices of bread and large pieces of crab meat. We were too busy to talk and while we ate I could hear small waves constantly lapping quietly against the river bank nearby.

When we had eaten the six crabs and all the bread we put out the fire, packed up and set off for home. Although it was very dark in the park, Tommy kept us on the track. We parted as usual near the edge of the park and I walked home tired, but full of joy; the expedition had been a very exciting adventure.

When I reached home Mother was already there. For some reason or other she had not had her usual evening meal with the Ely's. When she found out that I had been with Tommy for several hours and what I had been doing she seized a strap and thrashed me furiously.

Dot said I was crazy to have disobeyed Mother at that time. It was near the end of the year and I should know she was always on edge then. She was still, legally, a married woman and therefore could only get employment in the public service as a temporary teacher. Towards the end of each year she got more and more worried whether she would get an appointment for the following year. Dot said Mother was even more edgy than usual that year because she had applied for a position in a private school in Albany and was anxiously awaiting a response from the school.

Until Dot told me I was not aware that Mother was contemplating going to Albany. Such a move would take me away from Tommy and it didn't seem to make much sense – Mother had bought the 'house of our own' to give us a permanent home.

Because I was aware that Mother always talked to Dot before she took any important decisions, I was certain that Dot, if she chose, could tell me why Mother wanted to go to Albany. However as Mother, who had gone into her bedroom after thrashing me, had come out again I did not at that time press Dot to tell me. But, alarmed at the prospect of losing contact with Tommy, I was determined to get Dot to talk about it later on.

When I tackled Dot she chose to be communicative. She said Mother had bought the house in Wattle Street because it was relatively cheap – she could buy it without being overburdened with debt – it was near both a primary school and a secondary school and not far from both buses and trains. But after living in the house for a while, she thought it was, in her words, 'not a good place to bring up her family'.

When I asked what she meant, Dot said, 'Your mischief-making since we came here probably had something to do with it'. Then she went on to explain there were a lot of advantages for Mother if she could get the job in Albany. The salary was higher than Mother was getting in a public school –

she would have to supervise the homework of the boarders each evening but Mother was quite willing to do that; a four-bedroomed house in the school grounds was available at a low rent, and any daughters could attend the school – which catered for both primary and secondary education of girls – without fees. After talking to estate agents Mother was certain she could lease the Wattle Street house at a rental which would give her some income after the running costs and the regular repayments of the loan were met. And there was another advantage which weighed heavily with Mother – it would be a permanent job, she would be free of her annual anxiety and the constant transfers from one school to another.

The possibility of our moving to Albany shattered me; life without Tommy's companionship would be very bleak indeed. That night I lay awake on my stretcher for a long while fretting about Mother's desire to move from Perth and fervently hoping that the Albany school board would not select her.

On the Monday after the crabbing expedition Miss Denning sent me as usual to the grocer. Tommy was waiting at his gate and we trotted from his place to the grocer throwing the purse and the tennis ball between us. There were several customers in the shop but I caught Mr Barton's attention when I put the purse on the counter and he nodded. After we had been outside for some time, Mr Barton called and we went in. He said 'There's no money in the purse'. I was surprised but thought Miss Denning must have forgotten. I took the purse and Tommy and I went cheerfully back – Tommy dropping off at his place.

But when I gave the purse to Miss Denning and told her what Mr Barton had said she screamed at me 'What have you done with the pound note? Did you go the grocer on your own? Was Tommy Kelly with you?'

Without waiting for me to reply she went on 'You're two thieving scoundrels! I'll tell your mother and get the police onto you!'

As she seemed to be in an uncontrollable rage I left the house and went back to the shop to ask Mr Barton to look and see whether the note had dropped out when he opened the purse. Tommy went back with me. We were sure nothing had fallen out of the purse while we were tossing it to one another.

Mr Barton said he had opened the purse on the counter and there was a list but no money in it. Then, leaving me standing by the counter, he went into the storeroom. He did not seem to be at all concerned about the missing note. I was flabbergasted.

Tommy and I slowly made our way back to Wattle Street. When we got there we could see Mother and Miss Denning standing on the footpath outside my house. Leaving Tommy at his front gate, I went on alone, not only perplexed but by now pretty anxious.

As soon as I reached her, Mother said 'I knew Tommy Kelly would lead you into trouble, but I didn't expect robbery. Where's the money? What have you done with it?'

From the very beginning nothing I said seemed to make any impact on the two women; before long I was screaming out answers to their questions and denials to their accusations. The terrible inquisition ended quite suddenly when Miss Denning said to Mother, 'Your son was responsible for the pound note being stolen, you should give me a pound to replace it'. For a moment Mother said nothing, then she said 'Tomorrow evening I will ask Inspector Smith to get one of his men to investigate the robbery'.

Without waiting for a reply Mother seized my arm and walked me briskly through the open gate into our place. Inspector Smith was in charge of the Subiaco police district and I knew that Mother was coaching his son twice a week. Miss Denning also must have known of Mother's connection with Inspector Smith because she did not ask any questions as we passed close by her on the other side of our low front fence.

When we got inside the living room Dot greeted Mother with, 'There's a letter from Albany'. As soon as Mother read the letter the 'robbery' was well and truly put aside. The School Board wanted her to go to Albany by the night train either the coming or the following Friday, spend the Saturday with them and return to Perth on the Saturday night train. There was a cheque for the train fares and sleepers.

Mother decided to go to Albany on the coming Friday and immediately started to think aloud about things that needed to be done – postpone Eve's coaching to the Sunday, telegraph the School Board, get the railway tickets etc.

At tea all the talk was about the trip to Albany. I was fascinated by a lot of it. I had never before been present when Dot and Mother were discussing Mother's plans. At the beginning Mother was concerned as to whether there were some papers she should take with her, but Dot thought she had sent with her application all that were relevant – these, I gathered, included yearly reports on her work by School Inspectors and letters from the parents of children she had coached for exams. With the question of papers settled, they discussed what dress, shoes and hat she should wear, what bag she should carry and whether she should try and get her hair trimmed before she went. While I found the discussion interesting, I remained worried about the outcome of Mother's trip. Would it take me away from Tommy?

When Mother was getting ready to leave on Tuesday morning I asked her whether I should no longer help Miss Denning. For a while Mother went on gathering her things then she said, much to my disappointment, 'Go to her house as usual'.

On the way to and from school Tommy and I went over and over the events of the previous day. We were certain that the pound note had not fallen out of the purse while we were going to the grocer. What then had happened to it? Did Miss Denning not put a pound note in the purse? Did Mr Barton steal it? We could find no answer to the puzzle. I told Tommy that Mother, through Inspector Smith, hoped to get the police to investigate 'the crime'. Tommy and I tried to work out how that would be done and wondered whether the police, like Mother and Miss Denning, would automatically accuse us of taking the money.

I rather reluctantly went to Miss Denning's house after school. She said nothing about the missing pound note and seemed less aggressive than usual but, nevertheless, found a lot of work for me to do – all of it in the house.

When Mother came home she told me that Inspector Smith had said he would conduct the inquiry himself – which Mother said was 'very good of him' – and he would talk to me at home at about five the next day and I was to tell Tommy that Inspector Smith would come to his home between five and six.

On Wednesday, after I had done the chores for Miss Denning (which, once again, did not include any errands) and my homework, I sat at the living room window watching for the Inspector. There was no sign of him until after six o'clock when a black car slowly passed our house and stopped outside Miss Denning's. A tall man got out and went into Miss Denning's house. I kept an eye on the clock. It was twenty minutes later that the Inspector came to our front door. Dot let him in and left the two of us in the living room, though I think she was hanging about.

The Inspector was a quietly spoken man. He asked about the errand to the grocer on Monday, the jobs I did for Miss Denning and the sort of things I did with Tommy, but he also asked a lot of questions that didn't seem to have anything to do with the loss of the pound note.

Nearly an hour later, after I had had my tea, I went outside and to my surprise saw that the Inspector's car was, once again, outside Miss Denning's house.

On the way to school on Thursday morning Tommy and I discussed the Inspector's interrogation. Tommy's father was at home and the Inspector asked him some questions but his father was too ill to answer them. Tommy also said that not only did the Inspector ask him some strange questions but also asked to look at other rooms in the house. We both thought the Inspector had a peculiar way of trying to find out what had happened to the pound note.

When Mother came home on Thursday night she was looking very pleased. The Inspector had told her he was satisfied that the boys had not stolen the money.

When I asked Mother what happened to the pound note she answered, 'He didn't say', which seemed very strange to me.

On the way to school on Friday Tommy and I danced with joy and slapped one another on the back. Once again we speculated on the disappearance of the pound note. I was of the opinion that there was no note in the purse. I disliked Miss Denning so much that I thought she had concocted a cunning scheme to get money from Mother. Tommy, however, had doubts about Mr Barton's honesty. He said a neighbour who often shopped on Saturday mornings at the same time as him (Tommy) had told him that he should watch Mr Barton because a lot of people said he had tried to 'short change' them.

Just after lunch the headmaster came into the sixth class room, spoke to the teacher and then called Tommy out. As Tommy stood up he added, 'Bring your books and your school bag with you'.

Tommy went off with the headmaster and I was stunned. The Inspector had cleared us both of the charge of stealing, what was happening?

Before she left that morning Mother had told me to get a haircut. That involved catching a bus from beside the school to the Subiaco shopping centre, waiting my turn in the barber's shop and catching a bus back home. When I got home Miss Denning was out the front waiting for me. She had some extra chores for me to do that day and it was after six o'clock before I could go down to Tommy's house to try and find out why he had been called out of the class.

For the first time I went to the front door of Tommy's house. The knocker on it was similar to ours. After knocking several times I tried the handle. The door was not locked. When I opened it and went in I found myself in a living room with rather dilapidated furniture and an unpleasant odour.

A man was lying on an old sofa. His head was almost completely bald, having only a few long, untidy, brown hairs near each ear. He was a big man, his head rested on the top of the padded arm of the sofa and his feet were hanging over the other end of it. His eyes were closed but his mouth was open and a faint gurgling sound came out of it. His cheeks were puffed up. His shirt was open and the buckle of his belt undone. A large, round, white stomach protruded out of his clothes. On the floor beside the sofa were some empty beer bottles.

I could hardly believe that the man on the sofa was Tommy's father, but who else could he be? From near the front door I called out 'Mr Kelly' twice. The man did not respond. Then I shouted 'Tommy!' several times. The man did not open his eyes but his head moved a little and he made a grunting noise. I was certain that Tommy would have heard me if he had been in the house. After a few minutes I left and walked home feeling very depressed.

I did not say anything to Dot or Liz about Tommy or my visit to his home. I went to bed early but lay awake for a long time. The old man played mostly plaintive music that night. It was as though he was as distressed about Tommy as I was.

On Friday morning Dot had told me Mother had instructed her to keep an eye on me and not let me go off with Tommy. Dot then extracted a promise that I would do my chores and study on Saturday morning and not leave the house until after lunch. I kept that promise and then went down to Tommy's house. The front door was locked and there was no response to my knocking. I walked right around the house shouting out 'Tommy'. I didn't care whether his father heard me or not. As I was going around a second time a woman's head appeared over the side fence and said, 'You won't find Tommy there anymore. The Welfare people took him away'.

The head disappeared. I shouted out, 'Where did they take him?'

From somewhere in her backyard the woman shouted, 'Dunno'.

When I got back home I poured out to Dot all that had happened at the school on Friday and on my two visits to Tommy's house and asked her who were the Welfare people? why would they take Tommy? and what would they do with him?

Dot explained that the Government had a Children's Welfare organisation that took charge of children if the children's parents could not look after them properly. Foster parents were paid to take care of the children. I asked her if she could find out what foster parents were taking care of Tommy and where they lived, I wanted to see him. I was very upset and indeed shedding tears. Perhaps because of that Dot said she would try to find out.

Mother came home on Sunday morning in a triumphant mood; she had got the job in Albany and as the house would be available as soon as the school holidays commenced, she wanted to move there before Christmas.

All the family except me began excitedly preparing for the move. How terrible it was for me to walk to and from school and go on errands without Tommy, not to be able to crack jokes with him, talk about school work, teachers and other children with him, not to be able to romp in Kings Park with him. I kept pressing Dot to try and find out who were his foster parents. She told me on Thursday night she had got the phone number of the Children's Welfare Organisation and at lunch time on Friday she would go to the public phone near the school and ring up. How eagerly I awaited her homecoming on that Friday afternoon.

Dot said there was a lot of 'mucking about' with different people talking to her before she was put on to a woman that knew about Tommy. But when she got that far the woman asked what was Dot's relationship to Tommy and when she said 'none' but he was her brother's best friend the woman said she could not discuss Tommy's affairs with her.

After that set back I thought I could only find out what had happened to Tommy by going to see his father.

On Saturday morning as soon as breakfast was over I went down to Tommy's house. I didn't say anything to Mother or Dot.

After I knocked on the front door repeatedly for about five minutes, I tried the handle. The door was locked. I walked right around the outside of the house three times shouting out 'Mr Kelly'. There was no response from inside the house, nor did any woman's head appear over the side fence.

I plucked up courage, went into the house next door and knocked. The same woman came to the door wearing a long apron bespeckled with flour. I asked her where Mr Kelly was. She said, all in one sentence, 'The Salvo's have got him, drying him out, I'm very busy' and closed the door.

On Saturday evening Miss Denning came in and had an unusually long talk to Mother. The next day I got Dot to tell me what it was about. Miss Denning had been telling Mother about her troubles. Since arriving in Australia she had been living on an allowance from an aunt living in London. The aunt had suddenly died recently and the cousins who inherited the estate had greatly reduced her allowance. Consequently she was in financial straits. Although 'it would put her life at risk' she had to get some teaching work and she was asking Mother if she (Mother) would recommend her to parents who were wanting their children coached. Mother had apparently replied rather cautiously to Miss Denning's request – only agreeing to give her the names and addresses of some parents.

Soon after the school year ended we moved to Albany. Mother and the girls very joyfully, me very sadly.

Gradually memories of my year with Tommy faded as, assisted by scholarships, I passed through high school and the Melbourne and Cambridge universities and settled in England doing my research work. But the look-alike purse had brought back those memories very vividly. I was still sitting at the dining room table fingering the purse and wondering what sort of a life Tommy had had for the last thirty years when Marjorie returned from her meeting.

THE WOMAN AT THE WINDOW

It was Chris Stuart who told Tom that there were a number of brothels at the western end of Roe Street. Chris and Tom boarded at Mrs Chapman's house in West Perth, but having meals and living quarters under the same roof were almost the only things they had in common.

Chris was a handsome, debonair young man in his middle twenties, employed in the Customs Department, who owned a small car and had a busy social life outside his working hours. Tom, a plain-featured, unsophisticated youth of seventeen, had just finished his secondary education at a country high school. He was articled to an accountant in Perth and hoped by intensive study to complete in three years an accountancy course that normally took four. There were two younger children in Tom's family and his parents could provide him with very little financial support while he was in Perth. Tom's living expenses (very frugal though he was) left him with no money and his work and study left him with no time for any social life at all.

On one of the very few evenings when Chris remained in the boarding house dining room after the evening meal to talk to Tom (and Tom felt he could leave his study for a while and listen) Chris told a story about a raid made a year earlier, in 1922, by Chris and some other Customs officers on the brothels in Roe Street. The raid had nothing to do with prostitutes or sex, at least directly; its purpose was to try and find a Chinaman suspected of being an illegal immigrant.

After hearing Chris's story Tom changed the route by which he went to and from the city each day. He walked along Roe Street instead of Aberdeen Street. There were houses on only one side of Roe Street, on the other side was a wooden fence guarding the railway track. As Chris had made clear in his story the brothels were in seven terraced houses the front walls of which were only a few feet from the footpath. Chris had also mentioned that three of the houses at the eastern end of the terrace had been converted into one large brothel by making openings in the walls separating them and that the 'bouncer' employed in that brothel was the most villainous looking bruiser he had ever encountered. There was nothing much to see around the brothels when Tom walked past in the mornings or when he came back between five and six each Wednesday evening. But on the other evenings when Tom attended lectures at the Technical College and passed the brothels at about ten o'clock there was plenty to attract his attention.

It was March when Tom began using the Roe Street route and the evenings were warm. Usually at the door of each house there were one or two girls. Some of these wore rather vividly coloured evening dresses with long skirts, others were dressed with very short skirts. The tops of all the dresses were cut very low. The girls varied considerably in height, shape and age. As he passed Tom was greeted with remarks such as 'Hello dearie' and 'Like to come in for a while'. There were generally some other men going by, talking to girls or entering one of the houses. Sometimes a group of about half a dozen men would come down Roe Street from the city and go straight into one of the brothels. Several of the rooms facing the street were well lit and there were no curtains or blinds covering the windows. In one of the well-lit rooms there was a piano. Occasionally as he came down the street Tom heard, floating through the night air, a popular song sung by a group of male and female singers with a piano accompaniment. At other times as he passed a window of one of the well-lit rooms he caught a glimpse of men and women engaged in boisterous play or heard a loud conversation punctuated with gusts of laughter. Bright lights, singing, games, cheerful talk and laughter in brothels surprised Tom. But not all the rooms were well-lit, in some the lighting was quite poor and the closed windows were screened by blinds or curtains. The outward appearance of these rooms suggested that there was present inside them the sort of shadowy, sex-laden, serious atmosphere that Tom had imagined (until he began his evening walks down Roe Street) was part and parcel of everything connected with prostitution.

From the very first evening, a woman who sat knitting at the window of a house at the eastern end of the terrace caught Tom's attention. The room was well lit and Tom could see that the woman was probably between thirty and forty years old, with brown hair, dark eyes, a pale, clear skin and a well-proportioned face that always displayed a rather stern, but not unhappy, expression. She wore clothes of a kind that a neatly dressed suburban housewife might wear when out shopping or visiting friends. Her attractive features, the way she sat at the window and her tasteful attire gave her a kind of dignity that was difficult to describe and which in Tom's opinion brought a touch of elegance to the brothels. He assumed that she would attract a type of man who would not be interested in any of the other women he saw in Roe Street. Whenever Tom or some other male passed she looked up from her knitting but did not relax her calm but stern appearance. The poor municipal lighting in Roe Street probably made it difficult for her to get a clear-cut impression of any man passing by; certainly she showed no sign of recognising Tom as a regular passer-by.

Tom saw the woman three or four times a week. When she was not at the window he wondered what she was doing. Was she in bed with a man? Her absence did not divert his attention to any of the other women. He always continued his journey to the boarding house with her image in his mind and his heart buoyed up by the expectation that he would see her the next time.

The clothes that the woman wore and the occasional changes in her hair style became of great interest to Tom. Before the weather turned cold she would wear one of three cotton dresses and four blouses, in a fairly orderly rotation. In winter she would wear, also in an orderly rotation, one of three dresses of a heavier material or either a knitted cardigan or sweater over one of the blouses. With the spring came a new dress with a floral pattern, a new plain white cardigan and the light cotton coat of many colours she had been wearing the first night he had seen her and she had not worn since. The colours she wore varied widely but they were always soft-hued. He began to associate softness, not only with her choice of colours, but also (despite her rather stern expression) with her character. He thought of her as someone who would not easily yield to pressure but who also was a sensitive person with an underlying delicacy and gentleness. With the changes in her hair style and in the decorative combs she wore, Tom associated changes in her moods not evident in her impassive face. These mood changes, evoked by his fancy, filled out and made more intimate the personification of the woman he had created in his mind.

Before the autumn came to an end Tom had given a name to the woman at the window. He called her Rosamond after the comely fallen woman in Tennyson's poetic dream of fair women. While Tom did not find that the stern look of Rosamond impaired her attractiveness he nevertheless wanted very much to see her smile. From time to time he imagined her smiling. Her head was thrown back a little, her dark eyes were bright with laughter and there were charming little wrinkles on each side of them, her lovely red lips were parted and her shapely white teeth glistened between them. (He had never seen her teeth but he was certain that they were beautifully white and even and neither too long or too short).

Tom began to have dreams and fantasies (some of them erotic) about his Rosamond. In the world of make-believe and daydream he built around

73

Rosamond, he could relax after long hours of work and study. Also in this world away from facts and realities he could forget, for a while, the problems of living, working and studying in Perth on a pittance. Amongst the problems from which he was glad to escape was one caused by his physical changes. He was growing bigger, his shoulders were broadening and his chest swelling. He had only one suit; a suit his parents had bought for him just before he came to Perth. Its purchase was due, at least in part, to a remark made by the head of the accountancy firm during an interview with Tom and his father. Mr Casey had said, 'We expect all our staff to come to work in a business suit'. Every day it became more difficult for Tom to get into his business suit and more likely that the suit would burst apart while he was in it. But he could not see how he could get another suit. Oh! how he envied the well-dressed Chris with his many suits.

Tom had very little to do with his fellow boarder. Chris had his breakfast much later than Tom on working days and on Sundays slept in and did not have any breakfast at all. They occasionally met at dinner on Wednesdays but there was little conversation during the meal and Chris usually had an appointment later in the evening and hurried away when the meal was finished. On Saturdays and Sundays Chris played tennis each afternoon and attended some social engagement each evening. There was no basis for comradeship between the youth and the man. For his part Tom only rarely gave a thought to Chris but when he did he regarded with envy both his fellow boarder's clothes and his social life. He occasionally saw Chris at dinner or leaving the house dressed in a beautifully tailored suit, a well-cut shirt, an attractive tie and shoes of the latest style. Tom had none of these things. Although he really knew very little about what Chris did when away from the boarding house he was convinced that it included dining, dancing, playing tennis and love-making with beautiful women.

But as Tom became increasingly infatuated with Rosamond he ceased to conjecture about Chris's social life and to regard it with envy. By the late spring the extravagant passion Rosamond inspired in Tom was dominating much of his life. He spent some time, which he knew he should not, composing a poem to Rosamond. He did not find this labour of love to be easy. Although he had enjoyed most of the poetry he had studied at school he had not given much attention to the technique of writing poetry and getting an understanding of that technique delayed him. However he eventually expressed, in a poetical way that pleased him, his emotions when

74

he saw Rosamond at the window and met her in his dreams. While he was writing the poem Tom justified spending so much time on it by assuring himself that when his feelings were written down they would no longer divert him from work and study. But writing the poem made no difference, his thoughts still frequently took him away from the real world and its commonplace matters to the world of daydreams and fantasies where he lived with Rosamond, played with her, worked with her and each day heard her say in a voice so very sweet and low that she loved him.

On the second Saturday in December Tom finished his work at the office at noon and was walking along St George's Terrace when he saw Rosamond coming towards him in conversation with a girl sixteen or seventeen years old. The girl's face was so remarkably like the woman's that he had no doubt they were mother and daughter. After they passed him Tom turned round and followed them. They went into Barrack Street and when they reached the Esplanade entered it and sat on a bench. Tom passed behind them and sat on another bench about thirty yards away. After the girl and the woman had been talking animatedly for about five minutes Rosamond looked at her watch. Then the two of them sprang up, walked briskly over to the Barrack Street tram terminal and boarded a tram. Almost immediately the tram began its journey to Mt Lawley.

When the mother and daughter had disappeared Tom walked back towards Barrack Street. Passing the bench on which they had been sitting he noticed beside it a brown paper parcel. He picked it up.

Back in the boarding house Tom removed the brown paper wrapping and found a book of poetry. It was a copy of the book of poetry that he had studied in his last year at high school. He was convinced that the book belonged to Rosamond's daughter who had probably bought it that morning to study the poems over the long Christmas vacation and prepare for her next school year.

The encounter with Rosamond's look-alike daughter did not reduce Tom's infatuation with his first love or divert it to another. Up to this point his contact with both the woman and the girl had been at a distance and his actual knowledge of both was limited to what the eye could see. But it was the more mature version of the genes that he had found in the sex-charged environment of the brothels that had set alight the blaze of interest, affection and desire that burned within him.

Lying on his bed with the book of poems in his hand Tom decided that he would go into the brothel on Monday evening, explain to Rosamond how he had found the parcel and return it to her. Having made that decision he continued to lie on the bed for some time delighting in the thought that he would at last come close to Rosamond, talk to her, hear her voice, see her smile and perhaps even touch her. Probably, thereafter, she would wave and smile at him each evening as he passed by her window.

During the next two days it seemed to Tom that Monday evening would never come. At about ten o'clock he crossed over the railway lines by the horse shoe bridge and entered Roe Street. The night was still; the pale light from a half moon softened the harsh outlines of the unprepossessing houses and cast shadowy patterns on the uneven wooden pickets of the railway fence. Tom walked along with a springy step, his heart filled with the wonderful, joyful prospect.

When he reached the terraced houses Rosamond was there at the window. Without pausing Tom walked up to the front door of the brothel. Just inside, leaning against the wall smoking a cigarette, was a big, strongly built girl. She touched him on the arm and said, 'Hello duckie, we would have a lovely time in bed together'. Tom passed by her, walked a few steps down the passage and entered the front room of the house. Seated on a sofa along the back wall was a dark girl in a yellow dress with a very short skirt. She tapped the sofa alongside her bare thigh and said, 'Come and sit here dearie'. Ignoring her he moved towards Rosamond. As soon as Tom had entered the room Rosamond had turned away from the window. She now faced him across a table on which stood a black steel money box. Holding out the parcel Tom said, 'I saw you and a girl on a seat in the Esplanade on Saturday and after you left found this parcel alongside the seat'.

Looking steadily at him Rosamond said calmly, 'I was not in the Esplanade; that's not my parcel'.

Although surprised Tom went on, 'I opened the parcel and found it contained a book of poetry...'

Rosamond interrupted. 'Do you want a girl?'

He had not expected such a question and paused before saying, 'Oh no!' then, 'It is a school text book...'

Once again Rosamond interrupted, 'If you don't want a girl, get out'. She did not raise her voice but said this, like everything else she had said, in a quiet, clear voice while gazing sternly at him.

Tom thought if he could finish his explanation she would understand and he pressed on, talking hurriedly. 'I am sure it belongs to...' But he had only got that far when Rosamond asked, 'Do you want to be thrown out?'

Suddenly desperate and nervous Tom blurted, 'I'm sure it's your daughter's book'.

Rosamond turned towards the girl lounging on the sofa and said, 'Get Sid'. The girl sprang up and hurried out.

Tom stood silently by the table for a few moments astounded by the turn of events. Then, shocked and dismayed by the woman's coldness and cruelty and fearful of the bouncer, he fled from the room.

In the passage the Amazon-like girl jeered, 'Having a bit of trouble, duckie?' seized him in a bear hug and swung him around. Held firmly against the girl's breasts with his head on her shoulder, he could see a burly, grim-faced man striding down the passage towards him. With a great heave he broke away from the bear hug but in doing so burst open the seam at the back of his coat. The girl shrieked with laughter as Tom, with his torn coat flapping about his body, ran out of the house and continued to run across the road towards the railway. Sid followed him, but stopped at the edge of the footpath and shouted, 'If I catch you around here again I'll beat the bloody stuffing out of you'.

When he reached the railway fence Tom leant against it breathing hard. Across the street he could see the woman sitting at the window knitting.

BECOMING A TRADESMAN

His uncle and aunt slept in the room next to Ralph's. The wall between was not sound proof and Ralph couldn't help hearing snatches of their conversation and his uncle's coughing. The coughing was not very frequent or severe and it didn't disturb him until November and then, at first, it only caused him difficulty in getting to sleep; he seemed to be constantly waiting for the next bout of coughing. But before very long, when he got to sleep, vague but unpleasant images continually passed through his mind, disturbing his sleep and leaving him feeling unrefreshed when he woke. Then one night the vague images suddenly took a definite shape, that of a large, black man in black clothes standing close to his bed staring at him with black eyes. For some time the man stood perfectly still – then he leaned over Ralph and spat a stream of white fluid at Ralph's face. Just as the fluid was about to hit him, Ralph awoke in fright.

For a while after he woke Ralph couldn't overcome his apprehension of some immediately threatening evil. When he did, he made no attempt to go back to sleep but lay in his bed letting his mind drift through recollections of the events that had so unexpectedly led to his terrible predicament. He recalled the long train journey to Sydney with his father nearly two years earlier. When he was not dozing, his father had talked in a rambling sort of way, repeating several times his claim that all that had gone wrong with his life was because he had failed to become a certificated tradesman. That, his father said, had made it hard for him to get regular work, to remain for long in any one place, to get a decent house for his family, to frequent pubs because that was where he was likely to find someone who would give him a job. 'Something', he said, 'your mother never understood'.

Later in his rambling, his father both praised and abused his older brother, John. He said John had been determined to become apprenticed in some trade, had succeeded in doing that and, for the last twenty years, had run his own business, bought a nice house (which, however, his father had never seen), and had two daughters 'who were both married and well-off'.

But when his father next mentioned his brother he said the man was 'a pain in the neck', he didn't drink or smoke or have fun with the girls and went to church every Sunday. 'He was constantly preaching at me, telling me I ought to buckle down and try to get apprenticed somewhere. That was one of the reasons why I went off into the bush to see other places and have some fun'.

After saying nothing for a while, Ralph's father said, 'I let you stay in school after you finished primary and that's what made John interested in you'.

A silly statement, Ralph thought – they both knew that Rose, Ralph's sister was the one responsible for him being allowed to remain at school. Rose, six years older than Ralph, had become the housekeeper after their mother died. When their father wanted Ralph to leave school and find some work, Rose, who hadn't liked school and left as soon as she could, said she would leave the house and go off to find work if their father didn't allow Ralph to continue his schooling.

While his father dozed, Ralph recalled the ups and downs of his schooling. The 'downs' included nearly two years of frustration when he, who liked school, couldn't attend one because they were living in a shanty too far out in the bush. The 'ups' were solely the work of the wonderful teacher, Mr Parson, who came to the one-teacher school in 1913.

Ralph remembered being embarrassed when he had to tell the new teacher that he was just commencing Year Six, and being very surprised when Mr Parson, after immediately seeking the reason for Ralph's backwardness, thoroughly tested his capacity and keenness as a student.

And oh! what joy when Mr Parson, after helping him press on with Class Six subjects and finish them by the middle of the year, told him that if he stayed at school he would teach him five subjects in the High School curriculum because he hoped Ralph would eventually get to a High School, finish the subjects and sit for the Intermediate Certificate exam.

How wonderful it was to have Mr Parson set work for him – during the school hours and then stay after school for two hours each day to tutor him. Mr Parson's favourite subject was English; he encouraged Ralph to develop his vocabulary and before the lessons ended each evening, he encouraged Ralph to read aloud some poetry or prose. Though a little hesitant at first, Ralph recalled he soon came to greatly enjoy the reading.

Engrossed in his study, Ralph recalled, it was not until the second year of Mr Parson's term as the teacher at Pinbin that he became aware that his wonderful teacher was estranged from other adults in Pinbin.

At first Ralph thought adults might have been 'put off' by Mr Parson's odd appearance – he was a tall, thin man with large ears and a large nose, a small chin and eyes that always seemed half shut. But then he found that Mr Parson's behaviour was odd, at least by Pinbin standards – he didn't smoke or drink or attend any social, sporting or religious events and rarely spoke to anyone except his students. When Ralph talked to Rose about Mr Parson's behaviour, she told him that Mrs Wall (the postmistress) told her, and many other people in Pinbin, that every time Mr Parson received a pay cheque, he sent practically all the money to a woman in Sydney who wasn't Mrs Parsons. Rose dismissed the matter by saying, 'Mr Parson's behaviour is no great mystery; he has no 'spending money', so he just fills in his days teaching.

As the train wound its way through the Blue Mountains, Ralph's father, well awake by then, began to reiterate how lucky Ralph was. 'There are no boys in your uncle's family', he said, 'both his daughters only have girls. When he retires, you will run the business and when he dies, he will probably leave you a financial interest in it'.

Ralph paid little heed to his father's speculation. His concern was how well he would get on with his uncle and aunt.

He recalled that when he was very young, he had some difficulty distinguishing between Santa Claus and Uncle John as the giver of Christmas presents, because his parents referred to both, but at different times.

When he got older, Ralph found that money for the Christmas presents for both himself and Rose was sent to their parents early in December each year by Uncle John. With the 'Money Order' came a letter describing what had happened during the year to each member of Uncle John's family.

Ralph's mother had always written back, thanking John for the money and providing news of her family. After their mother died, Rose insisted that Ralph write the letters of thanks, letting Uncle John know what was happening to their little family.

Ralph realised that it was Rose's insistence that he write those letters that had brought the train journey to Sydney because in December 1915, he mentioned that Mr Parson had left at the end of his three year term and the high school lessons had ceased.

Within a few days, he had received a letter from Uncle John asking if he would like to come to Sydney, live with his uncle and aunt (Margaret), finish his study, sit for the Intermediate Certificate exam and then become apprenticed in the baking business.

Ralph remembered how excited he had been and how much he had wanted to accept the offer immediately. Rose was also excited and very pleased. But their father grumbled and said Ralph should get a job in Pinbin so that he could help his family. When Rose responded with the sharp edge of her tongue, their father, as usual, just grabbed his hat and disappeared.

Spurred on by Rose, who told him he could do what he like because he was fifteen now – a statement Ralph had gone along with, although he had some doubts. He had immediately written accepting the offer.

Ralph thought of Rose as the rhythm of the train made him sleepy. Rose was so sharp of tongue but so energetic, so direct and so reliable. Rose had made their ramshackle house a place of comfort and kept their lives from falling apart.

Soon after Ralph accepted his offer, Uncle John wrote to his brother offering to pay the rail fare for the two of them to come to Sydney and get Ralph 'settled in'. That seemed to placate his father and week later, they set off on the train to Sydney in high spirits.

The closer the train got to Sydney, the more nervous Ralph became. He had never lived, even for a short time, with anyone but members of his own family. He wondered what would be expected of him.

When he reached Sydney, he found that both his uncle and aunt were at the station to welcome him. Ralph was surprised to find Uncle John was a smaller man than his father, shorter and of lighter build. Aunt Margaret, however, was a large woman; 'buxom' was the word that came to mind. She was also much more talkative than Uncle John.

Ralph did his best to 'fit in'; listened attentively to everything said to him and insisted on helping with the housework – something he had always done when living with his mother and Rose. He was thrilled to find a small bedroom had been converted into a 'study' for him. It had a desk, a reading lamp and shelves for books. Uncle John told him not to hesitate to ask for money for any book or other equipment he may need.

Before Ralph had arrived in Sydney, Uncle John spoke to an Inspector of Schools and it was decided that the best place for Ralph to finish his studies would be the Technical College, because it had more flexibility in the teaching arrangements than a high school. The Inspector agreed to take Ralph to the Tech on the first day of the study year.

Ralph had arrived in Sydney wearing his only suit, a well-worn one, and with not much other clothing. During his second week, Aunt Margaret took him into the city to buy him some more clothes. She made quite a gala day of it, tram rides, visits to places of interest and pauses for cups of tea and for lunch at a very nice restaurant. Ralph was amazed and concerned about the beautiful new suit. 'For Sundays', she said.

Ralph soon found that Sunday was the great social day for his uncle and aunt. In the morning they went to the main service at the local Methodist Church; in the afternoon they visited relatives and friends or the relatives and friends visited them.

Uncle John and Aunt Margaret were important members of the church congregation; Uncle John was a Trustee of the local church and also of the state wide organisations. Aunt Margaret was the leader of a women's group. Ralph found later on that it was through his church connections that Uncle John was able to contact the Inspector of Schools. Ralph was invited to join the church's teenage brotherhood. He declined, saying he had a lot of study to catch up on, but hoped to join in the following year.

Ralph's cousins, Pat and Jill, made him very welcome and within a few weeks were treating him like a younger brother, teasing him in a light hearted way, bringing him into the games with their children, inquiring about his study and Pat particularly, from the questions she asked, showed she was genuinely interested in two of the subjects he was studying. Both girls also, like their mother, went to considerable trouble to produce special dishes and delicacies for him.

Every day when he returned from the Tech, he took Uncle John's advice and went for a long walk. His Uncle usually went for a walk at the same time, but insisted that Ralph walk without him. 'I am old and sometimes short of breath – you wouldn't get any worthwhile exercise walking with me', he said.

Not only did Ralph get on very well with his uncle, but a strong bond developed between him and his aunt. Having had only girls in the family, Aunt Margaret had encouraged Uncle John to bring Ralph to Sydney, had looked forward to having a boy in the house, but was not certain that she would 'hit it off' with him.

When she found that Ralph was very pleasant, always wanted to be helpful around the house, showed great appreciation for things she did for him and was an intelligent, thoughtful companion, she was delighted.

For his part Ralph felt he had never before experienced motherliness. His recollections of his mother were mostly of a bad-tempered woman,

83

frequently quarrelling with her husband and scolding her children. He had not realized that she was ill, constantly struggling to get food and shelter for the family and burdened with an unreliable husband.

Ralph worked very hard at his studies every evening except Sunday; he got high marks and praise from his teachers for his homework.

At the exam in November, none of the questions presented him with a major problem and he was fairly confident he would pass in all five subjects.

When the exam was finished, Uncle John suggested that he spend a week or so recovering. 'Go into town, take some ferry rides, visit the museums, whatever you want', he said. But Ralph insisted that he start his apprenticeship immediately.

The bakery, which was on a block of land behind Uncle John's house, faced a street containing mainly shops and warehouses. To get to the bakery, Uncle John went through a gate at the back of his house, across a lane and through a gate on the other side of the lane.

His uncle told Ralph that the bakery produced special, very high quality bread and buns (or rolls) to suit the requirements of some high class hotels and restaurants and a few retail outlets. No bread or buns were retailed from the bakery.

There were two men besides Uncle John working in the bakery, Joe Watson, a baker of about the same age as Uncle John, and a younger man, Claude Simpson, who performed all the non-baking tasks. Joe Watson was a very cheerful man, constantly making amusing remarks. He was also, Uncle John said, a very good baker from whom Ralph could learn a lot. Claude Simpson was quiet and very hard working. Ralph was amazed at the speed with which he chopped wood.

It took Ralph a little time to get used to the hours; he and Uncle John were both woken by alarm clocks at 3 am. As soon as they were dressed, they went into the kitchen and ate breakfast – prepared the night before by Aunt Margaret. By the time they got to the bakery, Claude had the oven fire going. Joe arrived at about the same time as Uncle John and Ralph. Both Joe and Claude travelled by bicycle. All the workers left the bakery at about 11.30 am every day except Saturday and Sunday. On Saturdays there was extra baking and they finished at about 1.30 pm. There was no work on Sundays.

Ralph had thought bread was made from flour and yeast, but found that the ingredients of even 'ordinary' bread (some of which was produced for the families of the 'workers' at the bakery) included other materials such as sugar, salt, oil and milk powder. For the various types of special breads a wide range of other materials such as honey, coffee, nuts, dried fruits and seeds were added. The quantities of all the materials used had to be very accurately measured.

Ralph soon came to like the atmosphere in the bakery. As the oven heated up, so did the work area. By the time he had finished his first lot of chores, the bakers were ready to start the kneading which Uncle John had told him he was to watch closely each day.

In the hot, floury atmosphere the two men worked rhythmically and silently except for an occasional short sharp comment or a quip from Joe Ralph was engrossed as he watched the finer parts of the process which his Uncle explained to him and which he need to get to know in detail.

Ralph had been working at the bakery for several weeks before he walked out into the street in front of the building and saw the sign – 'Campbell and Co Bakers'. He felt proud to be working for the Campbell company.

Ralph noticed that Joe had a cough somewhat similar to his uncle's. He thought that, being elderly men, they had both been unable to 'shake off' the effects of a bout of flu.

When, in January, the exam results were published, Ralph's confidence was justified – he had a good pass in all five subjects and would get the intermediate certificate.

When not working at the bakery, Ralph soon became very busy as a result of joining the church's teenage brotherhood. At first he was simply an enthusiastic participant in the activities, but by the second half of the year, he was a member of the executive, taking a constructive part in organising its activities.

His work as an executive of the teenage organisation brought him into contact with senior members of the church and he was pleased to hear Uncle John praised by some of them; one saying that Uncle John always seemed to be able to suggest a common sense solution to any problem.

One day early in November, the executive of the Teenage Brotherhood met with the senior laity of the church to get their approval and help in organising a picnic and gala day for the Sunday School children. When they were told that piece of equipment they wanted was not available within the church, Uncle John intervened to say, 'Leave the matter with me. I may be able to borrow one'.

As the boys were leaving after the meeting, Ralph overheard a conversation between two boys walking ahead of him. One said, 'Mr Campbell is always helpful'. 'Yes', said the other, then added, 'It's a pity he has the baker's disease!'

'What's that?'

'Haven't you noticed his cough? The father of a school friend of mine, Pat O'Reilly, is a baker and he has the cough; Pat told me a lot of bakers get it; its caused by flour getting into their lungs; they become a bit short of breath when they do anything very strenuous and cough regularly all day and night'.

Ralph was stunned. He walked home alarmed at the prospect of living a large part of his life short of breath and coughing regularly.

The feeling that he could not live like that grew stronger every day. But what should he do?

Should he now say to his Uncle that he didn't want to be a baker? But how could he do that after the great kindness and generosity of his uncle and aunt and his warm acceptance by the rest of the family. They all obviously expected him to continue the family connection with the bakery business. Would he lose all contact with his wonderful, lovable uncle and aunt? Would they regard him as an ungrateful, spoilt boy with whom they didn't want to be associated? What would happen to him? Would he be sent back to Pinbin? Would he end up like his father, a drifter, not trained to do any type of work?

Should he just accept flour in the lungs as one of the hazards of the work? Uncle John had apparently done that and was a good husband, family man and member of the church congregation. Flour in the lungs had not stopped Joe being a cheerful, likeable man.

Ralph couldn't get these worrying questions out of his mind. It began to affect both his work and his ability to learn in the bakery. It made him less attentive and sociable with his uncle and aunt at home and with other people. It began to disturb his sleep more and more until it made his nights unbearable.

His aunt noticed the change in him and asked him if he was unwell He said he was feeling a bit tired. His aunt suggested that he should ask his Uncle to let him take a holiday for a week or two. 'He would have no objection, he suggested it when you finished your exams', she said.

But Ralph realised that not working in the bakery wouldn't be a holiday for him. His terrible predicament would be uppermost in his mind wherever he went or whatever he did.

Ralph hesitated, then, feeling he could no longer stand the strain, said 'I'm worried about getting flour in the lungs'.

You should speak to your uncle about it', Aunt Margaret said.

Ralph thought his uncle would say 'It's nothing to get worried about – many bakers get it and live quite pleasant lives'. But after remaining silent for a while, his uncle said, 'You don't want to become a baker?'

'I don't think I could ever concentrate properly on the work', Ralph replied.

Once again his uncle remained silent for a while. Then he said, 'Don't say anything about this to anybody for a while. I'll tell your aunt and other people in due course. Just continue to work in the bakery'. He smiled and added, 'A few more days in the bakery won't do you any harm'.

Ralph was tremendously relieved by his uncle's quiet acceptance of his desire to give up the apprenticeship and although he had not given Ralph any indication of what he intended to do, Ralph felt certain his uncle intended to help him find some worthwhile future occupation.

To Aunt Margaret's great relief, Ralph became once more the pleasant young man she had come to know and whose unexplained depression had worried her greatly.

Christmas Day came and went. Ralph expected his uncle would tell his aunt as soon as the festivities had finished. He didn't. New Year's Day came and went. Still his uncle said nothing to anybody about the cessation of the apprenticeship.

Out of the blue one day, Uncle John said to Ralph, 'Would you be interested in being apprenticed to a French polisher?'

Ralph realised that his uncle had devoted a lot of his spare time searching for an apprenticeship that might be offered to him. He immediately said, 'Yes'.

Uncle John said, 'Don't rush into this, think it over for a day or two'.

Ralph didn't need to think it over. His father had convinced him that he needed to become a 'tradesman' to get regular work and he was extremely grateful to his uncle for getting him a second opportunity to become one.

The next day, when he told Uncle John that he wanted to accept the offer, his uncle said, 'Alright, we'll go this afternoon to see Mr Prosser, the manager of Blamey and Company'.

Mr Prosser seemed a brusque sort of man who obviously had a long standing association with Uncle John. He asked Ralph a few questions and then asked him when he would like to start. Ralph looked at his uncle. 'What about tomorrow?' his uncle said. Mr Prosser replied, 'That's fine. I'll see you here in my office at 9 o'clock in the morning'.

From snatches of conversation he heard that night, Ralph became aware that his uncle had told Aunt Margaret that Ralph was giving up his apprenticeship at the bakery. His aunt seemed upset. The last thing Ralph heard before he fell asleep was his uncle saying quite distinctly, 'He is the same boy whether he is apprenticed to a baker or a French polisher'.

Aunt Margaret didn't have her breakfast with Ralph the next morning. After serving him, she went back into the kitchen. When he carried his used crockery and cutlery out to the kitchen, she pointed to a bag on the table and said, 'There's your lunch'.

Ralph thanked her and dejectedly picked up the bag. As he turned to walk out of the kitchen, his aunt said, 'Good luck!' He turned back and she smiled He felt like rushing over to hug her but, not accustomed to showing affection he just smiled and said, 'Thank you'.

After the arrangements for the apprenticeship were completed, Mr Prosser explained the organisation of the company's operations. There were three sections, the retail household furniture shop, the retail office furniture shop and the workshop.

Mr Prosser said Ralph would be located in the workshop. In that section there were seven cabinet makers, the French polisher, Jack Smith and the odd job man, Ted Rimmer, all under the control of the foreman, Mike Taylor. The company made furniture for its own retail shops, for other retailers, for business organisations and it also repaired furniture.

Ralph would be taking over some of the odd jobs that Ted Rimmer performed. Mr Prosser explained that Blamey & Co didn't carry any substantial stocks of materials and fittings but had an arrangement with a nearby hardware wholesaler, Reith & Son, to supply on the following working day, any order they received from Blamey & Co.

Mr Prosser prepared an order every day for goods to be obtained from Reith & Son. Usually Ted Rimmer took these to the wholesaler's warehouse. 'As soon as you are settled in, I want you to take the orders to Reith & Son', he said.

Jack Smith was an elderly cheerful man who quietly hummed popular songs as he worked. When he finished a job, he always stood back from it for a while and then nodded his head and smiled.

However, he said very little to Ralph about the French polishing process and gave him only tedious jobs such as removing French polish or varnish from furniture brought into the workshop for repair.

The foreman, Mark Taylor, got Ralph to rough saw timber, sharpen tools and generally clean up the workshop. Ralph thought every apprentice was probably treated that way during his first year; he performed every job with enthusiasm and looked forward to the time when he would be taught the trade.

Each day Ralph took an order to Reith & Son. Inside the warehouse was a small counter and his order and those of other customers, most of whom seemed to be from hardware retail stores, were taken by a man called Jim who put them into several wire baskets on a desk near the counter. Jim also dealt with queries raised by customers.

To the left of the counter was an office which had a wall almost entirely of glass facing the counter. In that office sat a middle-aged man who came out to help at the counter when Jim was very busy. Before long, Ralph learned that man was Mr Reith, owner of the hardware warehouse.

Sometimes Ralph was asked to get a special type of material or fittings that were urgently needed from Reith's warehouse. These were obtained from either Jim or Mr Reith after Ralph carefully explained exactly what was required.

After he had been working for Blamey & Co for almost a year, Mr Reith stopped Ralph one day after he had collected some special fittings. 'You're a well-spoken young man. How far did you go with your schooling?'

'Intermediate Certificate', said Ralph.

'Where did you go to school?' asked Mr Reith.

'Mainly very small schools in western NSW, but I finished last year at the Tech in Sydney', replied Ralph.

Mr Reith nodded his head and walked off.

Ralph thought Mr Reith had asked the questions out of idle curiosity. However, when he arrived at the warehouse a week later, Mr Reith hurried out of office and asked Ralph when he usually took his lunch break. 'Could you come here one day soon during your lunch break and talk to me for a few minutes?' he asked.

Very surprised, Ralph arranged to come the next day Mr Reith took him into his office. 'I'm considering you for a job but first I want to clear up a few things. How old are you?'

'I turned eighteen in September', Ralph said.

'Are you thinking about enlisting in the army and going off to France?' asked Mr Reith.

'No! I'm a pacifist', said Ralph. That was said on the spur of the moment. Ralph had never considered he might become directly involved in the war and he certainly had no wish to join the army.

Obviously satisfied with his answer, Mr Reith informed Ralph that his country salesman, Barry Plant, wanted to retire in a couple of years. 'I'm looking for a replacement. What I have in mind is that you join this company, work for the packers but mainly get to know everything about every one of the products we sell here. Your teachers at the Technical College told me you were a very good student. So if at the end of a year I am satisfied, I will send you out with Barry Plant. Our country market extends right through New South Wales and just across the border into Victoria and Queensland, so it involves a lot of travelling'.

Then Mr Reith explained in detail what he expected the salesman to do when he was in the country as well when he was based in Sydney. He also told Ralph what his wages would be for the first year when he would be working with Barry Plant and when he became the salesman on his own.

Ralph was surprised how high the wages would be. Even the wage for the first year would be more than twice the wage he would earn as a second year apprentice at Blamey & Co. And his wage as the salesman seemed unbelievably high.

Mr Reith finished by saying, 'Bear in mind that you will have an opportunity to become an experienced commercial traveller and that good commercial travellers are always in demand. Please think about what I am offering you and let me know your decision within the next few days'.

As he walked back to Blamey & Co, one aspect of the offer was uppermost in Ralph's mind. Mr Reith had indicated that the skills he would acquire by getting and keeping customers for Reith & Son would be transferable; that he could expect to become an efficient commercial traveller capable of doing a good job elsewhere. His father's often repeated statement that it was difficult to get regular work if you didn't have a tradesman's certificate had made a considerable impression on Ralph. As a commercial traveller, he wouldn't have a certificate but would have to rely on 'word of mouth'.

The absence of a certificate worried him for a while but on further reflection he realised that any tradesman with a certificate wouldn't be able to rely on the certificate alone if he wanted to set up his own business or seek higher paid work; he would be dependent to a large extent on 'word of mouth'. Perhaps a certificate, although very helpful and legally required in many trades, was not essential to get regular work in some well-recognised occupations.

To avoid any possibility of Mr Prosser first hearing of Mr Reith's offer from another source, Ralph went straight to Mr Prosser's office to tell him about it and let him know he intended to discuss the offer with his uncle. 'I want to know very quickly whether you are going to continue with the apprenticeship', Mr Prosser responded.

Ralph was kept very busy during the afternoon, so he put the offer out of his mind. But on the way home Ralph wondered what his uncle's attitude to Mr Reith's offer was likely to be. His uncle strongly believed in the value of the apprenticeship system and the certified tradesmen it produced. Uncle undoubtedly considered his failure to get Ralph's father to take his advice would have contributed to his brother becoming a drifter. Ralph thought it likely that his uncle would endeavour to make amends with his nephew. Consequently his uncle would want him to continue his apprenticeship and Ralph was prepared to willingly do that, not only because he was very grateful for everything his uncle had done for him, but also because h greatly admired his uncle and had become very fond of him.

Ralph was unable to talk to his uncle until after the evening meal. Then, when they were alone in the dining room, he explained the whole thing from the beginning, the questions Mr Reith had asked and what he had offered Ralph during the lunch break that day. He also mentioned Mr Prosser's attitude when he had told the manager about Mr Reith's offer.

Uncle John asked Ralph whether the offer appealed to him. Because he was determined to do whatever his uncle wanted, Ralph replied 'I am uncertain. I find it difficult to weigh up the advantages and disadvantages'.

His uncle was silent for a while. Finally he made a decision. 'If you continue with your apprenticeship I have no doubt you will make a good French polisher, enjoy the work and live a quiet, happy life. But you won't be using and developing your real talents, which are not those of a craftsman. You are a good scholar, interested in a wide range of matters, always prepared to listen carefully, able to explain things very clearly and get on very well with people. Going out into the business world involves an element of risk but I think you will be able to handle that. Mr Reith obviously has a lot of confidence in you or he wouldn't consider you for the commercial traveller's job as such a young age. I think you should accept the offer. What do you think?'

His uncle's response was what Ralph really had wanted to hear but had put out of his mind because he didn't expect it. Elated, he could only agree.

Uncle John smiled and said 'I know you will make a good fist of it'.

Looking at his uncle across the table, Ralph's great affection for him was suddenly displayed in a surprising way; he burst into tears.

Aunt Margaret came into the room and seeing the tears running down Ralph's cheeks, exclaimed, 'Good Heavens! What has happened?'

Uncle John laughed and said, 'Ralph's going to become a commercial traveller'.

RURAL TALES

THE PARCEL

At ten past six on a Sunday evening early in April 1931 a family of four hurried down the steps of the overhead bridge at the Perth railway station onto platform three. Standing at the platform was the 6.15 pm train to Kalgoorlie. The train was an express as far as Northam and at that provincial town beyond the Darling Range it connected with several slow trains servicing a large part of the Western Australian farmland.

The first of the family to reach the platform was a lanky, rather sullen-faced youth of seventeen with an overcoat flung over one shoulder and carrying a suitcase. Just behind him was a round faced, plump boy of thirteen carrying a brown paper parcel about three feet long and one foot wide and having several bumps of no particular shape at the top and bottom. At least ten steps behind the boys were their mother and sister, a tall, authoritative looking woman and a pretty, petite girl of fifteen.

Although the train was not very crowded, the elder boy, whose name was Ralph, did not find a seat that suited him until he reached the second last carriage. Then he took the parcel from his brother, boarded the train, and made his way along the corridor to a compartment in which four men already sat close together with an overcoat spread across their knees playing cards.

For a minute or so after Ralph entered, the men's attention was diverted by the youth's attempts to place on the luggage rack above his seat the suitcase, overcoat and the awkwardly shaped parcel. Finding he could not place all of them on the same rack, Ralph, aware the men were watching him, nervously fumbled the parcel across to the rack on the other side of the compartment.

Having finally put away all his baggage Ralph dashed back down the corridor and left the train to receive a hurried kiss on the cheek and a hug from each member of the family. These farewell gestures completed he got back into the train and positioned himself alongside the window in the carriage door. His mother immediately repeated some instructions she had given him several times earlier in the day about what he should wear, eat and do while he was away. As Ralph murmured 'Yes mother' the guard blew his whistle and the train began to move. Ralph stayed at the window waving until his family were lost to sight when the train turned to the east just beyond the Beaufort Street Bridge.

Back in the compartment he settled into his corner seat and partially closed his eyes. He hoped to give the impression that he was asleep while he surreptitiously watched the four men at cards. It was not the card game but the players that interested him.

One of the men was considerably older than the others. The lower parts of the men's faces were reddish brown but their foreheads were surprisingly white, all were all clean shaven and had close-cropped hair. Each wore a shapeless pullover or a waistcoat over an open-necked shirt. Little could be seen of their pants under the overcoat but they all appeared to be very rumpled.

Much to Ralph's disappointment the conversation between the men was restricted to a few words necessary to forward the card game. But, at one stage some tension arose about the betting and this led to remarks such as 'Cut it out, you bastard. None of us have that sort of money now' and 'I'll have a crack at you with big stakes when we're comin' back'.

Ralph's observations tended to confirm what he had thought likely when he had first seen the compartment – that the men were seasonal farm labourers on their way to work for the planting season. They were the sort of men who would be his fellow workers and companions for at least the next few months.

Ralph perceived his future as a farm labourer with apprehension but was convinced that it could not be worse than his past as a discontented student. For as long as he could remember he had been terribly unhappy both at home and school and at loggerheads with his mother.

Ralph's mother Vera Burgess had been widowed eleven years earlier after six years of marriage. Both Vera and her husband had migrated from the eastern states in the early 1900s following the discovery of rich gold deposits in the barren hinterland of Western Australia. Neither of them had any relatives in the western state. Their marriage was not the culmination of a long, affectionate relationship between two loving people but a union 'forced' on the couple after a brief encounter when Vera became pregnant with Ralph.

During the marriage Vera's husband (an engineer managing a gold mine in the north of the state) had visited Perth, where Vera and the children lived, for only a short period each year. Consequently the children had seen very little of their father; the youngest, Jim, had never seen him.

Within a few weeks of her husband's death, Vera had engaged a woman to do the housekeeping and to look after the younger children during school hours, and had returned to teaching – an occupation which gave her great satisfaction, not because she was fond of children, but because she enjoyed the companionship of her colleagues and the sense of power it gave her.

Vera had begun her teaching career in the New South Wales public school system at a very early age. She had become a monitor at sixteen and a fully fledged teacher at nineteen. Three years later she had moved to Western Australia in response to advertisements inserted in the Sydney newspapers by the Western Australian Government offering highly paid positions to teachers.

A dogmatic person, Vera had readily accepted the system of teaching by rote prevalent at the time. For some of Ralph's primary education his mother had been his teacher at school and throughout his life she had been his strict supervisor for the long periods of study that she insisted all her children undertake at home.

Ralph was only vaguely aware of his mother's early life and knew very little about his father. His mother did not discuss these matters with her children and discouraged questions about them.

Sitting in the train, at last free from his mother and the school life he associated with her, Ralph did not feel the elation he had expected. He was not only anxious about his future but also puzzled and uncomfortable about his past. Why had Mary and Jim been able to get along with his mother and he had not? Why had he always seemed to be at cross purposes with his teachers? What had he done with the first seventeen years of his life?

These reflections did not continue for long. Worn out by the tension of the last few days he fell asleep.

•

It was after Ralph, at the age of three or four, added the word 'Why?' to his vocabulary and found frequent use for it, that he had begun to irritate Vera. Although his questions were generally brushed aside that did not deter him from continuing to ask. But when he went to school his teachers (one of whom was his mother) found his persistent calls for explanations exasperating and before long set out to silence him by scoring off him in front of the class. Faced with constant humiliation he gave up his search for the reason or purpose of things mentioned by the adults around him, lost interest in school work (doing only enough to just pass the exams) and withdrew to his own dream world. It was a world peopled by elfish creatures who exercised a mysterious power over men and women, a power which Ralph shared. His interest in supernatural beings was stimulated from the age of ten or eleven by stealthily reading a collection of books devoted to supernaturalism and left in his mother's care by a teacher who went overseas for a three year working holiday. As soon as she became aware of the contents, his mother had ordered all the children not to waste any of their time on 'that nonsense' – an order that had excited Ralph's curiosity.

Ralph's sister Mary and brother Jim accepted without demur the rote method of teaching at home and at school. Both were regarded by their teachers as outstanding pupils and in fact were invariably at the top of their class. But for Ralph it was a disaster. Eleven years of schooling and frequent whippings by Vera and various headmasters for truancy had turned an inquisitive, intelligent child into a sulky, rebellious youth with only a mediocre education.

Mary and Jim's progress at school had elated Vera; it was a source of permanent gratification, it enabled her to boast to her friends and acquaintances of her children's scholastic achievements. But even as she was speaking glowingly about Mary and Jim the thought preyed upon her mind that many of her listeners might be thinking, 'Ah! but what about Ralph?'. He infuriated her, she wanted to be unconditionally recognised as a good teacher and mother.

By the end of 1930 Ralph was determined to get away from home and began, without his mother's knowledge, and while still at school, to look for a job outside Perth. In the middle of the great depression it was extremely difficult for an inexperienced youth without outstanding educational qualifications to get a job anywhere. However, despite his nervousness and shyness, Ralph relentlessly pursued his objective.

Mrs Keating, a principal of Keating and Co, Employment Agency, began to take an interest in the boy after he had called regularly at the agency on Thursday afternoon for some time. She did not, like the employees of other agencies, dismiss his inquiries coldly and out of hand.

Ralph had started off trying to get a job in an office or shop but Mrs Keating had pointed out that there were many unemployed in every country town and any vacancy not requiring special qualifications was quickly snapped up by a local inhabitant. She considered that his only hope was seasonal work as a farm labourer but warned him that such work was hard, the hours long and the life rough. He said he was prepared to accept that. Mrs Keating thought he looked strong and fit and encouraged him to persevere although she knew that without experience the prospect of him getting even a farm labourer's job was not good.

The friendliness of the quiet, competent Mrs Keating, the first encouraging person Ralph had come across, strengthened his resolve and gave him more confidence.

When he entered her office one Thursday, two weeks after his seventeenth birthday, she greeted him with 'I have a job that might interest you'.

Extracting some papers she said, 'I have received a telegram from a farmer named Ted Miller at Lake Jane asking for a youth, no experience needed, willing to learn, conscientious, ten shillings a week and keep, to arrive at Lake Jane next Monday. That's all the information I have. But Mr Miller was a client of ours for a number of years when he owned a carrying business based on Northam. He was regarded as a good employer. Do you know anything about Lake Jane?'

'No'.

'It's well over two hundred miles from Perth, a new area, only opened up for farming about five or six years ago. The farmers are still trying to establish their farms; with the recent poor wheat prices they have had very little money to spare for housing and amenities. Living there could be very rough. The wage isn't much, but you can't expect anything better without experience. What do you think?'

'I'd like to take it'.

'Well it's yours. I'll fill you in on the travel arrangements'.

When Ralph told his mother about the job she shouted angrily, 'No child of mine is going to be a farm labourer'. There followed two days of fierce argument and threats from Vera that if Ralph went to Lake Jane she would have him brought back home by the police. But Ralph was as stubborn as his mother and finally she reluctantly agreed when he promised he would conduct himself at the farm in a way which would show the farmer and his family (Vera was not concerned about Ralph's fellow-workers) that he came from 'a well-respected and well-educated family'. One of the tasks Ralph promised to perform to demonstrate the respectability and education of his family was to go to dinner every evening wearing 'a well-kept suit'. To ensure that the trousers were always well creased his mother insisted that Ralph take with him a trouser-press.

Although the thought of walking into the labourers' quarters on a farm carrying a trouser-press made his blood run cold he had no alternative, he had to take the press with him.

•

Ralph slept for about an hour. When he awoke the train was slowing down and shortly afterwards made an unscheduled stop. He went into the corridor, opened a window and looked out. The name of the station was Clackline. He realised that they were quite close to Northam.

The stop was very brief. After the train started to move again Ralph remained at the window for a while to take his first look at the eastern side of the Darling Range, then he closed the window and returned to the compartment. The four men were still playing cards.

Ten minutes after the Clackline stop a uniformed ticket inspector entered and in a loud voice asked for 'Tickets please'. All the men quickly produced their tickets but Ralph could not find his. He had gone through his pockets once and was starting again when one of the younger men looked up from his cards and said to the inspector, 'I know he's got a ticket. I saw it in his hand when he came into the compartment'. All the other men spoke up saying they also had seen the ticket in Ralph's hand. The inspector said nothing. Ralph went on searching, carefully removing everything from each pocket.

One of the men said, 'He had the ticket in his hand when he looked out of the window at Clackline. I saw it as he went out of the compartment but now I think about it, didn't see it when he came back'. Another man backed up that statement by saying, 'Yes, he probably dropped it out of the train when he closed the window'.

By this time Ralph had completely emptied all his pockets and the inspector asked, 'Where are you going?'

'Lake Jane'.

'What's your name?'

'Ralph Burgess'.

'Well, you haven't got a ticket. I received a call from Perth to say your mother handed it in at the station after the train left. She'd forgotten to give it to you'.

The inspector got a note pad out of his pocket, wrote a few words on the top sheet, added his signature with a flourish and, as he gave the sheet to Ralph, said, 'Make sure you hang on to that. You have to change at Northam and Merryton'.

The four men had resumed the card game as soon as the question of Ralph's ticket had been satisfactorily settled. The inspector now turned to them and said with a laugh, 'You're a lying lot of bastards'.

All the men looked up from their cards and each of them acknowledged, with either a nod of the head or a grin that the inspector's observation was fair comment.

Ralph would have liked to thank the men for trying to help him but, feeling nervous and embarrassed by the inspector's reference to his mother, hesitated and the opportunity passed.

Quite soon after the inspector left the compartment the men stopped their card game and prepared to leave the train. While doing so they talked about the farms on which they had recently worked. At first Ralph was puzzled by their frequent references to 'cockies' but after a while realised that 'cocky' was a nickname the men used to describe the farmers who hired them.

When the train pulled into the Northam station Ralph delayed his exit from the compartment by opening his suitcase and poking around in it. As soon as the men had left he took off his tie and put it in the case. Then he closed the door of the compartment, got the trouser-press down from the rack, placed it on the seat and knelt down between the seats. He was just about to pick it up and hide it under the seat when the door opened and two women and a little girl appeared. For a moment the newcomers and Ralph remained silent and motionless. Then the little girl turned towards one of the women and said in a whisper overheard by all, 'Is he praying mummy?' Ralph rose from his knees, picked up his suitcase, overcoat and the parcel and stumbled out of the train. Directed by a porter he found his way to the Lake Jane train, still somewhat shaken by his unsuccessful attempt to dispose of the trouser-press.

•

A large group of young men joined the train just before it departed. Three of them took seats in Ralph's compartment, some others in the compartment next door and the remainder stood in the corridor. An alcoholic odour accompanied the men; they had apparently spent a large part of the day in

Northam exercising their right as bona fide travellers to be served with alcoholic drinks on a Sunday. Soon after the train started one of the men standing in the corridor began playing a mouth organ. His companions broke into song, singing or shouting bawdy verses to the tunes of several popular ditties.

To Ralph's surprise the other occupants, two men (one reading a paper and the other lost in thought) and two women reading magazines, remained apparently unmoved by the lewd words and indelicate descriptions of very private matters. Ralph listened intensely. Many of the verses were frequently repeated and he memorised a few in the hope that familiarity with them would prove a social asset later on.

All the choristers had left the train before it reached Merryton. On its arrival at that rail junction an announcement was made that the train which had just come from Northam would leave in ten minutes time for Bonyup stopping at all stations, and that the train which would pull into the platform after the Bonyup train had departed would leave ten minutes later for Lake Jane stopping at all stations.

•

Some of the passengers who had come from Northam and were going to catch the Lake Jane train went across the road to a hotel which was open for bona fide travellers. All the others except Ralph went into the waiting room alongside the station office. Ralph sat on a seat about twenty yards away from the office building. The only lights on the platform were near the office and at each end of the platform. None was bright and Ralph was sitting in semi-darkness. No one had seemed to notice him there. After looking around several times he pushed the parcel as far as he could into the darkness under the seat.

Feeling more at ease Ralph got his lunch box out of his suitcase. As he began eating he recalled that it was Mary who had made the sandwiches. Mary, so pretty, so serious, so conscientious and almost as lacking in humour as her mother, but probably the only staunch friend he had in the world. Always torn between affection for him and loyalty to her mother she had been an disapproving ally when he had needed aid to circumvent their domineering parent. But when any scheme of his had not succeeded she had invariably tried to help him as soon as the show-down came and had often diverted to herself some of their mother's rage.

102

From Mary his mind drifted to Jim. Always doing what he was told, always friendly, always wanting to please everyone and generally succeeding, always keeping out of the way when trouble was brewing. He could recall very little of Jim as a small child but for the last four or five years whenever the two of them had been able to get away from study together Jim had run with him (for as long as he could) in the park near their home or had played hand ball with him against the wall at the back of the house. Despite nearly four years difference in age and a marked difference in temperament they had readily accepted each other; they had needed each other, but Ralph realised that his need had been the greater because he lacked something Jim had, a knack of getting on with people.

Sitting in the semi-darkness with no one near him, recalling his life at home and his companionship with Mary and Jim, Ralph began to feel very much alone in the world and suddenly, although it was a mild autumn evening, quite cold. He put on his overcoat and pulled it tightly around him.

He wondered how different his life would have been if he had had a father. Only four-years-old when his father had visited Perth for the last time, and with no recollection of that or any other visit, he had always regarded himself as fatherless, as deprived of one of the necessities of life. But would his father have listened to him, answered his questions, talked to him, run with him, played games with him? Were fathers like that?

Ralph ceased to conjecture about the characteristics of fathers when he saw the Lake Jane train coming slowly into the station. It consisted of ten trucks (one a flat top carrying two tractors and the rest tarpaulin covered wagons), two rather dilapidated looking goods vans, one guard's van and two passenger carriages, pulled along by a small locomotive which seemed to be overloaded with coal and to be panting plaintively at the prospect of having to haul such a large, motley collection of rolling stock along more than a hundred miles of track.

Ralph picked up his suitcase and boarded the train as soon as it stopped. From a window seat in a vacant compartment he watched the people moving around on the ill-lit platform. He was a little tense, worried that someone might discover the parcel under the seat, now hidden from his view. But when the guard blew his whistle and the train began to move he relaxed.

His relief was short lived. The train had only moved a few yards when there was a great shout from one of the station staff: 'Hold it!' 'Hold it!' The guard stepped back on to the platform, blew three blasts on his whistle, turned his lamp to red and waved it. The train violently jerked to a stop. The railwayman appeared in the light of the train holding up the parcel and shouting at the top of his voice, 'The young fellow sittin' up there left this behind'. Heads appeared at all the windows and the railwayman shouted repeatedly, 'Where is he?'

Ralph realised he had no alternative; he had to go onto the platform and recover the trouser-press. When he gave the parcel to Ralph the railwayman said, 'You're very lucky; the light from my lamp just happened to fall on it when I was walkin' to the end of the platform'.

Back in the train Ralph put the parcel on the luggage rack and sat down feeling very dispirited and foolish. A large number of his fellow passengers had heard and seen it all. He was sure they thought that no one in his right mind could forget such a large parcel. Any of them that met him later on would recall the extraordinary episode at the Merryton station.

At the next station, Manmissing, a short heavily-built man with a very plain face dominated by a large red-veined nose, entered the compartment, threw his luggage on the rack and with one hand thrust out said to Ralph, 'I'm Nosey Parker'. Ralph shook his hand. 'I'm Ralph Burgess'.

'Where yer goin'?'

'Lake Jane'.

'Got a job there?'

'Yes'.

'I'm goin' nearly that far, to Swinbourne'.

'What's it like out there?'

'Dunno, never been out that far. But it's bloody hard to get a job anywhere now'.

Then a young man and a very attractive young woman with a baby in her arms entered. As soon as they sat down Nosey learned towards the man and said, 'G'day, I'm Nosey Parker'.

The young man responded, 'Jack Power and my wife Mary'.

Mary said, 'Hullo', then smiling and nodding towards the baby in her lap, added, 'And our son James'.

Jack looked towards Ralph. He rose rather nervously from his seat and said, 'I'm Ralph Burgess'.

Nosey asked, 'Goin' far?'

'Narara'.

'Not a bad sorta town. Yer live there?'

'For the time being. I work in a bank, the Bank of New South Wales'.

'Jist visitin' Manmissing?'

'Yes. My uncle has a property a few miles out of the town'.

'Dick Power?'

'Yes'.

'I've heard of him. Been there for a long time'.

'Yes. My grandfather settled there in 1900'.

Nosey's verbal voyage of discovery through the affairs of Jack Power was interrupted by James crying loudly.

Mrs Power immediately began to sing in a clear, musical voice, not lullabies, but Scottish songs. The singing almost instantly quietened James but it was sometime before he ceased watching his mother's face and closed his eyes. In the meantime his father had fallen asleep.

For about ten minutes the heavily booted left foot of Nosey went up and down in time with the beat of the music. Quite suddenly it stopped. And shortly afterwards intermittent snores informed those still awake that Nosey was asleep.

Ralph could see reflected in the carriage window Mary's head and shoulders. The handsome profile and graceful neck seemed to him to belong to a female spirit, a beautiful but insubstantial being, a fairy godmother endowed with the magical power of singing men to sleep and whisking their subconscious souls away from the worries of the world to an enchanting place.

With that thought in his mind Ralph gradually dozed off.

Sometime later both Ralph and Nosey were woken by the train suddenly stopping. Ralph was surprised to find that the Power family had left the train. Nosey took a watch out of his pocket, and when Ralph asked him the time, smothered a huge yawn and said, 'ten past two'.

They opened their windows and twisted around to see what was in action outside. The hamlet where the train had stopped bore the improbable name of Coocooing. There was no light of any kind beyond the station and very little within the station boundary. Two passengers could be seen disembarking under the half-awake attention of the guard and a drowsy member of the station staff.

After their train left the station Ralph and Nosey remained for some time looking out. High cloud obscured the stars, there was no moon, no light of any kind, nothing but darkness and the occasional glimpse of a stunted tree or wooden fence post caught in the light of the passing train.

Almost simultaneously the two passengers lost interest in the world outside and closed their windows. Nosey then said, 'I should've got a job 'round here!'

Puzzled, Ralph asked, 'Why?'

As he settled back to sleep again Nosey replied, 'The bloody cockies let 'em sleep in'.

•

Ralph could not get back to sleep. The closer he got to Lake Jane the more concerned he became about his ability to make a success of his job as a labourer; disturbing thoughts about his deficiencies floated in and out of his mind.

While he was trying to get a job he had been too busy stealing time from his 'duties' at home and school and inventing explanations for his absences, to think about the people for whom, and with whom, he might be working, or the type of work he might be required to do. After he got the job overcoming his mother's obstructiveness had occupied all his attention. It was not until he boarded the train that he began to think about what might lie ahead. It was only then that he began to realise how terribly ignorant of farming he was. He had seen, and admired, a few horses, cows and sheep but had never been really near any one of them. At home he would have loved a dog but had never owned one because his mother did not like them. Would he be afraid of the bigger animals if he had to manage them? He realised now that he knew nothing about farm equipment; he had never seen any cereals growing and could not tell wheat from oats or barley. Then there was the question of how he would get on with the other people at the farm. The few casual remarks the card players and Nosey had made about 'cockies' left Ralph with the impression that farmers were not considerate bosses. Would he have with Mr Miller the same sort of difficulties he had had with his mother and so many teachers at school? Would he be able to get along with the other labourers on the farm? He had had no experience of living closely with men or boys. His mother had banned such things as scouting and organised sport because they would interfere with study. On the very few occasions when he had been for any length of time in close company with boys of his own age outside the schoolroom he had not hit it off well with them. Reflecting on that background made him very nervous about his future with his prospective fellow-workers. How many labourers would Mr

Miller employ? How old would they be and would they take advantage of his inexperience to play practical jokes on him?

While Ralph agonised about his future the train continued its slow but sure way to Lake Jane. Whenever it arrived at a station Ralph lowered his window to see what was happening outside. At almost every stop after Coocooing the engine came past shunting a truck or a freight van from the front of the train to a suitable position in the station yard for unloading. Several times the firebox door was open and the firelight brilliantly illuminated the stoker, stripped to the waist, shovelling coal. Most of the time the driver hung well out of the cabin with his attention fixed on the shunter's light. The gradual shedding of trucks and vans had not resulted in the little locomotive pulling the train faster, it maintained its very leisurely, phlegmatic pace.

As Ralph was in no hurry to reach Mr Miller's farm, he drew some comfort from the train's slow rate of progress, grew fond of the panting, puffing locomotive and longed wistfully for the journey never to end.

After the train left each station Ralph kept his window open for a while hoping that he would be able to see something of the country through which he was passing. As the night wore on lights appeared here and there, some steady, others flickering like glow worms, and Ralph assumed that the farmers and their labourers had commenced their day's work.

When the predawn light came it was distorted and dimmed by a ground mist that gave the gaunt trees, low shrubs, sections of fence, sheds and small houses a light, airy, tenuous, almost spiritual appearance. But as the train drew close to Swinbourne the sun rose above the horizon, drove away the mist and revealed the passing scene in its substantive, everyday form. Where large areas of land had been cleared and Ralph could get a long view he saw a gently undulating landscape almost devoid of trees and shrubs. The only signs of human habitation were an occasional small, naked-looking house or outbuilding or a team of horses or a small tractor pulling a farming machine. Much of the countryside was uncleared and covered with thickets of shrubs or low trees through which protruded, singly or in small clusters, tall, stately trees whose unclad branches curved gracefully upwards to support flat, thin canopies of grey leaves.

At Swinbourne, Nosey, only half awake, pulled his bag from the luggage rack, and as he left the compartment wished Ralph success in his first job with 'Gu'd luck mate'.

•

For the final few miles of his journey Ralph was alone. He sat looking moodily at the trouser-press up on the baggage rack, considering whether or not he should throw it out of the window or hide it again under a seat. But the failure of his previous attempts made him hesitate. The guard might see him throwing it out and recognise it from his observation window in the van. A second attempt by Ralph to rid himself of the parcel might make the guard suspect wrong-doing and stop the train to see what was afoot or report the two incidents to the police at Lake Jane. And, as Lake Jane was the terminus, presumably the carriages would be cleaned soon after the train arrived and the package, if he put it under the seat, re-discovered. The experience at Merriton taught him that the whereabouts and actions of individuals were more likely to be observed in the sparsely populated country than in crowded Perth. Another unsuccessful attempt to get rid of the parcel by any means would get him an undesirable reputation before he even reached the farm. He decided that for the time being he was stuck with his burden.

Ralph had only just put his baggage down on the platform at Lake Jane and was looking around when a cheerful looking middle aged man with a sunburnt face and wearing overalls came up to him and asked, 'Ralph Burgess?'

'Yes'.

'I'm Ted Miller'.

Ted shook hands. 'Put your gear in the back of the truck'. He pointed to an old truck with low side boards, only a few yards off the platform, 'I've got to collect a parcel from the van'.

'Yes Mr Miller'.

Twisting around and glancing back at Ralph as he walked away Ted Miller said, 'Call me Ted'.

There was a short haired dog standing in the back of Ted's vehicle. It watched Ralph approach and moved over to sniff his hand as he put his baggage into the truck. Apparently satisfied with what it detected the dog wagged its tail and let Ralph pat its head.

While patting the dog Ralph looked across the road at the shopping and business section of the town: the Commonwealth Bank, Williams' General Store, Murray's Bakery, the Goldsborough Mort Office and the Royal Hotel. The hotel was the only two storied building and its verandah on the upper floor overlooked the Railway Station.

A man with a suitcase crossed the road and entered the hotel, smoke rose lazily from the chimney behind the baker's shop, a T-model Ford car drew away from the railway station and as it moved down the gravel road, left a thin cloud of dust hanging in the still morning air, a crow sitting on the fence alongside the station yard cried out loudly in a hoarse, cawing tone, 'Ka-Ka-Kaaa'.

When Ted Millet walked up to the truck carrying a small parcel and said, 'Hop in'. Ralph felt that the arrival at Lake Jane had been less stressful than he had feared.

As they were leaving town Ted asked whether Ralph had ever worked on a farm and when told he had not, asked, 'Have you ever been on a farm?'

'No'.

'Have you had anything to do with animals – horses, cows, dogs?'

'No'.

'Do you know anything about internal combustion engines?'

'No'.

'Can you drive a truck or a car?'

'No'.

After this Ted said nothing for some time. Glancing sideways it seemed to Ralph that Ted had lost his cheeriness, he looked quite solemn. Ralph's heart sank and his fears returned. Was Ted going to say already that he was unsuitable despite the inclusion of 'no experience required' in the telegram. Had Ted not expected to get someone so very inexperienced?

Ted then asked rather soberly, 'Are you just wanting some pocket money or are you thinking of making farming your life's work?'

As he asked the question Ted turned to look straight at Ralph.

The question took Ralph by surprise. When seeking a job away from Perth he had only been considering his immediate future not his whole life's work, but he certainly had not come to Lake Jane just to get some pocket money. After a slight pause he said, 'I think I intend to make farming my life's work'.

Once again Ted was silent for several minutes. Ralph sat pressing back against the seat fearing the worst, expecting that his halting reply had caused Ted to doubt the truth of his assertion. He was feeling very tired and sick with apprehension.

Ted broke his silence. 'Well I'd better put you into the picture. Normally I would plant the crop with Pat Riley helping me but a serious problem has arisen during the last month. My wife Sue, who is pregnant, has become very ill and the only doctor in the area cannot diagnose the cause. I want to take her down to the hospital in Northam next Monday and to remain with her until I am sure she is on the way back to good health. Pat is the best farm worker in the district. I have known him for a long while. We were mates in the war, we slogged alongside one another for nearly four years. But Pat now has an obsession, a need, from time to time, to go on a bender likely to last for four or five days. As long as you are here and can work satisfactorily with him I am sure he will not let me down – he is a very loyal bloke. I have taken a gamble, not on Pat, but on you and on Mrs Keating's judgement'.

Ralph was very surprised but heartened by the intimation that Mrs Keating, in offering him the job, had been willing to put at risk (even if only in a small way) her business reputation.

Ted went on to say, 'I am planting a very large acreage with wheat this year. It will be a long and hard job getting the crop in'.

Ralph said nothing for a while but feeling something was expected from him said, 'I'll do my very best'.

'That's fine', said Ted.

During the rest of the journey Ted was cheerful and talkative. He commented on the countryside, several of the farms they passed and some of the farmers who owned them.

For about a mile the road was alongside the edge of a huge, shallow depression. In the centre of the depression lay a pool of water, but the rest of its surface was covered by a white substance. Nodding in the direction of the depression Ted said, 'That salt pan is Lake Jane. After heavy rain it sometimes fills with water and looks like a real lake'.

Ralph noticed that the railway line had not terminated at the Lake Jane station but continued to go in an easterly direction parallel with the road on which they were travelling. When he asked about it Ted told him that the line he could see was an extension, made three years earlier, to a wheat-loading siding only a mile beyond the Miller farm.

As they passed, about fifty yards off the road, a small fibro house and a long shed, Ted said, 'Alf Blackall, my nearest neighbour, lives there. He's a nice bloke and a good neighbour. In the off season when either of us has a short-term job to do that needs more than one man we work together. Alf s a bachelor; single women are few and far between out here. When I met Sue she was a teacher in Northam. Her family have a dairy farm at Bornholm. That's about as far south as you can get unless you want to live in the Antarctic'.

Ralph was a little disturbed by the thought that a teacher, or ex-teacher, would probably have some authority over him while he was on the farm.

The Miller farm was only the second with a fence Ralph had seen since they had left the town. Hanging on a post beside the farm gate was a metal plate with the word 'Lamphanan' on it. When Ralph returned to the truck after opening and closing the gate Ted said, 'It was Sue's idea to name the farm Lamphanan after the town in Scotland where her father was born'.

A moment later he added, 'There is a rule you may not know. You must always leave a gate on a farm as you found it – open or shut. That is to control the movement of animals. I keep that main gate shut not to prevent animals getting out – I haven't got any yet. It's to stop rabbits getting in'.

When Ralph saw the farm house he was shocked. It was ugly; a square building with a flat galvanised iron roof, walls of hessian painted white and wooden windows in unsymmetrical positions that gave the farmstead a peculiar skewness. Behind the dwelling about thirty feet apart were two tents. Ted took Ralph to one of these and said, 'That's yours'. Inside the tent was a hessian mattress secured to a bedstead made of undressed timber. The other furniture consisted of four empty kerosene cases, three of them stacked on their sides to form shelving, the fourth upside down to provide a table alongside the bed. On the makeshift table was a hurricane lamp. Two folded grey blankets lay on the bed.

As Ralph took his gear out of the truck, Ted looked at the awkwardly shaped parcel and asked 'Do you play some sort of musical instrument?'

'No'.

Although Ted continued to look at the parcel in a puzzled way, he did not ask any more questions but said, 'When you have stowed away your gear, come over to the house and we'll get some breakfast'.

The inside of the house was as unattractive as the outside. There was no lining for the walls or the roof and the framework supporting them was made of the trunks of trees and saplings; the only dividing wall was of hessian supported by a sapling framework. There was a large cooking stove standing in a fireplace made of rough stone. The floor consisted of compacted soil raised about six inches above the surrounding earth and kept in place by rough timber and saplings. The most conspicuous piece of furniture was a large kitchen table.

At breakfast Ralph met Sue. She was not a young woman but probably ten years or so younger than her husband. Although obviously ill as well as pregnant she greeted Ralph with a wan little smile and asked a few polite questions about his train trip and his family. She did not remain at the breakfast table but excused herself and retired to the room beyond the dividing wall.

Shortly after breakfast Ralph found the toilet which, as a piece of architecture, stood in marked contrast to the farmhouse. It was a well-shaped building with walls of brown weatherboards, a peaked galvanised iron roof trimmed with white facia boards and a door of white tongued and grooved wooden panels. The inside of the toilet matched the outside; a level floor of well planed and varnished timber, a comfortable, neatly boxed in wooden seat with a hole deftly cut out of one sheet of timber and all the various sections of the dressed timber framework supporting the walls and roof joined by bolts recessed into the timber. Everything about the little building reflected the considerable care given to its construction. When Ralph remembered the trouser press hidden under the bed in his tent he came to the conclusion that if he was to wear well creased pants to any place on the farm, it obviously should be to the toilet.

Ted took Ralph out to the 'western paddock', a large unfenced area which Ted said had been ploughed six months earlier in preparation for planting with wheat. Knotted lumps of mallee roots littered about half of the ploughed ground. On the edge of the other half, attached to a tractor, stood a machine the most conspicuous part of which was the large rectangular wooden box straddling it.

Ted said the machine was a 'combine' and he explained how it worked. A row of metal tines (resembling small ploughshares) attached to rods beneath the box harrowed the soil (to break up the lumps caused by the ploughing) and cut grooves in the harrowed soil; seeds and superphosphate dropped through tubes behind the rods and tines from the box into the grooves, and a line of small rollers at the back of the combine pushed soil over the seeds and superphosphate.

Ralph, working from a narrow platform behind the box, had to keep both the seed and superphosphate in the box at an operating level and flowing steadily into the tubes. This involved from time to time closing the lid covering one half of the box, climbing over it, getting a bag of seed or superphosphate from a stack on a steel tray at the front of the combine, carrying it back to the platform and pouring the contents into the box.

In addition to replenishing the supplies of seed and superphosphate Ralph had to keep an eye on the iron wheels of the tractor and if the wheels either sank low or rose high in the soil, raise or lower the rods, tynes and tubes by means of a large lever alongside the box. Operating the lever Ralph soon found required all his strength.

Although the bags of superphosphate weighed the same as the bags of seed they were much more difficult to handle; the superphosphate was a very inert substance and it seemed to actively resist any attempt to move it.

The worst 'disaster' which befell Ralph while learning to work on the combine occurred when a bag of superphosphate slipped down the side of the box and got jammed between the wheel, the box and the lever. As he could not move the bag he jumped off the platform, ran ahead of the tractor and got Ted to stop.

Ted looked very annoyed and shouted, 'What the hell!' But then, after listening quietly to Ralph's rather nervously expressed explanation, went with him to the combine.

It took Ted and Ralph working together some time to get the bag of superphosphate from its jammed position. When that had been done Ted told Ralph that if the bag of superphosphate had stopped one wheel turning while the combine continued to move along for more than a short distance it might have damaged the rods and cogs connecting each wheel to the series of metal devices shaped like stars in the bottom of the box which guided the seeds and super into the tubes. Ted also said Ralph had done the right thing by jumping off the combine and getting him to stop the tractor. Before he returned to the tractor Ted greatly lessened Ralph's feeling of incompetence by saying, 'I always have trouble myself with those bloody bags of super'.

Ted's first reaction to this set-back had dismayed Ralph but this tolerance restored the boy's spirit. Ralph found during this first week, and later when he was working with Ted, that only occasionally was his boss's first reaction to any mishap one of annoyance and that the annoyance anyway was short-lived. Also that, Ted did his best to lessen the possibility of any mishap being repeated by discussing at some length how the mishap had occurred.

After some sandwiches under a tree alongside the paddock Ted told Ralph to collect the mallee roots and stack them by a rock outcrop. The boss then went off towards the farm house. There was no more planting work that day.

Ted picked up Ralph with the truck at the end of the day and they drove to a large three-sided shed close to the farmhouse but hidden by a cluster of wattle trees. Ted left the truck in the shed (which he said was the farm's workshop and storehouse) and they walked to the house.

On each of the following days the planting would be broken up by spells of collecting and stacking mallee roots.

As part of his coaching in planting Ted taught Ralph to drive the tractor. Once Ralph had mastered that task – the difficult bit being to correctly turn the whole outfit at the end of each row – Ted and Ralph changed positions on the combine and the tractor about every hour or so during each planting session.

The tractor burned as fuel kerosene, the truck petrol. Ted got Ralph to start both machines every day and also to drive the truck, under his guidance, to and from the paddock.

The first six days flew past for Ralph. Wanting to make a good impression he had applied himself wholeheartedly to every task he had been asked to do. Some muscles he had not been in the habit of using a great deal were a little sore but he had no other physical problems and he certainly did not suffer from homesickness.

During the evening meal on Saturday Ted told Ralph that he had picked up the work on the combine and the tractor very quickly.

With Ted's approbation ringing in his ears Ralph went to bed that night feeling very happy but wondering whether he would get on as well with Pat as he had, it seemed, with Ted.

•

On Sunday Pat arrived and took up residence in the other tent. He was a tall, thin faced, sober-looking, quietly spoken man who walked with a rolling gait. The next day Pat took Ted and Sue to the railway station in the truck. After they left Ralph went out to the western paddock to collect and stack the last of the mallee roots. About two hours later Pat came out to the paddock driving the truck with some bags of seed wheat and superphosphate in it. He said, 'You and I had better put a few of these wheat seeds into the ground'. Ralph noticed that while Pat did not smile he had something of a twinkle in his eyes.

And so began the planting partnership. Ralph soon found that Pat shared every bit of the work evenly with him, not only the planting but all the other chores around the farm and in the house.

114

The weather held and the planting went on for six days a week and from dawn to dusk every day except Monday. It was on that day the train from Perth arrived at Lake Jane and after lunch Pat and Ralph took the truck into town to buy, and charge to Ted's account, bread, vegetables (mainly of the root type but occasionally a cabbage), and fruit (mainly apples). Also from time to time they bought kerosene, petrol and tinned food.

The two labourers went out to the paddock each day with sufficient wheat seed, superphosphate and kerosene for the day's planting. As soon as the sun passed below the horizon they stopped the tractor, left the machines where they were and drove back to the house.

The mallee roots in the firebox of the kitchen stove smouldered throughout the twenty four hours and whenever Pat or Ralph wanted more heat they put tinder and some split wood into the firebox and opened up the flue. They had a hot meal each evening. Most of the food came out of tins, of which there was a large supply in the house, but the tinned food was augmented by whatever the male housekeepers had been able to buy in the town. While one of them prepared the evening meal, the other made sandwiches for the next day's lunch. As soon as they had cleaned up in the kitchen after the meal they returned to their tents and bed.

At the back of the house were three tanks into which flowed the water from the roof. On a two and a half feet high wooden platform alongside the tanks were kept an enamel dish, a tub, a dipper and a kerosene tin with its top removed and replaced by a wire handle. The platform and the equipment constituted the bathroom and laundry. On Sundays Pat and Ralph carried out more thorough personal ablutions than they did on week days and they also washed their clothes. The water from both the ablutions and the clothes washing was poured onto a plot of land called 'Sue's garden' which at that time contained a lot of broad bean plants narrowly separated from a row of geraniums. The ablutions, clothes washing and chores inside the house and in its immediate vicinity kept them busy practically all the morning.

On Sunday afternoons, after Ralph had written a letter to his mother, Pat and Ralph usually sat doing nothing on a large log in front of the house. At first rather cautiously Ralph began asking Pat questions. But finding Pat responded willingly, though slowly and carefully between puffs of his pipe, when he could, and simply shook his head and said, 'That's beyond me' when he couldn't, Ralph became more positive with his questions; for the first time he didn't feel inhibited about his hows and whys.

Pat's responses gave Ralph quite a lot of general information about farming and life on farms and some specific information about Pat's and Ted's lives. Both Pat and Ted had been farm labourers before the war – during which they had formed a strong attachment – but after the war, while Pat had continued to work as a farm labourer, Ted had used his deferred pay to start a carrying business, based on Northam. The business had prospered. But Ted had always wanted to own a farm and in 1928 had sold the business and had purchased land at Lake Jane. At the same time he had married Sue.

The house on the farm had been intended as a very temporary affair, Ted had plans drawn for a substantial home to be built on higher ground nearby. But building that home had been postponed when, with the onset of the depression, the price of wheat had collapsed. However Ted was still determined to develop the farm as quickly as possible without going into debt.

Ralph had noticed on a shelf in the kitchen a number of books about farming and the maintenance of vehicles and farm machinery. When he asked about them Pat said, 'I've never got much out of books myself but Ted's all the time making use of the stuff he gets from books and he has no trouble in explaining it to me or anyone else. Most of the blokes around here come to him with their farming problems'.

Pat made much of Sue. He called her a wonderful girl, who, when well, had accepted the rough life on the farm cheerfully and had been a great support for Ted. Now she was ill he was certain Ted would remain in Northam with her until she recovered.

Pat's remarks about Sue led Ralph to ask him whether he was married. Pat shook his head and said, 'I'd be no bloody good as a husband'. Ralph wanted to go on and ask him about girls and sex but when it came to the crunch, he was too shy.

Pat told Ralph he had been brought up as a Catholic but had lost touch with the church many years ago. Nevertheless, Ralph found he liked telling Irish stories or jokes that generally involved 'the church' or one of its frocked members. A mental impression of Pat that Ralph retained for many years was of him sitting on the log telling one of his Irish stories, his battered brown hat tilted back, his long weathered face almost expressionless, his blue eyes twinkling brightly, his big feet wide apart, his forearms resting on his knees and his body and head twisted slightly to look at his audience of one.

Ralph's own audience became the dog he had found standing in the truck at the railway station when he arrived at Lake Jane. It was a stray, who had appeared at the Miller's door a week earlier. The rather dejected looking animal was called 'Lament' by Sue. From the boy's first day on the farm the dog attached itself and followed him everywhere except into the house. When Ralph was working on the tractor or the combine, Lament spent most of its time dozing under a tree or in the sun (depending on the state of the weather) but sprang into action during the lunch break and when the work was finished. At night 'Lament' slept on the end of Ralph's bed and provided a welcome source of warmth for Ralph's feet on cold nights.

Each evening, before jumping up to its sleeping place, Lament stood waiting with its tail wagging expectantly, until Ralph, having taken off his boots, tossed them under the bed. Ralph liked to hear the noise the boots made when they hit the parcel hidden there; it provided a daily reminder of his good fortune in getting away from his miserable life in Perth.

There was before long, however, another reminder for Ralph of that life. It came in letters from his mother. To comply with his mother's instructions Ralph had written to her once a week. At first in her replies his mother had mentioned some of her activities and those of Mary and Jim and had not commented to any extent on his letters. But later on she had asked him to write less about his work and tell her about Mr and Mrs Miller, their family, the farmhouse, the other workers, how he was accommodated and the sort of meals he received. In a subsequent letter she had expressed considerable annoyance when he had not done that.

Ralph was worried about what he should tell his mother. How would she react if she knew that the farm house was made mainly of hessian and had a floor of compacted earth, that he slept in a tent on a makeshift bed with a dog as a foot warmer, that he bathed in a tub outside the house, that Mr and Mrs Miller had left the farm for an indefinite period, that the only person on the farm with him was a middle-aged labourer of Irish-Australian stock (a group his mother did not hold in high regard) who regularly needed to go on a drunken spree which lasted four or five days, that meals were prepared either by his fellow-worker or himself, that the tablecloth was made of newspapers and that he and his fellow-worker came to the table in their workaday clothes? If she became aware of the situation would she attempt to have him brought back to Perth?

After having grappled with the problem for a while Ralph decided to describe in letters to his mother a farm house, a Mr and Mrs Miller, a fellow-worker and living conditions on a farm which he considered would be acceptable to his aggrieved parent. He took care to describe Mr and Mrs Miller as hard-working and clean but not the type of people with whom his mother would want to be acquainted.

He was afraid if he made the Millers socially approvable, his mother might write to Mrs Miller with a view to striking up an acquaintance. Although a little concerned about what might be the long-term result of his deception, he nevertheless got a somewhat mischievous pleasure from giving his mother a detailed description of life at the homestead of his imagination while living in a very different way at the very different Lamphanan homestead.

There was one other animal besides Lament living on the farm, a pig. Although the pig was a sow Ralph nicknamed it 'Mr Piggott' because it had, like a headmaster of that name who had once caned him, large ears, a bald head, a long nose and small eyes. Mr Piggott spent his days putting on weight and he was very good at that occupation. Immediately before lunch every Sunday Pat and Ralph leant against the sty fence until Pat, who claimed to be a good estimator, announced the pig's weight. Ralph asked Pat to explain how he made his estimate and was soon able to form an opinion of his own and to question the expert's conclusion. This led to an interesting exchange of views on Mr Piggott's weight every Sunday.

One Monday when Pat and Ralph were in Williams' store Bluey Smith, who owned a pig farm on the outskirts of Lake Jane, came up to them and asked how the pig was going.

'Over three hundred pounds', said Pat.

'I am sending some pigs off to the market next Monday. I'll come over and collect it on Saturday'.

On their way back to the farm Pat explained that Ted bought a succession of piglets from Bluey and as soon as each was fat enough Bluey sent the fully grown pig to market with a batch of his own.

There was no animal loading ramp on the farm. Before Bluey came on Saturday, Pat and Ralph cleared the rubbish out of two narrow holes near the sty which were about two and a half feet deep and six feet apart. When he came Bluey drove the wheels of his cart down the sloping sides of the holes. The back plate of the cart was then lowered to form a ramp up which the pig could be dragged. Over three hundred pounds of fighting pig was very difficult to control. While Bluey and Ralph pulled the enraged and frightened pig by its ears Pat pushed the pig from behind. It was about half up the ramp when Pat began to cough and spit.

'Got a fly?' shouted Bluey above the squealing of the pig.

'Yes, straight from the pig's arse'.

In his endeavour to rid himself of the particularly unpalatable fly Pat relaxed his hold and the pig noticing that began to back-pedal furiously, dragging Bluey and Ralph with him down the ramp.

'Forget the pig's arse and the fly', shouted Bluey, 'or we'll lose the pig'.

Pat gave up coughing and spitting, tightened his hold and pushed with all his strength. Laughing and cursing they got the pig safely in the cart and the cart was driven out of the holes. The piglet which Bluey had brought as the successor to Mr Piggott was then put into the sty. With those transactions completed Pat and Ralph were able to continue, without any break, the pleasant Sunday routine of assessing the weight of the farm's pig in residence.

Just before lunch time one day not long after Mr Piggott had left, Pat and Ralph noticed dust rising slowly in the direction of the track from the Shire road to the farm house. They expected that their visitor, hearing the noise of the tractor, would make his way out to the paddock on which they were working. That did not happen. When they knocked off for lunch Pat said, 'While you boil the billy I'll go and see who is at the house'.

Pat returned and took a long drink of tea before he said, 'It's some railway blokes and they're taking away the dunny'.

Puzzled, and very concerned, Ralph asked, 'Why are they doing that?'

'Well, it belongs to them. They left it by the line three years ago when the gang that built the bridge over Cole's creek shoved off. After it had been there for six months, Ted and I sort of borrowed it'.

When they had finished their lunch Pat said, 'We'd better go and build another dunny'.

It took the two amateur builders a day and a half to construct the replacement toilet. They used some sapling poles Ted had stacked near the shed and they purchased on Ted's account from the store in town undressed timber to strengthen the framework, dressed timber to make the seat, galvanised iron for the roof and hessian for the walls. There was no door but a hessian screen on a sapling frame about two feet in front of the opening.

Ralph enjoyed the construction work and picked up from Pat some ways of using simple tools to shape and join timber and to get the correct angles and levels which Pat said was an important requirement for erecting any building.

When the new building was completed they walked a few yards away to get a good look at their handiwork. Pat said, 'It's not bad but I don't think the railway blokes would like it'. After a pause he added, 'Sue is going to miss the other one'.

Ralph was also sorry that the flash toilet had gone. But when his boots hit the parcel under his bed that night he was wryly amused by the thought that there was now no place on the farm where he might go wearing well-creased pants.

At fairly long intervals Ted wrote to Pat. The second letter brought the sad news that the child Sue had been carrying was still-born and that when Sue was well enough to travel Ted intended to take her to Perth to see a specialist. In the next letter Ted said Sue was going to have an operation. The fourth letter said Sue had had the operation but was having post operational treatment and consequently Ted could not say exactly when he would return to Lake Jane. He didn't say he was worried about the farm but asked how they were going.

•

As Pat's unbroken spell at the farm became much longer than either he or Ted had anticipated Ralph noticed that Pat was becoming somewhat tense during the visits to town. He seemed anxious to get their business done very quickly and to avoid speaking to any acquaintances they saw in the street or met in the store. Earlier some of these acquaintances had suggested they go into the pub for a few beers. Pat had always declined with remarks such as 'No time mate' or 'Got to get back to the farm'. But Ralph sensed that as the time without a bender went on Pat did not want to be faced with invitations to go into the pub and in fact probably found it difficult even to be near the pub. Back at the farm there was no noticeable difference in Pat's behaviour except perhaps that he drank a lot more water and tea.

It was the first week in July when the last letter came from Ted. The planting had finished a few days earlier and Pat and Ralph had started working on an internal fence which Ted had pegged out. The letter informed them that Ted would return on the following Monday after he had taken Sue down to her parents' home at Bornholm to convalesce. Both Pat and Ralph were pleased to hear that Sue was on the mend.

Pat told Ralph that he expected to leave Lake Jane the day after Ted arrived. This news brought home to Ralph that his own time at Lamphanan had nearly ended. Ralph realised that he had no prospect of another farm job before the harvesting season began in November and that, with his limited experience getting one then would be very difficult. When he left Lake Jane he would have accumulated only six pounds, not enough to live away from home for any length of time.

Also, with Pat's departure close at hand, Ralph suddenly realised that parting with him would be painful.

The two farm labourers, so very different in age, experience and background, required at short notice to work together without any supervision and do their own housekeeping, might have had difficulty in bringing about an effective working and living arrangement. But Pat and Ralph were able to quickly establish a suitable course of action and gradually develop a delightful comradeship that was of great significance to Ralph; he had never before got on so well with an adult.

On his return the first thing Ted noticed was the new dunny. He was very surprised. But when he had heard what had happened and had inspected the new building he congratulated the builders. Like Pat he said that the railway dunny would be missed very much by Sue. Ted seemed pleased with everything else he saw at Lamphanan and that evening produced a large fruit cake and several bottles of non-alcoholic cider to help them celebrate the successful planting of the crop.

When the time for separation came Ralph and Pat said goodbye beside the truck in which Ted sat ready to drive Pat into town. There, as they shook hands firmly, Ralph felt too close to tears to look at Pat's face. He was pleased to be left alone at the farm for the next two hours.

That evening when Ted and Ralph were having their meal, Ted said, 'Pat was very pleased with the way you worked'. After a while he went on, 'Would you be prepared to stay on for the off-season? I would want you to help me with the clearing, fencing and ploughing. I could only pay you the ten shillings a week and keep. Pat will be back for the harvesting. If you wanted to stay for that too I would be pleased to have your help and continue to pay you the ten shillings a week. And it should be good experience for you. Will you think about remaining here?'

121

Very touched Ralph did not require any time to consider Ted's offer. He immediately replied, 'I would like to stay for both the off-season and the harvesting'. He said no more but inside he was elated.

Ralph found living and working with Ted was quite different from doing those things with Pat. Pat was always quiet, good tempered and unassuming. While Ted was usually cheerful and helpful he was also a busy, bustling person and despite considerable self-discipline could not always control his quick temper. He shared the work in the field and house with Ralph but was always clearly the boss.

Ralph wrote his letters to his mother, and very occasionally a letter to Mary or Jim, at the kitchen table immediately after lunch on Sunday. On the first Sunday Ted said, 'Sunday afternoon is the time for my paper work' and got out some books and started work at the other end of the table.

Not wanting to sit around on his own and desiring to know more about the farm records and accounts, Ralph, as soon as he had finished his letter, offered to help with the paper work.

Ted said Sue had always helped him and then explained that he had three sets of books, the weather book, the diary and the accounts. Ralph was already familiar with the weather book. It hung on a nail near the door and each day while Ted was away either he or Pat had entered information in it after reading the rain gauge and thermometer.

Ted said that in the diary he recorded everything done on the farm – when, why and how it was done and with what result.

When they got to the account books Ted said that keeping comprehensive and reliable financial accounts was of fundamental importance to any business and recognising this he had immediately after the war completed Hemingway and Robertson correspondence courses in both bookkeeping and advanced bookkeeping.

The book-work did not take up all of Sunday afternoon and it was on the third Sunday that Ted suggested to his eager assistant that he widen his knowledge by reading the correspondence courses in bookkeeping.

Outside the house the first major task Ted and Ralph undertook was clearing an area of virgin country. Using a roller of large logs bolted to a metal frame and towed by the tractor, they knocked over the mallee thickets, brushwood and acacia shrubs. Then Ralph learned how to chop down trees, making sure that the trees all fell one way to assist securing a running fire when the burning took place. The smaller trees were felled at ground level, the larger trees at axe handle level. A few large trees were left standing to provide shade for the sheep Ted intended to graze later on.

The clearing went on for nearly two months then they began cultivating three hundred acres of fallowed ground which reached to the northern border of Lamphanan and abutted upon a large area of undeveloped land belonging to the Government. The three hundred acres had been left in fallow for two years and was now to be prepared for planting with wheat in the following autumn. The cultivating was done by a large disc plough pulled by the tractor.

As with all the work undertaken Ted explained why it was being done – in this case to preserve moisture and suppress the growth of weeds – and why it was being done at that particular time – because the soil had the right amount of moisture and the weeds had grown sufficiently.

Ted's explanations always helped make the farm work of absorbing interest to Ralph. Once Ralph had a good grasp of the cultivating Ted left him to it while he prepared the posts for fencing and carried out maintenance on the farm machinery.

As the cultivating advanced so did the spring and the vernal atmosphere induced Ralph to leave the farm during his lunch breaks and take short walks through the government owned bushland nearby. The most conspicuous signs of spring were the splashes of gold where the wattles were blooming. But there were other signs, small bright red flowers on trees covered with long green spikes, pale blue flowers on tall shrubs with narrow leaves pointing upwards, brown pea-shaped flowers on low growing fuzzy bushes and diminutive yellow, red and blue flowers on a variety of tiny plants nestling in the ground cover. Flocks of pink and grey galahs disturbed by Ralph's approach frequently rose ahead of him and gracefully wheeled through the bright sunlight as they flew to another feeding place; more vividly coloured parrots watched him come and go from perches high on the treetops, and large numbers of small birds flying rapidly and lightly about in the mallee thickets created a pleasant hum of noise with their ceaseless twittering.

The spring also brought two good falls of rain and on both occasions the ploughing had to stop for several days. During the interruptions Ralph gave Ted some unskilled help in the maintenance work he was doing on the header and the combine.

Ted took Ralph with him several times when he inspected the wheat that Ralph and Pat had planted in the western paddock. Fortunately the spring rain had been steady rather than heavy. It was growing strongly throughout the paddock and without any sign of disease. Ted became more pleased with the progress of the crop on each successive inspection.

While Ralph had been clearing and ploughing on the working days he had been studying the correspondence course on the Sundays and steadily becoming fascinated by the practice of keeping accounts. The attraction was increased by reading a pamphlet distributed by Hemingway and Robertson and kept by Ted in the suitcase containing the course study books. After stating that a full course in accountancy was available and that the course prepared students for the exams for admission to the Institute of Accountants, the pamphlet provided information about the type of work undertaken by accountants and the sort of positions open to persons admitted to the Institute.

Stimulating farm work, interesting study, a good relationship with Ted and the devoted attention of Lament gave Ralph a feeling of deep content he had never before experienced. And there was nothing in his mother's letters to disturb his contentment. She accepted without question his life in the imaginary farm house.

For five weeks after the ploughing was finished Ted and Ralph built fences. Nearly every day since he had come to the farm Ralph had performed strenuous work for short spells between periods of less arduous jobs. This regular but intermittent exercise had gradually strengthened and enlarged him. Making fences involved strenuous exertion the whole day and for a while Ralph went to bed with aching joints and muscles. But he was eating like a horse, he wrote to Mary. By the time the fencing ceased Ralph found the clothes bought by his mother in a size with a generous allowance for growth had become a much better fit.

•

At the end of November, Pat returned and the harvesting commenced. Ralph, after some coaching on how to operate the header and bag the wheat, shared all the tasks including driving the tractor and carting the wheat to the railway siding.

To his surprise Ralph found that bagging the wheat was the most difficult of the tasks. Ted told him that each bag had to contain one hundred and eighty pounds of wheat with a tolerance of two or three pounds and the wheat had to be tightly packed into the bag. If any bag was not well-filled

124

the lumpers putting the bags into either the stack or a railway truck at the siding would not handle it because of the risk of injury to themselves.

Pat patiently demonstrated the bagging process to Ralph the first time the header had a bin full of wheat. After the contents of the bin had been poured into eight bags. Pat took wheat out of one bag with a dipper and forced it into one of the other seven bags through a funnel with a very long tube which enabled the wheat to be tightly packed from the bottom up. When he was satisfied that the bag was tightly packed to a level which left just sufficient bag material above the wheat to seal the top Pat closed it with needle and thread in a way which ensured that there would be no movement of wheat in the bag. He repeated the operation until seven bags were filled and sealed.

Ralph at first became annoyed with himself when he could not immediately duplicate Pat's actions and get a tightly packed bag. But he soon overcame his annoyance, concentrated very hard, and by the afternoon was a competent bag-filler.

The three harvesters worked through the long summer days from dawn to dusk. There wasn't much talk even during the two short breaks for a meal beside the paddock but Ralph felt a valued part of the team.

Away from the work Ralph, who had been very pleased to see Pat again, found this spell of living with him different. There were three of them now to share the work, house chores and conversation. Also since they had parted Ralph had gained more confidence. And he had been gradually forming a plan for his future in preparation for which he wanted to study bookkeeping whenever he got an opportunity.

It was on the Sundays that the difference between the two periods was most apparent. In the morning when they had completed their washing and cleaning chores Pat and Ralph did once again lean on the pig sty fence and discuss the weight of the farm's pig in residence. But after lunch Ralph quickly wrote a letter to his mother, helped Ted for a while with 'the bookwork' and then studied bookkeeping. Pat sat alone on the log in front of the house smoking a pipe.

When the Sunday evening meal was finished Ted and Pat talked. Occasionally they were joined by a neighbour, generally someone wanting advice from Ted who stayed to discuss other practical farming matters or to gossip, reminisce or speculate about the future. Ralph did not join in these conversations but continued to work at the other end of the table on the correspondence course. However, occasionally something said caught his attention and he stopped to listen. A comment made by Ted during a discussion on the fate of a number of farmers with little or no capital made an indelible impression on him. It was that when a farmer without capital managed to remain on his farm, he and his family were often condemned to a life of ceaseless toil and wretched living conditions.

The weather remained fine. The harvesting went smoothly until Pat, after going to town with a neighbour one Sunday, did not put in an appearance for five days. When he did come back he looked very washed out. But despite his pallor and air of weakness he threw himself into the harvesting work, particularly into moving the pile of bagged wheat which had banked up while he was away.

Pat's lapse gave Ralph a feeling of guilt. He could not get out of his mind the picture of Pat sitting alone on the log in front of the house. On the first Sunday after Pat returned Ralph went out to Pat shortly after lunch and sat on the log. After telling one of his Irish stories in his old way Pat said he had a few things to do in his tent and that he was feeling tired and thought he would lie down.

On the following Sunday as Ralph was walking with him towards their log Pat stopped and for the first time put a hand on Ralph's shoulder and with his eyes twinkling turned him back towards the house and said, 'You have some important work to do in there'.

The harvesting was not finished until the end of January. Pat left soon afterwards. Although Ralph's affection for Pat was undiminished the second parting was not as distressing as the first.

After Pat had left, Ted and Ralph finished the fencing they had started earlier. Ralph was astonished how much easier he found the work. As soon as weather was suitable they burned off the timber and shrub material which had remained on the ground drying out since the clearing was done in July and August. But before starting the fire they set aside a small quantity of burnable material to provide fuel for fires to be lit around the tree stumps not destroyed when the main fire was put through the area.

On the Sunday after the big burn Ted told Ralph that he was going down to Bornholm at the end of the week to bring Sue, who had fully recovered from her illness, back to the farm.

Ted also said that Ralph with the experience he now had, should be able to get a job on a farm in one of the long-settled farming areas and be paid a good wage. To help him get such a job Ted said he would write to Mrs Keating to let her know what Ralph had done on the farm and also tell her that he was a quick learner and hard and conscientious worker. Ted suggested that Ralph return to Perth during the week following Sue's return and have a spell before he sought another job.

Ralph thanked Ted for the letter to Mrs Keating and for all the help he had received since he had come to Lamphanan. It was an expression of heartfelt gratitude. During the last week or so, knowing that he would soon have to leave Lamphanan, Ralph had thought back over his time as a farm labourer and felt thankful that the 'cocky' to whom Mrs Keating had sent him for his first job, had been Ted.

Ted's proposal that Ralph leave Lamphanan within a fortnight fitted in with the plans that Ralph had now developed. Although he had enjoyed working on the farm he knew he did not want to be a farm labourer for the rest of his life. He saw no prospect of ever owning a farm. He wanted to become an accountant. According to the Hemingway and Robertson pamphlet students could pay for their courses by instalments. He would leave Lake Jane with about twenty-five pounds, enough to pay the first instalment for his course and also pay for board for a while. He would go to Northam and book into a boarding house. Then he would make a one day journey to Perth, enrol with Hemingway and Robertson, talk to Mrs Keating and give her his address in Northam. After returning to Northam he would write to his mother telling her that during the off-season he expected to get some casual work on farms along the outskirts of Northam and that when not working he would study a correspondence course in accountancy for which he had already enrolled. Well away from his mother he wanted to work very hard at the task he had set himself.

Before he left to pick up Sue, Ted told Ralph to burn all the tree stumps which remained standing.

On the morning of his second day alone on the farm, during which Ralph intended to fire the biggest of the tree stumps, he pulled out from under his bed the dusty parcel and took it with him in the truck to where the tree stumps stood waiting to be destroyed.

When the fire around the biggest stump was burning fiercely Ralph took from the truck the parcel, still unwrapped, and tossed it into the flames. Oh! with what joy he watched it burn.

RAIN

Throughout the day the rain had drummed ceaselessly on the iron roof, filling the house with noise. Mary was edgy. The unceasing noise unsettled her and she feared that the river would soon rise and cut them off from their neighbours and the town.

Peter was away again. During the last six years, since he had been made a Justice of the Peace who could be called upon to undertake magisterial duties in the Cooma court, he went into Cooma whenever the work on the farm permitted and, lately, he had tended to leave a surprising amount of the farm work to Sandy. 'There's nought to do here that Sandy cannot manage just now', he would say. 'The name McPhee is highly respected in the affairs of the district and I must do my duty'.

But it was Betty whom Mary missed. Always a pleasant, cheerful person even when a small child, Betty had been for about ten years a wonderful companion. Helping with the work in the house or the chores outside, chatting about the little things that happened around the farm or in the district, Betty had seemed, most of the time, like someone of Mary's own age. The correspondence lessons, when Betty was in her teens, had been done by Betty and Mary as fellow students rather than as child and supervisor.

During most of the year that Jim was courting Betty, the close relationship between Mary and Betty continued practically undisturbed. But as 1st February, 1912, the date of the marriage, came closer, Mary's sense of impending loss and Betty's awareness of Mary's feelings affected their companionship. They were no longer as relaxed together as they had been for so many years; they became somewhat guarded in what they said to each other. Betty tried to avoid talking about the matter that loomed largest in her life just then, her impending marriage. The three months that had passed since the marriage had not lessened for Mary the aching loneliness that Betty's departure from the farm had brought.

The farmhouse was a lopsided rambling building, the end-product of several additions to a small cottage. The front of the house was not used as a means of entry by either the family or visitors. They all gained admission through a large lobby at the back which also functioned as the family dining and sitting room. The lobby was an extension of the original kitchen. It had two inside doors leading to other parts of the house and an open fire place in

129

which Peter's father had built a grate and flue of his own design. This iron structure helped the family keep a fire burning throughout the day and night in the winter.

When the evening meal was finished and Sandy had gone to his bedroom off the lobby, Mary sat at the table thinking of Betty and wondering when she would see her again. Jim, a surveyor employed by the New South Wales Government, had received instructions, just before his marriage, to move to Tamworth and the young couple had gone to that, to Mary far-off, town immediately after a honeymoon in Sydney.

Mary heard Sandy throw down his boots. Both he and his father had this habit. In a few minutes, Sandy would be asleep, dead to the world, until morning. Although only sixteen, he did a tremendous amount of heavy work around the farm. Each night he came in very tired, ate his meal in silence and went off to bed completely exhausted.

She and Sandy seemed to coexist in a frictionless way. She had never established with him anything like the very happy, amicable relationship she had had with Betty. Could she only establish a very close relationship with a girl? Had she not tried hard enough with Sandy?

Mary rose rather wearily from her chair and started to clean up after the evening meal. She had finished the dishes and was sweeping the floor when a loud double knock on the lobby door startled her.

The latch was a little stiff and another knock sounded before she had managed to open the door.

The light from the lobby showed a policeman and Bill Power standing on the step. The unusual position of Bill's hands attracted her attention immediately; the bright metal of the handcuffs shone in the light.

The constable asked her: 'Could we have shelter for the night, Ma'am, for ourselves and our horses?'

While the men were putting their horses in the shed, Mary threw some more wood on the fire and bustled about getting another meal ready. But her mind raced back to the stormy afternoon eighteen months earlier when Bill had knocked at the lobby door.

The men returned to the house. The policeman took off his hat and cape and hung them near the fire. Then, with a key taken from the pocket of his jacket, he undid the handcuffs. Bill rubbed his wrists before he removed his hat and old gabardine coat.

Except to occasionally mutter 'thanks', the two men did not speak throughout the meal. Neither offered any explanation about the handcuffs.

The policeman was a stranger and his big, burly figure made Bill look rather small.

Mary knew that Bill had long been suspected of having some connection with the sheep stealing which occurred in the district from time to time. Although Peter occasionally got excited about sheep losses from McPhee's farm, most, if not all, of these sheep had been discovered later on. On no occasion was it actually established that some sheep had been stolen from the farm. Usually a break in one of the fences had let the sheep get into the rough timbered land that bordered the farm. However, neighbours, whose farms were differently situated, stated in emphatic terms that sheep had been stolen from their properties and, ever since Peter had been a Justice of the Peace, he regarded any crime in the district as a matter of personal concern to him. On several occasions when he had mentioned the matter of sheep stealing to Mary, Peter had said such things as: 'That rascal Power will get caught eventually. We all know he's at it. He will get ten years inside and serve him right! We have got to stamp out sheep stealing. The confounded country helps them; so much bush to hide in'.

On the question of sheep stealing and many other matters Mary thought that Peter accepted too readily the opinion of the wealthier farmers who owned some of the properties nearby. But it was no good disagreeing with him; he would only become bad-tempered. It was difficult enough to get Peter to recognise her point of view, even slightly, in matters that seriously affected her life or that of the children. For many years she had not questioned, except in her mind, any statement that Peter made that did not directly touch upon the welfare of Betty or Sandy or herself. She had never expressed any dissent with Peter's opinion of Bill.

As Bill bent over the table, Mary noticed a few grey hairs near his temples. 'He must be over forty now', she thought. 'In ten years, he will be an old man'.

When the meal was finished, the two men took off their boots and jackets and sat near the fire drying the legs of their pants and their socks. The pistol in a holster on the policeman's hip looked ominous to Mary.

When she had washed up and put away the plates, cups and cutlery for the second time that evening Mary said, 'I had better bed you both down somewhere'.

'We will sleep right here in front of the fire', said the constable.

Mary got two blankets and two pillows and gave them to the men. She then brought in a large rug made from animal skins that normally covered some of the floor in the little-used front room. She spread the rug out in front of the fire.

Even when she said 'good night', Bill did not look at her, although he muttered 'good night' in return.

Mary left the door between the lobby and the front room ajar and went through to her bedroom which opened off the front room. Although she went into the bedroom, she stayed for only a few minutes, long enough to sit on the bed and rest for a little while, then to take off her shoes and blow out the light. On her toes she crept back to where she could see the men through the crack between the wall and the door. The noise from the rain on the roof drowned the occasional creak from a floor board as she moved.

Mary stood watching the men who, for a few minutes, continued to sit by the fire smoking the cigarettes they had rolled before she left the kitchen. Then the constable said, 'You and I had better go for a walk'.

The constable put on his jacket, cape and hat and Bill put on his old battered hat and gabardine. Both men pulled on their boots. The constable took the handcuffs down from the mantelpiece and coupled one part to Bill's right wrist and the other to his own left wrist. Fastened together in this fashion, the two men went out the door.

Mary waited. A few minutes later, the men returned and the constable undid the handcuffs. Fairly quickly, the men took off their hats, coats, jackets and boots, and arranged the blankets and pillows on the rug. The constable again fastened the handcuffs on to his left wrist and Bill's right wrist. Mary noticed that he put the keys in the pocket of his jacket and then hung the jacket on the back of a chair nearby. He reached over to the hurricane lamp standing on the table, lifted the glass and blew out the flame. When he had done this, he said to Bill, 'You will sleep there', and pointed to the pillow on his left. As they settled into their places, Mary saw, by the light from the fire, the constable undo the belt around his waist, take the pistol out of the holster and place this evil-looking weapon under his pillow.

As Mary continued to wait, the concern about Sandy's reaction she had felt ever since she first saw the two men outside the lobby door grew considerably. Although he had never talked to her about Bill she was well aware of the strong bond of affection between the two. When talking, working or playing with Bill, Sandy seemed a different person; his usual dour seriousness replaced with an animated cheerfulness that brought an unaccustomed sparkle to his eyes. Seeing Bill handcuffed to a policeman would certainly shock Sandy and very likely would overwhelm him with grief.

While she had been watching the men, Mary had not felt the biting cold but now her attention was no longer focussed on their movements, she began to shiver. The cold seemed unbearable and, after a few minutes, she crept back to her bedroom for a shawl.

Although she knew she could not afford to go to sleep, Mary felt so tired that she decided to lie down on the bed for a few minutes. Once on the bed, she fell asleep almost immediately.

She awoke with a start. How long had she been asleep? The only clock in the house, a large alarm clock, was in Sandy's room; he took it to the room every night to wake him in the morning in time to milk the cows. It was still raining. She may have been asleep for hours. She lifted up the blind and looked out the window. It was pitch black. She prayed that it was not too near dawn.

When Mary got back to the crack in the door, she could see by the pale light from the smouldering fire that the two men were lying quite still and apparently asleep. With her heart pounding fiercely, she crept into the lobby and came around the table towards the two sleeping figures. From a floor board on which she trod came a loud squeak only partly muffled by the noise from the rain on the roof. She stopped. The policeman moved a little.

It seemed unwise to proceed without first trying to see if the policeman was awake. Mary walked past the men to the fire place and, from this position, could see the men's faces with the light of the fire shining on them. The policeman's dark eyes were looking at her intently.

Mary turned round and put a large piece of wood on the fire. After standing for a while looking at the fire and regaining her composure she moved into the kitchen, poured some water into an enamel basin and, carrying the basin, made her way quietly back to the bedroom.

Was the policeman a light sleeper who was wakened by the noise from the floorboard or had she only dozed for a minute or two on the bed and not given the men time to get to sleep? Was Bill awake? She regretted she had not looked closely at him.

After a few minutes, Mary went back to the front room and sat down and watched the men through the crack in the door. She got very cold again.

To take her mind off her freezing feet and shoulders she let her thoughts drift back to the afternoon eighteen months ago when Bill came so dramatically into her life.

•

Peter had gone to Sydney for the first time to attend a conference of some country magistrates. He had been very thrilled to be asked to go and would be away for over a week. It had been raining intermittently for several days and the ground around the homestead was soggy and most things inside the house seemed damp. When she got up in the morning, Betty complained that she had a headache and a pain in her side. By lunch time, the pain and a feeling of nausea forced Betty to her bed.

With the cows to milk, horses, pigs and fowls to feed, wood to get in and a meal to prepare, Mary, even with Sandy's help, was so busy she was not able to look at Betty until late in the afternoon. She was shocked at the grey colour of Betty's face and was disturbed to find that she had been vomiting. Betty said the pain in her side and the headache were much worse.

Mary sent Sandy off on a horse with a message to the Williams' farm asking them to send for the doctor. About twenty minutes later, Sandy returned saying, 'The river is up beyond the black stump and Dad always says it's too dangerous to cross then'.

Jammed in at the end of the valley, the only two ways out of the farm were across the river or over the mountains. The long, tortuous track across the mountains was hardly passable in the summer and now, at the beginning of winter, with snow already on the mountains, would be completely impassable. It would not be possible to even find the track.

The weather had changed during the day from the intermittent showers of rain to a fierce storm with strong winds, driving rain and sleet. Crossing the river would become increasingly difficult and may be impossible for several days or a week.

Sheer panic seized Mary. For a while she could not think. Betty continued to vomit or dry retch and was writhing in pain. Forcing herself to concentrate, Mary examined Betty and found the centre of the pain was in the region of the appendix. Without attention from a doctor it seemed likely that Betty would die.

Either she or Sandy must cross the river. Even if one of them succeeded and Cliff Williams rode into Cooma, there was the problem of whether the doctor could possibly cross the river five or six hours later. But she tried to keep this worry out of her mind and to face the immediate problem or someone getting over to the Williams' farm

Sandy stood in the kitchen looking at her as she tried to weigh up the best course of action. Muffled groans from Betty could be heard above the noise of the rain.

Sandy could manage a horse much better than she could but he was only fifteen years old and he was obviously tired from a day's work around the farm. Should she leave Betty? Could she do anything for Betty if she stayed?

Mary decided that she could not risk Sandy's young life in the flooded river. There was no alternative but to try herself. 'Saddle Sophie for me', she said to Sandy.

'You cannot get across, Ma!'

'Do as I say', she snapped at him in a dogmatic manner and harsh tone of voice she never normally used.

Mary put on her only pair of riding breeches and an old pullover and jacket belonging to Peter.

As she was taking another look at Betty, a loud knock sounded on the lobby door. She thought it was Sandy letting her know that the horse was ready. When another, even louder knock sounded on the door, she cried out, 'Wait a minute!' Then Sandy rushed into the house shouting, 'Bill's here!'

In the winter and spring of 1910, Bill Power had worked on the farm erecting a new fence in the end paddock. Mary had not seen much of him because he had pitched a camp up near where he was working and only occasionally came down to the homestead to get some food or to see Peter. However, in some strange way, Sandy and Bill had become firm friends. Bill was doing the fencing job by contract but he occasionally took time off from the work to go riding or fishing with Sandy. These fishing and riding expeditions always took place when Peter was away in Cooma.

To make time for the expeditions Sandy had got up very early each morning and worked hard at his chores around the house and the farm.

Even while entering into a fencing contract with him, Peter had regarded Bill with suspicion. He had told her, 'The man's a good worker when he's willing to work, but he's mixed up with sheep stealing; mark my words!'

The fencing was finished before Christmas and Bill moved on. Neither she nor any of the family saw him again until the stormy afternoon in the following May. It hadn't occurred to her at the time to ask Bill why he was there or from where he had come. She realised now that he must have come from somewhere in the mountains. That day it was such a tremendous relief to have him there that nothing else seemed important.

Bill took a quick look at Betty and asked a few questions about her illness. While he ate some bread and meat, he sent Sandy out to feed his horse and to put a bridle on two of the McPhee horses. When this was done, he asked Sandy to get him two old horse rugs and a long length of rope. Mary remembered his request for a length of rope because every time she had seen Bill, he had a long length of rope coiled and fastened to the saddle of his horse.

Mary and Sandy watched Bill start off towards the river riding his own big grey stallion with two lengths of rope secured to the saddle and two horse rugs tied in front of the saddle. He was leading the two McPhee horses.

Then began the long hours of waiting, the nagging fear that help would not arrive in time.

Bill and the doctor arrived a little after 3.00 a.m. Both were soaked to the skin. Mary got out some clothes of Peter's and they changed into them.

While the doctor was examining Betty, Bill dozed by the fire, but when the doctor said he must operate immediately, Bill had sprung into action and not only helped in the preparations for the operation but also helped considerably during the actual operation.

When Betty was safely back in her bed, Bill lay down in the front room on the rug with a few blankets over him and slept for nearly twelve hours. It was while he was sleeping that the doctor, who had himself a great reputation in the district for courage, told her about the journey from Cooma.

Bill arrived in Cooma riding one of the McPhee horses and, on his behalf, the doctor borrowed a fresh horse from a neighbour. The ride to the river took nearly three hours through torrential rain and a bitterly cold southerly wind. Bill's grey stallion and the McPhee's mare, Sophie, were both tethered one hundred yards or more from the river in the shelter of a big copse of she-oakes and some acacia scrub.

As they took the saddles from the two horses they had ridden from Cooma and saddled up the other horses, Bill said, 'My stallion and this mare are both very good in water. They won't panic easily'.

When they reached the river and the doctor saw the width of the water and the strong rate of flow in the light of a flash of lightning he shouted to Bill, above the noise of rain and wind, 'It will be suicide to attempt the crossing. We cannot make it'.

Bill said simply, 'If I don't get across stay here until it falls. The Williams' place is about half a mile up the road on the right'.

More emphatically, he added, 'But stay until the river falls; that kid needs you badly'.

Bill explained to the doctor that he would go about fifty yards up the stream from the road to a belt of trees and start across the river from there. He took the doctor down the stream nearly a quarter of a mile and the two men made a gap in the fence that ran into the river at that point. Bill tied the two ropes together and fastened one end around his chest. The other end he secured to the saddle of the doctor's horse.

Bill showed the doctor the sort of knot he should tie and where he should secure the rope when his turn to cross came. They lowered a little the knapsack containing the doctor's instruments, which he had fastened to his back, so that when the time came, he could pass the rope more easily around his chest.

It was so dark that the doctor did not see Bill and his grey enter the water but he noticed the coil of rope begin to run out. When a flash of lightning showed the horse and rider in the river, they were well out and moving down stream so fast that the doctor had to set his horse into a canter to catch up to them. When he reached the gap in the fence, he saw them again, further across the river but still moving very fast downstream. He got the rope through the gap and continued down the paddock watching the coil of rope. Through the pelting rain and blustering wind he suddenly heard a shout; the rope was pulled tight and then relaxed three times. Bill was across.

In accordance with the instructions he had received from Bill, the doctor also started from the clump of trees. The water was so cold that a shock seemed to pass right through him as he entered it. The mare had to struggle to keep its head above water in the fast-moving stream and the surge was so strong that the doctor seemed always to be in danger of being swept away from the horse.

In the middle of the stream, the rate at which they went down the river frightened the doctor. However, the mare kept battling in the direction of the far bank and a cross movement in the current at one stage helped them considerably. They reached the other side of the river at a point where the stream had cut into the bank near a few gum trees. The horse could not get on its feet and was suddenly swept away from the doctor. Bill, who had ridden along the bank more or less parallel with the doctor, was only a few yards away. With surprising speed, Bill swung his horse around and pulled the doctor out of the water.

As soon as he was satisfied that the doctor was safe and uninjured, Bill jumped on his horse and raced around the trees and down the stream but he could not find the mare. When he returned, the two men mounted the big stallion and made their way to the McPhee's house.

It was six days after the operation before the crossing at the river became passable again. During this time, the doctor chaffed and became very irritable. However, Bill, with Sandy as his willing assistant, worked hard for the McPhees both inside and outside the house. Between them they quickly discovered what had to be done and did it; there was no need to ask them to do things. They took over so much of the work that Mary was able to spend a fair amount of time as a nurse and companion for Betty. With great joy she saw her quickly recover from the operation.

Each evening, Bill talked with Sandy; or rather Sandy talked to Bill. For Sandy poured endlessly into Bill's attentive ears stories about the birds, animals and plants in the valley and on the mountains near the farm. Mary had not realised how much Sandy knew about these things. He had never talked very much to anyone else about anything. Mary noticed that whenever Sandy was at a loss to explain clearly some part of his observations, Bill seemed able to help him out by asking questions.

While Mary was contemplating in her mind the scene in the lobby with Bill and Sandy talking near the fire, the doctor sitting at the table looking spasmodically through some old journals and occasionally jumping up and cursing the rain, a piece of wood fell forward in the fire place and a flame lit up quite brightly for a few seconds the lobby as it was now with the two men lying in front of the fire. Mary decided it was time to try once more.

•

On this occasion she avoided the badly creaking board and got to the policeman's jacket with practically no noise. The keys were easy to locate.

She watched the policeman closely as she took them out of the pocket. He did not move.

However, when kneeling down beside the two men, she became very nervous and had to bite her lip hard to stop her hand shaking. What if the policeman should wake and not Bill? Would Bill make a noise when she woke him? Should she undo the handcuffs and then wake Bill or wake him first?

She decided to undo the handcuffs first because she was afraid that if she aroused Bill, he might, while still half asleep, jerk the policeman's arm and awaken him.

There were five keys on the ring. She looked at the handcuffs in the shadowy light from the fire. There were two locks, one at either end of the centrepiece of the handcuffs. Three of the keys were obviously too large but it was difficult to tell which of the other two fitted the locks.

The policeman started to roll over. He pulled Bill's arm towards him and then could roll no further. He fell onto his back again. Mary held her breath. Was the policeman awake? She remained crouching down on her haunches, hardly daring to breathe.

After a minute or so, as the policeman did not move again, she selected one of the keys and tried it in the lock nearest Bill's wrist. It would not work the lock. She tried the other key and, to her great relief, the lock turned and the handcuff flew open. Bill rolled a little towards the fire and stood up. He must have been awake for some time and aware that she was there. He smiled at her and then began quietly gathering up his jacket, coat and boots.

The policeman started to roll over again. Mary slipped her wrist into the handcuff, clicked it shut and slid down into the position on the rug that Bill had just vacated. She pulled the blanket up over her head and lay perfectly still.

Although he made very little noise, she heard Bill leave the house and quietly close the back door. After that she heard nothing but the rain drumming on the roof. Bill probably led his horse away from the shed, she thought. She guessed he would take every precaution to avoid any noise just as much for her sake as his own.

When she was certain Bill had gone, Mary became increasingly concerned about her own position. If the policeman awoke she would be caught 'red handed' engaged in the crime of assisting a prisoner to escape.

Presumably the policeman would arrest her and take her to Cooma. Peter would never forgive her.

What would become of Sandy if, as seemed likely, she was sent to prison? He worked very well around the farm and doing some of the household chores when Peter was not supervising him, But became very sullen when Peter, in a dictatorial manner, ordered him about. A very untempered relationship had developed between the two and was likely to get much worse if she was not with them on the farm.

Mary forced the thought of her incrimination and imprisonment out of her mind, and to try and get some idea of how much time she was giving Bill to get well away from the house, began to count slowly up to sixty and mark off each minute on her fingers. After fifteen minutes the rain stopped. She waited for a while, hoping it would recommence. It did not. She counted out another ten minutes and then decided to try and release herself from the handcuff and return to the bedroom. Without the background noise of the rain drumming on the roof, every move of hers seemed to make considerable sound; the boards beneath the rug creaked as she shifted her weight, each change in the position of the handcuffs made a slight metallic sound. Just as she was about to put the key in the lock, the policeman rolled towards her so suddenly that she took fright and slipped down on the rug again and pulled the blanket over her head.

When she plucked up enough courage to try again, all went well until she opened the handcuff. It flew open with quite a noticeable noise. The policeman lifted up his arm and Mary remained kneeling beside him, hanging on to the handcuff until he settled down.

Moving carefully out of the kitchen, she paused every time there was the slightest creak from a floor board. For the first time in her life she would have welcomed the noise of the rain on the iron roof.

The long journey to the bedroom ended at last. She closed the door with a great sense of relief. Standing by the bed, Mary realised she was absolutely exhausted. She started to undress and had taken off her stockings and was lifting her dress over her head when a terrible noise shattered the silence in the house. Alongside the bed with her dress half off she stood rigidly, her heart pounding and her arms stiff above her head. It was a few seconds before she realised that the noise came from the alarm clock in Sandy's room.

A FAIR COW OF A COW

Alan threw down his cards and exclaimed, 'Three days wasted playing poker! Is the bloody rain never going to stop?' But it was not the rain itself but the strong south-easterly wind which prevented them from fishing; they could not cross the estuary bar while the wind blew strongly from that direction.

As the other three dropped their cards on to the table, Alan left his chair and went over to the window. Across the street he could see Bill Sorby with a note book in his hand, walking up and down under the awning in front of his shop apparently rehearsing a speech, or some Masonic ritual, for the meeting in Skene he had told the card playing fishermen he was attending that evening.

Bill owned the flat that the four men had rented for the first fortnight in July for the last nine years. They had come to Pretty Inlet each year because they considered the Lizard Reef about a mile off the shore was the best winter fishing ground along the New South Wales coast.

In addition to three flats Bill owned a general store with the attached dwelling and dairy and thirty acres of land on which he grazed some cows. It was only six months after he was discharged from the army following the end of World War I that Bill had become, by inheritance, the local postmaster, storekeeper, milkman and landlord of three flats.

Bill left most of the work associated with the positions he had inherited to his various assistants. However, one task that he had carried out himself for nearly twelve years while his wife Sheila was alive was milking the cows. Sheila had not liked cows; indeed she feared them and would have nothing to do with them. Bill himself had no great liking for cows or for the work associated with caring for them, feeding them, milking them and preparing the milk for sale. But he had found after his marriage that milking provided a soothing routine that he could pursue at his own pace away from Sheila's impatience, her restlessness, her pressure to get things done quickly, her constant demand that he 'hurry up'.

Bill had met Sheila in Skene a year before he had enlisted. Her prettiness had been the first attraction but he had soon come to admire also her intelligence and her willingness to undertake almost any task and get it done quickly. The latter quality, however, was not one he himself had possessed or had desired to possess.

During the three years Bill had been in France the mutual attachment had been strengthened by regular correspondence and they had been married a few weeks after he had returned. Probably because much of their intimacy had come from an exchange of letters rather than personal contact, Bill had no inkling that when they were man and wife Sheila would try to change him; that she would be unwilling to accept his slow, careful approach to doing things and his practice of spending a lot of time just talking to people. All through the thirteen years of their childless marriage, despite very little success, Sheila had persisted with her attempt to change Bill.

There was nothing special about Bill. He was of average height with a strong but ungainly body and a plain face. He had no great charm, no fund of interesting or amusing stories, no smart or witty rejoinders and no wise advice, and he made no substantial contribution to the affairs of the local community. Nevertheless he was generally liked. He had a great interest in other people's lives – not as an intercessor but as an observer. He could get most people with whom he came in contact to talk about their lives. He shared with them the experiences they had undergone both as children and adults, the work they had done, the folk they had lived with, their joys and sorrows and their successes and failures as bit by bit they revealed to him their personal history. Events, experiences and emotions that would have seemed hum-drum to many were fascinating to him. He never pressed people to talk about themselves but he encouraged them to do so with apt questions. He did not make any particular use of the information but on meeting again, even after a long interval, someone with whom he had chatted in his unconventional way, he could usually recall the person's name and the gist of what had been said.

It was typical of Bill that he joined the Skene Masonic Lodge mainly because he thought it would (and he soon found that it did) let him meet a large number of men who would be willing (with a little help from him) to talk about their lives. After reaching, in due course, a relatively low office in the order, he resisted many attempts to get him to seek higher office but he always gave meticulous attention to the duties of his humble office.

Bill's relations with the residents of the village and its environment were cordial with one exception. The exception was more of an absentee landlord than a resident. Rupert Southwell, whose one thousand acres abutted on Bill's thirty acres, lived mainly in Sydney although he had a very commodious home on his property at Pretty Inlet. In Sydney Southwell apparently led a busy social life because Bill frequently saw, photographs of him in the social columns of the Sydney papers. It was only in the summer that Southwell spent any length of time at Pretty Inlet and when he was in residence he usually had a number of guests who drove through the village in flash cars and moved about the inlet in Southwell's large motor boat dressed in fashionable holiday attire.

Bill had several reasons for disliking Southwell.

About four years after Bill had inherited the store and dairy Southwell had a large dam constructed right across a creek which flowed through Southwell's property before reaching Bill's thirty acres. The dam greatly reduced the flow to Bill's farm and resulted in the natural pool on his land almost drying up in the summer. Unable to get any satisfaction from Southwell, Bill had taken the matter up with the Department of Lands. But a long correspondence got him nothing but evasive replies. It seemed likely that Southwell had sufficient influence with the politicians and bureaucrats to ensure that his high handed action was not interfered with.

Another matter of concern was the state of the fence between the two properties. Repeated attempts to get Southwell to agree to share the cost of rebuilding the fence had not succeeded. Bill was particularly annoyed when the Southwell bull came through the fence and caused some damage to his property.

He also believed his ill-behaved neighbour to be dishonest. Southwell did not have a licence to sell milk to the public but Bill suspected that Southwell's milking contractor, under Southwell's instructions, was selling milk at a discount price to visitors to Pretty Inlet during the summer holidays – a time when the farmers in the district had their highest milk production and difficulty selling all of it.

Bill himself tried to be honest in all his personal and business dealings. But he occasionally found honesty a difficult virtue to practice. One such occasion had occurred a few months after Bill had bought a cow in calf. The cow when brought into the milking herd had caused considerable trouble. It had continually harassed the other cows in the queue to enter the milking bail, it had butted and kicked Bill and had badly bruised one of his legs. It had fought against having its leg tied up and had been slow in letting down its milk when restrained in that way. Fed up with the beast Bill had decided to sell it through an advertisement in the local paper but had had difficulty in finding words to describe it. While he had not wanted to claim for the cow qualities he knew it did not possess, he also had not wanted to use words which would make the bovine terror unsaleable. Much to Sheila's annoyance he had spent a lot of time mulling over the matter. Finally he had decided to describe it as 'a fair cow'. The use of a phrase capable of a twofold interpretation had left him conscience-smitten for about a year after a farmer living on the other side of Skene had bought the cow. But the farmer had not complained about his purchase.

Bill had always got on very well with the four fishermen. During each of their tenancies he had spent some time swapping yarns and sharing a few beers with them. He had become familiar with most aspects of each of their lives and had been able to catch up with new events during their successive visits to Pretty Inlet. Sheila had frequently asked, 'Why do you waste your time with those beer-drinking fishermen?' and had suggested that the men probably regarded the visits as a nuisance. But Bill in all his dealings with people was able to immediately sense when his presence was not desired or his inquiries not welcome.

Bill had by far the best of the three wireless sets owned by Pretty Inlet inhabitants and before he left for the lodge meeting he went over to the flat to tell the men the latest weather forecast – 'more rain and continuing south-easterly winds'.

Depressed by the forecast and with nothing else to do, the four men went to bed early. Awakened just after midnight by loud knocking Alan and Dick found Bill standing outside the front door dressed in gumboots and a mackintosh and holding a hurricane lamp. He told them in his slow, calm voice that while driving back from Skene his car headlights had shown one of his cows bogged at the edge of the creek, and, as he could not get it out by himself, asked if they would help him.

After some light hearted grumbling about being got out of bed in the middle of a wet, cold night to rescue a cow stupid enough to walk into a creek all four agreed to go.

Before setting off for the creek Bill half filed a large bucket with a pollard mash which he had already heated up on the kitchen stove. He told the curious men that he was afraid the cow might become exhausted and die if he did not keep up its strength.

As they squelched through the sodden paddock, the four men carried with them in addition to the hurricane lamp (which did not give them a great deal of light) and the bucket of mash, two ropes, a wide belt and a five foot piece of planking.

They found the cow deeply sunk in the mud and lowing pitiably. Always impetuous Dick lunged forward to have a closer look and found himself sinking in the mud. He yelled, 'Good God, it's quicksand!' His mates had considerably difficulty helping him out without getting stuck in the mire themselves. Bill on the third attempt managed to get the bucket of mash on the plank out under the cow's head and it started to eat.

The rescue operation then came to a halt. As the fishermen said they were afraid they would all be engulfed in the loose wet mire if they did not have some wide platforms on which to work, the five men stumbled back to Bill's place. They could not find anything suitable outside the buildings or in the sheds, but in the storeroom at the back of the shop there was a very large, well-made box in which Bill stored his reserve stocks of canned and packeted goods. Somewhat reluctantly he agreed to it being dismantled.

The rain had eased by the time the men got back to the creek with the pieces of the box. Working in the poor light was difficult and two of the fishermen fell into the mire and had to be rescued. But after an hour of hard work the cow was dragged out onto firm ground. Then the five men and the cow trudged back to Bill's house leaving the sections of the box to be recovered when the mire had dried out enough.

Bill invited the men to go into the kitchen, where the fire was alight, and help themselves from the bottle of whisky he had put on the table. He said he would join them as soon as he had washed down the cow and put it in the shed out of the cold wind.

Ten minutes later the kitchen door was flung open and Bill came in. The left leg of his trousers was untidily rolled up and blood from a cut just under his knee was dribbling down into his shoe.

The sudden entry of their host with his trousers in disarray and an injury to his leg stopped a conversation between the four fishermen about the possibility of getting out to Lizard Reef later in the day.

Watched by his silent, wondering guests Bill hobbled up to the table, poured himself a large whisky and said calmly, but grimly, 'That dammed cow belongs to Southwell'. Then, after drinking some of the whisky, added, 'And look what it's done to my leg. It's another fair cow of a cow'.

TRADE DEALS

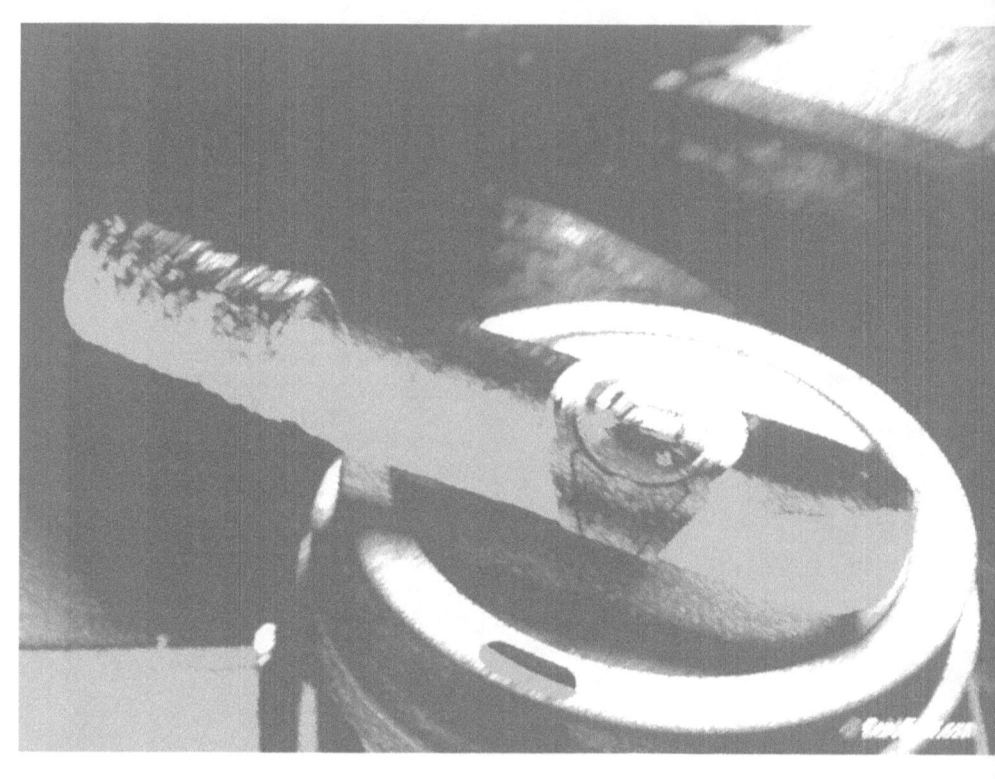

DRESSING FOR THE OCCASION

He introduced himself as Mr Loreto and said, 'I control the water supply to Havana and can guarantee that you will have water whenever you want it if you rent a flat in one of my blocks. I cannot give you a similar guarantee if you rent a flat anywhere else in the city'. As Len and I valued a reliable water supply fairly highly, we went with Mr Loreto to look at the flat he was prepared to lease to us.

The flat, on the second floor of a three-storied building, was commodious, the furniture was comfortable and the rent reasonable, so we agreed to lease it.

There was accommodation for a servant and Mr Loreto said he would 'supply' a good servant who spoke English and that she would be waiting at the flat when we returned with our baggage. When we arrived two hours later we were greeted, rather shyly, by a soberly dressed, handsome young woman named Marguetta, who, we soon discovered, worked at a tantalizingly slow pace but cooked appetising meals and kept the flat reasonably tidy.

The day after we moved into the flat Len, who was based in the Australian Embassy in Washington, flew home to spend the week-end with his family. That night I was awakened by two pistol or rifle shots being fired outside my bedroom window. I lay in bed for a few minutes after the firing ceased then slid off the bed onto the floor, crawled over to the window and very cautiously peered out. I could not see anybody. As I was making my way back to bed the buzzer on the front door began to ring continuously. I thought someone had come to tell me what was going on. When I opened the door, however, I was faced with a little man wearing a coat several sizes too big for him pointing a pistol at my stomach and jabbering in Spanish.

On my way to the front door I had passed the partially open kitchen door and had glimpsed, through the crack, Marguetta standing behind the door. I thought if I backed down the passage the gunman would follow me and be seen by Marguetta and that she would escape by the back entrance and get the police.

To my dismay Marguetta came out into the passage and began to talk in Spanish to the gunman. I thought that she must be a collaborator. Then she turned to me and said, 'He's the night watchman. He saw a man climbing towards your window and fired at him but the thief slid down a drain pipe and got away'.

I exclaimed, 'Why is he pointing that gun at me!' After a brief exchange in Spanish, Marguetta said, as the night watchman put the gun into a holster which had been hidden under his oversized coat, 'He had forgotten he had it in his hand'.

I went to my room, got a USA ten dollar note and gave it to the night watchman who left smiling, bowing and saying something or other in Spanish.

A few days later I saw Mr Loreto in the Pinos Club and told him about the foiling of the thief. 'Every time a new tenant comes into one of the flats the night watchman drives off an intruder', he said, unsurprised. He did not seem to be at all concerned about the possibility of the flat dwellers being injured by the little night watchman's bullets.

Amos, the delegation driver who was supposed to pick up Len and me at the flat at 8.15 each morning, was late on the first four mornings and Len and I had decided we would try and have him replaced. But on the fifth morning he saw Marguetta. After that he was never late again. Each morning he would arrive before eight and lean against the back door of the kitchen watching Marguetta at work until we were ready to leave. Not only did Amos become more reliable in the matter of time, but he also became more choosy in the matter of dress. For the first few days he had appeared in crumpled, nondescript shirt and pants and no tie. But for the rest of our time in Cuba he wore clean, well-pressed white pants, a brightly coloured shirt and a large bow tie, usually brown or yellow with black or white dots.

However Amos's conversion to punctuality and elegant dressing did not remove all the obstacles to our early arrival at the conference centre. That objective continued to be put at risk by the national pastime – playing dominoes for money.

On the way to the city and back Len and I had to cross a bridge, the centre of which was raised whenever a ship wanted to move up or down the river. The operator sat high above the bridge in a glass cubicle sheltered from the sun and rain by a green umbrella-like canopy. We soon came to realise he always had with him a domino playing companion. The two men absorbed in their domino game were clearly visible for a hundred yards or so along the road on each approach to the bridge. Both men wore battered-looking felt hats and when a game finished one of them (presumably the loser) would stand up, take off his hat and throw it on to the floor apparently with all the force he could muster. Without that outlet for their pent-up feelings both men might have died young from a stroke or heart failure. But with it they remained alive to torment dependent motorists including Len and me.

Sometimes when a ship went through the gap in the bridge the domino game must have been at a critical stage and the operator considered he could not afford to take his mind off the game to work the span-lowering mechanism. He ignored the blowing of horns by irate drivers, finished his game and, if necessary, took out his frustration on his hat, before attending to his duty.

•

The conference centre had been designed as a hospital but on its completion Batista, Cuba's dictatorial President, decided that the building, at least for a while, would better serve the interests of his country's citizens as a place for trade diplomats from around the world to confer than as a place for Cubans to be treated for sickness or injury. The building had been erected on a site previously occupied by a jail and the muscular security men who guarded the entrances and patrolled the corridors of the conference centre dressed in dark blue uniforms and ugly peaked cap looked remarkably like jailers who, when the jail was demolished, had remained in its precinct ready to haunt any new occupier of the site.

The aim of the conference (which involved 106 countries and was expected to last from November 1947 to March 1948) was to draft a charter for a world trade organisation. As is not uncommon during large international conferences delegates were each called upon to perform a task not directly related to the interests of the country they represented. I was asked to be the neutral chairman of a committee dealing with the special problems of land-locked countries. The other members of the committee were all from either a land-locked country or a country through which the imports and exports of a land-locked country passed. The need for a neutral chairman soon became evident. There was a lot of ill-feeling and distrust between many of the countries on the committee. The animosities were caused by disputes which varied greatly. An example is the dispute which flared up between Pakistan and Afghanistan. The Pakistanis claimed that Afghans crossed the rugged, poorly-marked border between the two countries posing as rural workers but spent their time robbing and murdering Pakistani citizens. The Afghans claimed their citizens were lured into Pakistan with promises of seasonal work on farms and were ill-treated and very poorly paid by Pakistani farmers.

Although none of the matters which caused these fierce disputes related to the work of the committee, at each meeting someone would make a remark which brought about an uncontrollable shouting match between several of the delegates. After a few weeks of trying to curb the unruly behaviour I adjourned the committee meetings indefinitely.

I then set out to draft the relevant chapter in the charter with the aid of one competent delegate from a land-locked country and another from a transit country. When we had a draft that satisfied the three of us we talked to each other country separately. After discussion lasting about a month, it was acceptable to all and I arranged for a meeting of the committee at 9 am to formally approve the draft. I confidently expected the meeting to last only a few minutes.

At 9 am all the delegates except Luis Alvarez from the Argentine were present. As Luis had not arrived by 9.10 I went to my office and rang his home – he had rented a house in a suburb some distance from the city. Mrs Alvarez who answered the phone, I knew had a poor grasp of English. When I asked where Luis was, she said he had lost his pants. The reason for Luis's absence from the meeting surprised me. It is not easy for a man to lose his pants; that article of his clothing is not one that he is likely to drop in the street without noticing, or, absent-mindedly, leave in a train, tram, restaurant, club or theatre. I repeated my question and got the same answer.

I then asked if I could speak to Luis himself but Mrs Alvarez said he could not speak on the phone because he had lost his pants. I thought Luis was being unnecessarily modest and also had been improvident in coming to Havana with only one pair of pants.

There were two other meetings I had to attend that day and I adjourned the committee until 6 pm.

When I came into my office at noon I found Luis, wearing a pair of pants, waiting for me. After apologising for his absence he told me what had happened.

On the previous evening he said he had worked late and when he got home after midnight his wife was in bed asleep. He had undressed with the aid of some light coming in through the bedroom window, hung his pants over the back of a chair, got into bed and fallen asleep almost immediately.

Sometime later he woke up. Lying in his bed he was astonished to see his pants slowly rise from the back of the chair and when about a foot above it move towards the window. At first he thought he was dreaming but then realised that his trousers were really leaving him. He jumped out of bed and went in pursuit of them.

The ground floor windows of every building in Havana had iron bars across them. Before Luis could reach his pants they had passed through the bars. Looking through the bars Luis saw a large black man snatch the pants off a hook on the end of a long thin bamboo pole, shove them into a bag and run away with the bag in one hand and the pole in the other.

In a pocket of Luis's pants was his wallet which contained very important personal and official papers. The robbery took place at 4.30 am and Luis spent the next six hours in discussions with the local police, police headquarters in the city, the Argentine ambassador in Cuba and by phone with people in Buenos Aires. It was only after he had finished all this that he remembered the committee meeting.

All the delegates turned up for the meeting at 6 pm and it was over in five minutes.

●

It was after we had spent a week in one of the large, flash hotels – which catered mainly for the Americans who came to Havana for their winter holidays – that Len and I decided to try and find a flat well away from the holiday entertainment area of the city. We hoped that the change in our abode would enable us to get to know some Cubans other than the conference delegates and learn a little about their manner of living.

The flat we had leased from Mr Loreto was in a 'middle class' suburb called Miranda. To the west of us the wealthy Cubans lived in large elegant houses. To the east of us, in the suburbs through which we passed on our way to the city, poor Afro-Cubans lived in dilapidated tenements.

Because Miranda was not a place to which tourists came, two strangers living in the suburb aroused considerable curiosity. Len and I did our best to get on good terms with people in the neighbourhood, none of whom except Marguetta (who had come from Jamaica to Cuba as a young teenager) spoke more than a word or two of English. Nevertheless with signs and smiles, the few words of Spanish we had acquired and the happy disposition of our neighbours, we got along quite well. We were regarded as Americans and nothing we could say or do seemed to change that.

On most Sunday afternoons Len and I spent an hour or two in a café not far from our flat. It was a meeting place for the locals and we soon established amicable relations with the staff and other customers.

In the cafe's juke box there were many records of dance orchestras playing rhumba tunes. When these records were being played – which was most of the time – some young couples would dance the Cuban national dance. It was warm in the café and the young men came there suitably dressed for dancing – above the waist they wore only a cotton singlet.

One Sunday two girls with smiles and signs – and considerable support from their companions – asked Len and me to dance with them

Neither Len or I had ever tried the rhumba but with a little coaching from the girls we soon mastered the two quick side steps and slow forward step in good time with the music but our hip movements probably left something to be desired, very seductive though we tried to be.

Word must have spread quickly that the Americanos were dancing the rhumba because passers by crowded into the café or stood outside looking in, clapping and stamping their feet in time to the music. More coins were put into the juke box and our attempts to leave the floor so that some others might dance were greeted with cries of dismay from both the girls and the audience. It became quite hot in the café and with great encouragement from the onlookers we stripped down to our 'Chesty Bond' singlets and were properly dressed for dancing the Rhumba café style.

Towards the end of our stay in the flat, in order to return hospitality, we held a cocktail party for members of other delegations. Word apparently spread that the Americanos were going to have a party and when the day came we found not only some of the locals on the footpath outside the apartment block watching guests arrive, but also that our neighbours in the next apartment block – whose living room windows faced ours at a distance of ten or twelve yards – had invited many friends and arranged chairs for them facing towards our flat so that they could all sip drinks and eat biscuits while watching us partying. The neighbours and their friends smiled and waved to us whenever we looked their way. Some of our guests seemed a little disconcerted by the onlookers but Len and I felt that the friends of our neighbours had paid us a compliment by coming to look on dressed in their best clothes, the women in cute little fashionable hats and the men with bright floral buttonholes.

•

Two days before the conference was due to end I received a cable from Australia. It instructed me to get to Brussels as fast as I could to be an observer at discussions to be held there by a number of European countries with the aim of creating a European Economic Community. I booked a passage to Brussels via London but the BOAC plane which was to take me from Havana to London went into the sea off Bermuda on its journey out to Havana. I flew in a small plane to Nassau so that after spending a night and day there I could fly to Bermuda on the regular service from Florida to Bermuda via Nassau.

Another guest at the Victoria Hotel where I stayed in Nassau was an English diplomat named Phillip Potter who was on his way home from Brazil. We agreed to have an early lunch together, go for a long walk and be back at the hotel by four o'clock ready to be taken out to the airport in the hotel's bus at quarter past four.

We got lost. At four o'clock we were hurrying along a rough road between two large sugar plantations when an old truck came out of a side track onto the road. The negro driver and another negro were sitting on a small wooden seat in the tiny cabin. We stopped the truck (which had an unpleasant smell) explained our predicament and asked the driver if he would take us to the Victoria Hotel. He did not seem very enthusiastic but after we offered him some money he agreed on the understanding that we would ride in the back of the truck – as far as we could see there was nowhere else we could ride.

When we got into the back of the truck we found where the smell came from – the tray was covered with bags of blood and bone manure. On these bags we sat while the truck went at full speed over the rough road.

We reached the Victoria Hotel at half past four. The bus, with our luggage in it, had left. The head porter got us a taxi and said he would phone the airport to say we were on our way.

At the airport we were rushed on to the plane and immediately we had boarded it the plane taxied out to the runway and took off.

The seat next to mine was occupied by a Hollywood actor whose name was, I think, Robert Newton. I had seen him playing 'Long John Silver' in the film *Treasure Island*. Before I sat down Newton drew as far away from me as he could and when the plane was safely in the air he rang for the hostess.

As soon as she was within earshot he said in a loud voice, 'I want a double whisky and another seat'.

The blood and bone dust which had found its way into my clothes gave off a pretty nasty odour and before long the passengers in the seats immediately in front and behind me had been taken to other seats. The departure of all these passengers to distant seats left me very comfortably situated. I could sort out my papers and stretch out in all directions without disturbing anybody.

When I arrived in Bermuda and presented myself at the immigration desk the officer moved back a bit, seized my passport, stamped it very quickly and shouted, 'Next please'. At the Customs counter the officer made no attempt to have any of my baggage opened. He quickly put some chalk marks on each piece and said, 'On your way'.

At the passenger exit I was joined by Phillip. He had also got through the Customs and Immigration formalities very quickly. He told me he too had had a pleasant journey in the plane; his seating companion had disappeared after walking down the plane and talking to one of the hostesses.

Phillip and I were staying at the same hotel, I for one night, he for several. The taxi driver taking us to the hotel did not engage in the usual over the shoulder conversation with us but concentrated on his driving and got us to our destination very quickly. At the hotel we had very speedy service from the receptionists.

Soon after I reached my room the valet called (no doubt under instructions from the management) and asked if I had any clothes I would like cleaned. He left holding my sports coat and flannel pants at arm's length. They were returned next morning smelling only of the cleaners.

The next day I boarded a Pan Am plane for Lisbon. The journey was not nearly as comfortable as the one from Nassau to Bermuda. I did not have anything like the same amount of room to stretch out and work on my papers. My seating companion talked non-stop when awake and snored non-stop when asleep. At Lisbon I nearly missed the Air France connection to Brussels because the Immigration officer spent such a long time examining the visas in my passport while carrying on a conversation with his colleague at the adjoining desk. My seating companion on the Air France plane ate garlic and complained at length about the incompetence of the Italian Government.

156

At Brussels it took so long to get through Customs and Immigration and from the airport to the conference centre in a taxi with a talkative driver that I was present for only the last hour of the first day of the meeting. I went to bed that night convinced that the most suitable dress for air travel was a pair of pants and a coat on which had been sprinkled, and well-rubbed into the cloth, some blood and bone manure.

THE IRISH CONNECTION

A series of international conferences which were held in London, Geneva, Havana, Annecy and Torquay in the late 1940s and early 1950s had two objectives. First, to establish an international trade organisation and, second, to permit a large number of countries to negotiate reductions in their Customs tariffs. The attempt to establish an international trade organisation foundered in 1950 when it became clear that the USA Congress would not agree to that country becoming a member of the organisation. But the negotiations to reduce the barriers to international trade continued under the oversight of an organisation known as the Contracting Parties to the General Agreement on Tariffs and Trade.

To this series of conferences the Australian Government sent a delegation which included three men of Irish descent, Kevin Doherty, Lew Murphy and Pat Ryan. The eldest of the three was Kevin, an assistant Comptroller-General of Customs in his late fifties who had not been overseas before he attended the first of the conferences. He had a settled inclination to make facetious remarks while maintaining an expressionless face; a type of humour not commonly practised by conferees during international deliberations. At the conferences Kevin was the Australian representative on the committee drafting the technical Customs sections required both for the charter of the proposed international trade organisation and for the regulation of the results of the Customs tariff negotiations. During the committee's deliberations, Kevin frequently produced one of his droll remarks while giving the impression of making a serious contribution to the discussion. It was a long time before the other members of the committee came to understand and appreciate Kevin's sense of humour. When they did, as we shall see, their response contained surprises for Kevin.

The humour in most of the facetious remarks Kevin made at the committee meetings could only be fully appreciated by someone conversant with Customs practices and jargon. But I don't think knowledge of these matters is necessary to recognise it in the example I will give.

The Cuban representative on the technical Customs committee (Antonio Mateas) brought to every meeting of the committee a large box of cigars which he handed around to the members. Kevin, who liked cigars and considered himself an excellent judge of tobacco in that form, said that Antonio's cigars were the best he had ever smoked. One day when the committee was to discuss rules to ensure that information marked on goods traded internationally (or the packages of such goods) gave the correct country of origin and description of the goods, not only Antonio but also the Canadian delegate, Lionel Jacobs (a non-smoker), came to the committee room with a large box of cigars. Around the middle of each of the Canadian cigars was the usual paper band incorporating an oval label which contained the following information; on the top was printed 'Tower of London Cigar', beneath these words was an illustration of the Tower of London and beneath the illustration were the words 'Made in Canada'. All the members of the committee who smoked cigars took a Canadian cigar as well as a Cuban cigar. The new provider of these symbols of high-living, Lionel Jacobs, was one of three members of the committee with whom Kevin had established very friendly relations and with whom he had a few drinks in the *Palais* bar each evening.

Soon after the discussion began Kevin got the chairman's permission to speak and said 'I want to draw the committee's attention to the fact that Canada is a country which is likely to supply goods which are incorrectly marked'. He then held up the Canadian cigar which he was smoking and added, 'This cigar is a good example of goods being incorrectly marked'. Lionel Jacobs did not wait for the chairman's permission to speak but burst forth. 'The Australian delegate has made an outrageous attack on a country which has established a world-wide reputation for correctly marking the goods it exports. It is nonsense to say that the cigars are incorrectly marked. While the label has the name "Tower of London" printed on it and also an illustration of the Tower of London, there is clearly no attempt to create the impression that the cigars are made in England because on the label, in the same size as the words Tower of London, are the words "Made in Canada"'.

When Lionel had finished speaking not a sound could be heard in the committee room. All the delegates except Kevin, who went on quietly smoking the Canadian cigar, appeared to be embarrassed by the dispute. After a moment or two the chairman said, 'Perhaps the Australian delegate would like to reply to the Canadian delegate's remarks'. Kevin carefully knocked the ash off his cigar, put the cigar down on the edge of the ash tray and then said, 'The Canadian delegate is under a misapprehension, it is not the words "Tower of London" to which I am objecting, it is the word "Cigar"'.

•

The other two men of Irish descent in the Australian delegation, Lew Murphy and Pat Ryan, were considerably younger than Kevin; both being thirty-four years of age when the conferences began. They were born and bred in Western Australia and joined the Federal Public Service in the middle 1930s when the Federal departments interested in international trade recruited some university graduates reasonably proficient in at least one foreign language. They were close friends, physically somewhat alike, large raw-boned men, but they had temperaments that were quite different. Pat was quick tempered, impatient and ambitious; a good footballer and an outstanding boxer. Lew was a bit of a dreamer, not governed by any desire for power or superiority but could pertinaciously adhere to his opinion or purpose if aroused; he kept himself in reasonably good physical condition by taking long walks and doing what he called 'physical jerks'.

Faced with a stay of at least six months at the conference in Geneva in 1947, Pat and Lew decided to move away from the hotel into which they had been booked by the Australian High Commission in London and live in a flat. However flats and servants to do household chores in them were very hard to get in Switzerland at that time. During the war and for several years after it the Government of Switzerland allowed into the country an influx of wealthy refugees and kept out poorer people – the type of people who were likely to do household chores in flats.

Eventually the two Australians leased a flat in a part of the town not frequented by tourists or conference delegates. Although they had only limited contact with the Swiss living around them, the contact they did have was sufficient to bring about a few changes in their habitual practices.

As soon as they took up residence in the flat they advertised for someone to regularly clean the rooms. They got no response and eventually settled for an arrangement under which the caretaker of the apartment building, Madame Rossi, undertook that work. For a while she also arranged help when they entertained in the flat. But as time went on they realized that this very fair-seeming lady regarded them as two rich foreigners who should be diddled at every opportunity.

Lew and Pat frequently had their evening meal at a café only a few doors down the street from the building in which their apartment was located. At first they did not realize that the café was a kind of club for the men (not the women) living in the nearby apartments. The café provided a number of copies of the local papers – secured to polished pieces of timber and kept in a large rack near the entrance – and many packs of cards and sets of dominoes for the use of its customers. At any time of the day a few of the local men could be found in the cafe. But the busiest times were in the late afternoon and evening during the week and throughout the day and evening on Sundays. Whenever a customer entered the cafe, or was about to leave it, he shook hands with all the other customers and both shook hands with, and inquired about the health of, Monsieur Barthelemy (the chef) and Madame Barthelemy (the cashier and general superintendent) and each of the staff. Although the regular customers usually spent several hours in the café each time they visited it, they normally had only one or two drinks of beer, wine or spirits and one or two drinks of coffee throughout that period. Occasionally the drinks were accompanied by a light meal of cheese or sausage sandwich or a cheese fondue. Less frequently a customer had a meal of meat and vegetables or salad. On Sundays some of the men brought their families (wives, children, grandparents, uncles and aunts) to the café for a midday meal, usually to celebrate some important family event. Except when they were participating in a family meal the men spent their time talking, reading or playing cards or dominoes.

Into this settled system of life there burst two foreigners, Lew and Pat, who hurried into the cafe, sat down without paying the usual courtesies to the customers already in the café and to Monsieur, Madame and the staff, ordered a meal of meat, vegetables, salads and desert (which by the standards of the place was a sumptuous feast) and at least one of the strangers (Pat) obviously fretted about the length of time it took to prepare the meal – something which did not seem to the local men, who intended to spend the whole evening in the cafe, to be any cause for concern.

While Pat fretted Lew took a newspaper from the rack and read aloud those articles he found interesting or amusing. The behaviour of the regular customers when they first came in and were about to leave the café caught the attention of both Lew and Pat, and after discussing the matter they decided on their fourth visit to extend the established courtesies to the other customers, and to Monsieur and Madame Barthelemy and the staff. This change in their conduct vastly improved their relations with everyone who worked in and frequented the cafe. Almost immediately Monsieur and Madame paid them the respect to which they were entitled as 'big spenders' by sitting at their table for a few minutes each time they were in the café and occasionally 'shouting' a drink for them. As they were no longer mannerless strangers, all the other customers, at first rather tentatively, but later with increasing confidence and cheerfulness, exchanged the usual courtesies with them on entering and leaving. When they suspected that Madame Rossi was exploiting them it was to Monsieur and Madame Barthelemy that Pat and Lew turned for help. The catering the café proprietors arranged was done very efficiently and at a reasonable price. The change in the catering arrangements had to be handled very carefully because Pat and Lew could not afford to be at loggerheads with so important a person as the caretaker of the apartment building. Their combined attempt to exert the art of a diplomatist was reasonably successful; Madame Rossi did not appear to bear them any ill will.

·

But it was not to fraternize with the Swiss that Lew and Pat had been sent to Geneva. At the conference Lew was the Australian delegate on a committee drafting some of the policy sections of the charter for the proposed international trade organisation. The other committee members were impressed with Lew's ability to compose acceptable drafts of their conclusions in the working language (English) and they asked him to be the *rapporteur*. In this position he worked closely with the chairman of the committee, a Frenchman named André Rudler. Pat was a member of an Australian team negotiating reductions in the Customs tariffs. A large part of his time was taken up by negotiations with the USA team and he became very friendly with two Americans, John Welham and Al Nixon. André, John and Al were frequent visitors to the flat Pat and Lew shared in the 'native quarter' of the town.

Australian delegations to international conferences held in far-away countries were (and possibly still are) frequently faced with requests from the Government for almost a day-by-day account of the conference activity in connection with some relatively minor matter of concern to a small group with a loud voice and considerable political power. One matter of this type, which was the subject of frequent cables from the Australian Government during the 1947 conference in Geneva, related to the Australian prohibition on the export of Merino stud rams. An influential primary producer group was anxious to ensure that the charter for the international trade organisation did not prevent the Australian government maintaining that prohibition. The question of whether or not the charter should disapprove of such prohibitions was a subject matter falling within the functions of the committee of which Lew was a member. He had to spend a disproportionate part of his time answering cables requesting information about the progress (or lack of it), the views of influential countries represented on the committee, the appropriateness of draft sections of the charter intended to protect the continuation of the prohibition and so forth. He did not want to distract the attention of the members of the committee from the other very important matters of concern to Australia, which he was putting forward on behalf of the Government and, having once raised the matter of the prohibition in the committee he did not pursue it any further during the first three months of the Geneva conference either in the formal meetings or, as suggested in the cables from Australia, in informal discussions with other members of the committee. He realized that eventually he would have to take the matter up again but hoped that that action could be postponed until after Australia's main policy objectives had been obtained. In the meantime he drafted enigmatic replies to the cables arriving in quick succession from Australia.

Towards the end of June various delegations began to hold cocktail parties to which all the delegates from the other seventeen countries represented at the conference were invited. These costly parties were justified on the grounds that they encouraged informal discussions between the delegates. No one was co-ordinating the dates chosen for the parties and on the 30th June both the USA delegation and the French delegation issued invitations to a party to commence at 5.30 pm on 13th July. The French chose that day because it was the Saturday before their national day, July 14th. On June 30th André Rudler told Pat and Lew that his wife and her twin sisters (two unmarried women in their early thirties) would be coming to Geneva for the week-end July 13th and 14th and he invited the two Australians to join them for a dinner-dance to be held on one of the Lake steamers on the night of July 12th. His invitation was readily accepted. Two days later John and Al asked Pat and Lew to a dinner at the Hotel Rhône which the American delegation was holding after its cocktail party. Pat and Lew had to decline that invitation but agreed to spend a large part of the cocktail period that day at the American party.

Shortly after 6 pm on July 13th Pat and Lew left the French cocktail party, at which they had met (and found very attractive) André's wife and her twin sisters, and made their way to the American party. Neither Pat nor Lew were normally heavy drinkers but by some means John and Al managed

164

to get Pat to consume a very large amount of Bourbon. The full effect of this only became apparent about half an hour after the Australians left the American party.

Pat and Lew met André and his bevy of attractive women at the ship's side shortly before 8 pm and the whole party went on board. André was acquainted with Monsieur Gellaty who organised the catering and entertainment on the ship. This rather pompous man told them that all the artistes who would be performing in the floor show had come from leading Paris night clubs, and that the majority of the diners were French people from 'across the border' who each year regarded the lake cruise as a perfect way to celebrate the French national day. He showed them to their table and from there pointed out some of the important French people on the ship. They included Monsieur Prevoir, a very broad shouldered, middle-aged man who had a much younger wife with a beautiful head of red hair. Monsieur and Madame Prevoir and their friends were already seated at a table on the edge of the dance floor.

At André's suggestion his party did not remain in the dining room but went to the bow of the ship. There they became the only occupants of two rows of comfortable wooden seats.

The ship left the wharf, cleared the small lake port and settled on a course close to the Swiss shore. Relaxing on the wooden seats the members of André's party did not talk very much. It was an hour and place for quiet enjoyment. While the ship moved steadily through the calm lake waters, the bland summer day came to an end and the stars glowed brightly in the twilight until the moon rising majestically over the snow-capped mountains dimmed all other heavenly bodies with her peerless light.

When the time came to return to their table for dinner Pat was found to be fast asleep. Lew tried to wake him but even when sober Pat was a very difficult man to wake. It was impossible to arouse him when drunk. Lew offered as an explanation for Pat's suspended consciousness that his colleague had worked hard in a stressful situation during the week and was completely exhausted. He then said that Pat would be very upset if they did not go ahead with the dinner without waiting for him.

Once the dinner began Lew did not for long remain disconcerted by Pat's fall from grace. He found the food very appetising, the conversation very lively and interesting, André's choice of wines excellent and the floor show entertaining. The fourth item of the floor show started with two very compact acrobatic men dressed in normal street clothes bumping into one another, as if by accident, and then as they bounced off, doing forward somersaults, back flips and neckrolls. After a few minutes they were joined by a third somewhat taller, rather angular man who maintained a very surprised way of looking while falling heavily himself and throwing into confusion his colleague's attempts to do difficult gymnastic feats. The audience took the third performer to their heart, gave him the nickname 'the clumsy one', and loudly applauded every move he made. André and his party, somewhat to their dismay, soon realized that the third performer was Pat. Still a little confused by the alcohol he had consumed, he had set out to make his way across the dance floor towards André's table and had become an unwilling participant in the gymnastic display.

All three performers moved quite rapidly in the general direction of André's table. When they neared the edge of the dance floor, Pat was jerked forward by one of the acrobats and, to keep his balance, thrust out his hand. It landed with such force on the head of Monsieur Prevoir that that important gentleman dropped a spoon full of fruit salad from which he was about to eat. Enraged by such objectionable interference with the ingestion of his food, Monsieur Prevoir sprang to his feet and gave Pat a strong hard push that sent him sliding across the floor into the lap of a corpulent young man who had turned his chair side on to his table to get a better view of the floor show. The combined weight of the two men was too much for the chair; it collapsed and spilled the men onto the floor with Pat on top of the young man. All this activity was greeted with continuous applause and shouts of 'Bravo the clumsy one' from the diners.

Pat got off the young man, leaned over and started to lift him up. The young man's friend, a pretty blonde girl, who had stood up when Pat crashed into the man's lap, walked around behind Pat, lifted the hem of her long evening dress above her shapely ankles, took a step forward and gave Pat a hard kick on the buttocks.

This unexpected attack from the rear caught Pat off balance. He dropped the young man and fell on top of him. The girl's vigorous footwork and Pat's return to the floor brought thunderous applause. Pat quickly rose to his feet without this time, attempting to assist the young man off the floor.

As soon as Pat had got entangled with Monsieur Prevoir, the two acrobats had stopped their act and during the subsequent events they stood scowling fiercely at the intruder. In this occupation they were soon joined by

Monsieur Gellaty. As Pat got up from the floor the acrobats and Monsieur Gellaty closed in on him and with much waving of arms loudly upbraided him for interfering with the floor show. Still regarding the stream of events as part of the entertainment, a chorus of cheers, jeers and cat-calls arose from the audience.

One of the acrobats waving his arms rather wildly hit Pat in the face with his open hand. From Pat's point of view he had been, in the last ten minutes, maliciously attacked by a number of people amongst whom the man who had now hit him in the face was quite prominent. Pat's temper was aroused and in a flash out shot his right to the chin – a punch which had won him several amateur light-heavyweight boxing championships. Down went the acrobat. Pat looked as though he was about to serve out the same treatment to Monsieur Gellatly and the other acrobat but they picked up their companion and retired hastily from the scene. Having settled one score Pat thought he should tackle another and swung around and shouted out, first in English (because, for the moment, he forgot where he was), and then in French, 'Who kicked me?' Several people who had stood up to get a better view of the action quickly sat down.

The girl who had delivered the kick had had to move away from her table to carry out her undertaking. She had remained away from the table first to acknowledge with a few bows the rapturous applause which her deed had brought forth and then to watch the dispute between Pat and his 'tormentors'. She now found herself stranded with Pat between her and her chair. Realising that this was not an occasion to stand on ceremony she flung herself into the lap of a man with a very long ornate waxed moustache who was sitting side on to his table. The man looked pleased at finding a very pretty girl on his lap but his wife, who was sitting beside him, did not share his pleasure. She unsuccessfully attempted to untwist the arms which the girl had wrapped around her husband and push the elegant female off.

Pat's question brought no response so he repeated it. For a moment there was complete silence then the wife of the man with the waxed moustache pointed to the blonde girl and said, 'She did it'. Pat did not connect the girl, so lovingly embracing the man on whose lap she was sitting, with the plump young man whose chair had been broken a few minutes earlier. That young man was still lying on the floor amongst the ruins of his chair forgotten by everybody during the recent stirring events. Soon after he landed on the floor the young man had seen his girlfriend move around behind Pat and deliver her kick. After Pat attempted to help him up and then dropped him, he had not risen because he was absorbed in the dispute between Pat and the acrobats and Monsieur Gellatly. When that ended quickly and forcibly and Pat shouted out, 'Who kicked me?' the young man remained on the floor because he considered it was a relatively safe place to be during the confrontation that was likely to occur between his girl friend and the large man with the powerful punch who didn't like being kicked.

Most of the people in the dining room waited in a state of eager expectation for Pat's reaction to the revelation by the wife of the man with the waxed moustache. They watched Pat as he stood looking at the pretty young woman who had struck him a hard blow with her foot, without, as far as he was aware, any provoking behaviour from him. Her action greatly puzzled Pat but he considered that there was no satisfactory response he could make to an attack by such an assailant. Much to the disappointment of the diners he walked past the girl and made his way to Andre's table.

A very crestfallen Pat took his seat at the table. The few things he could recall doing in the last two hours filled him with shame and he thought that he might have done other things even more shameful. He apologised to André and the ladies for his absence.

Before Pat had shouted, 'Who kicked me?' the audience had been under the impression that he was a clever, taciturn, French acrobat with a flair for creating comic situations. His shouted question had revealed him to them as an English interloper who ruined the routines of French acrobats, knocked down peaceful French citizens and created mayhem amongst French diners. The underlying French dislike of the English came to the surface and the audience booed him and shouted: 'Englishman go home' 'Englishman jump in the lake'.

By the time Pat sat down the majority of the diners were in a state of mind (or sobriety) which got much gratification from the type of slapstick comedy and rowdiness which had been a feature of the action in the dining room for the last ten or fifteen minutes and they were unwilling to forgo that gratification. After Pat was seated they carried on booing and shouting disapproving remarks at him in the hope that such conduct would provoke him into some entertaining response.

•

Lew considered that the diners had changed from lauding Pat to abusing him because they wrongly assumed him to be an Englishman and that this mistake should be corrected without delay. He suggested to Pat that the two of them stand up, say they were Australians and emphasise the point by singing 'Waltzing Matilda'. Pat very emphatically rejected the proposal but Lew, perhaps with his judgement a little clouded by the quantity of wine he had consumed, obstinately adhered to his purpose. He got up, pointed to Pat, announced that the two of them were Australians and not Englishmen and began to sing 'Waltzing Matilda'. To understand the effect this had on everybody on the lake steamer it is necessary to have a clear perception of Lew's training and experience as a singer.

Lew had a very powerful voice which he probably inherited from his father who had been an amateur singer of some renown. According to Lew's mother, Lew's father had also been a philanderer of some renown and because of that she had left him when Lew was eighteen months old. Lew's mother was of a puritanical disposition, she associated singing with philandering, did not sing herself and did not encourage Lew to sing. Lew greatly enjoyed the physical process of singing – the flexing of the muscles and sinews of his diaphragm, lungs and vocal chords, but, probably due to some ear defect, he did not have the delicate perception of the differences of sound and the judgement of harmony required if any person is to recognise and hold a tune. At the schools Lew had attended as a boy the children had been assembled each morning and taught to sing 'God Save the King'. After twelve years of practising Lew had mastered the tune of 'God Save the King' and by the time he went to the university he could sing the national anthem with the best of them. But that was the only tune he ever mastered. He frequently sang the words of other songs but always to the tune of 'God Save the King'.

At one time in the 'thirties when Lew and Pat were living in the same boarding house in Melbourne, Lew had come to the conclusion that there was no spirituality in his life and he had sought to remedy this by making regular Sunday visits to churches of different denominations. He had persuaded Pat to go with him on one of these visits. They had gone to a Methodist church about a mile from their boarding house. It was Lew's second visit to that church. During the singing of each hymn the huge volume of sound Lew was sending forth had quickly overwhelmed the singing of the choir and the congregation and the tune of 'God Save the King' had rung around the church. The organist had stuck grimly to the task of playing the correct tune but the small portable organ he was playing could not match the volume of sound from Lew and only occasionally had snatches of the tune reached the congregation. Pat had noticed at one stage that a few of the younger members of the choir were in tears as they listened to one of their favourite hymns being rendered unsingable.

Lew and Pat had been seated towards the front of the church and when they stood up at the end of the service Pat was surprised to see that the seats behind them, which had been full when they came in, were practically empty. On the way out, while shaking hands with the young clergyman, Lew had said, 'I liked your choice of hymns, they were all very singable'. A pained expression had passed over the clergyman's face but his Christian conscience had pricked him and he had set out to say, 'Thank you for coming and for your singing'. However he had not been able to force the last few words out of his mouth; he had spluttered and coughed and had then said, 'I think I have caught a cold'.

Lying in bed that night Pat had thought about, and had had compassion for, the young Methodist minister. He had considered that when Lew had expressed his appreciation of the choice of hymns the clergyman had feared that Lew had been contemplating becoming a regular visitor to the church and had thought that if that happened most of his congregation would desert it, the membership of the choir would fall below a workable level and no one would be prepared to play the organ. Pat had fallen asleep wondering to what extent the practising of religious rites by Christians in Melbourne would be abandoned if Lew continued his search for spirituality.

Memories of that Sunday evening nearly ten years earlier flooded into Pat's mind when Lew suggested that the two of them sing 'Waltzing Matilda' to the French diners; it caused him to promptly and emphatically refuse to participate in Lew's proposal.

The words Lew had begun to sing (he was making a rough translation from English to French as he went along) meant nothing to the French audience but the tune did because practically all of them had listened regularly to the BBC broadcasts during the recent war. They regarded the singing of the British national anthem by Pat's companion as adding insult to injury. They booed, whistled and shouted disparaging remarks. About twelve men and women got together in one corner of the room and sang the French national anthem at the top of their voices.

Sounds of the uproar reached the bridge and alarmed the Captain. Amongst the confused noise the captain could distinguish the singing of the

British and French national anthems and he thought that a riot might break out on the ship. He ceased maintaining a zigzag course on the return journey down the lake, rang down 'full speed' on the engine room telegraph and set the ship on the shortest course to Geneva.

The noisy audience did not disturb Lew. He greatly enjoyed his singing and was nearing the end of 'Waltzing Matilda' for the fourth time when a number of the audience noticed that the ship was rapidly approaching Geneva. When this news was broadcast amongst the rest of the audience all of them began to shout for the Captain to come and explain why the cruise had been cut short.

Lew considered that he should postpone his efforts to correct the assumption that Pat was an Englishman until after the audience had settled with the Captain the question of the ship's return to port. He sat down.

The uproar continued until finally Monsieur Gellatly, not the Captain, appeared on the musicians' little stage. Before speaking to the noisy assemblage Gellatly had a short conversation with the two musicians. Then he turned to the diners and said that the Captain had brought the ship close to the port because he expected bad weather. It was a fine, clear, still night and Gellatly's statement was interrupted by loud cries of derision. When these ceased Gellatly went on to say that the ship would continue to cruise in the vicinity of the port and, because this dinner-dance was a very special occasion for all the French guests, the ship would remain at sea for an extra half hour and the musicians would continue to play dance music and the bar would remain open throughout the extra period. He asked if the diners wanted to have an extra half hour on board. The question was answered with a wholehearted 'Yes!' and cheers.

After Gellatly's statement the atmosphere in the dining room changed. Lew did not recommence his attempt to correct the misunderstanding about Pat's nationality. With Gallic good humour the French diners now smiled and waved to Pat and Lew as they passed André's table and exchanged pleasantries with Pat, Lew, André and their partners on the dance floor. The last hour of the dinner-dance was a very enjoyable one. Before it ended, at André's suggestion, all his party agreed to meet on the morrow, weather permitting, for a picnic lunch in the gardens alongside the lake. The weather did permit.

•

By August 1947 the technical Customs committee had been meeting regularly for about six months, two months in London and four in Geneva.

Members of the committee had become accustomed to, and appreciative of, Kevin's poker-faced banter; they considered that it brightened the otherwise pedestrian discussions. On 10th August the delegate for the Netherlands circulated a paper for discussion in the committee the next day. This paper referred to the work done by botanists and horticulturists in the Netherlands which had resulted in the development of some bulbiferous plants having very special characteristics. It proposed that a clause in the technical customs section of the charter for an international trade organisation be drafted in a way which would permit the Netherlands Government to control, and if necessary, prohibit the export of certain bulbiferous plants.

Throughout the conference all the members of the Australian delegation came together for a meeting first thing every morning. At the meeting on the morning of 11th of August it was agreed that Kevin should support the Netherlands proposal but request an amendment to the clause drafted by the Netherlands. The amendment would allow the Australian Government to control the export of merino stud rams on the grounds that this was a special type of sheep which had been developed in Australia. The Australian delegation considered that there were marked advantages in having the question of the prohibition of the export of merino stud rams dealt with in the technical Customs committee rather than in a committee dealing with policy matters.

Before the technical Customs committee started its meeting later that morning Kevin asked the chairman to allow him to speak immediately after the Netherlands delegate had introduced his paper. When Kevin spoke in favour of the idea put forward by the Netherlands delegation and proposed that the clause drafted by that delegation be amended by adding Australian merino stud rams after Netherlands bulbiferous plants there was much laughter from the committee members. Delegates from several other countries got permission to speak. Each proposed that the clause drafted by the Netherlands delegation be amended to allow export controls over certain goods or services which they said had been specially developed in their country. The United Kingdom delegate proposed the addition of 'rising damp'; the USA delegate 'business know-how', the French delegate 'illicit love'. Kevin spoke again in support of the Netherlands proposal and the amendment he had put forward. His thoughtful way of speaking and grave countenance delighted the delegates of all countries other than the Netherlands and brought loud bursts of laughter. The chairman did not consider it was worthwhile putting the Netherlands proposal to the vote; it was lost on the laughter.

Lew, who on the morning of 11th August thought he was rid of the problem of the prohibition of the export of merino stud rams, by the evening found he was once more encumbered with it.

•

The conference ended on 20th September. A draft charter for an international trade organisation had been prepared for consideration by fifty-two countries at an international meeting starting in Havana on 21st November 1947. The draft did not include any clause which would specifically allow the continuance of the prohibition on the export of merino stud rams but it did include clauses which met most of the Australian Government's major objectives.

All members of the Australian delegation except Lew returned home in the latter part of September. Lew remained in Geneva as a member of a small steering committee which was to work with the secretariat in developing details of a plan to handle the major issues at the Havana conference. The weekend before Pat was due to leave Geneva Lew went looking for new accommodation. His search was facilitated, and the type and location of the lodgings he sought influenced by the transport available to him after the conference ended.

Throughout the Geneva conference transport for the Australian delegation was provided by a small fleet of British cars shipped over from England and driven by English girls wearing bright green uniforms. The cars and the girls were part of a VIP transport unit established in England during the war which remained in being for a few years after the war. The Australian delegation arranged for one of the cars and its driver to remain in Geneva after the conference ended to provide transport for Lew. With this transport at his disposal Lew decided to look for accommodation in a hotel in a small town in one of the French provinces near Geneva. After two days of searching he found what he was looking for in the Hotel Beau Regarde on the northern outskirts of St Varent.

The hotel was owned and managed by Madame Guiseard. She was a short stocky woman, about forty years of age, plain looking, brown haired and blue eyed, with a shrewd but cheerful way of running her business. Monsieur Guiseard was an accountant working in Lyon. He came home to the hotel on most weekends.

Lew enjoyed gossip and whenever he had time to spare while staying at the Hotel Beau Regarde he chatted to members of the staff and the guests. From these sources he learned that the Mayor of St Varent was ill-disposed towards Madame Guiseard. This feeling arose out of the circumstances in which Madame had bought the hotel from its previous owner. A close friend of the Mayor who had lived in St Varent all his life wanted to buy the hotel. He started negotiations with the owner but before any agreement was reached Madame Guiseard arrived in the town and offered a price which the Mayor's friend was unwilling or unable to match. After the stranger from Lyon had taken over the hotel the Mayor began to call her 'a blood sucking foreign parasite' and other unpleasant names and he tried to discourage the local people from patronizing the hotel. But Madame's cheerful efficiency soon gave the hotel a good reputation and much to the Mayor's chagrin its patronage by the townspeople increased and it became popular with travellers. Madame ignored the Mayor's name-calling and attempts to intimidate the people living in the vicinity of the hotel and concentrated her attention on the effective management of her business.

While Lew listened to gossip about the dispute between the Mayor and Madame Guiseard he little thought that before long he would become involved in it.

The Hotel Beau Regarde was a building of three storeys with a single storey flat built alongside it and connected to the main building by a short passage. The flat provided the living quarters for Monsieur and Madame Guiseard. There was one bathroom on each floor of the hotel. In accordance with the custom of most hotels of this type throughout western Europe the door of the bathroom was kept locked. Any guest wanting a bath had to order it from the chamber maid and pay for each bath. Most European guests at these hotels took a bath about once a week and on the other days washed at the hand basin in the bedroom. When Madame found that Lew wanted to bath every day she suggested to him that he use a bathroom which was situated off the little passage between the hotel and the flat. This bathroom was readily accessible from Lew's bedroom because there was a staircase (normally used only by the staff) situated near his bedroom which led down to the entrance to the passage. Madame had said that the bathroom off the passage was a 'private' one and it would be available to Lew whenever he wanted to use it.

Once the bathing arrangements had been satisfactorily settled Lew found the accommodation at the Beau Regarde much to his liking and he began to look with increased interest at the Savoie district of France in which he was now living. From the window of his bedroom on the first floor of the hotel Lew could see a large area of farmland stretching away to the mountains in the east. The division of land and the methods of farming seemed more closely related to the middle ages than the twentieth century. The land was divided into small fields encompassing only one or two acres and each of these was sown with a different cereal or vegetable crop, the farming equipment was of an elementary nature pulled by a horse or manipulated by a man or a woman, there was no sign of machinery such as tractors, harvesters, complex ploughs or cultivators. The work done in the fields by the men and the women was of a back-breaking nature and could not have been very productive. What Lew saw from the window of his room in the hotel and from his car when travelling to and from Geneva supported the claim which had been made by the French government during the Geneva conference that, for both social and economic reasons, many sections of the primary industries in France had to be restructured and developed. Lew considered that the Australian Government could hardly argue against the restriction of imports of primary products by France (and probably some other European countries) to assist the restructuring of primary industries while at the same time it (the Australian Government) imposed high Customs tariffs to help the development of Australian secondary industries. But he wondered if a major aim of the proposed International Trade Organisation – to substantially increase the production, consumption and exchange of goods throughout the world by reducing Customs tariffs and other barriers to international trade – would be realized as long as its charter (under a variety of 'special provisions') allowed new barriers to international trade to be erected on the grounds that they were needed to restructure or develop secondary industries or branches of agriculture.

Lew's long lasting stay at the Beau Regarde soon came to the Mayor's attention and when that important official heard of the Australian's daily bathing habit he decided that it gave him a chance to cause Madame Guiseard some bother. He sent her a note saying that the foreigner staying in her hotel should not be allowed to have a bath every day because it imposed

175

an unnecessary strain on the town's water supply. Madame ignored the Mayor's note. A few days later the Mayor ordered his staff to turn off the water going to the northern part of the town for an hour at the time that Lew normally took his bath. The Mayor expected that his order would put to inconvenience not only Madame but also many people living in the northern part of the town who patronized the Hotel Beau Regarde against his wishes.

Madame and her staff were not prepared to submit to such tyranny and took it for granted that Lew would not wish to yield to the despot. They decided to outmanoeuvre the Mayor by changing from day to day the time at which Lew took his bath. He was sometimes woken at six o'clock in the morning and told 'now is the time to have a bath'. On other days he was urged to have a bath immediately on his return to the hotel after work – an event which occurred at varying times. On some days Madame and the staff got him to take more than one bath so that they could be sure that they were engaging the Mayor from a position of strength. As a result of the various elements in the strategy adopted Lew found himself having baths at times which varied from six in the morning to midnight.

At whatever time a decision was taken that Lew should have a bath it was always accompanied by a flurry of activity; Lew undressing quickly, Madame and the staff getting the bath filled with water of the right temperature and towels warmed and properly arranged in the bathroom. From the beginning of Lew's stay in the hotel Madame had been concerned at the risk he ran of catching the dreaded disease 'the cold' by taking a bath each day. To reduce that risk Madame said he should always dry himself on towels warmed to the right temperature. Two towels were provided; a large one in which he could envelope himself and a smaller one with which he could give more specific attention to the drying process. All the Mayor's opponents recognised that it would be a terrible disaster if Lew caught 'the cold' while the struggle with the Mayor was in progress. Consequently the greatest possible care had to be taken with the towels and Madame herself undertook that critical task. Madame was convinced that the moment when anyone in a hot bath would leave the water could not be predicted because the decision was not made by any logical process but as a result of an immediate perception of the mind without reasoning. Therefore towels heated to the right temperature had to be available throughout the time that Lew was in the bath and to ensure this Madame constantly ran in and out of the bathroom checking the temperature of the towels and replacing any that were too cold. While Lew was in the bath every member of the staff left his (or her) work for a short time, hurried to the bathroom and from the door shouted, 'Vive la liberté'. Lew, lying in the warm water shouted back in his great raucous voice, 'Vive la liberté'. To the delight of the staff Lew's great cry for freedom from injustice carried across the road outside the hotel and filled the living rooms of the houses on the other side of the street.

Throughout the remainder of Lew's stay at the 'Beau Regarde' the trial of strength between the Mayor and Madame Guiseard and her staff continued. From the point of view of the citizens of northern St Varent this great contest ranked with the storming of the Bastille as a glorious example of the determination of the French people to resist oppression by despotic rulers.

At the beginning of November Lew left his accommodation in St Varent and his work in Geneva a well-washed man. He made his way to Havana via London and New York. In Havana he again caught up with Pat and the two of them set out to find a flat in the 'native quarter' of that town. But what happened in Havana is another story.

THE CONFESSION

At midday Mike and I caught one of the buses that supplied the public transport along the western side of Lake Annecy. Well before we reached the village of Menthon we could see the Chateau de Menthon – a typical medieval castle standing on an isolated hill. Surmounting the very high exterior wall of the castle was an attractive array of turrets, towers and spires, some built on top of the wall, others obviously the upper part of buildings inside the wall. On the eastern side, the exterior wall ran along the edge of an almost perpendicular rock formation that constituted most of the top of the hill.

Opposite the village a steep narrow road zig-zagged up towards the chateau and we ate the lunches supplied by the hotel as we walked along it. After zig-zagging for more than a kilometre the road (and Mike and I) went through a high, arched tunnel-like opening in the chateau wall, which was about five metres thick at this point. Inside the wall the road ran past three cows grazing in a field of long grass and led us to what was obviously the main family dwelling, a large stone building with a lawn in front of it protected by a hedge and gate from the grazing animals.

At that time (1949) the Count de Menthon was the French Ambassador to Canada and he and his family were living in Ottawa. We were shown over the chateau by the retired family tutor – an old, grey-haired, slightly stooped man whose name I think was Lavon. He told us that he was a bachelor and had been allowed to remain in the chateau and given a pension when his services as a tutor were no longer required. Lavon had quite a good command of the English language but was obviously somewhat out of practice in its use. He frequently paused in order to recall the English word he needed to express himself clearly.

We were taken through several splendid living rooms and also the beautiful chapel with its ornate stone columns and arches and colourfully painted ceiling depicting biblical scenes. But what I remember most clearly is the long narrow room in which Bernard de Menthon (later Saint Bernard) was imprisoned in 941, the portrait of the saint that hung there and the account of Bernard's life that Lavon gave us while we were in the room.

Bernard was born at Menthon in 923. When twelve years old he went to a Monastery in Paris for his education and returned to the chateau at the age of eighteen. While Bernard was in Paris his father, the Count, arranged a marriage between his son and Marguerite de Molans, the daughter of a neighbouring nobleman in the same line of business as the Count de Menthon – robbing (or taxing) commercial caravans moving between France and Italy. Bernard was determined to become a monk and refused to marry Marguerite. His father locked him up in the narrow chamber on the first floor of the chateau and sent for Marguerite.

Lavon tried to convey to us something of Bernard's predicament and his reaction to it. He said that the young man spent the time he was locked up either pacing up and down the length of the room or on his knees praying for help that would, in Lavon's words, 'Save him from a fate worse than death'.

On the eve of the marriage Bernard went out through the window of the room and climbed down the almost vertical rock face below the chateau wall. (We looked out the window and found it hard to believe that anybody could climb down that rock face.) Search parties mounted by his father were unable to find Bernard who made his way to Rome where he joined the monastical order of Saint Augustine.

He became the Vicar-General for Aosta and established a hospice first at the summit of the Alpine pass now known as the Great Saint Bernard pass and latter at the summit of the pass now known as the Little Saint Bernard pass. For hundreds of years the monks in the hospices gave hospitality to all travellers moving through the passes. They also trained and used dogs for rescuing lost travellers. The hospice at the Great Saint Bernard Pass is at a higher altitude than that of any other permanently occupied human habitation in Europe.

Hanging on a wall in the 'Ancienne chamber de Saint Bernard' was a portrait of the Saint. It was a copy. The original painting, done by a colleague and close friend of Bernard, was found in the sixteenth century to be deteriorating and could not be preserved for much longer. So that all would not be lost a leading artist was brought down from Paris to copy it. The painting depicted Bernard in a monk's robes kneeling beside a window in his cell at the Great Saint Bernard Pass hospice. Through the window of the cell could be seen a cloudless sky and a flight of swans. The inclusion of the latter surprised me. Lavon agreed that it was highly unlikely that swans would be seen at such a high altitude but said their inclusion was symbolic; that swans were regarded as the embodiment of purity and innocence. I did not doubt that the swans were symbolic but their inclusion in the portrait of a monk intrigued me because from time immemorial in the mythology of most European countries attractive maidens were able to take the shape of a swan for part of their lives.

The portrait was not a flattering one but an interesting visual description of a middle aged man. He had a broad face, wrinkled skin, large nose, high brow, thick lips, black curly hair and dark eyes filled with a sad thoughtfulness. The affection of the painter for his subject seemed apparent in the underlying drawing of the figure, in the tilt of the head, the form of the lips and the shape and the position of the hands.

When we left the chateau to walk back to Annecy the sky was blue, the wind light and the sun bright. It was a lovely summer's day, made the more lovely by the view we had from the chateau hill of the placid bluish-purple lake, the agricultural plain with its irregular pattern of green, brown and yellow fields, the dark fir tree covered mountains, and the towering, rugged, snow-capped alps.

This walk was one of many I had in France with Mike. He was a man of my own age whom I had known slightly in Canberra but got to know much better in Annecy where we were drawn together by a shared fondness for walking. Mike was energetic, impetuous, kind-hearted, intelligent and talkative. He was also an ardent Roman Catholic.

For the first six weeks of the conference we were able to go for long walks only on Sunday afternoons. But these weekly walks enabled us to explore the villages and farmlands on the narrow plain between the lake and the mountains to the north and east of Annecy. The inhabitants of those rural regions spoke only a provincial dialect; they probably could not understand any Parisian French and certainly not the French Mike and I spoke with an Australian accent. Although, when we endeavoured to enter into conversation with a 'local' it was apparent that he (or she) could not see any meaning in what we said, Mike (who had a sense of pride in his ability to speak French) persisted in trying to communicate by means of the spoken word rather than by hand and body movements and facial expressions.

We had planned the trip to the chateau de Menthon as our first Sunday journey along the western side of Lake Annecy. However, a sudden break in the conference routine enabled us to make the bus ride and walk on a Saturday. We were to find that the change from a Sunday to a Saturday for one of our long walks caused an unexpected complication.

We had covered about two thirds of the return journey from the chateau and were off the road for a while walking on an open grassed area alongside the lake when two swans and three cygnets in arrow formation flew over our heads pointed in the direction of Annecy. No doubt they intended to join the colony living around the two bays of the lake and the connecting canal on which the town was situated. The birds in this colony, who spent most of their time squabbling over scraps of food left by human beings, seemed far removed from an embodiment of purity and innocence, despite their smooth, pure white bodies and their long graceful necks.

Soon after the swans were out of sight, the weather changed dramatically. A strong westerly wind sprang up, dark clouds raced over the sky and it started to rain. As we made our way in the rain down the main street of Sevieux we could see members of the local community, in ones and twos, moving in and out of the large church which dominated the buildings in the village. This activity apparently struck a chord in Mike's mind because he said, 'It will be too late for confession when we reach Annecy. Would you mind if I went into this church?'

I didn't mind and I entered the church with Mike not only to get out of the rain but also to satisfy at least some part of my curiosity about the confessional sacrament of the Roman Catholic Church.

On the left hand side of the church was a long wooden pew with seven people sitting on it facing the confessional area. With astonishment apparent on their faces the seven people watched Mike and I join them on the pew. During the next quarter of an hour whenever a confessant left the confessional, the person on the end of the pew took his (or her) place and we all moved up one position. Every few minutes one or two newcomers joined the queue on the pew. Before long the number waiting increased to eleven. Amongst them were three teenage girls. One of the girls had an abnormally long neck. She was pretty and, except for her neck, well formed, but wore a sullen expression and paid no attention to the other people in the church; she spent her time staring gloomily at the church wall. The long neck, the well-formed body and the pretty face suggested to me that she was a mythological maiden whose transformation from a swan to a young woman left something to be desired and that the poor conversion weighed heavily on her mind.

Eventually the time came for Mike to enter the confessional. He walked over and disappeared behind the padded door. A minute or so later the door of the confessor's cubicle flew open, a big young man in a priest's robes stepped out, opened the padded door and pulled Mike from within the penitent's compartment. Holding Mike by one arm he hurried up the outside aisle of the church. At the end of the aisle he turned to the right and after taking about ten paces in the new direction opened a door in the wall so constructed as to be hardly noticeable at first glance. He steered Mike through the opening and quickly followed him. The door closed.

Everyone in the church, except the mythological maiden had eagerly watched the progress of the confessor and penitent. After the two had disappeared I found that several of the prospective penitents were surreptitiously glancing at me. Apparently they wanted to see what effect the dramatic treatment of my companion was having on me. If they were able to read in my face my feelings they must have learned that I was as astonished as they were.

After what seemed an abnormally long time for a confession, the priest and Mike reappeared. But while the priest hurriedly retraced his steps back to the confessor's cubicle Mike slowly and thoughtfully made his way to the centre aisle of the church and then absorbed in some cogitation, slowly continued to move towards the main door.

I was so engrossed in watching Mike that I overlooked the fact that all the other people sitting on the pew assumed that I was a penitent waiting to confess. My attention was drawn to this fact by the man sitting next to me standing up saying in an urgent tone of voice 'Monsieur! Monsieur!' and pointing to the door of the penitent's compartment. I stood up, and saying 'Non! Non!', tried to wave him into the compartment. This resulted in several other people standing up, saying in chorus, 'Monsieur! Monsieur!', and signalling that I should enter the compartment without delay.

The door of the confessor's cubicle opened, and out jumped the priest. He seized my left arm firmly but not painfully and started to lead me up the outside aisle. I did not resist the Priest's imperious action – mainly because it presented an opportunity to learn a little more about the confessional sacrament – but I justified my action (or lack of it) on the grounds that it would be unseemly for me to wrestle with a priest in his church and I could withdraw from the sacrament immediately (well, almost immediately) after the priest let go my arm, without doing anything improper.

The priest's kidnapping of his walking companion brought Mike out of his reverie. He stopped his slow progress down the centre aisle, turned towards the priest and me, leant over the pews and shouted in his best

183

French 'Stop! He is a protestant! (pause) And an atheist!' If the priest understood that contradictory description of my religious characteristics, he ignored it. He pressed on with our passage down the outside aisle. When we turned the corner at the end of the aisle I was able to look back at the waiting penitents. All of them, including the mythological maiden, were standing up facing in our direction. Undoubtedly Mike's shouted call to the priest had raised to an even higher pitch the onlookers' interest in the unusual proceedings.

Finding his verbal intervention was unsuccessful, Mike returned along the centre aisle, paid his respects to the altar, then ran towards the 'secret' door. His arrival coincided with ours. Mike grabbed my right arm. It seemed likely that I would be the rope in a tug of war. But to my surprise the priest let go my left arm, swung around and headed back towards the confessional area; he abandoned my sinful soul to the machinations of the devil and any other perpetrators of evil that happened to be around.

Being under the impression, I am sure, that he had rescued me with difficulty only just in the nick of time from an experience that I would consider to be unpleasant, Mike, in his kind-hearted way, made every effort to get me out of the church as soon as possible.

Once outside we set off for Annecy walking steadily through the wet, windy, evening. My friend seemed withdrawn, deep in thought. It was unlikely that the weather curbed Mike's talkativeness. On earlier walks whenever rain fell, the dampness seemed to encourage Mike to argue intensely about many things. Some of the views opposed to mine he expressed in these arguments he clearly held from conviction, but most of them I think he adopted for the sheer pleasure of arguing.

The only vehicle we encountered on this stage of the journey was a truck that swept past us at speed on the outskirts of Annecy and added water from the puddles on the road to our general dampness. This broke the silence between us; we sent in the direction of the truck some Australian curses and then fell into a discussion about a book, the name of which neither of us could recall, but which commenced by recounting that a frowsy chamber maid each morning after washing the front steps of an inn flung the water from her bucket straight out without moving from where she stood, thus putting at the risk of a wetting any pedestrians passing by.

We had entered the town and were walking along the road running parallel with the canal when we came upon two swans and a three quarter grown cygnet uttering shrill, strident cries while standing alongside another cygnet lying on the ground. After saying to me 'keep those birds away' Mike knelt down on the wet road alongside the cygnet and began to examine it. To attract the attention of the swans and avoid their beaks, I did a sort of Irish jig in front of them. However, just as Mike loudly announced to all and sundry (which consisted of the three swans and me), 'It's dead', one of the swans bit my well-intentioned companion on the leg.

Without any further ado Mike and I raced towards our hotel about twenty metres away. While running, Mike favoured one leg and complained about my failure to protect him while he was engaged in his clinical examination. We entered the hotel foyer not more than two metres ahead of the swans, dashed into the lift, slammed closed the telescopic lattice door and pressed the fourth floor button. We left it to the hotel receptionist to explain to the swans that there was nothing much to be gained by continuing to chase two rather ragged Australians.

On the fourth floor we told Louise, the cheerful, plump, middle aged chambermaid on night duty that we had forgotten to collect our keys from the reception desk. She playfully wagged a finger at us and let loose several 'la! la! la!'s' in a rising crescendo before walking down the passage, unlocking our bedroom doors and agreeing to run a bath for each of us.

We ate late and during the early part of the dinner talked shop. However, while we were both waiting for a serving of 'Compote des fruits', a dessert that was a specialty of the hotel's restaurant, Mike referred to the confession he had made at Sevieux. He said, 'I suppose you were surprised by what occurred during my confession'.

I admitted that I was surprised and he went on, 'The priest seemed an uneducated fellow, he didn't understand a word of real French; he ended up taking my confession in the church office with the aid of a book he dug out of a cupboard after pulling out and searching through a mass of reading matter'.

Somewhat puzzled I asked, 'What sort of a book? A dictionary?'

'No, it had all the common sins in several languages', he replied; then added with a touch of pride, 'You see "the church" is prepared for every eventuality'.

THE COPPER PROBLEM

There were three works of art hanging in Harry McGauran's office: two oil paintings of local landscapes and a pencil drawing of a boy wearing a paper hat. All were the work of Harry's wife Ruth who had established, both locally and in Sydney and Melbourne, a reputation as a competent artist. The office, large and well-furnished and with a fine view of the lake, the northern suburbs of Canberra and Mount Ainslie, befitted the head of an important Australian Government Department.

Harry was good-looking, tall and well built but had a club foot. It was, however, only slightly bent upwards and outwards and when wearing his special boot he could walk vigorously and fast and he had always liked to walk. Although the standard of health required for entry into the Australian Public Service was very high it did not preclude someone with a club foot and Harry had entered the public service immediately after obtaining, from the Melbourne University, a degree with economics as his major subject. Clever, hard-working and very ambitious, he had succeeded in constantly catching the attention of those senior civil servants, and later also those ministers, who he considered could help him advance in the Public Service. His assiduity had paid off. At the early age (by Australian standards) of forty-one he had been appointed the Secretary of the Department of Commerce and Industry.

In 1966, a year after he had become Secretary, at three forty-five on a beautiful Canberra spring day as he was preparing to leave his office, one of the two phones on his desk rang. When he answered it his secretary said, 'Phillip has rung to say the Minister is on his way back to Canberra with the Prime Minister in the V.I.P. plane and wants to see you as soon as he gets here. The plane is expected at Fairbairn in half an hour'. Thanking her he quickly picked up the other phone and dialled a number. A woman answered by giving, in a musical tone of voice, a phone number, but when Harry said, 'I can't come this afternoon. "My man" is returning to Canberra and wants to see me as soon as he gets here', she said in a less musical way, 'Damn him! You said he would be away for several days!'

'Yes! Something pretty important must have happened. My darling I'm sorry but there's nothing I can do about it. I'll ring you in the morning'.

Harry pulled out of a drawer in his desk a copy of the Minister's itinerary. It showed that he was lunching in Sydney that day (Monday) with Clive Britten, the Executive Chairman of the North-West Mining Company, staying the night in Sydney, flying to Queensland the next morning, then spending three days visiting ship-building yards and factories in Brisbane, Maryborough and Townsville before returning to Canberra on Friday. Nothing in the itinerary gave Harry a clue as to why the Minister was returning so unexpectedly. Half an hour later Harry walked over to the Minister's office in Parliament House and while waiting there thought about the Minister (Joe Goldrick) and his relationship with him.

Goldrick was generally regarded as tough and fearsome and Harry believed he had gained that reputation because of his appearance – a big man with a long face, a jutting jaw and usually a serious look – his abstemiousness, his habit of taking to task everyone (including business executives, members of parliament and industry delegates) who came ill-prepared to see him (he himself asserted that he never went to any meeting without doing 'his homework') and his ability to constantly overcome opposition in important discussions by his grasp of the subject matter and his staying power.

A teetotaller, non-smoker and staunch family man, Goldrick claimed to follow high, moral principles but Harry had discovered he was prepared to leave the moral high ground to further his own and his party's political aspirations.

Whilst Harry did not like some of Goldrick's characteristics he had found working with him interesting and productive because the Minister – unlike some of his predecessors who wanted simply to keep out of trouble – earnestly endeavoured to get things done, insisted on being well-briefed, listened very carefully to the advice Harry gave him and usually won the tactical battles in the cabinet room.

Goldrick was Deputy Prime Minister and the Prime Minister's confidant and Harry was aware that the closeness of the two men had helped him (Harry) get his present position. When Harry's predecessor had retired, both the Public Service Board and the Secretary of the Prime Minister's Department had recommended that the Chairman of the Tariff Board be appointed Secretary of the Department of Commerce and Industry. Goldrick had taken a strong liking to Harry (who, as Deputy Secretary of the Department of Commerce and Industry, had worked hand in glove with him for several years) and he had persuaded the Prime Minister to support Harry's nomination.

However Harry was not content to remain for long in his present position. He wanted to become Secretary of the Prime Minister's Department, the most important, prestigious and highly paid position in the Civil Service. He knew he would only have a good chance of getting the job in three year's time (when the present Secretary would retire) if he had Goldrick's support and the Conservative Party was in office. Although the Conservative Party, in an election held during an economic recession ten months earlier, had only narrowly scraped home – it got forty-five seats to the opposition's forty-four – Harry believed that it would easily win the next election which was likely to be held when the economy was once again buoyant.

Harry's reflections ended when the Minister arrived and told Harry that in Sydney he had learned of two impending events which could bring down the Government within a few months.

During lunch Britten told him that the North-West Company had found a new lode containing a very large amount of easily extractable copper and by the end of the year it would be producing the lowest cost blister copper in the world in sufficient quantity to meet the whole Australian demand and that was what it intended to do.

'There is no need for me to tell you, Harry', the Minister said, 'that, unless we can stop them, North-West will close down the Four Star Mine in Tasmania and the Pardoo Mine in Queensland – each of which I think now supplies about a third of the Australian demand.

'When I asked Britten why he would not export two-thirds of his output and continue to supply only a third of the Australian demand he told me that he would be failing in his duty to his shareholders. He said, because the prices of blister copper, refined copper and copper products in Australia are much higher than the "world" prices the company's shareholders could, with justification, call for his head if he sold two-thirds of the company's copper overseas at a price much lower than that available if the copper was sold in Australia.

'Whilst it's not fear of complaints from his shareholders – an apathetic lot – but the opportunity he sees of getting more money for himself that's driving him, there is no doubt about Britten's intention.

'I tried to unsettle him by reminding him that the production of the very high cost copper and copper products in Australia was only possible because high customs tariffs protected them from overseas competition and

189

that the Government could remove the high tariffs.

'He laughed. He said if the tariffs were removed North-West would still be better off selling all its copper in Australia but, because high tariffs had been imposed by all Australian Governments since Federation to encourage the development of Australian industries, no government would start dismantling the high tariff protection in the face of vehement opposition from industrialists, trade unions, investors etc. and the widespread public support these people could quickly organise.

'Although Britten is obviously determined to capture the whole of the Australian market for copper, before we parted I got him to agree not to make any public announcement about North-West's intention and not to take any specific action to secure the whole Australian market until I had had an opportunity to assess the effects of such a move.

'After the lunch I went to the Sydney office pretty perturbed. I'd hardly arrived before I received a telephone call from the Prime Minister telling me that Tom Downer, the Member for the electorate of Lachlan, has terminal cancer and intends to resign at the end of the present Parliamentary session. Practically every elector in Lachlan is dependent in one way or another on the Pardoo mine. So we've got to keep that mine operating or we'll be out of office and the Socialists in, early next year'.

The Minister got out of his chair and strode up and down his office for a while, then asked, 'I'm right aren't I, we can't, under the Constitution, subsidise the production of a product in some states and not others, so we can't subsidise Pardoo and Four Star and not North-West?'

'Yes'.

'To get into office the Socialists would promise the Lachlan electors the world and under their Party's platform the Government could take over the mines'.

Harry asked, 'Wouldn't the prospect of the Conservatives losing office and the Socialists with, as you point out, an anti-private enterprise approach in the Party Platform, make Britten change his mind?'

'No', said the Minister. 'I've known Britten since we were at school together, while we are not close friends we've maintained contact. He prides himself on his ability to do deals with both Conservative and Socialist Governments in both the State and Federally. As you know he has wrung railway extensions, freight subsidies, cheap electricity and water etc. from both political parties'.

The Minister went back to his chair, flung himself into it and said, 'We're in a critical situation and I want you to concentrate on the problem Harry and give me your ideas when I return to Canberra on Friday. I've discussed it with the PM but no one else. We've got to keep it under wraps, at least for the present'.

Harry returned to his office, told his secretary he was not to be disturbed and sat there for an hour or so thinking, jotting down notes and finally preparing a list of the information he wanted. That done he telephoned for his executive assistant, Helen Waite. When Helen arrived he gave her the list and said, 'Drop everything else, get me the information on this list. It'll probably mean going to both Sydney and Wollongong but I want you to have it ready for me by Wednesday evening'.

The next morning Harry telephoned 'My Darling' just before ten o'clock and told her 'his man' had given him a very knotty problem to resolve by Friday but he might be able to see her on Thursday afternoon. 'Would you be free then?' he asked. She said she would.

'My Darling' was Edna Jennings. She had been a fellow student and a friend of Ruth McGauran at secondary school and at Melbourne University. The two girls were different both in appearance and personality. Ruth, tall, with a good figure and a handsome face, was reserved and contemplative. Edna, short, thin with a rather plain face but attractive blue eyes, was lively and inquisitive. They were complementary. While at the University the girls had met and paired up with Harry and Jeff Jennings who were also good friends. After Harry and Jeff joined the Australian Public Service the friendships between both the men and women had continued and had resulted in Harry marrying Ruth in November 1951 and Jeff marrying Edna a few months later.

The two couples lived in the same suburb in Canberra and continued to be close friends, regularly going on outings together, combining to provide the transport needs of all the children for school, sport and other entertainments and always sharing a beach house in a South Coast town during the summer holidays.

Jeff, clever, a steady but rather laid-back worker, was not as ambitious as Harry. Also, unlike Harry, he much preferred the company of men to women. A foundation member of the Treasury Five O'clock Club – a group of civil servants mainly, but not entirely, from the Treasury who met in the back bar of the Canberra Hotel every day after work and had a few drinks before going home – Jeff occasionally drank a bit too much at the five o'clock sessions and that did not please Edna. But despite (or perhaps because of) his very occasional drinking bouts and his avid reading of detective stories, Edna considered Jeff to be a husband and father of 'fair average quality'.

It was during the 1962/63 summer holiday that the 'affair' between Harry and Edna began. One day Jeff and Ruth took all the children on a fishing expedition at which Ruth intended to sketch and Jeff to read while keeping an eye on the young fishermen and fisherwomen. Harry and Edna remained at the beach house, Harry to work on his car, Edna to do some housework and prepare the evening meal. After he had finished the work on his car Harry, in singlet and shorts, greasy and dirty, came into the house. Edna told him he looked a dreadful mess. When Harry said, 'Yes, I'll get under the shower and clean up' Edna asked, 'Would you like some help?' It took Harry a moment to grasp the significance of that question but when he did he said, 'I'd love some help'. After showering they went to bed together for the first time.

Harry found Edna was an exciting sexual partner but their relationship was not predominantly sexual. Harry liked to hear Edna's exaggerated, droll accounts of everyday events. And whereas Ruth seemed always too busy with her painting and drawing or the children to listen to anything Harry had to say about his work, Edna was very interested, prepared to listen to him at length and sometimes through her questions gave him the nub of a new idea. By talking freely to her about his work Harry satisfied a great deal of Edna's curiosity about the activities of civil servants and politicians and with his playful comments and charming manner Harry always made Edna feel attractive even when dishevelled. Harry and Edna had always talked together a lot – often with the children playing, Ruth painting and Jeff reading nearby – and they continued to do that after they became lovers. Opportunities to be together by themselves were few but as their romantic relationship developed, being together in the same place amongst other people, even when not able to talk together, always kindled in them a delightful piquancy most keenly felt when they caught each other's eye. Neither of them wanted to disrupt their marriages, and from time to time each was assailed by a sense of guilt about their adultery, but both felt it added a quality to their lives which they could not now do without.

•

On Wednesday evening Helen Waite gave Harry the information he had asked her to obtain. After going through it with her and telling her to collect, analyse and tabulate by the following Monday a wide range of statistical material (which he wanted as 'back-up data') he completed the outline of his plan.

Early in the afternoon on Thursday Harry rang Edna. She said she would like to go for a walk with him. He pointed out there had been heavy rain overnight and it would be wet under foot. 'I'll wear my heavy walking shoes', she said and they arranged to meet in a car park in Civic at four o'clock.

When he picked up Edna Harry suggested that they walk in the pine plantation surrounding the hill on which stands a monument to the Fairbairn air disaster. He told her that when a single man living in a boarding house in a northern suburb he had sometimes driven out to the plantation and gone for long walks amongst the then young trees. Edna was delighted. She said she had never been into any of the pine plantations.

Harry drove along the back road to Queanbeyan and when he reached the memorial drive going up the hill to the monument, turned on to it. About two hundred metres along the drive he saw a gravel track going off to the right through the trees. He swung the car around on to the track and stopped about fifty metres in from the drive.

As soon as he stopped Edna said, 'Tell me about the problem the Minister gave you on Monday and what you are going to do about it'. Harry explained the problem then said 'To resolve it I am going to persuade the North-West Company to export three-quarters of its copper output as a part of a scheme by which the company will be reimbursed for the lower price it will receive for that copper with money provided by the Australian consumers of copper products'.

'How on earth can you do that?' asked Edna.

Harry said nothing for a moment then said, 'I'd better first explain the working arrangements for copper production in Australia.

'At the mine site the copper is extracted from the ore, treated to remove other metals and formed into large, rectangular cakes of what is called blister copper. These cakes are sent to a plant in Wollongong where they are refined by an electrolytic process and formed into marketable shapes: billets, bars and ingots. The plant in Wollongong is owned by the Port Kembla Electrolytic Company which charges each mining company a fee for the work it does. The ownership of the copper remains with each mining company and the copper is sold by those companies on the basis of delivery available from the Wollongong plant.

'There are two features of the Australian economic environment I expect to help the implementation of my plan, which I should tell you about.

'A wide range of goods, including all those containing any substantial amount of copper, have a level of protection under the Customs Tariff greatly in excess of that needed to keep even the highest cost producers profitable. (These very high levels of protection were enacted as an emergency measure during the 1930s depression and have not been removed.) Because the levels of protection are so high the prices of products containing copper can be raised considerably without any chance of competition from imports.

'The second feature is this. In Australia the operations of a number of companies are completely controlled by one man who usually has the position of Executive Chairman of Directors. The other directors are all stooges selected by the controller and the rest of the shareholders are completely apathetic. Clive Britten controls the North-West Mining Company and David Pickering controls the Port Kembla Electrolytic Company. Consequently the implementation of my plan will have to be negotiated with two people only, not two boards of directors.

'The key to the plan is the changes I will propose to the fee the Port Kembla Electrolytic Company charges the mining companies to refine their blister copper. I'll suggest that the North-West Company be charged less than the present fee and the other two companies be charged more. The total amount of money received by the Port Kembla Electrolytic Company will remain unchanged. The higher charge will force the Pardoo and Four Star Companies to raise the price of their refined copper. North-West will also sell its refined copper at the higher price and profit considerably thereby. The higher price of refined copper will be passed on through the different stages of the production of goods containing copper. Since there is no price competition between Australian manufacturers and since the high Customs duties prevent any competition from overseas suppliers, the consumers will have to pay the higher price of the finished goods'.

Harry looked at his watch and then said, 'It's nearly half past four. We'd better go for our walk. I will tell you more about the plan as we go'.

The sun was shining brightly, there were no clouds and a fresh westerly breeze was blowing. Harry and Edna entered the forest full of joy; it was a wonderful time and place to be together. The ground under the trees was still wet from the overnight rain but the pine needles thickly covering it made walking quite pleasant. As they walked along hand in hand they became aware of a sobbing and moaning of the wind as it passed through the pine tree tops. This mournful sound, so inconsistent with her own feelings, caused Edna to ponder, 'Why are the trees so sad on such a lovely day?'

Edna continued to question Harry about his plan. She asked him whether the consumers were likely to protest about the increase in the price of copper goods.

'I don't think so for three reasons: firstly I envisage that the rise in the refining fee for Pardoo and Four Star copper will be made in three steps spread over nine months; secondly only a few final consumer goods containing copper have a high copper content; and lastly because Australian consumers have got used to regular increases in the cost of practically everything and think that these increases are completely offset by nominal (but not real) wage increases won for them each year by their union bosses or salary increases granted executives and other senior staff by their employers. But I'll be in a better position to answer your questions next week; by then I'll have much more information on products and prices'.

After being silent for a while Edna asked, 'Will the plan be made public?'

'No'.

'Has anyone in the Department worked with you on the plan?'

'No. But Helen has obtained a lot of information for me. She is very good at that; she's charming, shrewd and very persistent'.

'Also very pretty', said Edna.

'I don't regard that as a disability'.

'But I do', said Edna.

'I believe you're jealous of her!'

'I'm jealous of every pretty girl that gets near you'.

Harry laughed. 'You've no need to be. I have the pretty, charming girl that I want'.

Edna pulled him towards her, hugged and kissed him.

They walked on briskly and soon came to an open space – a large number of trees had been removed. To their amazement they saw near the trees on the opposite side of the opening a woman lying on the ground, they stopped, then, both feeling apprehensive, walked towards her. Because there were very few pine needles on the ground their shoes sank into the wet, clayish soil, slowing their progress and increasing their anxiety about the woman. When they reached her there was no longer any doubt. She was dead. Horrified by what she saw, Edna said in a low voice, 'How dreadful! Look, the red hair and the striped blouse, it's the missing Muriel Jones! The poor young thing! What should we do?' Harry put his arm around her and said, 'We can't do anything for her. We'd better get away'.

As they walked back through the trees, both now in a sombre mood, Edna said, 'We will have to tell the police where the poor young woman's body is'.

'Yes. I'll do that. But we must be careful not to do anything that will upset Ruth and Jeff'.

When they came out of the forest onto the gravel track they found that just behind their car was another with its doors open and three young men in it drinking beer from stubbies. They had apparently been on a drinking spree for some time because they shouted at the couple some very obnoxious remarks such as 'Having a bit in the trees?' 'Did you have it lying down or standing up?'

As soon as Harry and Edna were in their car, Harry hurriedly started the engine, turned the car and drove off. As he was going down the Memorial Drive towards its junction with the Queanbeyan road he was annoyed to see in the rear vision mirror that the car with the three men in it was close behind, possibly intending to follow him.

When he reached the junction Harry looked to the right; there was no vehicle in sight. He looked to the left and saw a car coming from Queanbeyan. He decided to go straight across the Queanbeyan road and turn in front of the on-coming vehicle and thus put some distance and another car between him and the young men.

But he had just moved forward when he realised that the car coming from Queanbeyan was travelling very fast. He jammed on his brakes and almost immediately there was a loud bang and a jolt as the young men's car hit the back of his.

When Harry got out and looked he found very little damage had been done to his car, just a dent in the bumper bar. But the tow bar on his car had badly damaged the radiator on the young men's car – a new-looking Holden – and water was pouring out of it.

The driver of the young men's car was very upset and the reason for that became apparent to Harry when they exchanged information about driver's licences, car ownership etc. The car belonged to the young man's father. As nobody was hurt the only legal obligation the two drivers had was to each report the accident to the police. Harry told the young man that he would ask the police to get a tow truck sent out to tow the Holden away. All three of the men said they would wait with the Holden car for the arrival of the tow-truck. They'd sobered up a lot and made no more unpleasant remarks.

Although the prospect of the young men continuing to be a nuisance to Harry and Edna had been removed by the accident, the other distressing event – the finding of Muriel Jones' body – overshadowed the pleasant part of their afternoon together and left them both saddened. When he stopped the car to let Edna out Harry would have liked to have hugged and kissed her and given her some reassurance but the Civic parking area, very busy between five o'clock and six, was too public a place.

Sitting in his car after Edna had gone Harry thought about his obligation to report to the police the discovery of Muriel Jones' body. Should he do it immediately? As he had to report the car accident without delay he would be making the two reports at the same time. His report about the collision would have to be consistent with that of the Holden driver and therefore he believed he would have to state that he had a passenger in his car and probably give her name. He was certain that the discovery of the body would be regarded by the local media as a sensational news item and to make the most of it the journalists would delve for every detail. With the vehicle accident reports available in the police station it was likely that the journalists would ascertain that Edna was with him in the pine plantation and therefore his afternoon tryst with Edna could become headline news in the local paper and on the local television and radio. He decided not to report the finding of the body immediately but work out a way of doing that later.

After reporting the accident he drove back to his office. But before starting work he thought for a moment about ringing Edna just to say a few words, to empathise with her after the disturbing experiences they had had. But then he realised it was after six o'clock and not only would her children be home from school but possibly also Jeff.

•

197

When Harry discussed the plan with the Minister the next morning, 'his man' liked it and he agreed that they must first convince Britten that if he did not go along with the plan the Government would take control of the marketing of blister copper and ensure that North-West supplied only one-third of the Australian demand.

But then the Minister asked, 'What about Pickering? Government control would not affect his activities even if it was extended to cover refined copper, so the threat of it will not influence him and yet the plan will not work if he doesn't cooperate'.

Harry said, 'If Britten is interested in the plan he may be prepared to force Pickering to cooperate – and I have thought of a way he could do that. The Germans have invented a new method of refining copper blister which reduces considerably the amount of electric power required. Presumably Pickering is aware of this much cheaper method of refining but is not interested in making the large capital expenditure required to put in the new type of plant as long as there is such very high tariff protection for copper products. The North-West Company is now producing sufficient blister copper to provide an economic 'through-put' for a refining plant. Britten might be prepared to indicate to Pickering that he has been considering building a new German type of refining plant, probably in Newcastle (which is the port nearest to the North-West mine) and would build one if Pickering did not cooperate with the plan – North-West could easily raise the capital'.

The Minister said if Britten liked the plan he would probably be prepared to tackle Pickering but he then wondered whether 'the people' from Pardoo and Four Star were likely to cause trouble.

Harry said if there was any indication of trouble someone would have to point out to 'the people' that their livelihood would be at risk if the plan was not implemented and obviously Britten would be the best person to do that. 'Britten is the key', he added.

The Minister sat back in his chair for a minute or so silent. Then he told Harry he wanted him to discuss the plan with Britten as soon as possible.

That wasn't the way Harry wanted the matter to be raised with Britten. Harry and the Minister both realised that if details of the plan became widely known there would be a public outcry. Neither wanted to be regarded as the originator and main activator of the plan. If any trouble arose the Minister wanted to be able to say that the plan was presented to him by the civil service, that he probably should have looked at it more closely but he was very busy at the time and let the civil servants go ahead. Harry wanted to be able to say that the plan arose in the course of discussions with the Minister spread over several days in which a number of proposals were discussed, including subsidies for the less efficient mines and even government control of them, but eventually the Minister wanted this particular plan implemented and it was his duty to carry out the Minister's orders. Harry believed that he would be much better situated were any problem to arise if he got the Minister (with him, Harry, simply at his side) to explain the plan to Britten.

He told the Minister he thought that Britten was much more likely to believe that implementation of the plan was very important and urgent if he (the Minister) raised the matter with Britten. But the Minister said he would be too busy during the next week and he wanted the plan discussed with Britten without any delay.

As Harry was about to leave the office the Minister said, 'I'm going to tell the PM about the plan but nobody else. We've got to keep it under wraps. You will have to be careful'.

Harry said, 'I'm the only person in the Department that knows about the plan'.

'Good', said the Minister.

When he returned to his office Harry first of all rang Britten, who agreed to have lunch with him in Sydney on Monday. Then he rang Edna. It was too risky to refer directly to the events of the day before but he did say he 'had not passed on the information' but would tackle that matter early next week when he returned from Sydney.

When Harry explained the political situation and outlined 'the Minister's plan' to Britten. the Executive Chairman said he didn't want 'to get mixed up in it', that he was entitled to have all his blister copper refined and sold in Australia.

Harry said that no Australian government would be prepared to see two longstanding, isolated communities wiped out when they provided most of the electors in two key electorates; that he was certain a way would be found to prevent it even it if involved a Conservative Government in making an exception to the Party's private enterprise policy.

Britten held his ground saying that the plan didn't make economic sense. 'If the whole of the Australian requirement was met by using the low cost North-West copper sold at the Australian price additional Australian wealth would be generated and, although that wealth would in the first instance be in the hands of the North-West shareholders, those shareholders would spend practically all of it in Australia and the whole community would benefit'.

With a smile Harry said, 'The whole Australian community would benefit more if North-West sold all its copper to Australian users at the "world price", but politics not economics will decide this issue; you must surely see that'.

For a few minutes Britten said nothing then he asked how Pickering could be persuaded to cooperate and in reply Harry put forward his scheme based on a threat that North-West Mining Company would establish a refining plant using the latest technology. Harry got the impression that Britten rather liked that idea.

Britten agreed to give the plan 'careful consideration' but added that a decision would have to be made quickly because, if North-West was going to export blister copper, arrangements would have to be made for overseas sales.

Determined to get the Minister directly involved in the discussions Harry told Britten that, because Parliament was sitting, the Minister had been unable to come down to Sydney to explain the plan to Britten himself. However he wanted to carry the discussion forward and give details of the plan himself. 'Would it be possible for you to go to Canberra in the near future?' he asked. Britten, looking at his diary, said the only possibility was Thursday morning but he would have to return to Sydney on the midday plane. Harry agreed to get in touch with the Minister during the afternoon and let Britten know whether Thursday morning would be suitable.

Harry rang the Minister, told him that Britten was considering the plan but wanted to speak to him personally – 'presumably to satisfy himself that the plan was regarded as essential by the Government' – and would be able to come to Canberra on Thursday morning. The Minister agreed to see Britten during that morning.

Back in Canberra on Tuesday Harry rang Edna and told her he had worked out a way of 'getting the information passed on to the right quarter'. She was very relieved, she said.

•

On Wednesday, after studying the 'back-up data', Harry was less confident than he had been when outlining the plan to Edna and to the Minister that the substantial increases in the prices of copper products would be accepted without protest by the consumers. To lessen the likelihood of protests he now wanted the Minister to ask Britten to accept something less than the full difference (after allowing for the difference in the cost of refining) between the prices of refined copper in Australia and overseas. Harry was of the opinion that the Minister could get Britten to accept a lesser amount. He believed Britten would go along with the plan when he was convinced that the Government would directly intervene in the marketing of blister copper if he didn't, and once committed to the plan Britten would be as anxious as the Minister to avoid the public exposure of it which consumer protests against the increases in the prices of copper products would probably bring. Harry had worked out that if Britten received about 75 per cent of 'the difference' the resultant price rises for copper products would not be likely to bring consumer protests and he mentioned that figure when he raised the matter with the Minister later that day. However the Minister, who seemed rather agitated, wanted to put aside the whole question of Britten receiving less than the full difference. He said, 'The PM has just decided that the by-election for Lachlan will be held on the third Saturday in February and it's absolutely essential that there should not be the slightest rumour of a situation developing which could close down the Pardoo mine. You and I have got to get Britten to accept the plan without delay. Perhaps after the by-election we could get Britten to accept some fine tuning; by then only the first price rise would have occurred'.

'No Minister', said Harry. 'If we do not stick strictly to the commitments we make with him now I think Britten will pull out. Then we'll have a terrible situation with both Pardoo and Four Star involved'.

Nodding his head the Minister said, 'Alright! If we're going to tackle Britten on this we've got to do it now. But if he objects we'll have to agree to him getting the full amount'.

'Because Britten likes to haggle', said Harry 'I suggest we start with an offer of two-thirds'.

'No, that might scare him off. We'll start with three-quarters' said the Minister.

•

Harry met Britten at the airport on Thursday morning and drove him to Parliament House where the Minister saw him immediately. The Minister explained at length why the government could not accept the closure of the

Pardoo and Four Star mines and also why the plan Harry had outlined to him was the best way of resolving the problem.

Britten asked, 'Would the North-West Company receive the same amount of money for the blister copper it sold overseas as it would have received if the copper had been refined and sold in Australia?'

Harry expected the Minister to explain why he thought it necessary for the North-West Company to receive only 75 per cent, but he said, 'Harry has all the figures. I'll get him to go through them with you'. Then, after looking at his watch, added, 'I've got to get ready for a Cabinet committee meeting. I'll leave you in Harry's capable hands. He'll let me know what the two of you have decided'.

Harry realised that the Minister had withdrawn from the discussion at the critical stage in order to leave him (Harry) with the responsibility of getting the plan accepted. He didn't like it but didn't see there was anything he could do about it.

The discussion was continued in Harry's office and after much argument Britten agreed to seriously consider the plan with provision for reimbursement of only 80 per cent of the difference in the return to the North-West Company with the copper sold overseas instead of in Australia. But before deciding whether he would 'go along' with the plan he wanted to discuss it with Pickering. Harry willingly agreed on that point. Britten then said he would make his decision early in the following week.

Britten left by taxi for the airport; he said he could see how busy Harry was. After Britten had gone Harry sat back in his chair and stared unseeing at the shimmering lake for a minute or two, more tired than he had expected.

•

On Saturday morning Harry suggested to his family that they have a picnic on the following day and go to a new place, the Fairbairn Pine Plantation, in which he said he had had many pleasant walks when he was single.

Harry's suggestion was discussed on the phone between his children and the Jennings children and between Edna and Ruth. Places for picnics were always put to the vote and on this occasion the majority wanted to go to the Cotter – Ruth wanted to sketch there too. Edna – well aware of the reason Harry wanted to go to the Fairbairn Pine plantation – had pushed as hard as she could for that venue and had to conceal her disappointment when it was not accepted by the majority.

After the failure of his picnic plan there was no opportunity for Harry to tell Edna what he intended to do about informing the police of the location of Muriel Jones' body until the following Tuesday. Ever since he had joined the Public Service Harry had occasionally worked back in his office at night and in the last few years the first Tuesday night in each month had become one of those occasions. On that same night in every month Edna attended a meeting of the YWCA Board of Management and after it finished (usually about 9.30) went to Stirling Park where Harry waited for her. During their assignation on the Tuesday night after the picnic at the Cotter, he told her that throughout the next weekend Ruth would be in Melbourne attending an exhibition with her art group. With her away he would go for a walk in the pine plantation by himself and after sighting the body report the location to the police.

By Wednesday there was good progress in resolving the copper problem. Britten rang Harry during the morning and said he and Pickering had agreed to go ahead with the scheme as it had been settled between him (Britten) and Harry. Britten also said he had spoken to 'the people' at Pardoo and Four Star and they would not create any trouble.

When Harry, concealing his intense satisfaction, reported the outcome to Goldrick, the Minister, after telling Harry he had done a wonderful job in resolving so quickly so difficult a problem, added, 'I am lucky to have such a capable civil servant as the head of my department'.

Later that Wednesday when Harry had finished discussing some other business with the Minister, Goldrick said, 'You should listen to the media news at lunch time tomorrow, Harry, because the PM will be making an important announcement'.

Harry did listen and heard the Prime Minister announce he would be retiring in eight months' time when he reached the age of seventy and his retirement then would give his successor (who, he said, undoubtedly would be Joe Goldrick) more than a year to make his mark as Prime Minister before the next election. Harry was delighted. With Goldrick – who held him in such high regard – as Prime minister he was certain to be appointed Secretary of the Prime Ministers Department when the present secretary retired.

Harry woke up early on Saturday morning, got up quickly and pulled back the curtains. The sun was just coming over the horizon, there was no wind, it was a perfect morning for walking but he was not looking forward to the one he had to make. He went out, picked up the paper from the lawn and took it back into the kitchen. When he removed the wrapper he saw a large heading across the front page – 'Muriel Jones' Body Found in Forest'. He almost jumped for joy. What a great relief! How pleased Edna would be too! He decided to make a cup of coffee before reading the article reporting the discovery. While he was making the coffee his younger daughter Ann came into the kitchen in her nightdress and said, 'You're up early, Daddy!'

'Yes! It's a lovely day. We should go somewhere. All think about where we could go'.

'I'll wake the others and tell them', said Ann and hurried off.

Coffee in hand Harry sat down at the table and began to read the article. A forester had found the body on Friday afternoon but the police had not released the news until 10pm because there was some important evidence in the vicinity of the body which they did not want disturbed by journalists or sightseers. The body had been found in an area which was treeless because the trees had died and been removed. In the clay soil there were distinct footprints of a man and a woman going to and from the place where the body was lying. Police experts had made moulds of the footprints. The man had a club foot and was wearing a boot specially manufactured to fit it. Since there were in Australia only a few manufacturers of boots for people with club feet and they all kept a mould of each of their customer's club feet, the police expected to be able to track down the man. The police also said they were surprised to find that there was a possibility of both a man and a woman being connected with the disappearance and death of Muriel Jones.

Harry swung back in his chair and exclaimed, 'Oh! My God!'

WHIMSY

THE PRUNER'S FUNERAL

When I was six years old I was shown my well-loved Uncle Tom lying in a coffin and soon afterwards was taken to his graveside funeral. That unpleasant experience left me with a great dislike of funerals. So much so that I didn't go to another funeral until Roy McGregor, a friend of mine who loved pruning, died nearly forty years later.

I want to explain why I went to Roy's funeral and what happened at it.

In March 1936 Pat and I, newly married and both only twenty-one years of age, came from Western Australia to Canberra. Because I worked in the public service we were allocated a government house in Charles Street and we moved into it in June.

There were two pear trees, three apple trees and twelve rose bushes in the garden. I knew such trees and bushes had to be pruned in the late winter but had no idea how or when.

On the Saturday morning after we moved in the front door bell rang and I found on the doorstep a short, stockily-built, grey-haired man who said, 'Roy McGregor is my name. I live five doors down the street. I used to do the pruning for Clive Reid (the previous tenant). I was wondering if you would like a bit of a hand'.

I invited him in.

When I asked what sort of an arrangement he had had with Clive Reid he said, 'I just came whenever some pruning was needed and got stuck into it'.

'But what about the financial arrangements?' I asked.

'Good heavens! I don't want to be paid, I like pruning'.

The following Saturday Roy came with a barrow, two secateurs and a rake. As he pruned each fruit tree he explained to me what he was doing and how the pruning would not only make the tree more productive but also ensure it maintained a lovely well-balanced shape. When he finished each tree he raked up the cuttings and put them in his barrow. 'I'll burn them in my furnace', he said.

As he was raking up around the last tree I asked him what he would like to drink and he said, 'If you have some whisky I'd like that but I'll drink anything'.

Fortunately I had a bottle given me as a 'going away' present. I was not a whisky drinker myself but from that time on I always had some whisky in the house and for the next three years after each pruning session we sat for an hour or so in the sunroom at the back of the house and drank and talked. During those talks I learned a little about Roy's life.

He had been born and bred in Arbroath on the east coast of Scotland. His father and grandfather were stone masons but he didn't like working with stone and became a carpenter. Wanting to live in a warmer climate, he, his wife June and his eleven year old son James migrated to Australia in 1920. Working first in Sydney, then in Canberra he finally got a permanent job with the maintenance section of the Department of Interior. His son James, he said, was working in the Commonwealth Bank in Tamworth and had already got accountancy qualifications by correspondence and was studying for a Bachelor of Commerce degree from the University of Queensland also by correspondence. He said he and June saw very little of James because their studious son had to go to the University in Brisbane each year during his annual leave and was very busy in Tamworth with his study and bank work during the rest of the year. Roy also told me that for several years June had suffered severe and frequent migraine attacks which none of the doctors they had gone to had been able to prevent and that because of June's illness he and June did not 'get out and about very much'.

•

The war came. In 1939 I enlisted in the Air Force and was away for over five years. In her letters to me Pat, who had a slight physical impairment, mentioned the help Roy gave her and after a while said she did not think she would have been able to carry on without him. He pruned the trees and roses, mowed the lawns, chopped the wood, replaced the tap washers and light globes, cleared the blocked gutters and down pipes – and did it all so very cheerfully, she said. She also said that he praised the biscuits she regularly made to a recipe of her own – a sure way of getting her approbation.

From Pat's letters I also learned that Roy retired from the civil service in 1941, having reached the age of sixty-five and that James had become a junior partner in an important accountancy firm in Brisbane in 1943 and a year later had married the daughter of one of the senior partners.

A fortnight before I returned to Australia June died and so by the time I arrived back in Canberra Roy was living alone. It soon became apparent that he was drinking more heavily than he had when June was alive. He made his neighbours aware of this by occasionally wandering up and down Charles

Street singing Scottish songs in his rather pleasantly-accented voice. Alcohol did not, however, make him reckless or quarrelsome; he was never a nuisance.

Also Roy did not let alcohol interfere with his pruning. Whenever there was some pruning to be done he always arrived at my place quite sober. But at our drinking and talking sessions after each pruning, whilst he didn't get drunk, he certainly drank more whisky than he had at the prewar sessions and I sometimes broke up a session by saying I would walk home with him.

In the winter of 1949 Pat and I got new neighbours, a rather boisterous young couple, Bill and Helen Ingram. They said they were not interested in gardening but told me that Helen's brother who had also moved to Canberra had bought a forty acre block near Hall and intended to plant a lot of fruit trees on the block. 'Bloody madness' said Bill. 'He's working like a nigger preparing the ground'.

Two weeks later as Pat and I were driving out just after lunch to do some Saturday shopping we saw, parked on the Ingram's drive, a Holden car and a large trailer containing eight well-developed young fruit trees. When we returned two hours later the car and the trailer were still on the drive but as I drove slowly past the trailer I could see that the trees had been severely pruned,

I was working in the front garden later that afternoon and I could not help hearing a conversation which occurred between a young man (who obviously was Helen Ingram's brother) and Helen.

Helen's brother shouted excitedly, 'Christ almighty! What's happened! These are not my trees! Mine were twice that size!'

Helen loudly but calmly said, 'Don't be stupid. The beer's affected your sight'.

'I tell you they're not mine! I bought the biggest trees in the nursery!'

'Go and look at the labels'.

After a minute or two Helen's brother exclaimed 'Some bastard has cut large pieces off them'.

'Nonsense, the bits would be lying on the ground'.

'I know what I bought'.

'You don't, you're drunk'.

'I tell you some bastard has been at them. They're not half the size!'

'Well, you had better go home before they disappear entirely. I'm going in'.

Soon afterwards the car and the trailer backed out of the drive and went off down the road.

Helen's brother certainly had justification for feeling hard done by. A large part of the foliage of his fruit trees had disappeared but when he had told his sister she had not believed him. The pruning had been beautifully done, undoubtedly by Roy. Probably he had wandered down the street slightly intoxicated, seen the trees and had been unable to resist the temptation to prune which such a large number of unpruned trees had presented. However his severe pruning would not have done the trees any harm, it would have got them off to a good beginning.

Roy started to drift down to our place more often. Pat would give him some tea and frequently send him home with a casserole. We began to feel responsible for him, particularly as he was starting to become frail. Before long he had to give up pruning, first the trees and then the roses. By the middle of the 1950s I was pruning the trees and roses in both my garden and his under his supervision. His health continued to deteriorate and in 1956 he told me he would like to go into a nursing home. At my instigation James came to Canberra. He was, I found, a pompous pain-in-the-neck who left the whole task of getting Roy into a nursing home to me.

On my third visit to Roy in the nursing home he gave me a metal flask and asked if I would fill it with whisky for him. Although alcohol was not allowed in the nursing home, knowing that Roy was never troublesome when under the influence of alcohol and that the flask did not hold a large quantity, I regularly filled it. Some of the staff probably became aware that Roy was getting whisky but they took no action to prevent it – probably because he was in a single room and never a nuisance, also they may have liked his singing.

During his second year in the nursing home Roy told me that an Anglican priest, who earlier in the year had begun to make regular visits to the home, was 'a good bloke, easy to talk to and very interested in what I did in Scotland and after I came to Australia'. I was pleased to find that Roy, who did not have many visitors, got so much pleasure from the clergyman's visits. I sometimes saw the tall, cheerful-looking priest talking to patients when I was making my way to or from Roy's room, but did not have an opportunity of talking to him.

One day in the spring of 1959 when I visited Roy I found him much more propped up with pillows than he had been before and his voice much weaker. As soon as I sat down he produced the flask from under one of the pillows, gave it to me and told me he didn't want it back, that he would like me to keep it. 'It may sometimes remind you of me', he said.

I told him I would be delighted to have the flask but I could get it from him later on. He, however, insisted that I should not bring it back, 'I don't want the whisky any more and someone else might get it if you don't take it now'.

We then chatted about the usual things until, as I got up to leave, Roy, who knew I avoided funerals, said 'Perhaps a friend, who for a very long time shared both pruning and drinking with me will share my funeral with me'.

His peculiarly put request surprised me and touched me. I said, 'I am sure he will, but it won't be for a long time yet'.

Roy smiled, dropped his head back onto a pillow and said 'Good oh!'

He must have known that the end was near because five days later he died. Pat was in Western Australia with her mother who was ill. When I rang her Pat was quite upset – she too had grown fond of Roy.

James must have arranged by phone from Brisbane for the cremation, the funeral service in the crematorium chapel and the notice in the *Canberra Times* giving the time and place of the funeral. He made no attempt to get in touch with me.

The day before the funeral I bought a 'Helen Traubel' (one of Roy's favourites) growing strongly in a fairly large black pot and pruned it very carefully but lightly in the way I had once seen Roy prune to trim an unpruned rose in the spring.

The funeral was scheduled for 9.30 am on the Friday. I went early and arrived at the crematorium before nine o'clock. The door of the chapel was wide open. I went in. The coffin had one large floral wreath on it. I put the rose bush in the pot with a plastic tray under it on about the centre of the coffin then took Roy's flask out of my pocket and carefully poured whisky over every part of the rose bush. That done, I left the chapel and waited on the verandah for the arrival of the other mourners.

At twenty past nine a short, black-haired undertaker's man wearing a dark suit and with a grave expression stationed himself alongside the middle of the coffin. By that time there was waiting outside the chapel seven couples and two widows – all of whom lived, or had lived in or near Charles Street, also two women who were old friends of June McGregor and three elderly men who told me they had worked with Roy in the Department of Interior.

A minute or two later James, his wife and his three daughters arrived. James made himself known to all the mourners but even in carrying out that simple process his pomposity, which had irritated me on the previous occasions I had been with him, was evident.

At 9.30 the Anglican minister so well-liked by Roy carrying a small suitcase hurried onto the verandah, nodded to James, went into the chapel, talked for a moment to the undertaker's man then left the chapel through a door at the back, presumably to change.

The mourners led by James and his family followed the clergyman into the chapel but at a much slower pace.

My floral tribute to Roy stood out conspicuously. It must have quickly attracted the attention of James because, after settling his family in the front row of seats, he strode over to the undertaker's man, pointed to the flower pot and asked in an undertone (which, because there was no noise in the chapel could be heard by everyone), 'Who put that there?'

The undertaker's man (also in an audible undertone) answered, 'It must have been one of the mourners, sir'.

'Don't you know which one?'

'No! there's no card, sir'.

(That answer by the undertaker's man surprised me. Being unused to funerals, I was not aware that cards were attached to funeral floral tributes).

Not having got from the undertaker's man the information he wanted, James turned slightly and slowly scanned the mourners – presumably trying to discover which one of them was likely to put a flower pot on a coffin. Then he fixed his gaze intently on Roy's three ex-work mates who were sitting well back in the chapel and across the aisle from the rest of the mourners. Some of the mourners, apparently wondering what was engaging James' attention, twisted around and also looked in the direction of the three men. Under the stern gaze of James and the inquisitive gaze of many of the other mourners the three men looked uncomfortable.

However James diverted everyone's attention by sniffing very audibly and then exclaiming loudly in an accusatory way to the undertaker's man, 'There's a strong smell of alcohol!'

The undertaker's man said, 'Yes, it comes from the rose bush, sir'.

James stiffened, evidently very annoyed; he probably had never heard of a rose bush with an alcoholic odour and thought that the undertaker's man was 'having him on'.

There was a strained silence for a moment which was broken by the undertaker's man stepping back a pace and saying, 'Will you smell the rose bush, sir?'

Apparently still unwilling to believe that the alcoholic odour was coming from the rose bush and not from the undertaker's man, and perhaps not wanting to run the risk of looking foolish in front of his family and a group of mourners by sniffing fruitlessly around a rose bush, James continued to stare fiercely at the undertaker's man who obviously very annoyed by James' offensive behaviour, stared fiercely back at James.

For what seemed a long time, but was probably only about thirty seconds, there was absolute silence in the chapel. I, and very likely most of the other people in the chapel, waited rather excitedly for the outcome of the deadlock between the two men.

James broke the deadlock by moving closer to the coffin, leaning over and sniffing at the rose bush. He quickly straightened up, turned to the undertaker's man and exclaimed, 'This is dreadful! It shouldn't be here! You should remove that pot plant!'

The undertaker's man looked alarmed, presumably fearing he could be embroiled in a dispute between the chief mourner and one or more of the other mourners in the chapel. 'But it must have been put here by some of the other mourners, sir', he said.

Before James could respond to the objection of the undertaker's man the clergyman, wearing rather elaborate vestments, came hurrying into the chapel through the door at the back of it, took two steps towards the rostrum then stopped, looked towards the fuming James, and loudly cleared his throat.

With noticeable reluctance James accepted the clergyman's hint and walked to his seat. Before sitting down, however, he stood for a moment with his back to the clergyman and with a very stern face stared over the heads of the other mourners towards Roy's ex-work mates.

At least the first part of what followed was presumably a typical Christian funeral service. James read a brief summary of Roy's life (which to my great disappointment did not mention Roy's love of pruning), the priest consoled Roy's family and friends with readings from the bible, led them in prayers, and – with a very fine voice – in the singing of a short hymn. But it was the last part of the service that appealed to me. The priest said that during his visits to the nursing home he had enjoyed many chats with Roy, hearing about his life in Scotland and Australia and his love of improving the growth and beautifying the shape of trees and shrubs in his own and other people's gardens by careful pruning. 'From these talks', the priest said, 'I got a clear impression of the sort of life Roy led and I want to end the service by reading a verse from Gray's 'Elegy written in a country churchyard' because Gray, with his description of the kind of life led by the villagers buried in the country churchyard, had captured the essence of Roy's life'.

This is the verse he read (I found it in one of Pat's books of poetry):

Far from the madding crowd's ignoble strife
Their sober wishes never learned to stray;
Along the cool sequested vale of life
They kept the noiseless tenor of their way.

After reading the verse the priest looked towards the undertaker's man and nodded his head. The coffin began to sink below the chapel floor. For the last few seconds of the funeral all that could be seen was the well-pruned 'Helen Traubel' rose bush drenched with whisky.

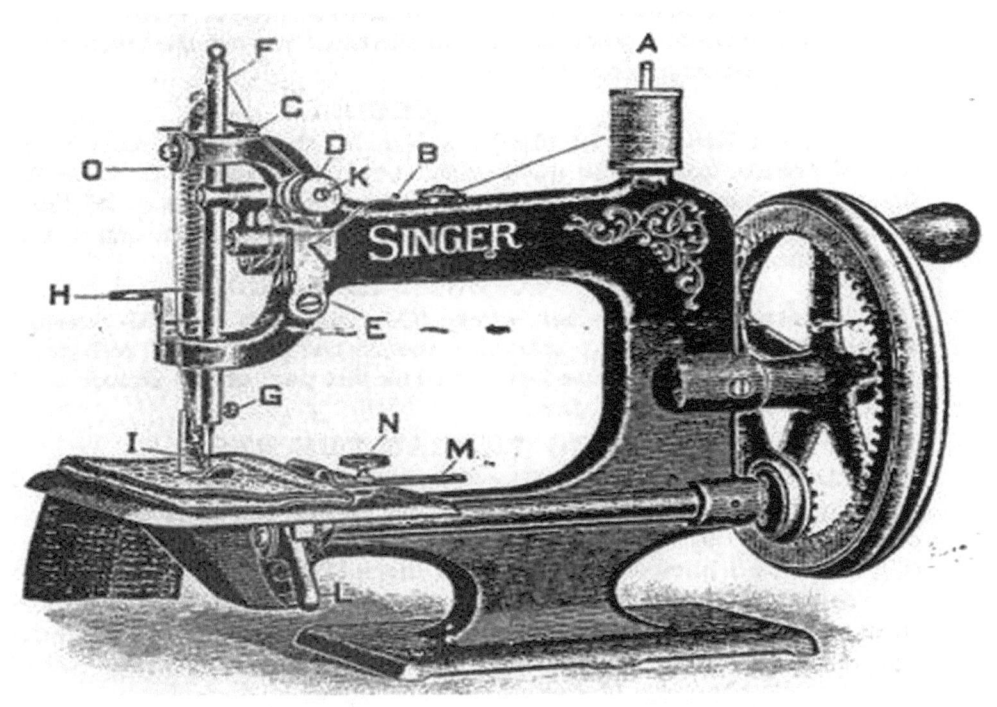

A 13/16TH INCH BUTTONHOLE ATTACHMENT FOR A SINGER SEWING MACHINE

In the spring of 1958 the strong westerly winds came later than usual. One lovely, still, September morning before the winds came, while waiting for my porridge, I sat looking through the window at the tapered tips of the next summer's foliage splitting the remnants of the last summer's clothing which still clung to many of the deciduous trees. On a tattered grey branch of the Chinese elm a brilliantly coloured parrot stood on his left leg eating red cotoneaster berries from an overhanging bunch he held in place with his right foot. I had started to speculate on the circumstances in which Australian parrots might have first discovered that the fruit of the exotic cotoneaster tree was edible when my wife suddenly said to me, 'Why won't you let the Singer people import a 13/16th inch buttonhole attachment for my sewing machine?'

Members of the Parliament, businessmen, trade union officials, mayors of cities and official representatives of a wide range of trading, manufacturing, and social organisations were constantly asking me somewhat similar questions but this was the first time such a question had been put to me by a member of my family. I replied, 'Every four months the Singer Company is given authority to import goods of an agreed type up to a specified value. It presumably uses the authority to bring into Australia those goods which it considers can be sold most profitably; apparently that does not include any 13/16th inch button hole attachments or sufficient of such attachments to meet all the local demand'. But my answer did not finish the discussion. By the time I had given a short dissertation on why the import controls were necessary to help overcome Australia's balance of payment problems and how they were administered the parrot had finished its breakfast, wiped its beak on the branch of the Chinese elm tree and flown off crying, 'chink' 'chink'.

Four weeks after the breakfast conversation I went overseas to attend a six week GATT conference in Switzerland and after that to England, Canada and USA for some bi-lateral discussions about special problems. Amongst the papers I carried with me was one on which was written in my wife's handwriting: '13/16th inch buttonhole attachment for my Singer sewing machine'.

While I was in Switzerland I located a Singer sewing machine shop but was told by a saleswoman that it did not have in stock a 13/16th inch buttonhole attachment, that there was not much demand for an attachment of that size but I should have no trouble getting one in the USA.

It was not until I reached San Francisco in the middle of December that I had another opportunity to try and purchase the buttonhole attachment. But my schedule provided for a very short stay in that city. I flew into San Francisco on a Friday afternoon and was booked to leave for Australia at 8am the next morning. Bookings for Australia were very heavy at that time and if I did not catch the plane the next morning I would not be able to get home before Christmas.

I arrived at my San Francisco hotel at 4.30 pm. From the telephone book I ascertained that there were three Singer sewing machine shops in the town area and, after jotting down the address of each of these and getting directions from the head porter, I hurried off towards the nearest.

When I reached the shop I found that the whole front wall and the entrance doors were made of plate glass. Through the glass I could see a broad sweep of nice grey carpet, polished timber tables on which were displayed sewing machines and accessories and along one wall many sets of drawers made of highly polished timber. It was an attractive looking shop. I went in and asked a saleswoman with striking red hair for a 13/16th inch buttonhole attachment. She went through some drawers at the back of the shop and then moved to the front of the shop and started looking through another set of drawers. I knew that all the shops in San Francisco would close at 5.30. The red haired woman's search seemed fruitless and I decided to try and get the attachment at another Singer shop. While attempting to hurry away and at the same time explain to the saleswoman why I was leaving, I walked into a glass door. I staggered back several paces with blood pouring out of my nose onto the nice grey carpet. Two shop assistants led me to the back of the shop and sat me on a low, cushion-topped stool. Other members of the shop's staff and several customers crowded around and gave advice quite freely: 'sit him up higher', 'lay him down', 'put ice down his back', 'put salt around his nose'. One of the customers, apparently a veteran from the Korean War, said it reminded him of an incident during the battle for Panmunjom and he then proceeded to describe the battle. After about five or six minutes a man leaned over me, said he was the manager and that he had not been able to get an ambulance from the City hospital but had arranged for one to come from the Port hospital.

The ambulance came. Although I said I was quite capable of walking out to the vehicle the ambulance men insisted that I get onto the stretcher and be carried out.

At the Port hospital the doctor who attended me was a long, lanky, young man well over six feet tall. He recognised my Australian accent and asked me the name of the ship to which I belonged and whether I had been in a fight. I told him that I didn't belong to any ship, hadn't been in a fight and that I had been trying to get a 13/16th inch buttonhole attachment for my wife's Singer sewing machine. The doctor, after putting a cotton plug in each of my nostrils, told me to breathe through my mouth and also said that in due course I would get two black eyes and a swollen nose. When the long, lean practitioner had finished his medication a hospital clerk ordered a taxi for me.

The taxi arrived and I asked to be taken to my hotel. The driver, an oldish man, was uncommonly quiet for an American engaged in that occupation. After driving in silence for about ten minutes we reached the shopping area. I saw that the shops were open although it was well after 5.30pm. When I expressed surprise the taxi driver told me that for about ten days before Christmas the shops remained open until 9.30 pm. I got out my note book and told the driver to take me to the second Singer shop on my list. The quiet American was, however, of a caring disposition and, although it was against his financial interests, he tried to persuade me to go straight to the hotel. He pointed out that I had just left the hospital and said that I did not look in good shape. I insisted on going to the Singer shop.

The second Singer shop was practically identical with the first. It had the same plate glass front wall and doors, the same nice grey carpet, the timber display tables and sets of drawers. From the taxi parked at the kerb I could see everything that was occurring in the shop. After I entered the shop I had to wait for about five minutes before a shop assistant could attend to me. Within a few seconds of making my request for the buttonhole attachment I sneezed and the cotton plugs shot out of my nose. Blood poured down onto the nice grey carpet. Once again members of the staff led me to the back of the shop but this time they provided a chair for me to sit on. Customers and staff gathered around. Some gave advice, others asked questions about the blood-letting and a few just stood and stared.

I had been on the chair for only a few minutes when the driver of the taxi forced his way through the small crowd and told me that as a result of a radio call he had made to his base the police were sending a patrol car which would escort the taxi at high speed to the Port Hospital. Aided by one of the staff and accompanied by some of the spectators I made my way to the taxi. As soon as I was in the back seat of the vehicle the driver gave me a copy of the evening paper to hold in front of me so that the blood still dripping from my nose would not fall on my clothing or on his taxi. By the time these arrangements were made the police car had stationed itself in front of the taxi.

We set off and were soon speeding through the streets of San Francisco. I marvelled at the willingness of the local police force to provide an escort so quickly and without any pernickety questioning. The police car had its siren wailing and blue and red lights flashing; the taxi driver kept his horn blowing presumably to identify his vehicle's connection with the police car. I sat in the taxi with the afternoon paper held in front of me. I kept looking straight ahead to reduce the possibility of spilling blood on my clothes or on the taxi but out of the corner of my eye I could see the people on the footpath. They all stopped walking and stood on the edge of the pavement to watch the noisy procession race past. I tried to guess their thoughts as they stood there. Were they wondering why a man sitting in the back seat of a taxi, apparently reading the afternoon paper, should be driven through the town at great speed with the aid of a police escort?

At the hospital the doctor who had put the plugs in my nose attended me again. He replaced the lost plugs and then put a wide piece of sticking plaster across my face. It reached from just below my eyes to just above my mouth and almost from ear to ear. He said the plaster would keep the plugs in place. When the doctor had finished his work the hospital clerk got another taxi for me.

I told the taxi driver to go to the address of the third Singer sewing machine shop on my list. I had not exhausted the possibility of getting the buttonhole attachment from the second shop but thought my re-appearance there might disturb the staff and retard the procurement of the attachment.

The driver of the taxi was a very talkative man of about thirty years of age, who told me his name was Joe. Although it was a warm evening he wore a woollen pullover and a strange woollen cap or hat. He prefaced practically all his remarks with the phrase, 'I reckon'. He began our conversation by saying, 'I reckon the bears will eat 'em on Saturday'. My questions revealed that he did not consider that weekend visitors to a nearby

219

national park would be devoured by grizzly bears but that a San Francisco baseball team would easily defeat one from Los Angeles. As we drove along he 'reckoned' that Eisenhower was a hopeless President who didn't know what was going on in the country, that two local politicians were closely associated with the Mafia, and that wearing wool, particularly on your head, reduced the likelihood of getting high blood pressure.

The third Singer shop looked like the other two but was larger and had a more elaborate display of sewing machines and other goods. Soon after I entered I sensed an uneasiness amongst the staff. They all seemed to be keeping their eyes on me rather than on the goods they were trying to sell or the customers they were trying to serve. The first saleswoman that became free made a bee-line for the toilet, or some other refuge behind a door marked 'Staff Only', before I could catch her. I came to the conclusion that the Singer organisation had alerted the staff in all its shops to look out for a tallish, thin, red haired, balding man in his forties who, soon after placing an order for a buttonhole attachment, would douse the carpet with blood. I stationed myself between the remainder of the staff and the door marked 'Staff Only' and swooped down on a young saleswoman as soon as the customer she was serving left her. When I gave her my order the girl moved towards the large set of wooden drawers, walking sideways like a crab with her head pointed in my direction. I followed her astonished at the apprehensiveness of the staff. After all there was a limit to the amount of blood I could spill on the carpet in Singer sewing machine shops.

The saleswoman began to look through the articles in the wooden drawers but she seemed to be shaking at the knees and it was apparent that her mind was not on the job in hand, so, my patience exhausted, I asked to see the manager. With an obvious sense of relief the saleswoman raced away and after giving a hasty knock on the door labelled 'Manager', opened the door went in and closed the door behind her. I remained in the vicinity of the wooden drawers. After a few minutes the door opened and a middle-aged woman, whom I presume was the manager, stood in the partially opened doorway with one hand on the door. She looked in my direction and shouted across the room, 'I understand you want to see me, sir!' As I walked towards her I could see that the nice grey carpet ran on into her office. The way the manager stood in the doorway suggested that she had no intention of letting me into that room; she was not going to risk the carpet in her office being soiled. When I reached the door I told her that I wanted to buy a 13/16th buttonhole attachment for a Singer sewing machine but had been having considerable difficulty getting one. She said, 'It'll be no trouble sir, we have some. The clerk will get you one straight away'. She stood aside to let the young saleswoman return to the display room. As the girl was moving past me I asked the manager the price of the attachment. She replied, 'Twenty cents'. I said in a quite loud voice, 'To hell with the expense and Australia's balance of payments problem, I'll buy two'. My loud statement, most of which was probably incomprehensible to everyone in the shop, startled the manager and the saleswoman. The former quickly pulled the door almost shut and peered at me through a very narrow aperture, the latter leaned for a moment against the wall staring at me and then walked quickly to the set of drawers. I decided not to follow the girl because I felt my presence near her might distract her from her work.

The young saleswoman located two of the buttonhole attachments fairly quickly, turned in my direction, held them above her head for a second and then walked over to the small counter in the middle of the room. I joined her there and gave her a fifty cent piece. While I waited for her to ring up the sale on the cash register and give me my change I noted that all the remainder of the staff in the shop stopped what they were doing and looked in my direction. They continued to watch me as I strode out of the shop joyfully clutching my two 13/16th inch buttonhole attachments.

When I joined Joe in his taxi he said, 'I reckon with that plaster over your face, they all thought that you were going to stick up the joint'.

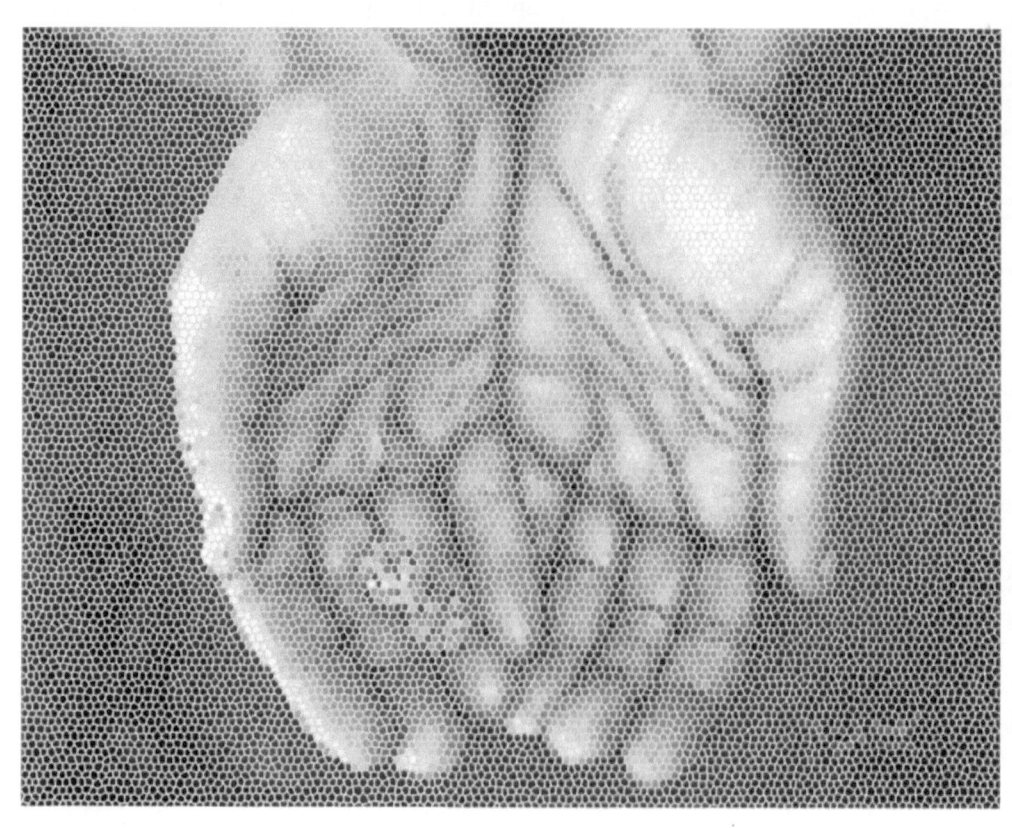

THE REVELATION

Clarrie Rogan was a very short, rotund man with a plump face clean shaven except for a long, thin, almost semi-circular moustache of which he was very proud. He spent quite a lot of time tending that growth of hair, trimming and brushing it twice a day and constantly stroking it to make sure each hair remained in its right place.

Clarrie's regular attention to his moustache did not seriously interfere with his work as a clerk in the Sewerage and Water Commission. He performed that work quite competently but did not give any indication of having the ability or the desire to undertake more responsible work.

A shy bachelor, Clarrie lived in a flat in Manly which he had inherited from his mother, a large voluptuous woman who had dominated him for thirty nine years until her death in 1955.

Just after his fortieth birthday Clarrie was appointed superintendent of the local Methodist Church Sunday school. He was given that position after more than twenty years as the teacher of an intermediate class at the school.

In the Sunday school classroom Clarrie had devoted practically all his attention to a series of stories based on incidents from the old and new testaments. He knew those stories very well because he had frequently heard them told at home and at Sunday school. Both his parents had been Sunday school teachers and had loved to tell the bible stories in a plain, uncomplicated form. Clarrie's interest in religion did not extend much beyond those simple stories. He was, however, very pleased with his elevation to superintendent. The job, as he performed it, was within his capacity. It involved drawing up a teaching roster, maintaining a list of relief teachers (and arranging for one of them to take over a class when the regular teacher was ill or on holidays or could not be present for personal reasons), going into the classrooms while the lessons were in progress to get from each teacher the pennies collected from the children and securing and distributing the materials and equipment required to operate the school.

While his mother was alive she had bought Clarrie's clothing. A parsimonious woman, she had bought 'off the hook' drab, ill-fitting suits of poor material, and cheap shirts, shoes, ties and hats. Dressed in such clothes Clarrie had no chance of appearing well-groomed.

But two years after his mother's death Clarrie branched out. He had a suit made of very good material by one of the better Sydney tailors and bought an expensive shirt, tie, shoes and hat to complement the suit. He also arranged to take most of his annual leave as half days off on alternate Fridays. On each of those Fridays he began to arrive at work in his new attire and to leave the office immediately after eating the cut lunch he brought each day. He began to spend the afternoons walking around the streets of inner Sydney examining goods in the better class departmental stores, speciality shops and bookshops and gradually even drinking coffee in one or two of the more expensive cafes. Then before the late afternoon rush commenced he would catch a bus back to Manly.

Clarrie got a feeling of exhilaration and independence, of being 'a man about town', from the half days spent in that way.

Clarrie's first appearance at the office very well dressed came as a great surprise to his fellow workers. After he had, on several alternate Fridays, arrived at work 'dressed up' and been away from the office for the whole afternoon, Clarrie became the subject of gossip throughout the office. In the opinion of the gossipers Clarrie must have been having an affair with a married woman. His supposed involvement in a romantic intrigue gave him much greater status amongst many of his fellow workers.

Before long the semi-jocular remarks made from time to time by his male colleagues and the more interested glances he received from some of his female colleagues made Clarrie aware not only of his higher standing but also of the reason for it. Becoming a man of mark for any reason, however misplaced, was very pleasant and gave added zest to his Friday afternoon-off routine.

One Friday in September 1960 Clarrie ended a pleasant few hours as a fashionable idler in the city by catching the 4.20 pm bus to Manly. Amongst the passengers already in the bus were Mrs Williams and her five year old son Tom, a strongly built child whose outstanding physical characteristic was a very loud, high-pitched voice.

Mrs Williams sat reading the *Women's Weekly* while Tom kept an eye on the passengers from a vantage point gained by standing on his seat.

Tom's attention became engrossed with Clarrie as soon as he stepped up into the bus and he watched him carefully as he passed by the Williams' seat and sat down two rows behind and on the opposite side of the aisle. Then Tom pointed at Clarrie and shouted excitedly, 'Look Mummy! There's Jesus! There's Jesus!'

That cry attracted the attention not only of his mother, but also of everyone else in the bus. Men stopped reading their papers, women stopped reading their magazines, non-reading passengers stopped staring out of the window and the conductor stopped collecting fares. Most of the occupants of the bus craned their necks round to catch a glimpse of the person Tom was pointing out.

Mrs Williams, after a quick glance over the back of the seat at Clarrie, said, 'Sh! Sh! Get down from there'. But Tom, aware of the interest his statement had aroused and somewhat hurt because his mother seemed unimpressed went on proclaiming in his loud, high-pitched voice, 'He is Jesus Mummy! He is Jesus!'

Soon many people in the bus became convinced that there was a passage in the bible that said: 'When he comes again a child will recognise him'. Once Tom had drawn their attention to Clarrie they could see something supernatural in the plain, middle-aged, little man sitting so quietly in their midst. They considered it was to be expected that Jesus would re-appear in a form distinctly different from that of His first appearance and in which only an absolutely innocent person, like a young child, would recognise him.

Clarrie's apparent composure in the face of Tom's repeated announcements (a composure which seemed to many to confirm the genuineness of the revelation) was not due to his calm frame of mind. In fact he was stunned by Tom's outburst and was sitting in a state of shock.

The bus was an express for the first part of its journey and, as it made its way through the inner northern Sydney suburbs, there was no movement of passengers in or out of the vehicle to disturb the growing excitement within it.

Mrs Williams, getting a firm hold on Tom, tried by physical force to stop him shouting and get him down from his perch. But he clung to the back of his seat and went on proclaiming the good news – 'He is Jesus Mummy! I have seen him Mummy! I have seen him! He is Jesus!'

Some passengers viewed with alarm the mother's attempts to man-handle her son. They began to wonder if they should intervene to protect the young disciple. Had not Jesus made it clear during his first sojourn amongst humans that family considerations should not be allowed to stand in the way of those who wanted to be his disciples?

While the concerned Christians hesitated to intervene, Mrs Williams with her superior strength and weight overpowered Tom, got him down from his vantage point and with him in a less conspicuous position hissed, 'Why are you calling that man Jesus? Wherever have you seen him?'

Tom replied stoutly, 'He is Jesus! I've seen him at Sunday school when he gets the pennies we've given the teacher for him'.

'What do you mean 'for him'?'

'For Jesus, Mummy'.

AUNT MOLLY SHOULD HAVE A TURN

Although I think of her as Aunt Molly I am not related to her. She is Ida Forbes' aunt not mine. I first met her when both she and I were visiting Ida. Very tall and gaunt, she was rather restless – her head nodding, shoulders shaking and arms waving – but seemed to be of a whimsical disposition. After poking fun at the business of selling books (Ida's occupation) she asked me whether I knew any middle-aged women who walk in their sleep, what make of clothes-washing machine I had and whether I used 'wonder' soap.

When she had left the house Ida told me that her aunt was a pensioner who had recently moved into a flat in the next suburb and was seeking someone to share the flat with her. 'There is a difficulty', Ida said. 'My aunt is a sleep-walker. She goes into the laundry and starts up her washing machine and keeps it working for much of the night. A woman did share the flat with her for a few weeks but left saying she was being driven crazy by my aunt's sleep-walking. Aunt is now trying to find another sleep-walker who will share her flat. She needs someone else in the flat because she has a serious heart problem, but God knows what sort of bedlam two sleep-walkers in the same flat would create.

'Aunt Molly spends a lot of day time as well as night time in her laundry. She loves her washing machine and washes everything within sight. It's her main amusement or diversion, and she says the soothing sounds calm her down'.

Ida's description of Aunt Molly's means of entertainment interested me. I am a bachelor and I too launder my clothes at home. Hearing of Aunt Molly's fondness for her washing machine led me to pay more attention to mine and I soon began to enjoy the sounds it makes – the burble (like the flow of a small waterfall) as the bowl fills up, the rhythmical beat (that invites one to dance) as the dirt is forced out of the clothes, the gushing of the dirty water as it leaves the machine, the whirring (like a strong breeze blowing across a sea shore) as the clothes are given their first rinse, the splashing (that reminds me of children playing in a pool) as the clothes are given their deep rinse, and finally, the roaring (like a mother elephant's call to her young) as the clothes are spun dried. For a short time between each activity there is no sound at all and through those silences I wait with pleasant expectancy for the next activity.

Many people (both men and women) who seek a companion by advertising in the 'Personal Column' of the local paper or by paying a large fee to a 'Match Maker' could instead give proper attention to their washing machine. They would then find they already had in the house a clean, honest, reliable, cheerful and interesting companion who would never complain if they came home late or slightly under the weather, or spent money foolishly or burnt the toast, and who also could easily be 'turned on' when they felt the need for excitement.

But I must return to Ida and her aunt. I see Aunt Molly only rarely but I am in constant contact with Ida — she and her husband Chris are my neighbours. They own a bookshop in Fyshwick and that enterprise (which does not seem to be very profitable) keeps them at work for very long hours for seven days each week and, during the eight years they have lived next door to me, they have not taken a holiday. For the last ten months I have gone to great lengths to try and get them to take one. I have offered them the use of my cottage at the coast, have said I would take my annual leave whenever they wanted to go away so that I could look after their shop in their absence and I have worked there for several week-ends to become familiar with the management. Though they have warmly thanked me for my offers, have agreed they need a holiday and will go down to the coast, they have not yet gone.

It is not my concern for the welfare of Ida and Chris that drives me in my attempt to get my neighbours to take a holiday but my concern for the welfare of Aunt Molly.

No! I am not being fully frank. Although I am very concerned about Aunt Molly, do want to give her a turn and make sure she can continue to enjoy her life-long recreation, my underlying motive is the preservation of my Viburnum.

You see my Viburnum is a unique plant. It has many of my own characteristics. It is tall, handsome, dignified and modest (it produces only the tiniest flowers). Also, like me, it wants to be a once-only phenomenon and has no desire to spawn any progeny – it has never produced any seeds.

This magnificent plant stands alone in a narrow strip of lawn between my concrete driveway and a white Colorbond fence which separates the side of my block from the rear of the Forbes' block. The white backdrop of the fence sets off beautifully the lovely dark green foliage of the Viburnum. Undoubtedly the plant's roots draw most of their sustenance from a piece of

229

uncultivated land at the back of the Forbes' house. Because Ida and Chris have very little time at home they have no garden. Neither have I for that matter; both of us have only lawns and we both get a local lad to cut them. The Forbes' lawn covers all the ground around their house except for a patch at the back. That patch is bounded on the northern side by their laundry, bathroom and toilet, on the eastern side by the back of their garage, on the southern side by the Colorbond fence and on the western side by a small lawn in the middle of which is a Hill's clothes hoist. Presumably the Forbes have left that piece of land uncultivated because it is not visible from the street or from anywhere inside the house except the laundry.

Last year I took six months of my long service leave and travelled right around Australia. When I returned I found my Viburnum drooping. I could find no reason for that until I looked over the fence and saw there had been some digging in the Forbes' uncultivated piece of ground.

When I asked Ida were they intending to plant something there she said that the digging had been done by a girl who for a while had worked in the book shop and whose much loved cat had died. Because the girl lived in a flat she had asked the Forbes if she could bury the cat in their yard.

The amount of ground which had been disturbed made me doubt Ida's explanation, indeed I was almost certain something bigger than a cat had been buried. Not wanting to upset Ida by appearing to link the two questions I let a week go by and then asked about Aunt Molly's health. Ida told me her aunt had died not long after I left for my trip. Undoubtedly it was Aunt Molly the Forbes had buried at the back of their house.

Burying a loved one in the garden is not uncommon in Canberra. Many public servants, having spent their working day wrestling with the nation's problems, find it comforting to come home from the office, see through a window a loved one's resting place and recall, often with a tear, a sigh or a smile, something the loved one has said or done.

However because there is a law prohibiting garden burials (the families of several Ministers have shares in undertaking companies) these activities are kept very quiet. Nevertheless groups of people interested in visiting the burial sites have formed clubs which regularly arrange such visits for their members. Because of the prohibition the burial site visitors disguise the real purpose of their organisations by calling them 'Garden Clubs'.

During the cold weather (and Canberra has a lot of cold weather) the clubs maintain fellowship between their members by meeting in the warmed rooms of religious or social societies. Here they are pleasantly put to sleep by the droning voice of some 'gardening expert' (of which there are a great number in Canberra).

When the warm weather returns the club members cease to hibernate and set off to inspect the new graves and to renew their acquaintance with the old ones.

The Canberra do-it-yourself societies adorn the graves of their loved ones with beds of Agapanthus because these plants readily adapt to the changes occurring in the level of the ground over a grave. Purple flowering plants are grown over the graves of public servants, mixed purple and white over the graves of the wives of these illustrious men and white over the graves of ordinary citizens.

To help conceal the real purpose of the 'garden clubs' the members also visit gardens without graves. On these visits they walk slowly through the garden occasionally stopping near a shrub or flower bed and by pointing, nodding and crouching to create the impression that they are interested in the flora.

Do-it-yourself undertaking is now an important recreational cottage industry in Canberra. It could also become a valuable tourist attraction. Canberrans should press for self-government and when that is obtained, repeal the law against disposal of bodies in any place other than a cemetery or crematorium. As soon as the law is repealed the local government could follow the practice of many town councils, which, by erecting a large model of a banana, sheep, cow etc. at the entrance to the town, advertise the town and the district's main tourist attraction. Where the roads into Canberra from Melbourne and Sydney meet there could be erected a gigantic sculpture of a public servant in the elegant but comfortable attire used when one of these distinguished gentlemen is put into his last resting place. It should show a well-dressed, tall, handsome man in a thoughtful pose – as befits someone who throughout his working life has borne great responsibility for the welfare of the Australian community – lying at an angle to the horizontal with sculptures of a few large purple Agapanthus around him – sufficient to make it clear that it is the last resting places of the important men that the tourists are being invited to see, not live public servants. (Of course a member of the public could only see a live public servant by appointment.)

But developing the cottage industry of do-it-yourself undertaking as a tourist attraction is admittedly something for the future. In the meantime I have got to deal with the problem created by Aunt Molly's burial in the Forbes' backyard. I have no objection to that site as her last resting place, indeed I think it is a very suitable one with its proximity to the Forbes' laundry. But the way they have buried her is causing trouble for my Viburnum. Obviously she has been buried with her feet near the laundry and her head near the fence. That irritates her, makes her very restless and her constant movements disturb the roots of my Viburnum. She needs to be put the other way around so that she can hear the delightful and soothing sounds of the washing machine working away in the Forbes' laundry. Everyone who loves a washing machine will understand Aunt Molly's distress.

The Forbes, who are not public servants or members of any 'garden club', cannot be aware that garden burials are commonplace in Canberra. I believe that they did not bury Aunt Molly in their backyard because they wanted her last resting place to be nearby, but because they could not afford to have her buried in a cemetery. They are very touchy about their income (or lack of it) and would take offence if I told them I knew they had buried Aunt Molly in their backyard and that I wanted to turn her around. My only hope of turning Aunt Molly around in time to save my Viburnum is to persuade the Forbes to go away within the next week or two.

Can anyone help me get the Forbes to take their holiday immediately so that, before it's too late, I can give Aunt Molly a turn?

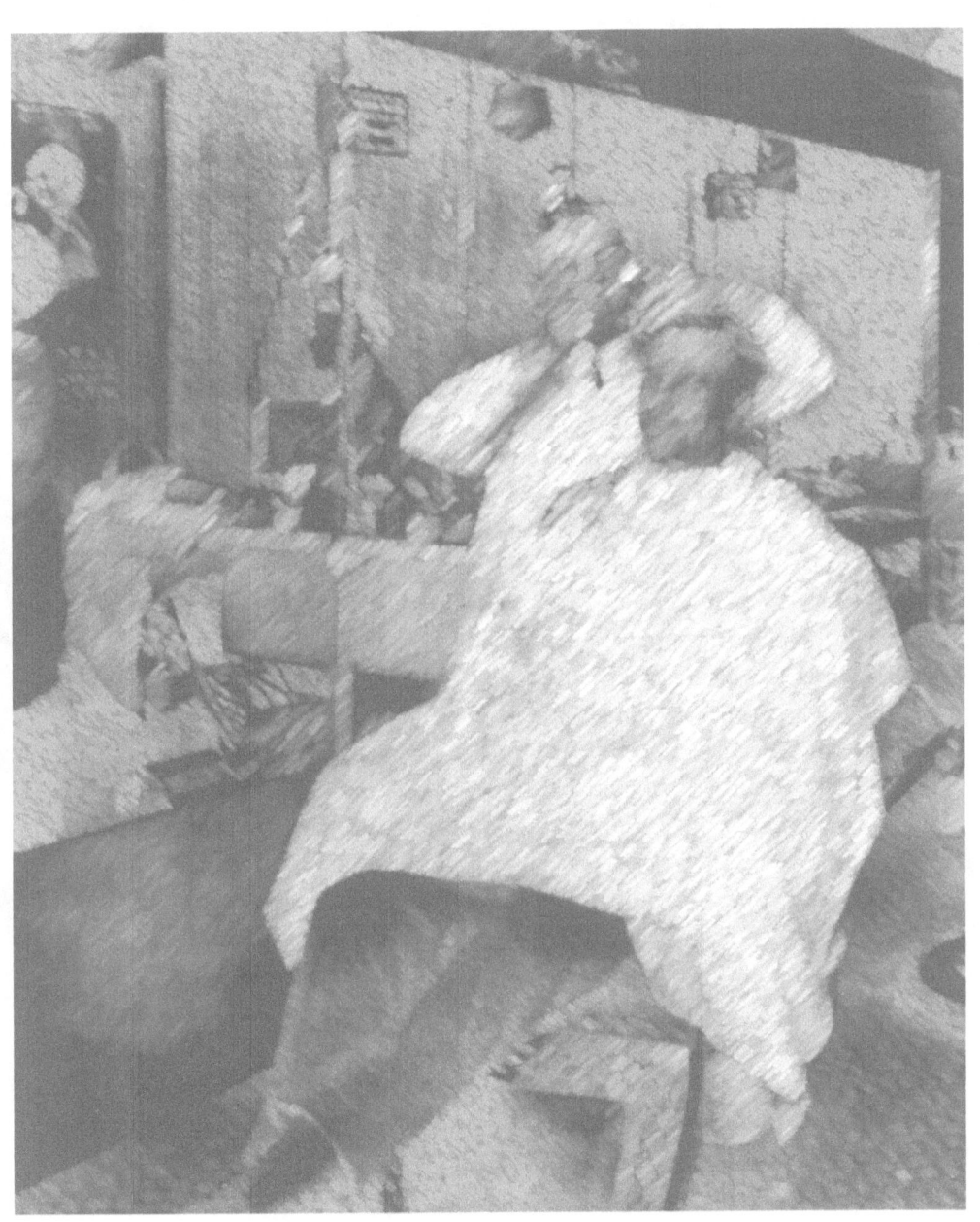

MY BARBER

When I was in my late teens and early twenties I had my hair cut by Mike Shanahan. He plied his trade in a small room next to a secondhand book shop in Civic Centre. One advantage of having Mike as a hairdresser was the time it saved and time was something I often ran short of. Not only did Mike speedily cut hair but he also saved time by not indulging in such unnecessary frills as trimming the hair protruding from the ears and nose or shaving the edge of the hair line.

Besides being a barber Mike was a prominent actor in the local repertory society. He was particularly interested in Shakespearian drama and was frequently chosen by the society to fill a leading role in the major productions and public readings of these plays. When acting he was restrained, he did not use grand gestures or extravagant variations in the tone of his voice but expressed great sensibility by more subtle means. He had a marvellous memory and while cutting hair frequently rehearsed the various parts he played in repertory. If at any time he was not actually playing in a current repertory show he went through the dialogue of a part he had played earlier or he practised a part which he hoped to play later.

Mike was a bachelor, middle aged, a big man with a long face, aquiline features and a rather brooding expression which, however, changed to one of warmth and merriment when he smiled. He walked with a slight limp the result, some returned soldiers told me, of a wound he had received in the 1914-18 war. He was regarded by most of his customers and acquaintances as an aloof person; he was not very communicative and did not readily tolerate ordinary social chit-chat, even in his shop. If normal barber shop subjects – horse racing, football, local gossip – were raised there, he ignored them.

Whenever he was not playing a part in repertory Mike joined a group which had a long wet lunch at the Civic Hotel every Saturday. I was one of that group and in the course of those lunch-time get-togethers found that Mike and I shared an interest in 19th century English novelists. Often the two of us sat in a corner of the bar for an hour or two discussing the authors and their works.

There was one other circumstance in which I regularly met Mike. He closed his shop for fifteen or twenty minutes at lunch time each week day and went for a walk on City Hill. I worked in Civic and when our lunch-time breaks coincided I joined him in the walk. Neither of us found walking in silence uncomfortable; when we did talk it was generally about books and writers.

Sometimes at about four o'clock on a Saturday afternoon when he was in the Civic Hotel Mike would ask, 'Anyone want a haircut?' For repertory buffs such an offer was hard to refuse because on those occasions the hair cut would be an unhurried affair during which Mike would bring every bit of his great acting skill to bear on the portrayal of some leading Shakespearian character. The chosen few could spend the remainder of Saturday afternoon in his company enjoying his portrayal.

On one such Saturday, a month before Christmas in 1933, Tony Eggleton and I accepted Mike's offer of a haircut and the three of us walked to Mike's shop. Just after we entered the shop a stranger appeared and asked if he could get a shave. Mike waved him into the chair.

The character Mike had chosen to play was Romeo but the stranger was an uncultivated fellow who did not willingly accept the part of a silent Juliet. During the first five minutes he twice attempted to leave the chair. Both Tony and I showed our displeasure at the distraction his movements caused and Mike had to use his strong personality and large physical presence to restrain him. Not unduly disturbed by the early distractions, Mike went on with the shaving and acting and in the last quarter of an hour the man made no attempt to leave the chair. But I noticed that on one or two occasions, such as when Mike with an open cut throat razor in his hand lent over him and said very tenderly, 'Speak again bright angel, for thou art as glorious as this night', the stranger pressed himself hard against the back of the chair and blanched a little.

When both the shave and the portrayal were finished the stranger's face was so covered with the bits of cotton wool Mike had used to dry up small cuts on his face that he could have obtained a position as Father Christmas in any leading department store without any further ado. But the stranger did not seem to appreciate the new opportunities for employment which Mike had opened up for him. He was reported as having said later that evening in a hotel that he had been held down in a chair and nearly skinned alive by a raving lunatic of a barber aided and abetted by two equally crazy customers.

Looking back now at those, for some, halcyon days I realise that we may have seen Mike's Saturday afternoon performances through rose coloured glasses. Before each performance the customers as well as the barber had enjoyed a long wet lunch. Also Mike's hair cutting on those Saturday afternoons often fell well below his normal standard; on occasions friends who met me during the week following a Saturday afternoon haircut greeted me with remarks such as 'Good God! What's happened to your hair?' The story the reluctant Juliet told about the shave he had received spread like wild fire through the small town Canberra was then. The poor quality of the Saturday afternoon haircuts and the shaving incident were not good advertisements for Mike's business which began to fall off. They seemed also to affect the invitations Mike received to perform in the repertory shows; he was no longer offered major parts. Mike's problems were increased by a decision he took in May 1934 not to continue cutting children's hair. I was with him when he took that decision.

I went to the shop late one Monday afternoon and found Mike cutting the hair of a small boy. The boy was sitting on a box placed on the seat of the barber's chair so that Mike could reach his head without bending over very far. A woman, probably the boy's mother, was sitting right on the edge of a chair staring at Mike in a rather frightened way. She had a small, very pale face but a big, strongly-built body.

Mike was in splendid form and, as I sat down, he was saying, 'Look in upon me then and speak with me or, naked as I am, I will assault thee'. The small boy was sobbing quietly but deeply; tears were falling down his cheeks in endless succession. Obviously Mike was conveying to him, with tremendous force, the terrible tragedy of Othello.

Mike lifted the clippers above the boy's head and exclaimed, 'Behold a weapon. A better did never sustain itself upon a soldier's thigh: I have seen the day that, with this little arm and this good sword, I have made my way through more impediments than twenty times your stop'. His voice fell and he continued, 'But oh vain boast! Who can control his fate? 'Tis not so now'.

The clippers moved steadily over the boy's head and, leaning forward to cut the side hair, Mike said, 'Be not afraid though you see me weaponed. Here is my journey's end; here is my butt and very sea mark of my utmost sail'. He pulled himself up to his full height so suddenly that the mother moved back instinctively on her chair. 'Do you go back dismayed? Tis a lost fear; man but a rush against Othello's breast, and he retires. Where should Othello go?' Mike moved round to the other side of the barber's chair and now faced the mother across the boy's head. 'Now, how dost thou look now?' Raising his head he looked straight at the woman, 'Oh! ill-starred wench! Pale as thou smock! When we shall meet at compt, this look of thine will hurl my soul from heaven and fiends will snatch at it – cold, cold, my girl, like thy chastity'.

Having finished the first run over the boy's head, Mike moved to a cabinet fastened to the wall to change the blade in the clippers. In this position, with his back to us, Mike continued to fill us with the terrible agony of Othello's sorrow. 'Oh cursed slave! Whip me ye devils from the possession of this heavenly sight! Blow me about in winds! Roast me in sulphur! Wash me in steep-down gulfs of liquid fire!'

While he was saying this the mother jumped up, lifted the small boy out of the chair and fled from the shop. Mike continued, 'Oh Desdemona! Dead! Oh! Oh!' He finished changing the blade, turned round and stared at the vacant chair.

'What's happened to the kid?' he asked.

'Shot through in his mother's arms', I replied.

To my surprise Mike ran quickly out of the shop after his absconding customer. I was surprised because, up to that time, Mike had always adopted a 'take it or leave it' attitude towards his clients. He didn't advertise his business; he didn't encourage people to enter his shop by word or deed and didn't seem at all concerned if someone came in, looked around, and walked out.

After a few minutes Mike returned and leant up against the barber's chair. He remained there looking down at the floor.

I thought he was getting into the right frame of mind to face up to Lodovico's question, 'Where is this rash and most unfortunate man?' and at any moment expected the unhappy, bitter, disillusioned Othello to say, 'That's he that was Othello; here I am'. But Mike said, 'I'm fed up! That's the last time I'll cut a kid's hair'. He lifted the box from the barber's chair, dropped it on the floor, flung himself into the chair and gazed despondently at his reflection in the mirror on the wall.

I considered it likely that Mike was fed up with more than the cutting of children's hair. Technically he was a good barber (when sober) but the work did not uplift him intellectually or suit his personality and he had grown impatient with it; also for the last six months the repertory society had not given him any opportunity to use his considerable talents as an actor and that had vexed him.

For a while there was a complete silence in the room then I said, 'I'll see you tomorrow, Mike'. He didn't reply but as I walked out he lifted one hand

and waved it wearily. When I reached the door I looked back; Mike still sat looking at his reflection in the mirror.

As I made my way across the old sheep paddocks towards my room in Glebe House I thought about the scene I had left behind. Did Mike see in the mirror the ghost of a much younger Mike Shanahan full of the hopes of a youth on the threshold of adulthood? Did he wonder what had become of that youth and those hopes? I would have liked to have known more about Mike's life before he came to Canberra but he resisted attempts to draw him out on that subject. However, he had on one occasion told me that he was an only child and that his father had been a barber and had insisted on him taking up that occupation.

When I reached my room I lay down on my bed. At first Mike was uppermost in my mind but gradually I began to think about my own past and speculate about my future; about what my life might be like when I reached Mike's age. Would I be as disappointed as Mike seemed to be? My meditation was cut short by the sound of the dinner gong.

•

During the next twelve months I had about ten haircuts, none on a Saturday afternoon. Mike dropped out of the group which regularly had lunch in the Civic hotel. He no longer appeared at repertory shows, either in the cast or in the audience; he ceased rehearsing parts while he was working in his shop; he became more and more withdrawn. From the odour of his breath it was plain that Mike was drinking every day, presumably when alone in his lodgings and in his shop. But, at this stage, the drinking was not having any marked effect on the standard of his work. I thought that an opportunity to play a worthwhile part in a play might help bring Mike out of his depression. I spoke to two prominent members of the repertory society with whom I had had some contact. However both seemed to consider that I was questioning the 'professionalism' of the society in selecting casts for its shows. Perhaps my approach was clumsy; I felt that my intervention was likely to do Mike more harm than good.

Late one Saturday morning in June 1935, when the sun was hidden by a heavy fog and the frost which had formed during the night still lay like white sheet on the ground, I walked across the old Glebe farm paddocks to Civic for a haircut. When I entered the shop Mike was sitting in a chair very close to the heater reading 'The Lonely Plough' by Constance Holm. I sat alongside him and for quarter of an hour we discussed the book. No other customer came in. During the discussion Mike mentioned that he had first read 'The Lonely Plough' in 1917 when he was in an army hospital in England and that a year later, while on leave from his unit, he had spent a week in the marshlands of northern England in which the events in the novel are located. Those casual remarks about his war time experiences were the only references he ever made to the war.

As he prepared to cut my hair Mike quoted a line from the short poem with which Constance Holme finishes her book, 'Who hath remembered me? Who hath forgotten?' and said, 'Perhaps those words have a special meaning for me just now. I am leaving Canberra shortly'. When I asked him where he was going he ignored the question and stood looking at me with the old twinkle in his eyes. Then he said musingly, 'Three thousand ducats: well' and so began the negotiations for a loan to Antonio with which Shakespeare introduces Shylock to the audience and reveals the money-lenders hatred for rich Christians, like Antonio, who lent money without charging interest and reviled Jews for not doing the same.

With sensuous enjoyment I sat quietly in the barber's chair while Mike shared with me Shylock's bitterness when his daughter ran away with her Christian lover and took some of the Jew's jewels and money with her, the impetus these losses gave to his desire to avenge, by persecuting Antonio, the wrongs done him by Christians, his gloating over the financial disasters that befell Antonio, his refusal to yield to any intercessors seeking Antonio's release from his bond, his fawning praise of Portia when she argued that 'the Jew may claim his pound of flesh', the marked change in his attitude when Portia faced him with the obligation to shed no blood and take neither more or less than a pound of flesh, his sudden desire for a cash settlement, his despair when confronted with a judgement which would bring financial ruin and his final acceptance of an ignoble discharge from the Court.

All the while Mike carefully combed and cut, brushed and trimmed my hair. At no time did his concentration on either his acting or haircutting relax. After Shylock left the stage he made the finishing touches to my hair and held a mirror behind me so that I could get an overall view of the results of his work.

During the next ten days several friends asked me who had cut my hair and seemed surprised when I told them they were looking at an example of Mike's handiwork. On the eleventh day I was sent to Sydney to fill temporarily a position vacated by the sudden death of an officer. When I returned to Canberra two months later I found Mike's shop closed. I paid a visit to his old lodgings in O'Connor but the only information his former landlady gave me was that he had left Canberra six weeks earlier and she didn't know his present address.

A WELL TRAINED EXECUTIVE TAKES THE CAKE

The cake was baked by my Aunt Ruby. Aunt Ruby was not the sister of my father or mother but a childless friend of both my parents who had acquired the title of Aunt. The honorary title was much deserved. Aunt Ruby hit it off very well with young children. She spent many hours reading to them, playing simple games with them and encouraging them to draw and paint. She bore with tolerance the damage they sometimes caused her utensils and furniture and their bursts of noisiness and mischievousness. She greatly valued the title of Aunt and liked the children to call her husband 'Uncle Joe'.

Uncle Joe was an easy going, amiable man who, as a general rule, preferred beetles to children. However, when we visited our honorary relatives, he often spent some time discussing beetles with my young brother who was favourably disposed towards those insects. Both Aunt Ruby and Uncle Joe were undemonstrative people but everyone who knew them well was aware of a strong bond of affection between them.

Aunt Ruby was a compulsive fruit cake maker. She did make other types of cake but less frequently and it seemed to me much less enthusiastically. To ensure that she was always in a position to make a fruit cake whenever the desire seized her, Aunt Ruby kept, in a room beneath her house, two steel garbage bins, one containing packets of flour (plain, self-raising, wholemeal) and sugar (raw, brown, white, icing) and the other containing dried fruits (raisins, currents, sultanas), dates, almonds and bottles of rum.

Both Aunt Ruby and Uncle Joe were Methodists and, in common with all devout members of that religious denomination at that time, abstained from the use of intoxicants, but my honorary relatives allowed themselves some exceptions to this abstinence. One was the inclusion of rum in the production of fruit cakes; Aunt Ruby was too conscientious a cook to leave out an essential ingredient. The other was the use of rum for medicinal purposes; for that purpose they drank rum every day. Such a substantial breach of teetotalism by two committed Methodists calls for an explanation.

In the 1920s Aunt Ruby and Uncle Joe had taken a holiday in a sugar growing district in Northern Queensland. Both being of an inquiring nature they had set out to learn all they could about the growing of sugar cane and the manufacture of various products from the cane. This involved not only visits to sugar farms and mills but also to a rum distillery. A very well built, rosy cheeked, healthy young woman had taken them around the distillery and in conversation with them had said that for over six years she had taken a tablespoon of rum in hot water every morning and, as a consequence of this, had not had a cold for all that time. Aunt Ruby had no faith in medical practitioners but an almost unbridled faith in remedies and preventive measures recommended by other people, particularly if the person making the recommendation was a living example of the effectiveness of his or her prescription. After the visit to Queensland, Aunt Ruby and Uncle Joe took a tablespoon of rum in hot water each day with their breakfast. It did not prevent one or the other, or both of them, from occasionally getting a cold but on each occasion Aunt Ruby was able to point to some rash action taken by Uncle Joe which she said had caused the aberration and which she also said would be avoided in the future.

Aunt Ruby loved shopping and in particular buying things at a 'special' price. When she located a bargain she would generally buy a quantity of the product which far exceeded her likely requirements for a reasonable time ahead. One result of this was that there were periods when the ingredients for making fruit cakes overflowed the two bins and much fruit cake making had to take place. The cake recipe provided for only a small quantity of rum and when, as a result of my Aunt's purchasing habits, there was a superabundance of that commodity she increased the consumption by putting two tablespoons of rum in Uncle Joe's daily potion. She considered this gave him greater protection from colds. It may or may not have done that but it did affect his career in the Victorian Public Service and his standing in the local Methodist congregation.

Prior to World War II the officers in each of several Victorian Public Service departments were predominantly of one particular religious denomination – in one department Roman Catholic, in another Methodist and in a third Church of England or Congregational. The system of recruitment and promotion in the public service tended to perpetuate the religious partiality in the various departments.

The department in which Uncle Joe worked was dominated by Methodists. The head of his section, the chief clerk, Harry Reid, was a leading layman in the suburban Methodist church to which Uncle Joe and Aunt Ruby belonged. Harry Reid was an intractable teetotaller who advocated total abstinence from intoxicants by everyone; he possessed a nose capable of detecting the slightest trace of alcoholic fumes. Early one morning in 1932 Harry Reid had sent for Uncle Joe and, as they together closely scrutinized a document he had, to his great surprise, noticed an odour remarkably like that associated with alcoholic liquors. When he had asked Uncle Joe whether he had been drinking, my honorary relative had at first said 'no', but then, remembering his hot drink at breakfast had said he had drunk some rum as a safeguard against colds. The chief clerk had regarded Uncle Joe's claim that he used rum as a prophylactic as a subterfuge and had been very displeased when he had discovered that my Uncle had drunk rum every day for several years.

Promotion in the Victorian Public Service was almost entirely on the basis of seniority but during the 1930s Uncle Joe was passed over for promotion on several occasions. Uncle Joe was a member of the council of his local Methodist church and when other members heard (presumably from Harry Reid) of Joe's rum drinking habit they branded him a backslider and requested his resignation from that select group of holy men. None of these events seemed to unduly disturb Uncle Joe. He had never been an ambitious man and had a greater interest in the beetles he collected than in either the public service or the church. He bore no ill will towards Aunt Ruby the instigator of the rum drinking. He clearly recognised that Aunt Ruby always had his best interests at heart even if some people might doubt the effectiveness of the methods she chose to promote those interests.

In 1957 when I returned from overseas Aunt Ruby asked me to stay with her for a while. I found that she had aged perceptively in the four years I had been away. Her previously strong, slim body had got much leaner and she looked quite frail. Her hair had got thinner and greyer and she stooped a little. But she remained energetic, bustling through her household chores and working in the garden with vigour as well as with tender loving care. She was still fond of company and gossip and although she did not have a keen sense of humour could occasionally make a very funny comment about a matter under discussion.

I had arrived at Aunt Ruby's house in time for afternoon tea and she had ready for me a lovely fruit cake. On the second day of my visit she cooked another for a luncheon party being held in Canberra three weeks later (on Saturday 28th September) to mark the seventieth birthday of her sister Muriel.

Aunt Ruby rarely did only one thing at a time. When cooking the cake for her sister's birthday party she also cooked 'to use up the heat' a stuffed beef roll and baked potatoes, pumpkin and carrots. Many and varied were her activities in the kitchen that day – soaking raisins, currents and sultanas, chopping up dates, sifting flour, beating eggs, sugar and butter (first separately, then together), soaking almonds, grating orange and lemon peel, measuring out cinnamon, nutmeg and salt. All those activities related only to the cake, they were mingled with the preparations for the baked dinner – peeling and cutting up potatoes and pumpkin, chopping up and mixing together onions, celery and parsley, crumbling bread and mixing spices. The end-products of this stage of the work, temporarily stored in a variety of containers, were distributed along the kitchen benches in what seemed an indiscriminate way. How the mixture of onions, celery and parsley did not get into the cake, or the batter of eggs, sugar and butter not get into the meat roll, remains a mystery. But no such disaster occurred and the outcome of the cooking was a lovely light brown fruit cake about one foot square and three inches thick and a delectable baked dinner.

During the next few days a neighbour skilled in these matters came into the kitchen on several occasions and gave the fruit cake first a coating of almond paste and then of icing fondant. Finally she decorated the cake using a 'pure' icing sugar mixture called Royal icing.

Aunt Ruby intended to take the cake to Canberra when she and Uncle Joe went to the national capital for the birthday party. But unfortunately ten days before the date set for the party Uncle Joe fell ill and had to go into hospital. As Uncle Joe's illness was found to be of a serious nature it was soon apparent that neither he nor Aunt Ruby could attend the party.

At that juncture Aunt Ruby could have packed the cake in a box and sent it to her sister's house by one of the carriers operating between Melbourne and Canberra. But that was not the way she managed these matters. Aunt Ruby believed that any person travelling from one place to another should be prepared to carry parcels for friends or relatives. I don't think she ever moved away from Melbourne or returned to it without carrying a great load of packages which she had collected from friends or relatives at her place of departure for delivery at, or near, her destination. Aunt Ruby was convinced that any article delivered 'in person' (even if the person was not the donor) had a worth not to be found in one delivered by a commercial carrier.

It did not take my Aunt very long to press someone into her service to take the cake to Canberra. That someone was her sister Muriel's son Robert, a forty-eight year old bachelor.

Most of Aunt Ruby's male relatives were steady, fairly cautious men who worked in one of the many Australian public services or in a bank or the teaching profession. Robert, who was in the Commonwealth Public Service in Canberra, was less steady and cautious than Aunt Ruby's other male relatives, not because he was very adventurous or courageous, but because he did not recognise that his physical and mental powers were not above the average. It was as a result of his overconfidence that Robert sometimes trod where, if not the angels, at least the people with better judgment, feared, or did not desire, to tread.

By his late thirties Robert had progressed to a lower management position. He remained in that position for ten years, gradually becoming very discontented with the lack of promotion. Then came what seemed to him an important break-through. He was selected to undertake a six months course at the Australian Staff College. The Staff College, which was located on the outskirts of Melbourne, was, in the first few decades after World War II, the only institution in Australia specializing in the training of executives for industry and the public service.

Some of Robert's colleagues said (behind his back) that he was being sent to the Staff College to get him out of the department so that another officer could be tried out in his job. But these remarks may simply have been an expression of the envy a few fellow officers felt at his selection.

The six months course was scheduled to finish on Friday 27th September and Robert agreed to collect the cake from Aunt Ruby's home that night so as to be ready to fly to Canberra the next morning at eight o'clock. While waiting for Robert to collect the cake Aunt Ruby gave serious thought to the type of travelling container in which the cake should be carried.

For as long as anyone could remember Aunt Ruby had attended every fete organised by a school, church or charity within reasonable distance of her home. At each fete she spent a considerable amount of time examining the goods for sale on the various stalls and always purchased some of them. The consumable items were either given away immediately or eaten by Aunt Ruby and Uncle Joe. A niche was found in the main part of her house for a few of the durable goods but most of them were stored in the room under the house awaiting the discovery of some way of using them. From time to time when a friend or relative happened to mention in Aunt Ruby's presence the lack of something she was able to find in the room under the house an article which would make good the shortcoming. With great joy she gave the article to the person in need of it. Occasionally a recipient of Aunt Ruby's generosity found that my Aunt's gift did not fit an essential condition the acceptor had in mind and the article concerned found its way back onto a stall at a fete. Aunt Ruby greeted the article like a long lost friend, purchased it and restored it to its former place in the room under the house.

To ensure that the fruit cake was not damaged in transit to Canberra Aunt Ruby got out from amongst the durables under the house an attractive solid leather suitcase about eighteen inches square and six inches thick. She firmly packed the cake (enclosed in greaseproof paper and a cardboard box) in the leather suitcase using rolled up newspaper and old cloth as the packing. When she gave the cake in its travelling container to Robert, Aunt Ruby told him that he could keep the suitcase. Although the suitcase took Robert's fancy he was surprised and somewhat dismayed at the size and weight of the parcel.

Robert did not travel light. He dressed well and always carried with him a wide range of articles to assist in his toilet. Consequently the personal baggage he was taking back to Canberra from Melbourne reached the limit of that allowed free carriage for one passenger. When he checked in at the airport on Saturday morning he was told that he could not take into the cabin of the plane both the elaborate executive brief case he had purchased while in Melbourne and the leather suitcase containing Aunt Ruby's cake; one of these had to be put into the hold and he would have to pay an excess baggage fee for its carriage.

Robert had a parsimonious attitude towards any expenditure that did not affect his own well-being. Having to pay for the transport of Aunt Ruby's cake to Canberra was not at all to his liking. As he considered that he now had at his finger-tips all the skills of a well-trained executive, he decided to use those skills to avoid being charged the excess baggage fee. He asked to see the supervisor and when that official arrived gave him a soul-subduing lecture on the need for executives at all levels 'to manage' – to face up to problems and resolve them in an imaginative and constructive way and not behave like clerks and simply apply existing regulations to all situations.

During the course of the lecture Robert said that he needed his brief case in the cabin of the plane because he had some important business matters to attend to and that the other small case should remain with him because its contents were very valuable. Robert was very pleased to find that his lecture attracted the attention of a number of people – counter clerks and baggage handlers with nothing else to do and passengers waiting to be called to board their planes. He was certain that he gave the lecture with the clarity, calmness and patient behaviour towards interjections by the supervisor that one could expect from a well-trained executive. However, the supervisor remained unmoved. Robert recalled that a leading businessman who was visiting lecturer at the Staff College had demonstrated how an executive could 'with single minded concentration on achieving his objective', reach a successful conclusion in difficult negotiations. He tried to emulate the businessman but only succeeded in blustering. It was to no avail. Robert finally had to pay the excess baggage fee. When he had done, the attractive leather suitcase with its very tasty content was sent on its way to the aeroplane.

The case did not turn up in Canberra and a thorough search by the National Airlines of all its branches did not locate it. In due course Robert received from the airline quite generous compensation.

NAVY BLUE

A MARVELLOUS ENCOUNTER

The taxi arrived at the hotel on time and was driven by a rather elderly, cheerful-looking, sprightly man who jumped out quickly and helped me put my baggage into the boot. There was something vaguely familiar about him. When all the baggage was in and we had both got into the front seat, the driver turned towards me. 'I don't thuppothe you remember me, thir', he said. As soon as he spoke I did remember him.

In March 1942 I was on leave in Adelaide when a signal came appointing me gunnery officer on HMAS *Fairfield* and instructing me to join the ship in Sydney.

When I got there and reported at Rushcutter I found out that the *Fairfield* was not expected for several days, that accommodation had been arranged for me at the Officers Club in Kings Cross, and that, apart from reporting to Rushcutter each day, I was free to do what I liked until the ship arrived.

My unexpected freedom did not last long. Before I had finished dinner in the club that evening I was called to the phone and instructed to report to Rushcutter immediately with the gear I needed for about three days at sea.

When I arrived at the base I was told that an officer on HMAS *Astra* – the duty ship on the examination service off Sydney Heads – had suddenly become seriously ill and that I was to replace him for the next three days. The naval launch that took me out to the *Astra* picked up the sick officer to take him ashore.

The *Astra* was a lightly armed ex-merchant ship. Its captain, a Reserve Officer with merchant ship experience, after explaining at length how the examination work was carried out, told me I would be keeping the Middle and Afternoon watches.

The helmsman on duty for those two watches was a tall, thin, middle-aged, solemn-looking Able Seaman named Miller who had a small but distinct speech defect. He could not pronounce an 's' or a 'z'. Instead of pronouncing those letters he uttered a soft, drawn-out 'th'.

For about half of my first watch the captain remained on the bridge – presumably to satisfy himself that I could handle the ship and carry out the examinations. After he left, the watch-keepers in the bridge area were a lookout, who was also a signaller, in each of the wings and Miller and I in the control centre. During the watch there were a few periods of considerable activity while we examined a ship, and long periods of quiet while we steamed up and down a stretch of the New South Wales coast that was free of navigational hazards.

At breakfast the next morning the first lieutenant said, 'You've got Noisy Miller as your helmsman. He's an odd fellow, but you'll find him a dammed good man to have at the wheel when you've got some difficult manoeuvring to do'.

'How did he get the name 'Noisy'?' I asked.

'Because he's as quiet as a mouse. Rarely says anything, a real loner, but not a sulky person. He's spent a lot of time in the service, came into it through the *Tingara*'.

Mention of the *Tingara* brought to my mind Potter Power the ex-*Tingara* boy in my year at the Naval College. He was a year older than the rest of us but fitted in quite well and formed a very close and lasting friendship with two of the other boys in the year. Power was the only *Tingara* boy I knew who became a Commissioned Officer. From Power I had learned that the *Tingara* was a ship moored in Sydney harbour, used by the Navy to train boys to become seamen. The boys, who were accepted for training at the age of thirteen, lived, worked and studied on board the ship. Those who successfully completed the course were given the rating of 'ordinary seaman' at the age of seventeen and then signed on to serve twelve years in the Navy.

Later in the forenoon, while I walked up and down the quarter deck to get some exercise before the afternoon watch, the first lieutenant's reference to Miller as a loner was uppermost in my thoughts, because I was aware that I was called a loner by colleagues who had known me for a long time. When I first realised that term was applied to me I was surprised but after some introspection considered that its application was justified. Although I had always

252

enjoyed spending some time alone (and had found I could be alone, if I wished, in the presence of others) I had got on quite well with the people with whom I worked, played sport and socialised.

However, during none of my activities with others had I wanted to get very close to anyone. I had greatly valued my feeling of independence which not having intimate acquaintances gave me. I was a loner.

Thinking about this trait in my character once again as I paced up and down the quarter deck I began to wonder why I was a loner. Was it due to the environment in which I had grown up or was it due to my parents?

My mother and father had parted when I was six years old and I never saw my father again. My only distinct recollection of him was of him walking out the front door and banging it behind him. For some reason which I never understood, my mother took my young brother and me from Brisbane, where we had all been living with my father, to Perth, which was about as far away as she could get from, not only her husband, but also from her other relatives and friends – perhaps that was her purpose. My mother had been a teacher in Brisbane before she married and about a year after we arrived in Perth she got a job as a teacher in the Western Australian Public School system.

Because my parents did not get divorced my mother (as a married woman) could only be employed as a temporary teacher and she was moved each year, from one school to another. Whenever she changed schools we changed our house. A lot of our furniture suited this nomadic life – wooden packing cases in a variety of sizes which served as wardrobes, cupboards and side tables when we were in a house and containers when we moved. Throughout my primary school years I went to and from school with my mother and had only limited contact outside the classroom with other children. We did not get to know the neighbours very well because we did not live near any other family for very long, and my mother had no time to spare from her teaching and housekeeping and my brother and I from the home study and household chores she imposed upon us, to cultivate friendships with the neighbours.

Soon after I passed from primary to secondary school, at the age of twelve, I was accepted for entry to the Naval College. It was my mother's idea that I should go into the navy. She told me it was a wonderful chance to see the world, to have an interesting job and be an important man. But I think she really saw it as an opportunity to get me completely off her hands, she was fonder of my brother than me.

I entered the Naval College as an apprehensive, secretive, watchful, inquisitive boy but adjusted faster to the highly regimented, strictly disciplined lifestyle that did some of the others who entered at the same time.

I have in the drawer of my sea-chest a photograph taken six months after I entered the college that reminds me of the beginning of my life in the Navy. It shows the twelve cadet-midshipmen in my year in their blue, double breasted, brass buttoned uniforms standing 'at ease' on the steps of the Cadets' mess. Each cadet stands with his feet the same distance apart, his arms stretched stiffly down, his closed hands pressed against his pants, his face expressionless, his head held rigidly upright and his officer's cap facing squarely to the front. Above the line of caps, in bold lettering on the face of the mess building, is the college motto *By obeying we learn to command.*

Because I came to the college with no experience of socialising with boys of my own age (or with any boys at all except my young brother) I carefully watched what the other boys did and listened to what they said to each other. I was more of an observer than a participant in most of the social activity of my colleagues.

The aim of the Naval College system of instruction and discipline seemed to be to produce officers who were interchangeable – each of them certain to react in much the same way in any particular circumstance pertaining to warships or the Navy. I accepted the system and succeeded in it, being near the top of my year when we graduated. To do that I had to get on quite well with the other cadets and the officers. I did, but remained emotionally detached from all of them, not particularly liking or disliking any of them.

It was much the same after a graduated and went to sea. I had occasional brushes with others, of course, but I generally hit it off quite well with my compeers, senior officers and the lower ranks but made no intimate friends.

The watchful, inquisitive approach I had adopted when I first came to the college developed into a strong and continuing interest in the everyday life – the friendships, quarrels, joys, frustrations and chicanery – of the people around me. As I grew older my known lack of intimates and empathy with others' affairs, seemed to encourage both men and women with whom I came in contact to talk freely to me about themselves, their friends, enemies and acquaintances while I remained reticent about myself.

The Naval way of life had appealed to me while I was at the College and after I graduated and went to sea I liked it more and more. I liked both the theoretical and practical side of the work. I liked the sea, its beauty, its restlessness and the challenges it constantly presented. I liked the precise, rhythmical marching and the stirring martial music of the ceremonial parades. I liked the clubbish, impersonal atmosphere of the wardroom messes in both the ships and shore establishments. I liked the many opportunities to play sport and I liked the wide range of social activities available to an 'unattached' naval officer. And since the war had come I liked the feeling I had of being well trained for the job in hand.

Ever since I had reached the age of puberty I had enjoyed the company of girls as a form of entertainment. They provided light-hearted interludes in the generally more serious male part of life. For quite a long while I had trouble satisfying my sexual desires. It was in England while on a gunnery course that I had my first sexual experiences; they were with a woman in her late twenties who was the wife of a senior officer. To become intimate with her I had to play a part in a romantic intrigue in which she took her part much more seriously than I did mine. Fortunately my return to Australia enabled me to break off the affair without too much drama. But I was determined not to get involved in any more such affairs.

My next sexual experience, in Sydney a year later, was a one night event in the back of a car after a dance. It was not very satisfactory. Soon after that I saw an advertisement for an escort service. When I contacted the service I found I could choose a place unlikely to be frequented by any of my acquaintances to 'entertain' the girl for a while and then take her to a room in a guest house recommended by the service. All the girls I 'escorted' during the next few years were presentable and by and large good sexual partners. With my active social life and the occasional use of the escort service I got what I wanted from women as companions and sexual partners but remained free of care and passion in my relations with them.

Recollections of my parents and the environment in which I had spent my boyhood and early manhood did not provide an answer to the question in my mind. My thoughts kept drifting back to Miller. I had not worked closely with a loner before. I wondered what had made him a loner, and such a silent a one; was it his speech defect? I decided to try and break through his taciturnity – I liked getting people to talk about themselves. If it did nothing else the attempt would occupy me, and hopefully Miller, during the long quiet periods of our watches together.

My next watch was in the afternoon and the Captain kept appearing on the bridge – perhaps just for the pleasure of being there. It was an afternoon typical of many that I can recall when it was a joy, even under wartime conditions, to be at sea off the New South Wales coast in the late summer – the bright sunshine, the fresh northeasterly breeze, the comfortable roll of the ship in a moderate swell and the view across the bluish-green, white topped waves to the gracefully curved golden beaches separated by rugged, brown, yellow and black steep sided cliffs and gently sloping rocky ledges.

With the Captain on the bridge, or nearby, I could not indulge in a personal conversation with Miller.

During the second middle watch we kept together I told Miller that a cadet in my year at the Naval College had been a *Tingara* boy and mentioned some of the things Power had told me about his year on the training ship. I asked Miller whether he had enjoyed his time on the *Tingara*. His response was simply, 'It wath alright'.

When I asked him whether he joined the *Tingara* because he was keen to go to sea he said he was 'puthhed' into becoming a *Tingara* boy by his grandmother. That enabled me to explain that it was my mother who had pushed me into becoming a cadet at the Naval College. I then talked about my experiences when learning seamanship and asked about his.

Miller responded haltingly at first by referring to the 'seamanship' he had to do as a waste of time – the scrubbing of decks with bucket of water and a stiff-bristled brush and the polishing of brass work. But after a while I was able to get him to talk about more interesting instruction in seamanship. Twice our conversation was interrupted by the examination of a ship but after each break he needed only the slightest encouragement from me to return to his seamanship experiences. Though he spoke slowly and tonelessly, he obviously was beginning to enjoy the reminiscing and he laughed a little when recalling his first attempts to heave the lead during a day the boys spent at sea on a destroyer – but said it was not a laughing matter at the time. Near the end of the watch we were able to commiserate with one another for having to learn to sail as member of a crew of a cumbersome, dipping-lug cutter – a very common naval teaching practice that was more likely to turn budding seamen (both officers and ratings) away from sailing than encourage them to them to learn the finer points of the art.

The next afternoon was sunny and the Captain once again hovered around the bridge but having broken the ice with Miller, I felt free to ask him one or two more personal questions and learned that he was a bachelor and had been outside the service for about eight years during the 1930s.

It was during the latter part of the last watch we kept together that Miller talked freely and openly about his life. I think that the remarkable break away from his usual reticence was brought about not

257

only by the relationship we had established during the previous watches but also by an incident which had occurred during the last watch.

When I first came on board the *Astra* and the Captain explained the examination duties to me he mentioned difficulties with what he called 'rogue' ships. The 'rogues' were some ships that normally plied between the Mediterranean or Middle East and Asian ports. A number of them arrived in South East Asian waters in February and early March 1942 and finding that the ports for which they had been bound had been captured by the Japanese, they fled to the east and south convinced that Japanese surface ships were pursuing them and Japanese submarines were lying in wait for them. It was during the examination of one of these ships that the incident occurred.

The night was very dark and heavy rain further reduced the visibility. Shortly before one o'clock the lookouts drew my attention to a ship only vaguely visible coming down from the north. I put on the examination lights and made towards it. I tried to contact it by W/T and a signal lamp but got no response. As we got nearer, I could make out sufficient of the ship through the rain to establish that it was large and steering a rather erratic course. As I could still get no response from my W/T and lamp signals I decided to get close enough to use the loudhailer. When I was nearly in a position to do that the ship made an alteration of course that instantly put the two ships in danger of collision.

I switched on my navigation lights – these were not used under wartime conditions but I thought it was necessary immediately to give the 'rogue' the clearest indication of my position and course.

Then, apparently, the rogue's captain, realising that he had put himself on a collision course with me, that there was very little room between us, that if we both tried to avoid the impending disaster the situation might become even more dangerous, blew four blasts on his fog horn – an international signal 'keep out of my way I cannot keep out of yours'. When I heard the signal I assumed that he intended to hold his new course and reduce the speed of his ship as much as possible, and I took action accordingly. My assumption seemed to be confirmed by another signal from him – three blasts on the fog horn, 'am going astern'.

It was a close shave. The big ship's bow, bearing down on us at considerable speed, was only a few yards away from *Astra*'s port quarter as I swung the examination ship, going full speed, around it. Then, with both ships still moving very fast, I had to pass right down the rogue's port side so close to the big ship that I could not move the *Astra* even a yard more away from it without smashing the *Astra*'s stern against the side of the rogue. Only Miller's very prompt and accurate carrying out of my orders and his ability to hold a steady course prevented us from being sunk.

When we were out of the dangerous situation and I had established communication I found that the rogue was originally bound for Batavia. The captain explained that he was steering a zig-zag course and constantly altering the zigs and zags to confuse Japanese submarines and that he was not familiar with examination lights. He also said that his W/T operator, who was also the only morse code reader on the ship, was ill. All of which was not a very satisfactory explanation of his dangerous behaviour. He did, however, apologise for nearly sinking us.

When I had cleared the ship I told Miller it was very fortunate for the crew sleeping peacefully down below that he had been at the wheel. For the first time in our acquaintance he smiled.

Soon afterwards there was a rapid change in the weather; the rain stopped, a westerly wind blew away the heavy clouds, the full moon shone brightly and the visibility became very good. I felt more relaxed and probably so did Miller. A personal conversation between us became possible for the first time during the watch we both knew would be our last together.

Miller seemed, once he had begun to talk, to need to, and his story came out in bursts, though still in an almost expressionless tone. It was triggered off by my asking why it was his grandmother who had pushed him onto the *Tingara*. I could see him screwing up his face for a moment before he said 'There wath no one elthe'. He went on to say his mother must have died when he was very young because his grandmother frequently told other people in his hearing (generally when she had too much to drink) that his father came down from the bush, dumped him, less than four years old, in her lap, and then 'the bastard' cleared out and since then had never been seen or heard of.

Miller said he and his grandmother had lived in a house in Redfern, renting two rooms and sharing the kitchen and bathroom with other tenants. There was a lot of quarrelling, drinking and rough, noisy parties in the house. The only other relative he ever heard of was his mother's sister who occasionally wrote to his grandmother. This 'Aunt Gerty' lived way out in the west of Queensland in a town called Longreach.

As Miller saw it, when his grandmother heard about the *Tingara* she seized the opportunity to get rid of an unwanted responsibility in a way which could be seen to bring credit to her, and she paraded Miller around Redfern telling everyone what she had achieved.

I was surprised both by the candour with which Miller spoke of his relationships and also his willingness – even eagerness – to continue to talk.

He went on to say that when he joined the *Tingara* he got a fair amount of 'chaffing' about his speech defect but after a while that died out. He considered he got on 'well enough' with the other boys. He did not get into fights with any of them (and he said fights were not uncommon) but he also did not form a close friendship with any. It was much the same he said after he went to sea. He 'got on' with members of his 'part of ship' and the crew generally but did not have any particular friends. He said alcohol did not 'turn him on' and when ashore he stayed away from the pubs around the port areas where his shipmates were likely to gather.

When I asked him what he did when he was ashore he first said, rather wryly, 'kept away from Redfern', which suggested he had no pleasant recollections of his boyhood there. After a pause he said he made his way to the suburbs in the various towns he landed in. When he mentioned the names of some of them I realised they were middle class districts. In these 'suburbs' he merely walked around looking at the houses and apartments wondering what it was like to live there. He said he often had a meal, or drank some coffee, in a local café, watched the people, tried to guess what they did for a living, whether they had families and how they got on with their husbands or wives and their children. Later on, he said, he took lessons at a driving school, got a driver's licence and, in some ports, hired a car and drove around the suburbs. He said he liked driving.

There were breaks in his reminiscences, some when I needed to turn the ship around at the end of each leg of our ocean track, others when Miller seemed to be considering what else he wanted to say. Fortunately, after we cleared the rogue no other ship required clearance until near the end of the watch.

Miller said he didn't enjoy being in the Navy, he just 'put up with it'. Both on the *Tingara* and after he went to sea he took each day as it came, worked steadily but, I gathered, not enthusiastically, at the various tasks he was given. By the time he was twenty-one he had been promoted to Able Seaman but he was not promoted further because, he believed, senior officers considered his speech defect might prevent him giving clear orders quickly in an emergency.

He said his sixteen years in the Navy had been forced on him and he resented it.

Now Miller seemed oblivious of his loquaciousness, talking sometimes even rapidly, though tonelessly.

He had left the Navy as soon as his time ran out. Unfortunately, that was just after the great depression started and because he had been locked away in the Navy since he was thirteen, he found himself completely ignorant about life outside. He had thought on leaving the service he could get a job without much trouble.

By hitching rides in motor and horse-drawn vehicles, jumping the rattler and walking, Miller moved around New South Wales and Victoria looking for work. Occasionally he got casual work but it was not until 1938 that he landed a regular job, working night shifts as a taxi driver – as he said he liked that, his voice brightened. But when the war broke out he was called up from the Naval Reserve for active service.

He was silent for a few minutes. Then, as a ship could be seen approaching from the East, he shrugged his shoulders and said, 'I don't thupothe thingth will be any better after the war'.

The last half hour of the watch was taken up with the clearance of two ships.

I left the *Astra* at nine o'clock that morning. In the launch travelling back to Rushcutter I thought about Miller. There were a lot of gaps in his reminiscences but it was clear that there were similarities between his childhood and youth and mine. However I had passed through those stages of my life without a speech defect, in much more pleasant and inspiring surroundings and with the opportunity to train for a career that I liked. We were both loners, but while Miller remained in great measure isolated from people even when living cheek-by-jowl with large numbers of them, I enjoyed socialising with a wide range of both men and women while managing to avoid any close attachments.

I wondered what Miller thought about during his long silences. I also wondered about his relations with women. He left me with the impression that he had no ties of any sort with any woman other than his grandmother. Was he celibate? Did he sometimes visit the brothels that operated so conspicuously in the vicinity of most of the ports? I thought fate had treated Miller unkindly in the past and was not likely to treat him any better in the future.

The *Fairfield* arrived in Sydney that afternoon. I joined it and soon forgot Miller and his reminiscences.

•

As Miller drove us through the city centre in the peak hour traffic twenty-five years after we had been on watch together, I recalled the impression of Miller I had formed in 1942. He seemed different now and I wondered whether the change had been brought about by his taxi work – I remembered it was a job which he had enjoyed before the war.

I did not want to ask him questions while he was driving in heavy traffic and my thoughts drifted away from him to my own situation, to what had happened to me in the intervening years. I had done very well, I had got to the rank of Rear Admiral and the position of Deputy Chief of Staff, the second highest position in the Australian Navy. I had left the service on reaching the retiring age six months before making the trip to Melbourne. Being a loner had probably helped my career. I was able to make quite objective decisions about promotions and appointments and, having no entanglements, was prepared to take up any appointment in any place and at short notice if required. I had continued to enjoy a wide range of social activities. My attitudes towards women and my relations with them had not really changed. Meeting them socially remained an entertaining diversion from the more serious matters even when my female companions were expressing views on public business, backbiting and speaking daggers, or more recently, thumping the drum of women's rights.

I had continued to use the escort service (which had remained in business although the management and the girls changed from time to time). When I was in my early fifties, one of the girls, whose name was Barbara, had made a strong impression on me. She was older than most of the others, probably about forty, an attractive looking woman with a good figure, a delightful sense of humour and a charming manner that seemed to please irresistibly. I began to ask specially for her and to arrange my use of the service to fit in with her availability. But she used her pleasant, amusing, smart talk as a barrier between us through which I could not penetrate. I could not tell what were her thoughts, her feelings. She had a calm, unconscious pride which enveloped her always, like an elegant cloak. I was unused to being thwarted, and particularly, so charmingly. For the first time in my life I got really annoyed with a woman and for over six months avoided her. When, once more, I asked for her I was told she had left the service. I tried every means I could hit upon to track her down but could not even find out her real name. She was gone, apparently forever.

Since I retired I have had plenty of social engagements and, on a regular basis, had done some work with a community welfare organisation but I seemed to be just filling in time. The contact I had with other people through my social engagements and welfare work did not satisfy me. I craved for something more. For the first time in my life I was feeling lonely.

•

We reached the freeway and Miller, turning towards me, said 'I was certain it would be you ath thoon ath I received the order to pick up Admiral Bedlow'.

I asked him whether he had been driving taxis ever since he was discharged from the Navy.

He laughed, 'You were a great one for questionth thir' and then told me he had only returned to taxi driving twelve months earlier when he had reached the age of sixty-five and retired from the Civil Service. He was doing taxi work, he said, to earn some extra money to help his daughter through university. His daughter was now sixteen, doing very well at high school and determined to become a doctor. He said he owned the taxi and only worked five shifts a week because he was too busy to do more. He employed drivers for the other shifts.

Miller seemed to have changed dramatically, not only was he cheerful, he was much more assured, talkative and busy. And he had a family.

When I told him I was pleased he had done so well and developed so many interests, he said it was all due to his wife Pat whom he had 'the good fortune' to meet when he was fifty years old.

Miller made much of his wife. He said she was a wonderful and loving person – eleven years younger than him – who, in addition to working five days as a typist, had, until two years before she met him, willingly looked after her widowed mother crippled with arthritis.

He went on to say that Pat, in her cheerful way had encouraged him to do all sorts of things – many of which, he said, someone like me would probably consider commonplace, but they were not that for him.

When I was with Miller on the *Astra* I had got the impression that he had no contact with women and didn't seem to desire any. Now I found he was married and had a family. My old curiosity was re-aroused. How had he become acquainted with Pat and got to know her well enough to propose to her? I asked him how they had met.

He said 'It wath in a marvellouth way, I will tell you about it'.

Miller's description of his marvellous encounter with Pat made a lasting impression on me and I will try to put it down exactly as I heard it.

Miller said 'Thoon after I wath dithcharged from the Navy I found that, ath an ex-thervitheman, I could get a job in the Federal Public Thervithe. I applied and wath appointed to a pothition of clerical athithtant in the Taxation Department in Melbourne. Though it wath fairly lowly paid and rather routine work, it thuited me.

'I boarded with an elderly couple living in Dennith, a thuburb about five miles north of the city. There wath a lot of overtime available in the Department and I worked three nighth every week. I didn't need the extra money – I put it in the bank – but working overtime wath ath good a way ath any to fill in the eveningth. When not at work I thpent my time reading detective thtorieth, helping my landlord in the garden, walking in Northcote park, which wath near my lodging, and on thaturday evength going to the movieth – I liked wethternth and muthicalth.

'Every working day I went to and from the city by train. There were about twenty people who each morning got aboard the thame train ath I did at Dennith thtation. Pat wath one of them. When I did not work overtime I often thaw her on the late afternoon train coming back to Dennith. In the last year or two before I met her I did occasionally thee her on the train that left the city at ten o'clock at night. I took little more notice of Pat than I did of the other paththengerth.

'While in the train I uthually read one of my detective storieth. It thaved me getting into converthationth. Many of the other paththengerth read either a book or a newthpaper; only a few of them thpoke to one another.

'One evening Pat and I were travelling home in the thame carriage on the ten o'clock train and it thtopped between Wethtgarth and Dennith. The latht of the other paththengerth mutht have got out at Wethtgarth. I put down my book and peered out of my window to thee why the train had thtopped. There wath nothing to thee. I turned away from my window and there wath Pat sitting oppothite me about three feet away and we were looking at one another.

'It wath for me an unexpected and uncomfortable thituation. I wanted to break away from it by picking up my book and tharting to read again but that theemed rude, tho I rather hethitatingly thaid "It altho happened latht week."

'For perhapth a thecond or two Pat continued to look at me and thaid nothing, then thhe thaid, mimicking me. "It ith a nuithance ithin't it?"

I had got uthed to occathional unpleathant remark, but I wath thhocked, appalled that thith pleathant looking woman thhould jutht thit there and amuthe herthelf at my expenthe.

'It muthh have thhown in my face becauthe thhe thaid, "Pleathe do not be upthet, I think we both have the thame trouble."

'Once again for a moment we remained thilently looking at one another, then we both began to laugh'.

•

Miller put me down at the entrance to the Ansett terminal. Flying back to Sydney thinking about what had happened to Miller and to me during the last twenty-five years and what lay ahead for each of us, I began to feel envious of Miller and his marvellous encounter.

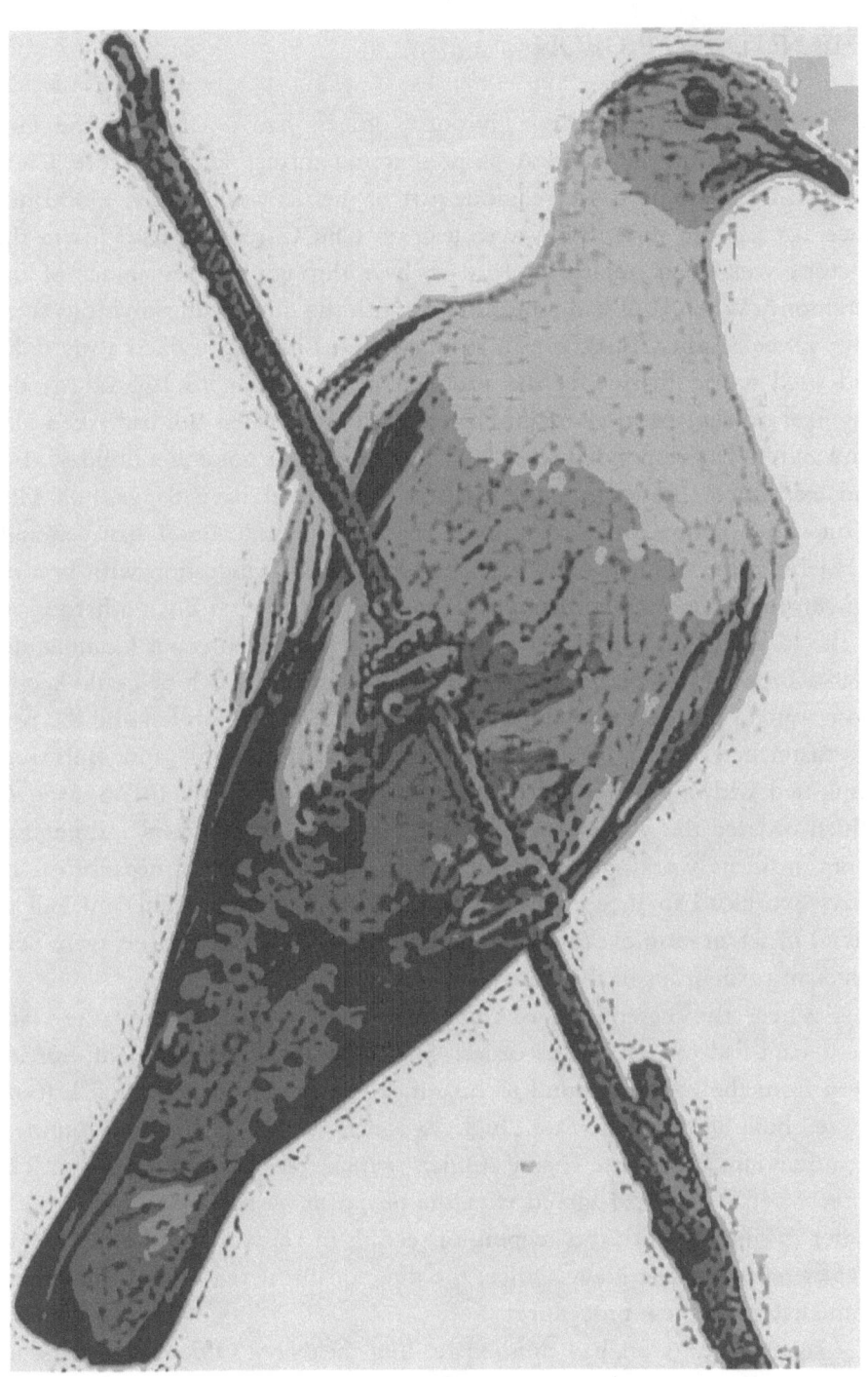

THE NUTMEG PIGEON

As soon as each of the three divisional officers had reported to the First Lieutenant that his division was 'all present and correct' and the padre, Clem Dine, had commenced the religious part of the daily ceremony, Doc Buck once again began surreptitiously to lean on Cliff Corey and Cliff found the doctor's weight an unpleasant load to bear through the remainder of the ceremony. When Cliff had remonstrated with the doctor after divisions were over a week earlier, Buck merely grinned sheepishly and walked away. Cliff had tried to rid himself of the problem by suggesting to Bill Edgar, the engineer officer, that they might change places but, when Bill had asked him why and he had responded with, 'Oh! A change is as good as a holiday', Bill had exclaimed, 'Jumping gauge glasses! We would have to get the First Lieutenant's permission, and I don't know about you, but I have enough problems with "number one" without getting into a discussion with him on a damn fool proposal like that'. Cliff was tempted to give Buck a hard blow in the ribs with his elbow but the First Lieutenant, Lieutenant Commander Merve Egan, always placed himself in a position from which he could keep a close watch on the three divisions of seamen fallen in on his left and the row of unattached officers fallen in on his right. Both Cliff and Bill were displeased with a decision by the Commanding Officer of HMAS *Melville* which ordered the writers working under Cliff and the stokers and engine-room artificers working under Bill not to attend 'divisions' because of the heavy workload in those 'parts of the ship' and ordered Cliff and Bill to attend to set an example to the 'ship's company'. The two officers were very reluctant participants in the daily parade.

When the ceremony of divisions was completed and the First Lieutenant had roared out the order, 'Ship's Company dismiss!' Cliff hurried away from the parade ground to his office – a typical five-roomed Darwin house built on seven foot high wooden stilts. There he found a memorandum from the Navy Office which pleased him greatly. The Director of Supply had agreed with the proposals he had made two months earlier to simplify both the keeping of records in Darwin and the sending of regular reports to the Navy Office; the director instructed him to implement immediately the new procedures.

By the time Cliff had finished reading the Navy Office memorandum Writer Williams had placed the customary cup of coffee on his table and as he sat sipping the coffee Cliff turned his thoughts back to the time when he had decided to enlist in the Navy.

Early in January 1941 he had met in George Street Sydney, David Campbell who, a few years earlier, had lectured to him in accountancy at the East Sydney Technical College. David was dressed in the uniform of a Lieutenant-Commander in the Royal Australian Naval Volunteer Reserve. He suggested to Cliff that he apply for a commission as a Paymaster Sub-Lieutenant in the RANVR saying, 'the "Pay" officer's responsibilities include ensuring that equipment, consumable stores, clothes, food and pay are supplied and accounted for. Without efficient "Pay" officers the Navy can't function. You are a dammed good accountant and could always see the shape of the wood as well as the trees. We need people like you'. Cliff agreed to think about the matter and get in touch with David later on. He had in fact been for several weeks pondering over the question of whether he should enlist in one of the armed services.

Cliff at the time was twenty-six years old, married, with a daughter Patricia aged seven months. Because of his deep involvement with family affairs, work and study Cliff had not given any serious consideration to the war and its gradually increasing impact on his life until late in 1940.

The members of his family in whose affairs Cliff was deeply involved included not only his wife and child but also his parents. Immediately after their marriage in 1912 Cliff's mother, Isobel, and father, Tom, migrated to Australia and a few weeks after landing in Melbourne, Tom got a job as a shop assistant in a large departmental store. He remained in that job until 1929 when the family, which by this time included their only child Cliff, moved to Sydney after receiving medical advice that the climate in Sydney was less likely than the climate in Melbourne to bring on the severe attacks of asthma to which Isobel was prone. In Sydney Tom once again found employment in a large departmental store but, when the economic depression began at the end of the year, he was retrenched and could not get any work throughout the 1930s. Tom's unemployment greatly dispirited both Cliff's parents and resulted in Tom developing a mental disorder from which he never fully recovered.

Cliff was fifteen when the family moved to Sydney and he lost contact with the boys and girls with whom he had grown up. In Sydney, in addition to working very hard at his studies, he worked long hours as a messenger for the local chemist. Consequently he had very little opportunity to make new friends of either sex. He was studying at a boys high school and his contact with girls of his own age was minimal.

Two months after his seventeenth birthday Cliff gained a good pass in the university matriculation examination and was appointed a clerk in the Federal Taxation Department. During the next nine years he improved his career prospects by qualifying as an accountant and undertaking a part-time course at the Sydney University for a Bachelor of Arts degree, and added to his responsibilities by marrying and begetting a child. His wife Marjorie had joined the Taxation Department as a typist at about the same time as Cliff had joined as a clerk. She was a pretty blonde girl with a shapely figure who lived not far from Cliff's home in Rockdale. The two formed an attachment when they met at a departmental social function and after that Cliff spent with Marjorie most of the very limited time he could spare from his work, his study and his efforts to brighten the lives of his parents. On week days Cliff and Marjorie often lunched together in the Domain and during week-ends walked along the foreshore of Botany Bay or swam in the Brighton-le-Sands baths. Occasionally they went into the city on a Saturday night to see a film. Cliff was attracted to Marjorie by her pretty face and good figure and also by her plain, unaffected view of life, her earnestness, her desire to be better informed about things going on around her and her reliance on him for an explanation whenever anything came to her notice which seemed beyond her comprehension. After he had been married to Marjorie for a while Cliff found she was much slower than he was in grasping mentally any complicated matter, but she always doggedly pressed him for explanations until she felt she fully understood the matter. The continued requests for explanations tried his patience. Also her limited imagination sometimes prevented her realising that somebody's point of view could be vastly different from her own and in these circumstances the remarks she made, or action she took, although well meant, could lack sensibility.

A few days after the conversation in George Street, Cliff contacted David Campbell and as a result he received a commission as a Paymaster Sub-Lieutenant in February 1941. He did a general training course at the Flinders Naval Base followed by six weeks work at the Navy Office in Melbourne before he was appointed to HMAS *Brisbane*, an old light cruiser built during World War 1. He served in the *Brisbane* for twelve months and during that time the ship operated in the Indian and Pacific Oceans escorting convoys and searching for German raiders disguised as merchant ships. There were a number of alarms and many hours spent closed up at action stations, but no action. In May 1942 he was promoted to lieutenant and appointed to HMAS *Melville*, the Darwin naval base, in charge of supply and accounts for the 'ship's company'.

On his desk in the Darwin office Cliff had a photograph of Marjorie. As he sipped his coffee he felt a loving closeness to her. He recalled the many happy hours they had spent together, their private jokes, their joyous play with Patricia; he heard the tunes she hummed and the snatches of songs she sang when doing the household chores, he saw her at work in the garden where she turned the drab area around the house they rented in Coogee into a colourful but very irregular display of flowers and shrubs.

Cliff's reverie was interrupted by a telephone call from the Commanding Officer of HMAS *Melville*, Captain Edward Morris. Cliff had never received such a call before, and the Captain had only spoken to him in person on two occasions. Captain Morris was a Royal Navy Officer who emigrated to Australia when he retired and volunteered for service with the RAN when war was declared. He applied very strictly the naval precept that a commanding officer should avoid familiarity with all members of his ship's company. The purpose of the present call was a pleasant one; it was to compliment Cliff on the work he had done to improve the keeping and reporting of the 'ship's' accounts.

The next day at divisions Doc Buck began to lean on Cliff as soon as the religious part of the ceremony began and he maintained his leaning posture throughout the singing of the hymn. Just after prayers had commenced the Yeoman of Signals walked onto the parade ground and gave a signal to Merve Egan. After reading it the First Lieutenant strode off in the direction of Naval Headquarters. As soon as he was safely out of sight Cliff, with his elbow, gave the Doc a hard hit in the ribs. The Doc grunted, hastily retreated three or four yards behind the line of officers and then charged into the back of the engineer officer. The force of the blow propelled Bill Edgar forward into the arms of Clem Dine, who, having finished the religious service, had turned round ready to resume his place in the line of officers.

The ship's company was delighted to see a particularly pious padre and a publicly proclaimed atheist in a warm embrace on the parade ground. Doc Buck, apparently satisfied that by his action he had indicated his dislike of being hit in the ribs, walked off towards the hospital. When Bill Edgar and Clem Dine had disentangled themselves and returned to their correct positions in the parade the senior divisional officer gave the order, 'Ship's Company dismiss!'

Cliff, pleased that he had been able to strike a blow for the freedom of the individual, hurried away to his office, his coffee and his work. He had arranged to speak to Surgeon Lieutenant Commander Horace Buckingham at ten o'clock about the new accounting procedures. When he entered the main hall of the hospital he saw Horace on the other side of it talking to Chief Sick Bay Attendant Martin and was struck by the contrast in the physique of the two men. Martin was a well-built man over six feet in height, with broad shoulders, a deep chest, strong legs and arms, a round rosy face and thick wavy black hair. Horace was short, not more than five foot three or four, with a slim body, thin bandy legs, a long pallid face, large ears, thin brownish grey hair and a wispy brownish grey beard which grew mainly on his chin.

Horace sang out, 'Come along purser, I am just about ready for you' and led Cliff to his surgery. Warrant Officer Blain, the captain of a navy tug, was sitting alongside the table in the surgery and as he sat down Horace said to him, 'I think you have got dengue fever'. Doc Buck who was looking in through the open window guffawed loudly. Both the patient and the surgeon looked around to see if the Doc was going to offer a second opinion. He didn't; but Horace modified his diagnosis but saying, 'It might be the flu; we will soon find out I am going to put you in bed'. He rang his bell and when sick bay attendant Jones appeared, said, 'Admit Warrant Officer Blain'.

After the patient and the attendant had left Cliff came forward, sat down alongside the desk and started to get some papers out of his brief case. While he was doing that Horace opened the top drawer of the desk, pulled out a large carrot, walked over to the window and gave it to Doc Buck. He watched the Doc eat the carrot then pulled down the window and stood for a while exchanging grimaces with the doctor through the glass.

At Cliff's request Chief Sick Bay Attendant Martin and the hospital storeman, Petty Officer Weldon, were present during the first half hour of the discussion. After they left Horace was called away to deal with an emergency in the hospital. Cliff agreed to wait awhile and he walked over to the window to watch Doc Buck eating grass alongside the edge of the road. He recalled the first day that the donkey, which had appeared unexpectedly and mysteriously in the town, walked on to the parade ground and occupied the position at the end of the officers' line which was officially allocated to Surgeon Lieutenant Commander Buckingham. Horace had a special dispensation from the Captain under which he could be absent from divisions if his services were required urgently at the hospital. Many matters demanding

Horace's urgent attention apparently arose between eight and nine in the morning because he rarely attended divisions.

After his first appearance the donkey came to divisions with commendable regularity and always stood in the Surgeon Lieutenant Commander's position. The animal resembled Horace in many respects. He was short, perhaps a few inches shorter than Horace, he had thin bandy legs, large ears, a long face, thin greyish hair and a wispy brownish-grey beard growing from his chin.

Clem Dine considered that the donkey's body did not contain a soul that could be saved and that its presence at divisions distracted the attention of members of the ship's company when their minds should be concentrated on religious matters. He asked Merve Egan if action could be taken to prevent the animal from coming to divisions. The First Lieutenant said that both he and the Captain considered that the donkey was well behaved and provided a diversion for the seamen who had very little to brighten their lives while in Darwin. 'Also', the First Lieutenant added, 'the Captain has the normal English gentleman's fondness for horses and dogs and in the absence of any horses in Darwin all his love of equine animals is bestowed on the donkey'.

Clem's attempt to keep the donkey away from divisions was hard to understand because the animal seemed to be of a religious turn of mind. He rarely attended the first part of divisions which involved some platoon drill and officers' inspection but arrived in time for the prayers and hymn singing. During prayers he generally bowed his head in submissive respect for the almighty and during the singing of hymns made many valiant attempts to join in with the rest of the ship's company but had some difficulty in getting the correct intonation.

The stand-in for Surgeon Lieutenant Commander Buckingham was given the name of Doctor Buck not only because he occupied Horace's position in the line of unattached officers, generally remained in the vicinity of the hospital (where Horace frequently fed him on such delicacies as carrots and Chinese lettuce), and looked like Horace but also because of his behaviour during air raids.

Doctor Buck could not fit into a slit trench and when the sirens were sounding obstinately resisted all attempts to get him into a sand-bagged area. Consequently he was always in the open when an air raid was in progress. While the bombs fell and the ack-ack guns fired Buck aimed fierce kicks in the direction of the Japanese planes. The view was widely held that if the Japanese planes ever came down low enough the doctor would create widespread destruction amongst them. The Kittyhawk fighters which took off from RAAF strips along the Stuart Highway never seemed to have much effect on the bombers and many of the ship's company placed their faith in the Doc in the event of a low level attack. However, when such an attack did come – just after the Kittyhawks were replaced with Spitfires – Buck forgot which side he was on and while the Zeros rushed over the town with their canons and machine guns firing he charged into the sandbagged area in which the telephone switchboard was located and with two well-aimed kicks put all the telephones out of action. When the matter was discussed after the raid the Captain considered that, in the heat of the moment, anyone might make the sort of error Buck had made.

Cliff finished his discussions at the hospital just before noon. On his way back to the office he caught a glimpse of a dog scurrying past the hospital boiler house. This surprised him because no dogs had been seen in the town for many months. Lots of dogs were left behind when the civilians hurriedly evacuated the town after the first air raid. During the subsequent air raids the dogs, greatly agitated by the sirens blowing, ack-ack guns firing and bombs bursting, leapt into the nearest slit trench and soon discovered that biting any humans they found there relieved their nervous tension and gained them more space in the trench. There were many calls for drastic action against the dogs. The Captain's strongly expressed love of the *Canis familiaris* species gave them protection from any official action but one by one the dogs began to disappear. Soon after each dog dematerialised there was more than the regulation amount of meat in the stew in the seamen's mess. The cook in that mess was a man of Yugoslav origin who came to Australia in the 1920s and learnt his trade cooking at miners' camps to the north east of Kalgoorlie. In that part of the country anything that moved and wore no clothes soon found its way into the cooking pot. The seamen enjoyed the dietary supplement although the eating of it was often accompanied by remarks such as, 'Take care, that's the big Boxer bastard and he is bloody likely to bite a large piece out of your intestines on the way through'.

The Captain soon noticed the diminution of the dogs and ordered the First Lieutenant to conduct an inquiry. The young seamen with the most innocent-looking faces and the most plausible sounding tongues came forward and said that they had seen soldiers in the unoccupied parts of the town carrying what appeared to be large meaty bones and therefore it was likely that the dogs had been lured away to help the soldiers kill kangaroos, round up buffaloes, look for wombats or whatever it was the thousands of soldiers were doing out there in the bush. When the Captain received the First Lieutenant's report he sent off a strongly worded signal to the General Officer Commanding at the Army Headquarters Adelaide River. The GOC sent an equally strong reply pointing out that the town was built on a peninsula, that the narrow neck connecting it to the rest of the northern territory was heavily mined and that a company of military police guarded the only track through the minefield; consequently, the GOC said, no soldiers could get into the town with or without large meaty bones. In his next signal the Captain said that whenever the Navy were showing a rather better than usual film in the open recreation area on a Saturday night many soldiers could be seen sitting on the roofs of nearby houses watching the film so it was nonsense to say that they could not get through the minefields. The exchange of signals between the senior officers of the two fighting services went on for some time. Copies of the signals were secretly circulated in the seamen's mess as a sort of literary supplement to the regular official Navy news-sheet. Despite the counter measures taken by the First Lieutenant, which included small squads of seamen regularly patrolling the unoccupied parts of the town, the dogs continued to disappear and eventually not one could be found in the Darwin area.

Although Cliff spent the next few days constantly moving around the base trying to impart a clear understanding of the new accounting procedures amongst all concerned in the various 'parts of the ship' he did not see again the dog which had so unaccountably appeared near the hospital boiler house. But a dog in the town was no longer likely to create any difficulty because it was nearly six months since the last air raid and no further raids were expected.

On the following Saturday the Captain was to be the guest of the Wardroom Officers' Mess. Early that day a momentous signal from the Navy

Office arrived. It said that all the male car drivers, writers and some of the W/T operators were to be replaced by Wrans and that the Darwin hospital was to be upgraded, turned into a combined services establishment and manned mainly by female service personnel.

In the afternoon a meeting of senior officers was held. Considerable consternation was expressed. During the last one and a half years much time and effort had been spent preparing for an invasion by Japanese men and now they were faced with an invasion by Australian women. This was not the way faithful followers of naval practices expected to be treated.

The Captain stayed longer than usual in the Wardroom after dinner that night and the port and sherry decanters circulated more frequently. The discussion in the latter part of the evening was concentrated on the impending arrival of the women. Most of the junior officers did not share the dismay of the senior officers but each felt that this was not the occasion on which he should express his views on the matter. The Captain said he was thoroughly familiar with every paragraph of the King's Regulations and Admiralty Instructions and there was nothing in the comprehensive directions to naval officers which provided for the situation in which they now found themselves. The First Lieutenant, while not claiming to have anything like the Captain's detailed knowledge of the regulations and instructions, supported his commanding officer's appraisal of the situation and said, 'We will have to wrestle with this difficult problem without the appropriate guidance from the highest naval authorities'. A few days after the dinner, the 'appropriate guidance' arrived in the form of a flood of regulations and instructions from the Navy Office.

The first contingent of women was flown in three weeks later. It included eight writers and twelve drivers as well as nurses and sisters. The writers and drivers were under the charge of a Wran officer named Kathleen Watson. Kathleen was a thirty-year-old Englishwoman, the wife of the senior executive in Australia of an international oil company. She was very attractive in appearance and demeanour but had unusual colouring for an Englishwoman, very black hair and a lovely white skin – no delicate pink cheeks. Kathleen messed with the hospital sisters and was appointed liaison officer between all the female members of the ship's company and Cliff's department.

Cliff arranged for Kathleen to meet him in his office once a week to discuss ongoing matters of supply and accounts. He saw her at other times in various parts of the base but never attempted to get into a conversation with her. However, the way in which the official matters were discussed at the weekly meetings gradually changed. Kathleen introduced a little quiet humour into her remarks and Cliff enjoyed making a return in kind.

Throughout his time in Darwin, Cliff went for long walks whenever he had an opportunity, sometimes with one or more other officers but often on his own. His favourite walks were in the unkempt, bomb damaged, botanical garden and he became interested in the great variety of birds he found there. Petty Officer writer Walter Dunn had a book about Australian birds and Cliff, with the aid of the book, was able to identify a number of the birds he saw. One Saturday afternoon, about six weeks after the women arrived in Darwin, Cliff approached the botanical garden from Myilly beach and after entering it unexpectedly came upon Kathleen standing watching a bird paddling in the small lagoon. He was very surprised to see Kathleen in such a place on her own. From gossip in the Wardroom mess he was aware that her company was in great demand not only from naval officers serving in HMAS *Melville* and in ships in the harbour but also from army and air force officers, stationed in various establishments along the Stuart highway, who now frequently visited Darwin. He would have passed her by after saying 'Good afternoon' but she stopped him and asked if he knew the name of the bird in the lagoon. He did; it was a grey-tailed tatler. This led to a discussion about other birds she had seen earlier in the afternoon and a rather amusing attempt to identify some of them. They walked through the garden trying to find a bird whose strange appearance had particularly perplexed Kathleen; they ended up spending the afternoon together and on their way back to Myilly Point agreed to go for another walk the next day.

Cliff expected that Kathleen would regard her week-end association with him as an ephemeral affair and did not look forward to any further fellowship of that kind with her. He was mistaken. At their next regular official meeting she asked whether they could go for another walk during the following weekend.

Cliff had never contemplated having with any woman the rapport he soon had with Kathleen. She was straightforward and uninhibited, knowledgeable on many matters, very quick at seeing a point, a lucid speaker and an intelligent listener. She had a sense of fun similar to his. Each of them could refer to some of the things the other said or did mockingly but affectionately. Despite the harmony of their relationship, however, Cliff remained a bit bewildered as to why she had, as it were, plumped for him as a companion when there were so many men seeking her company who were more handsome, vigorous, important, urbane, learned and covered with glory as a result of their wartime exploits.

Whenever they were both free of official duties they went for a walk whether the sun shone or the rain fell. Cliff enjoyed all these walks but it was the one during which they first saw the nutmeg pigeon that remained most vividly in his memory for many years afterwards. After lunch on a Sunday they set out to walk around Fanny Bay to East Point and return to Myilly Point by the same route – a walk of about twelve kilometres. There was not likely to be anyone else on the beaches because the sea wasps which had come into the harbour at the beginning of the 'Wet' still infested the water and made it too dangerous for swimming.

When they left Myilly Point the tide was out, the waves flopped lazily onto the sand and nothing seemed to move except the tiny sand pipers who constantly ran from one place to another to peck at specks of food. Cliff and Kathleen ambled along talking intermittently of many things but, possibly because they had attended a church service in the morning, they drifted into a discussion of religion. Neither of them could accept as divine any being worshipped by the followers of any religion of which they had some knowledge; neither of them could comprehend what they really were other than a composition of chemicals; they speculated about the purpose, if any, in each of them spending (hopefully) about seventy years in their present form as a part of the planetary system.

By the time they started on the return journey from East Point the thirty-foot tide was racing in and coming with it were several schools of fish. From time to time they stopped to watch the flocks of seagulls attacking the fish from above the surface of the sea and the porpoises breaking out of waves to take breath while attacking the fish from below. When they drew level with the seaward side of the botanical garden they turned inland, entered the garden and sat down on the trunk of a fallen tree. To their left wild nutmeg and quondong trees cast long dark shadows across a patch of grass. To their right little lilac crested wrens, chasing insects, moved swiftly in and out of a clump of acacia trees adorned with yellow tipped buds. In front of them two large butterflies flew slowly in a circle and with the bright sunshine on their translucent bluish–green wings they were as soft and light and colourful as flying flowers. A white bird with flashes of black on its tail and wings descended quickly through a gap in the trees, flew past the butterflies and settled on the stump of a dead tree only about three or four yards from Cliff and Kathleen. It stood there for a while looking very beautiful with its contrasting colours, shapeliness and well balanced posture; then it took off and flew inland.

On the inside of the cover of Walter Dunn's book of Australian birds was a full page picture of a nutmeg pigeon. Cliff had looked at the picture on many occasions and admired the striking contrast in the pigeon's colouring and the sense of dignity in its stance. He was therefore readily able to recognise the bird when he saw it in the garden.

After the nutmeg pigeon flew away Cliff and Kathleen returned to the beach. They walked leisurely, stopping frequently not only to watch the seagulls and porpoises but also to look back along the beach at the changing shapes the constantly moving rays of light from the slowly setting sun formed on a rugged rocky outcrop that jutted out into the sea. The only sounds to be heard were the shrill cries of the seagulls feeding and the ceaseless grumble of the waves breaking. They felt themselves to be an integral part of the lovely evening and when the sun reached the western horizon it seemed to pause for a moment just to watch them, rapt in an enchanting contentedness, take their last few steps along the beach and reach the path that wound its winsome way through the flowering shrubs to the top of Myilly Point.

Three days later a signal arrived from the Navy Office appointing Paymaster Lieutenant Barry Jones to Cliff's position in HMAS *Melville* and instructing Cliff, after he had handed over to Jones and taken three weeks leave, to proceed to Port Moresby. A signal the next day from HMAS *Rushcutter* advised that Jones would arrive in Darwin in a fortnight's time.

During the next two weeks Cliff and Kathleen went for three more walks in the botanical garden. On the first of these they saw the nutmeg pigeon again. It was feeding on the berries of a quandong tree and flew off as they approached the tree. Cliff considered that the beautiful colouring of the bird and its poise had a similarity to some of Kathleen's distinctive qualities and he began to refer to her as the nugmeg pigeon. She regarded the nickname as a compliment.

Jones arrived, and with his arrival the clear and forceful recognition that their separation was inevitable and imminent. Their encounter seemed unbelievably brief and the charm of it something they would never forget.

They agreed to keep in touch, but only by exchanging cards at Christmas each year.

At the end of 1944 Cliff was still in Port Moresby and Kathleen was still in Darwin and the Christmas cards they sent each other were purchased in the armed services canteens.

In May 1945 Kathleen wrote to Cliff saying that her husband had been appointed to a senior position in the Company's headquarters in London and that after obtaining her discharge from the Navy she had been flown to England by the RAF. She gave Cliff her address in London.

In October Cliff advised Kathleen that he had been demobilized and had returned to the Taxation Department and his home in Coogee. Early in December Cliff purchased a folded sheet of cartridge paper. On the outside he drew in Indian ink a picture of a nutmeg pigeon and on the inside he printed the usual seasonal greetings. Each year after that he sent to Kathleen a Christmas card on which he had drawn a picture of a nutmeg pigeon.

TRAVELLERS' TALES

A JOURNEY AROUND THE WORLD

Six weeks after my thirteenth birthday I became a cadet-midshipman at the Royal Australian Naval College – the only Western Australian among the twelve boys selected that year. The journey by train between my home in Perth and the Naval College at Jervis Bay, which I made four times each year, took five days and five nights and involved seven changes of train. In December 1925 I 'passed out' from the college, was promoted to Midshipman and sent on home leave two days ahead of the rest of the cadets because I had to join a ship in Sydney on 4th January 1926 and, even with the extra two days leave, would be in Perth for less than one week.

On the Sydney to Albury section of my journey home I shared a sleeping compartment with an elderly man who introduced himself as 'Smith' and said he was going to Kalgoorlie. He had an English upper class accent with which I was familiar because all the officers at the College had a similar accent – they were Englishmen on loan from the Royal Navy.

When I told him my name he immediately asked, 'Did your grandfather live in Notts?' When I replied, 'No, in Ireland', he said 'I asked because your name is unusual and the only McCurdy I have previously met lived in Notts. When I was twenty-one I made a journey around the world to try and get some information needed to help him. He was in serious trouble'.

Nothing more was said about the journey around the world that night or the next morning when Smith and I shared, with four other men, a compartment in the train between Albury and Melbourne. As we were leaving the train at Spencer Street station Smith said to me, 'We will probably see each other again tonight'.

I passed the time in Melbourne in the usual way – taking a trip on a cable tram, spending in a restaurant in Collins Street the cash allowance for lunch which the Navy provided and walking in the parks on the edge of the city. Throughout the day Smith's reference to his journey around the world floated in and out of my mind. I wondered what sort of trouble the McCurdy living in Notts had been in, what countries Smith had visited, what he had done in each of them and whether he had got the required information.

When I boarded the Melbourne to Adelaide train I found Smith and I were once again sharing a compartment – that was not unusual, passengers travelling all the way from Sydney to Perth often shared a sleeping compartment in each of the trains with the same fellow passenger. After we had settled in I asked Smith if he would tell me about his trip around the world to help my namesake.

He smiled and said, 'Old men's tales usually bore young men but if you are really interested I will try and recall what happened. You must bear in mind that it all occurred fifty years ago'. He paused then said, 'It will take quite a while because I will have to explain how the need for the journey arose – but we both will have time on our hands during the next few days'.

It was actually during the nights not the days that Smith talked to me. We were both too busy during the days. Perhaps I should explain why that was so.

There were on the train two boys and three girls, all of about my own age, who lived in Western Australia but were students at private schools in Melbourne for the last two years of their secondary education. None of my other journeys to or from Perth had coincided with one of theirs. We first got together on the narrow gauge train between Peterborough and Port Augusta. Every carriage of that train had an open platform at each end and we stood on one of these alongside the large waterbag (with an enamel mug attached to it by a long cord) provided by the caring railway authority to relieve the thirst of passengers. On the rocking platform the six of us chatted while the train for the first three hours – with the driver blowing many a cock-a-doodle-doo to brighten the lives of the farmers – meandered through the wheat fields of the northern plateau and then, to all appearances in a much more serious mood and with a great deal of puffing and blowing, struggled up and down the sparsely vegetated, rugged, rocky hills of the Flinders Ranges. A stop was made at every station – seemingly to let the train crew and the station staff engage in a leisurely conversation. At each of these stops the other two boys and I got down onto the ground (there were no platforms) to stretch our legs and when the train started to move again climbed back on board in a rather nonchalant manner to impress the girls.

In the much more luxurious 'trans-continental' train between Port Augusta and Kalgoorlie we got together in the lounge car or one of the sleeping compartments. At each of the long stops when water and coal for the locomotive were picked up, the six of us spent the time talking to the families of railway workers we had met on previous journeys. At one of the stations – I think it was Deakin – the 'tea and sugar' train was standing on the loop line. Some of the locals, who had postponed their shopping, showed us through the mobile shopping centre with its wide range of merchandise and services; an outing which the girls seemed to find particularly interesting.

Late each afternoon while the girls were changing for dinner the two boys and I spent about one hour in the habitat of the cigar and pipe smokers – the parlour car right at the rear of the train – mainly because my newly-found friends liked to smoke cigarettes in that very adult setting.

Smith, who like most of the other passengers had dozed off in his seat during the hot afternoon journey from Peterborough to Port Augusta, was more lively on the trans-continental train. He played bridge in the lounge car each morning, had a short nap in the sleeping compartment after lunch, then went to the parlour car where he and a group of men spent their time talking, apparently about business matters.

Neither Smith nor I ranked our singing ability highly and each evening when, an hour or two after dinner, the vocalists, aided by a piano-playing passenger, were going full blast, the two of us quietly left the lounge car and went to the sleeping compartment so that Smith could tell me more about his voyage around the world.

Smith was a fairly plain looking man but had a pleasant manner and a particularly attractive smile. His story interested me greatly at the time and most of what he said still lingers in my memory nearly seventy years later. I would not like it to be lost and have decided to write it down before I pass on.

•

Smith's story.

In 1875 I turned twenty-one, inherited considerable property and came down from Oxford. I was at a loose end without any idea of what to do with my life. My Uncle Jack, a London solicitor and my guardian, suggested that I go to the colonies to try and get some information needed to help a client of his named McCurdy who was in serious trouble.

Before McCurdy got into trouble all that my uncle knew about his life prior to his arrival in London was that he had been a drover in New South Wales, then a prospector, and finally the owner of a gold mine in Victoria. My uncle said that when he first saw McCurdy he was a relatively young man, probably in his middle thirties, tall, well-built, good looking with plenty of black, wavy hair. (Perhaps I should mention my uncle had barely a hair upon his head.)

Uncle Jack specialised in commercial activities and McCurdy came to him for assistance in investing his (McCurdy's) capital and in finding a home. He wanted an elaborate one – a landed estate with an attractive manor house, good stables and well established, tenanted farms, all in a district where there was a competent hunt club. My uncle found such a home in Notts, not very far from the main city in the county, Nottingham, through the good offices of an old friend of his, Wilson, a solicitor in Tonborough a small town very close to the estate.

A family named Somers had owned the estate for nearly two hundred years but the last member of the family to live in the Manor House (known as The Pillars), a compulsive gambler and an alcoholic, had been forced to sell the whole estate to pay off his debts and obtain a small income while he continued to live in Italy. Fortunately for the alcoholic owner and his creditors the estate was not entailed.

Because my uncle had to go down to The Pillars from time to time to discuss investment matters with his client and after each discussion spent a day or two with his old friend Wilson, he (my uncle) became well informed about McCurdy's life in Notts.

On arrival in the county McCurdy was not made welcome by the other landed gentry. When they heard that the new owner of The Pillars was a colonial with an unpleasant cockney-like accent who had made a fortune mining gold in Victoria, they decided not to call upon him.

However, when the fox-hunting season started McCurdy turned up at a meeting of the local hunt club, introduced himself to the Master and told him he was the new owner of The Pillars. The Master, named Duren but generally referred to by his friends as 'the Squire', was a widower whose whole life was bound up with horses and hunting. He judged every man by the horses he owned and the way he rode. He was impressed by McCurdy's horse and his seat and he invited him to join the hunt. Being hard of hearing the squire always talked very loudly and the invitation was heard by the group of huntsmen and huntswomen and all the onlookers who had gathered to see the start of the hunt.

McCurdy was a very good horseman and a bold one. He was that day one of the small group of huntsmen first in at the death. The squire, also a member of the group, shouted across to him, 'An excellent run, Sir! You took both Hardy's hedge and Simpson's gate. Very few members are prepared to take either of them. We are pleased to have so daring a rider among us, will you join the club, Sir?'

McCurdy did join the club.

On the second hunt McCurdy was once again among the first in at the death. The squire, much impressed, said, 'I usually have a few friends to dine with me after the hunt. Would you care to join us?'

McCurdy willingly accepted the invitation. The same invitation was extended to him after each hunt. The squire's dinners were purely male affairs. The small group who regularly attended them found McCurdy a very pleasant companion. He drank rather less than the others but carried that off quite well. He told interesting and amusing stories and listened attentively to others' stories. When they were in a roistering mood he could sing along with the best of them. He was genuinely interested in learning how other landowners ran their properties and several of the squire's guests liked to talk shop.

Before long he was dining in the manor houses of the squire's friends and meeting their wives. Then, landed gentry other than the squire's friends called upon him — especially men with several daughters of marriageable age and an anxious wife. Gradually McCurdy's social circle widened not only amongst the landed gentry but also outside that high-nosed group. He invited to The Pillars the leading townspeople (which included my uncle's friend Wilson) and their wives and some of the well-to-do tenant farmers and their wives.

McCurdy did not cut himself off completely from Victorian affairs while living in England. He had copies of the Melbourne *Age* daily paper sent to him in batches and from reading them got some idea of what was happening to the people he knew in the colony. It did not make him want to return to Victoria. He had enjoyed his life in England from the beginning and that enjoyment had been greatly increased as a result of his admission to the fox-hunting club. He had found the sport exhilarating and it had led not only (through the Master's invitations to dinner) to his social acceptance by many of the landed gentry but also to his friendship with Marjorie Harrison.

Marjorie, a very good and bold rider, was the only daughter of Sir Henry Harrison, Bart, who owned the largest estates in the county and whose family had for many generations been regarded as pre-eminent among the local landed gentry. Sir Henry kept a good stable but was 'too busy' to hunt himself. It was legal matters that kept Sir Henry busy. He sat on the bench in Nottingham much more often than any other magistrate. He attended all the periodical sittings of the assize in Nottingham and was very friendly with the judge on the circuit – his honour spent at least one weekend at the baronet's manor house whenever he was in the county. Sir Henry's sons did not make much use of the horses in his stable; his eldest son lived on another property twenty miles away from the main family estate; his younger sons were rarely at home. One was in the Indian Civil Service, the other up at Cambridge. Consequently Marjorie had plenty of excellent horses to ride and, being an out-of-doors person, made good use of them, not only for hunting. Much to her mother's chagrin she would not take part in the normal female social activities. Animal husbandry and farming practices were what interested her and she rode around the family estate, sometimes with the steward but often on her own, to see what was being done and to talk to the farmers. She attended the markets in the district and was quite a competent judge of stock and cereals.

It was inevitable that Marjorie and McCurdy should be attracted to one another; both were fond of horses and daring riders; both were good-looking, outgoing and good company. Before long they discovered they had something else in common, a keen interest in all aspects of farming. Within a few months they were riding together not only to the hunt but also to look at farms, attend local markets and see something of the picturesque countryside.

Lady Harrison soon heard that McCurdy had become Marjorie's constant companion. When she failed to get Marjorie to desist from her outings with McCurdy the baronet was alerted and issued an edict that she should not be with McCurdy except during the hunt. The edict was not obeyed. Instead McCurdy called upon Sir Henry to ask for his daughter in marriage. Sir Henry was astounded; he refused to consider such a marriage.

A month later, Marjorie eloped. She and McCurdy were married at Gretna Green. Sir Henry, greatly enraged, announced that none of his family would have anything to do with her; that she was an outcast from respectable society.

One or two of the landed gentry families who had visited The Pillars when McCurdy was a bachelor declined an invitation after he married. But within a few months the McCurdys had established a reputation as good hosts and their social circle gradually widened beyond that enjoyed by McCurdy as a bachelor.

In a copy of *The Age* printed four months after his wedding McCurdy was very surprised to see an article reporting his wedding under the heading 'Ex-Melburnian marries English socialite'. The article gave an exaggerated account of the luxury living he and his wife enjoyed at The Pillars and the 'very romantic' circumstances in which he and Marjorie were married against her father's wishes. McCurdy wondered who had provided the information on which the article was based.

One morning ten weeks after the second anniversary of the McCurdy's wedding, a man who gave his name as Burke and a woman arrived at The Pillars and asked to see Mr McCurdy. McCurdy told the butler to show them in. Later the butler, when questioned, said that when he showed the two visitors into the study McCurdy received them with a smile and a handshake. The butler also said when about quarter of an hour later he responded to a ring on the study bell McCurdy, obviously very annoyed, told him to show the man and woman out and never again admit them.

Soon after his unwelcome guests had left, McCurdy sent a telegram to my uncle asking him to come down to The Pillars at the earliest possible moment. Surprised at getting such an urgent call, my uncle came down on the afternoon train.

When my uncle arrived at The Pillars and was shown into the study he found both McCurdy and his wife there looking much more sombre than he had ever seen them before.

McCurdy told him that a man named Pat Burke and a woman named Mary Brines had come to the house that morning and tried to extort a large sum of money from him under a threat of exposing a 'secret' marriage between him and Brines. They produced what they claimed was a photograph of the marriage certificate and asserted that the original was in Brines' possession.

McCurdy said the two were scoundrels who knew perfectly well that there had been no such marriage. He then explained his connection with both the visitors.

(Smith paused for a moment, then went on to say, 'These connections were important. I heard them not only through my uncle repeating what McCurdy had told him but also later on from McCurdy himself'.)

McCurdy said from 1850 to 1855, when he was in his teens and early twenties, he and Burke had been in a team of drovers which regularly brought cattle down from the high country to the market at Albury. The third member of the team, and the head drover, was a slightly older man, Matt Hesse from Queensland.

The licensee of the largest hotel in Albury, the Grand Hotel, was Mary Brines' father, Jim Brines. Mary was a few years younger than McCurdy, a very pretty girl and a very smart one too. By the time she was in her early teens she was doing all the book keeping and running the office of the hotel. Her mother had died when Mary was born. Her father was ambitious for his pretty daughter, he frequently told her that with her beautiful face and good figure she would be able to marry a very rich husband.

McCurdy said he never was a heavy drinker and while his two mates were spending time in Brines' bar he and Mary went for walks, despite opposition from her father – Mary was very strong-willed. Mary's and McCurdy's favourite walk was on the western edge of the town near a wooden church with a small cottage attached. The buildings belonged to the Californian Evangelical Church whose pastor was the Reverend Hugh Jamieson. The bogus wedding which the two conspirators called a 'secret' wedding, doubtless on the grounds that the bride and groom would want to hide it from Mary's father, was, according to the copy of the wedding certificate, performed in the Californian Evangelical Church by Pastor Jamieson on 6th June 1855. After the two lovers (which McCurdy admitted they were at the time) helped Jamieson recover his mare called Mary which had one day escaped from the home paddock, Jamieson always joked with them when he met them in the town or near the church that he had promised McCurdy to help him recover his (McCurdy's) Mary if she ever escaped. McCurdy said he mentioned this horse incident as he thought it might be useful in identifying him and Mary when the clergyman was questioned about the bogus wedding.

In October 1855 McCurdy and Burke decided to give up droving and look for gold. Two years later they found considerable alluvial gold, including small nuggets, along the bank of a creek. When the alluvial gold ran out they sank a shaft near the creek's source and discovered a reef with a seam of gold running through it.

The capital they had obtained from the alluvial gold enabled them to have a company, Hillside Limited, in which each of them held 26 per cent of the shares, floated in London to mine the reef.

Once the mine was in production Burke spent practically all his time in Melbourne 'living it up' on the huge income he was getting. McCurdy continued to live close to the mine and in daily touch with the manager, accountant etc. and also with a team he had set up to systematically explore some adjoining leases the company held.

After five years it was clear that the reef on which the company was working would cut out in a year or so. When told of the situation by McCurdy, Burke suggested that, while the price was high, they sell their shares on the London market by a rather shady method he had devised. McCurdy did not agree, partly because when the reef ran out a short time afterwards, both their reputations would be destroyed among the mining fraternity, investors and the community generally, but also because he had a hunch, and at that time it was no more than a hunch, that they would find another reef. Burke had no faith in McCurdy's hunch and wanted a lot of money quickly. After several discussions McCurdy agreed to buy Burke's batch of shares at the London market price.

Nine months later a new reef was found; then only four months after that an even richer second reef. The price of Hillside shares rocketed. Burke asked McCurdy to let him buy back the 26 per cent of the shares he previously owned for the price at which he had sold them. McCurdy did not agree. Burke took the refusal very badly and spread a story in Melbourne that McCurdy had cheated him out of his holding in Hillside.

While prospecting, McCurdy had kept in touch with Mary by letter. Eighteen months after they started corresponding she wrote to him from Melbourne saying she had a job in the Capital Hotel and that she had left Albury because she was fed up with being ordered about by her father and wanted to live in a big city. A few months later McCurdy went down to Melbourne and spent two days at the Capital Hotel. Mary was the book keeper but also worked part-time in other departments. She said that the hotel was ill-managed and it seemed to him that it was. During the establishment of Hillside Limited and after the large mining operations commenced, McCurdy was in Melbourne from time to time and always stayed at the Capital Hotel because he enjoyed Mary's company and it was convenient. About two years after she was first employed at the hotel, Mary became the manager and under her management the hotel improved considerably.

McCurdy said he had proposed to Mary Brines in May 1855. By then he had saved a bit of money and had his eye on a 400 acre block in the lovely high country where he could breed horses for stock work – he was

291

fond of horses and had a lot of experience working with them, breaking them in and training them. He told Mary he would be able to build a small house on the block. But Mary said she was not going to rough it with any man anywhere. She wanted to live in a big city in a large house with servants to do the hard work. It was soon after Mary refused to marry him that he had gone off to search for gold, hoping to find a lot and get Mary to change her mind.

As the manager of a middle-of-the-road hotel, Mary met men from a wide range of social positions and her beauty attracted many of them. She enjoyed having a lot of men admiring and entertaining her. When she had first mentioned her activities with other men, McCurdy said he had become jealous and for a second time had proposed marriage but Mary had only laughed. As the years went by McCurdy became less jealous of Mary's 'other men'. He continued to find her physically very attractive and usually good company but began to have reservations about her character. She seemed selfish and, from remarks she made about men and women with whom she came in contact, spiteful. One night, after he had lost interest in having her as his wife, Mary mentioned the proposals he had made and said now they were both older and knew one another better she would marry him if he asked her again. He suspected that her willingness to marry him had been greatly influenced by learning that he was a very rich man. An article in a daily paper a few weeks earlier had referred to his huge holding of Hillside shares and to the investments he had made in other companies and property.

McCurdy said Mary's proposal had brought the relationship between them to a rather unpleasant end and before very long he had become aware that she was saying nasty things about him to her friends and acquaintances. Meanwhile Burke had continued to tell everyone who would listen that he had been cheated out of his shares in Hillside. McCurdy had considered suing Burke for defamation but had decided it was not worthwhile and, except for refuting it when his attention was drawn to the untruth, had ignored it.

After the break with Mary, McCurdy said he had become increasingly fed up with his life in Victoria and finally had decided to leave the colony, devote much less of his time to investing his large income and try to live a more interesting life somewhere in England.

Having explained to my uncle his involvement with Pat Burke and Mary Brines prior to their calling upon him at The Pillars, McCurdy had gone on to say that both of them were vindictive and if not successful in getting money from him were likely to pursue their false claim with the object of wrecking his life. But even if they did not do that he wanted them charged with blackmail. He was not going to leave any rumour that he was a bigamist unanswered. He said it should be possible to prove that the marriage had not taken place and that the document they had produced was false.

McCurdy agreed to my uncle's proposal that he (my uncle) would return to London immediately, engage the services of a solicitor specialising in criminal cases and also a barrister specialising in that field, and that he bring the solicitor back with him in a few days time.

Burke lost no time in taking action against McCurdy. Only an hour or so after he left The Pillars he sent a note to Sir Henry Harrison saying that he had evidence that McCurdy had married Mary Brines while in Australia and that he and McCurdy's legitimate wife would like to speak to him.

Harrison saw them the next day and flew into action. He took the two into Nottingham and got one of his magisterial colleagues to listen to their story and look at the alleged certificate of marriage – the original being produced on that occasion. Urged on by Sir Henry, the magistrate had a constable go out to The Pillars the next morning and bring McCurdy into the court house. There he was brought before the magistrate on a charge of bigamy. The magistrate ordered that he stand trial at the next assize due in a fortnight's time, not leave Great Britain and be released on bail of one thousand pounds.

News of the charge brought against McCurdy spread like wild fire through the district. An urgent telegram from McCurdy brought my uncle back from London together with the specialist solicitor. After several days of communication with London authorities they had the trial postponed until an assize six months later on the grounds that any earlier trial would not enable the defence case to be prepared. But my uncle said getting the trial delayed had been very difficult.

It was after the arrangement for the later trial had been made that my uncle asked me if I would go out to the colonies to get the evidence needed to disprove the claim put forward by Burke and Brines.

I readily agreed and my uncle took me down to The Pillars to discuss the matter with McCurdy.

At The Pillars McCurdy described his connections with Burke and Brines and my uncle referred to some inquiries he had made in London.

My uncle had gone to the Registry of Births, Deaths and Marriages to ascertain what was known there about the recording of these events in the colonies. He was told that a central registry had been established quite early in Victoria (largely because a man with considerable experience in that type of work in England had gone to the colony as a prisoner) but that central registry was not established in New South Wales until 1856. Records of the earlier marriages in New South Wales were understood to be still kept in the 'authorised place' (usually a church) where the marriage took place.

With McCurdy's permission my uncle had taken a photocopy of the marriage certificate and some of McCurdy's signatures to a writing expert. The expert had said that the signature on the certificate was a good imitation of McCurdy's signature and any attempt to refute the certificate on the basis of the signature was not likely to succeed.

McCurdy and my uncle agreed that when I reached the colonies I should go first to Albury, look at the records in the Californian Evangelical Church and if there was no record of the marriage between McCurdy and Brines on 6th June 1855, get a statutory declaration signed by the clergyman of the church to that effect. If Jamieson was still the clergyman I should ask him to make a statutory declaration that he knew both McCurdy and Brines and had never been the celebrant for a marriage between them.

I should contact Matt Hesse, who was shown on the certificate as one of the two witnesses, the other being Burke, and ask him to make a statutory declaration that he had never been a witness to a marriage between McCurdy and Brines.

When those two tasks were completed I should go to Sydney and get a statutory declaration from the New South Wales Registrar of Births, Deaths and Marriages that the record of every marriage in New South Wales before 1856 was kept in the authorised place where the ceremony was performed.

The tasks seemed to me to be straight forward and I did not expect any difficulties.

I stayed for one night at The Pillars. Despite the great strain which the charge of bigamy must have imposed on them, both McCurdy and his wife remained sociable and cheerful throughout my stay. I left determined to do everything I possibly could to get the evidence needed for McCurdy's defence.

I sailed from London a week after my night at The Pillars and eight weeks and two days later arrived in Albury. There I suffered a great set back.

The Californian Evangelical Church had been burnt down in March 1862 and all the records lost in the fire. Jamieson had left Albury soon after the fire and had never returned.

The blow was softened a little for me by the attitude of the Albury people. Dressed in the attire normally worn by an English gentleman visiting the countryside, I was very conspicuous. The local people, in what I was soon to find was the unreserved manner of most colonials of all classes, asked me what I was doing in Albury and when told, many tried to help me. Several who had known both the Brines and McCurdy recalled seeing Mary and McCurdy together. None had heard of their marriage. A woman who claimed to have been a close friend said Mary had told her 'in confidence' of McCurdy's proposal in May 1855 and she thought any wedding would have been secret because Mary was under twenty-one and Mary's father would have opposed the marriage. If there had been a secret marriage it would most likely have been performed in the Californian Evangelical Church because that church was not fussed about marrying girls under twenty-one without the written permission of their father and also because the leading members of the church were teetotallers and not likely to be in contact with Mary's father.

The Mayor of the town and the main stock and station agent in the district, Mark Stubbs, said that he remembered Matt Hesse quite well and knew he had left the district, but as he had lived on a property in the high country, someone up there was sure to know where he had gone. To my amazement Stubbs offered to take a few days off and drive me up to the high country in his gig. He told me to bring 'my swag' as the trip would take several days.

On the way up to the high country we spent a night at a sheep station. The owner lent Stubbs a horse for the second stage of the journey so that Stubbs' horse could rest. It was an example of the helpfulness and comradeship which I found was common amongst certain classes of people in the colonies.

We spent two days in the high country. Hesse had lived in a stockman's hut on a property owned by a man named Law who told me Hesse had returned to Queensland. Law said a cousin of his was married to Ted Dickie who had a property in the Maranoa River area for which Hesse was heading and that he would write to Dickie saying that I would be up there shortly trying to get hold of Hesse.

Armed with that information I returned to Albury with Stubbs.

It was to Sydney I went next. There I learned, from clergymen of other denominations, that the Californian Evangelical Church no longer had any pastors in the colonies and that Jamieson had returned to the headquarters of his church in San Francisco soon after the buildings in Albury were burnt down.

I went to the Registrar of Births, Deaths and Marriages and got a statutory declaration signed by the Deputy Registrar confirming that the record of every marriage performed before 1856 was retained in the authorised place (usually a church) where the ceremony had been performed.

While in Sydney I also tried to find Mary's father, Jim Brines, as I had been told in Albury that he had gone to Sydney when his lease of the Grand Hotel ran out, but I had no success.

Getting to the Maranoa River area and in contact with Ted Dickie took a week.

Ted Dickie and his wife Win had a son James, a little older than me, and a daughter Jane, a little younger. The whole family treated me as one of them. They lent me riding gear and clothes suitable for the climate; they taught me local customs and teased me about my accent and my somewhat formal manners. Ted and I made a number of trips in search of Hesse. We visited several properties and were made welcome at all of them. On one trip Ted and I took a pack horse and camped out – a wonderful experience.

Ted brushed aside my concern about the amount of his time being taken up with my affairs and said he was enjoying the search and was full of sympathy for the McCurdy couple.

Eventually we found a brother of Matt Hesse, Tom Hesse, a blacksmith in a small town about a hundred miles from the Dickie's property.

Matt Hesse occasionally wrote to his brother and in a letter Tom had received about a year before Dickie and I found him, Matt had said he was about to set off as head drover on the longest cattle drive ever undertaken – from a property in the centre of Queensland right across the north of the continent to land near the Western Australian coast. He expected it would take three or four years and the owner of the cattle, who was going with them, expected to move the cattle around after they got to the west to find the best piece of land on which to settle. Consequently, Matt said, it would be a number of years before he would be in touch with Tom again.

Tom was surprised that we had not heard of Matt's great undertaking. He said 'It was in all the papers' and promptly produced several cuttings sent to him by relatives and friends. I noticed one of the papers was published in Melbourne so I had no doubt that Burke and Brines were well aware that Matt Hesse would be uncontactable for several years.

The months I had spent in Queensland had not provided any information helpful to McCurdy. Perhaps I had stayed there too long. But the people I had met had been so charming and so helpful, the weather so lovely, the countryside so unusual and so open and Ted Dickie so eager to show me special features of the natural environment and also of the work carried out on various cattle stations to improve their output, that I had not made any attempt to press on with the search for Hesse at a fast pace.

By the time I got back to Sydney there was just over two months left before the assize would be sitting in Nottingham. I immediately got a berth on a ship sailing for San Francisco a few days later.

The way of life, the weather, the feeling of freedom and space and the relaxed friendliness of the people in the colonies had made a great impression on me. I was determined to come back.

During the journey to San Francisco I thought about the progress I had made (or not made) towards the success of my undertaking.

The situation I had found in the colonies obviously had not been anticipated by McCurdy or my uncle; they certainly had not expected that all the records held in the church in Albury would have been destroyed, that Hesse would be uncontactable for several years or that Jamieson would have left the country and his present whereabouts be unknown. With this state of affairs there was no chance of getting any evidence in the colonies which would cast doubt upon the genuineness of the marriage certificate produced by Burke and Brines. I was sure that the conspirators had been well aware of the situation in the colonies when they embarked on their conspiracy. What they could not have anticipated was that I would go to the colonies, not a hired enquiry agent who probably would have returned to England when he found no evidence was available in the colonies. I had not taken a contract to do a specific job, was free to go where I liked, had plenty of money of my own and no ties requiring my presence in England. Consequently I considered I should be able to find Jamieson wherever he might be, remind him of McCurdy and Mary Brines through recalling the 'horse called Mary incident', and get him to make a statutory declaration that he had never married McCurdy and Brines.

I travelled across the Pacific Ocean – which lived up to its name throughout the voyage – confident that during the next stage of my undertaking I would get the evidence needed to help McCurdy.

The day after I arrived in San Francisco I went to the headquarters of the Californian Evangelical Church. There I got the shocking news that Jamieson had died three years earlier. I was told that soon after he returned from Australia he had been sent with a young clergyman named Simpson to establish a branch of the church in Bermuda. After six years on the island he died and was buried in Hamilton, the capital of Bermuda. I sat for a while quite stunned in front of my informant, an elderly clergyman, then asked, – I don't know why – 'What did he die of?'

'Pneumonia, if you want to know more about his death perhaps you might like to write to Simpson; he was with him when he died. I will give you Simpson's address'.

I left the headquarters clutching a piece of paper containing Simpson's address in Bermuda. A bit of information of no use whatsoever to McCurdy. I had ended up after nearly five months of searching and travelling three quarters of the way around the world with not a skerrick of information which would cast doubt upon the veracity of the marriage certificate produced by Burke and Brines and having no prospect of getting any information. I was very depressed.

I went across the United States by train; not as I had expected when I planned the journey – enjoying the wonderful opportunity of seeing a lot of the great continent – but endlessly going over what I had done and conjuring up things that I might have done. How could I go back to England and tell McCurdy, Mrs McCurdy and my uncle, all of whom seemed to have had so much faith in me, that I had achieved nothing.

In New York I spent the first eight days just wandering around the city and visiting the offices of various shipping companies asking about berths on ships going to England and when offered a berth saying, 'I will think it over and come back'. I kept putting off taking the final step which would commit me to returning to England empty handed. On the ninth day I was offered a berth on a ship sailing a week later to Liverpool via Bermuda. I took it although the clerk pointed out that the ship was a freighter with accommodation for only four passengers and consequently I would not have much company, the passage would be slow and the scheduled time of arrival in Liverpool only approximate. The clerk also said, in response to my question, that the ship was expected to remain in Hamilton for about two days but the actual time would depend on the cargo available.

I realised that going to England via Bermuda made no sense. How could talking to Simpson be of any help? Nor was I likely to learn anything useful by looking at Jamieson's grave. I was not grasping at straws, there were clearly no straws around to grasp; I was only delaying as much as I could my arrival in England where I would have to face the McCurdys and my uncle.

The lovely scenery as we came around Spanish Point into the big well-protected bay and moved up to the wharf at Hamilton did not relieve my despondency. After lunch I went ashore, found the Californian Evangelical Church and in an office there, the Reverend Arthur Simpson. When I told him I was interested in Jamieson I found he was an admirer of Jamieson and quite eager to talk about him. What he said did not provide me with any useful information; boiled down it was that Jamieson had come from a family prominent in the Presbyterian Church in Scotland, his grandfather, father and elder brother had all been or were Presbyterian clergymen. Although Jamieson was of a religious turn of mind, he disliked Presbyterianism, fell out with his father and at the age of eighteen migrated to the USA. Within a few years he had become a clergyman in the Californian Evangelical Church. Simpson said if I would like to see Jamieson's grave he would be very happy to take me out to the cemetery on the following morning. I had nothing else to do so I accepted his offer.

We drove to the cemetery in Simpson's trap. Jamieson's grave had on it a gravestone similar in shape and inscription to a great many headstones in a great many cemeteries around the world. Looking at it did not lessen my despondency. As we were returning to Hamilton through North Village, Simpson asked me if I would like to come to his house which was alongside the church, meet his wife and have a cup of coffee. I accepted his invitation. Anything that might for a short time divert my mind from its endless deploring of my failure was welcome.

Jamieson, who had been a bachelor, had lived with Simpson and his wife and both of them seemed to have been fond of him. To my disappointment the conversation over the coffee did nothing to divert my mind, it centred on Jamieson. But after a while a remark by Mrs Simpson caught my attention. Mrs Simpson said never mind what time Jamieson finished his day's work he meticulously wrote up his diary before he went to bed. I asked what had become of it. Simpson said that at the end of each year Jamieson had shipped off to his brother in Scotland all the diary books. There was a number of them because Jamieson covered what he had done each day in great detail. Simpson believed Jamieson's main purpose was to inform his brother of everything he was doing and how he was doing it.

In response to questions from me, Simpson said he did not know when Jamieson had started keeping the diary but he thought it likely that he would have recorded every wedding he had celebrated after he had become a diarist.

At this point I told the Simpsons the purpose of my journey. They became so interested in my story that they insisted I stay to lunch. I left the Simpson's home with the address of the Reverend Hamish Jamieson and with my outlook brightened by the possibility that the diary could provide the information needed to clear McCurdy of the charge of bigamy. But it could only do that if Hamish Jamieson had kept his brother's voluminous diary intact and Hugh Jamieson had started his daily record of events before June 1855, had clearly been in the habit of recording every marriage he celebrated – which it might be difficult to establish to the satisfaction of a judge and jury – and had not recorded a marriage between McCurdy and Mary Brines on 6th June 1855.

I went immediately to the Hamilton Post Office to send a cable to my uncle telling him about the diary and giving him the address of the Reverend Hamish Jamieson, but the clerk in the post office told me that Bermuda was not connected to the trans-Atlantic telegraph cable. Nothing could be done to try and locate the diary until I reached Liverpool. The time of the ship's arrival there now became very important.

The ship remained in Hamilton three days instead of the two originally scheduled and then was further delayed by bad weather. It did not arrive in Liverpool until the afternoon before the sitting of the assize in Nottingham. I raced ashore and sent a telegram to my uncle care of The Pillars telling him about the diary and that I intended to go to Edinburgh as quickly as I could.

I arrived in Edinburgh early the next morning and, very anxious and excited, got a cab from the station to the Reverend Hamish Jamieson's house.

The servant who answered to door bell said that the Reverend Jamieson was busy and I should come back in the following week, or, if the matter was urgent, see the minister in the next parish whose name and address she would give me. I explained that it was not as a minister but as the brother of the late Hugh Jamieson that I wanted to see the Reverend Jamieson and that the matter was very, very urgent. After talking to her for a few more minutes, getting nowhere and becoming increasingly concerned, I pushed my way into the house. The poor, frightened servant girl ran off leaving me in the hall.

The Reverend Hamish Jamieson came into the hall obviously (and I suppose rightly) very annoyed. When he realised that he was unable to get rid of me he listened to what I had to say. After I had explained my problem he explained his – he was the chairman of an assembly or conference of the Presbyterian Church which was running right through the week and he had no time to attend to anything else. But he took me into his study, said he had given all the diary books to Professor Fordyce at the Edinburgh University to assist in some research work, immediately wrote a note to the professor asking him to let me look at the diary and hustled me out of the house.

I got back into the cab and ordered the driver to go as fast as possible to the university. Although feeling a little relieved now, I knew that the diary had not been lost or destroyed. I was very anxious to find out quickly whether its contents would help McCurdy; I had to get a message to my uncle before the trial finished.

When I got to the university I found that Professor Fordyce was in London. His research assistant was located and he said he would take me to the diary. It was a long walk. On the way there the assistant removed one of the uncertainties about the diary's usefulness; he told me it had been commenced in 1850. With that uncertainty removed, I realised that I had reached the critical point of my six months journey. Excited and worried, I wondered whether it would be possible to establish that the marriage certificate was a fraud just by reading the diary.

As the books were in good condition and kept in chronological order, it did not take me long to find Jamieson's record of the events on 6th June 1855. There was no wedding between McCurdy and Brines or anybody else. Jamieson had spent the day visiting the families of two parishioners living on properties some distance from Albury. He had left his home at 9.30 am and had not returned until 8 pm.

It was a wonderful discovery for me and, of course, for the McCurdys.

After explaining to the research assistant why it was essential that I take the book containing the record of events on 6th June 1855 with me to the Nottingham Court House, I got his reluctant agreement. He would not let me take more than the one book.

I would have liked either the Reverend Hamish Jamieson or the Professor to have accompanied me to Nottingham to help establish the genuineness of the diary. But that was obviously not possible.

I only had time to send a brief telegram to my uncle saying that the diary clearly showed that the marriage certificate was a false document, before I caught the train to Nottingham.

Sitting in the train I felt both elated and exhausted as the events of the last six months floated in and out of my mind. It was hard to believe that I had travelled so far, seen so many places, met so many people and been so confident, enlightened, happy, shattered, despondent, hopeful, anxious, determined, aggressive, excited, worried and jubilant in so short a time.

Oh! what a warm welcome I got when I arrived at the Court House just after 5 pm. The jury was out. The McCurdys, the defence lawyers and my uncle had all been dismayed by the judge's summing up in which he had dismissed my telegrams, saying they should not be regarded as evidence.

After they had both looked through a substantial part of the diary book, the barrister and solicitor for the defence asked to see the judge in his chambers and when he agreed they took me with them.

The judge first looked at the diary for a few minutes then he said, 'Anyone could have written this, what evidence is there that it's authentic?'

I was called upon to explain what I had learned in Bermuda and Edinburgh about Hugh Jamieson's diary but, before I started, McCurdy's barrister suggested to the judge that the barrister for the prosecution be asked to come in.

He was asked and did come. So I was able to tell both the barristers and the judge everything I had learned on my journey relevant to the trial.

When I was about half way through, a member of the court's staff came in and said the jury had reached a verdict. The judge told him that the jury were to remain in the jury room until he sent for them.

When I had finished and answered some questions the judge told me to leave and I returned to my uncle and the McCurdys who were waiting anxiously in the foyer.

About then minutes later the defence barrister and solicitor came up to us looking extremely pleased and said the trial had been aborted and the jury discharged but a new trial would commence a week later. At that trial both the Reverend Hamish Jamieson and Professor Fordyce would be required to give evidence.

A few days after the first trial had been aborted it became common knowledge that the verdict the jury reached was 'guilty'. Hearing that added to the anxiety of the McCurdys while they waited for the retrial. On the day of the retrial, however, Burke and Brines did not appear at the Court House. It was postponed for five days, the police being instructed to search for the two witnesses for the prosecution. When they could not be found a warrant was issued for their arrest on charges of perjury and blackmail. At the same time the charge of bigamy against McCurdy was officially dropped.

Burke and Brines were never found.

•

On the last full day of my journey home as the train crept past the pitheads of several mines and made its way slowly into the station at Kalgoorlie, Smith said good-bye and wished me success in my naval career. Then, after smiling in his very pleasant way, he added, 'I have something in common with the namesake of yours that lived in Notts; I own a large part of a gold mine'.

THE CANNIBAL IN THE FAMILY

Both my mother and father grew up in Southampton but Dad did not hit it off very well with Mother's family and that, I believe, was the main reason why they migrated to Australia soon after their marriage. Because of the strained relationship I knew very little about Mother's two brothers until the elder, Tom, suddenly appeared in 1925 at our house in the Melbourne suburb of Westgarth. Mother said it was very good of Uncle Tom to come all the way from Geelong – where his ship was berthed for just two days – to find us in Westgarth.

Dad, a commercial traveller, was on one of his long trips and Mother was busy with housework and looking after Lucy who was ill, so loquacious Uncle Tom spent most of his time talking to me. I was sixteen and quite eager to hear what the big, bearded captain of a merchant ship had to say about where he had been and the adventures he had had. However it was not his own experiences that left a lasting impression on me but what he told me about those of his young brother, my Uncle Eustace. Some of the stories he told were so astounding that I interrupted him to question their veracity. Our conversation, when he began to talk about Uncle Eustace, went something like this:

'Do you, like most men with the Burn's blood in them, want to go to sea and become a ship's officer?'

'No! I couldn't climb up masts and such like things. I'm afraid of heights'.

'You must be like Eustace. He has always been afraid of heights. Perhaps you'll follow in his footsteps and become a priest, a missionary and a cannibal'.

'You're kidding! He can't be a cannibal!'

'He is, he told me so himself'.

'When was that?'

'When we met in Port Moresby in 1909, my ship *Minerva* put into the Port only to discharge a few crates of cargo from London. As I was leaving the shipping agent's office, to my great surprise, I bumped into Eustace hurrying past. He was in Port Moresby for an important discussion with the Papuan Mission's Vicar-General. We hadn't seen one another for twelve years so had a lot of news to exchange but, because of our urgent engagements, little time to talk. Just as we were about to part I asked him how he got into the missionary business. He said, in his usual cheerful way, that he became both a missionary and a cannibal by accident.

'There was no time for to hear more but I am sure Eustace meant what he said, though I doubt whether either of his achievements occurred by accident because I found out a year later that he did not become a missionary by accident but as a result of an amazing skill he developed. He could send a mug of beer along a bar counter with just the right amount of spin to stop the beer overflowing and just the right amount of forward motion to stop the mug right in front of the customer who had ordered it'.

'You're having me on! How could such a skill make him a missionary?'

'I'm not having you on and if you'll listen I'll tell you. In 1910 the *Minerva* had a major engine problem which held her in Port Adelaide for three weeks. To fill in the time I decided to learn what I could about Eustace's activities in South Australia. Mother (your Grandmother) had mentioned in a letter that another young priest, Will Ransome, had travelled out to South Australia in 1898 with Eustace but whereas Eustace wanted to go into the wild bush country to preach, Ransome wanted to stay in Adelaide.

'I found Ransome, who in 1910 was the curate of a parish in the city, very willing to talk about Eustace. He said that shortly after arriving in Adelaide they were both taken for an interview with the Bishop. The Bishop told them that they must always wear a clean, well-starched clerical collar. The sight of a clerical collar, his lordship said, subdued even the most ill-behaved colonials and made even the most ungodly of them consider their future and their need for salvation. So emphatic was the Bishop that Ransome and Eustace, the next day, spent money they could ill afford on the purchase of extra clerical collars. A clerical collar, or the absence of one, Ransome said, played an important part in Eustace's career.

'Ransome introduced me to two of his parishioners who in 1898 had been living in Oodnadatta (then a newly-established rail head town about 600 miles north of Adelaide) to which Eustace was sent soon after his interview with the Bishop. What those two men and Ransome told me gave me quite a good understanding of Eustace's work as a soul-saver in South Australia.

'I was told that Oodnadatta was established by the South Australian Government to enable cattle from a huge area of grazing land – northern South Australia, southern Northern Territory and south-western Queensland

– to be entrained for transport to the Adelaide cattle market. The cattle were brought to holding paddocks around the town by teams of drovers. There were only a few permanent residents in Oodnadatta but large numbers of drovers constantly came into it for just one day with pay in their pockets and a vehement desire for beer. It was the bars that kept the two hotels in the town profitable but they were both required by law to have considerable accommodation for overnight customers – most of which was never used. The existence of this unused sleeping space had an important effect on Eustace's activities in Oodnadatta.

'When Eustace (well-equipped with clerical collars) arrived in Oodnadatta he asked the station master where he could get accommodation and the Railway Hotel was recommended.

'Apparently, at first, Eustace regarded the hotel as only a temporary abode but the proprietor and his wife (Bill and Dot Kerr) were so kind to him he established himself there permanently. The Kerrs provided him free of charge with two rooms (one of which, near a side entrance to the hotel, he used as an office), they charged only a small amount for his meals and laundry and Dot ensured that his clerical collars were always beautifully starched.

'Every Sunday Eustace held, in the school, a service which was attended by the few parishioners living in Oodnadatta. He was not an evangelist and he did not interrupt the nomadic drovers' beer drinking with proclamations of the gospel. Having time on his hands and few calls on his stipend he was able to frequently hire a horse and buggy and pay overnight visits to, and hold services at, many cattle properties in the Oodnadatta area.

'All went well for two years. Then Dot became seriously ill and Bill had to take her down to Adelaide. Before they left Oodnadatta he promised not to leave her side until she had regained good health. Bill considered that the only person he could trust to run the hotel in his absence was Eustace and Eustace felt morally bound to accept that responsibility. All Bill's capital was tied up in the hotel and he would need to have the income from it sent to him regularly to pay for the couple's living expenses in Adelaide and Dot's medical expenses.

'As the bar trade was the life blood of the hotel and Bill was the barman, it was essential that Eustace took on that job himself. But though he quickly learned the technique of serving the beer he could not match Bill's hearty handling of the customers.

'Having the Bishop's instruction firmly in his mind, Eustace wore a clerical collar while serving in the bar. Although he was, as usual, quietly cheerful, the clerical collar, the Church's symbolic reminder of how rigorous was the journey to salvation constantly caught the eye of the customers and damped their spirits. As word spread amongst the droving teams that a parson wearing a clerical collar was now the barman at the Railway Hotel, all the drovers took their custom to the Dominion Hotel. Before long the few commercial travellers who from time to time had stayed in the Railway Hotel followed the drovers to the Dominion to ensure that they had some company while drinking. Nobody now came to the Railway Hotel.

'With no money coming in Eustace could not pay the cook or the laundress and they left. Besides Eustace the only person in the hotel was Nellie a half-caste girl who worked there as a maid and had nowhere else to go.

'Eustace, who had stopped hiring a horse and buggy to visit cattle properties, sent off to Bill all of his stipend except that needed to buy food for Nellie and himself. But that money did not meet the Kerr's financial requirements and both Bill and Eustace were filled with anxiety.

'Every day except Sunday Eustace opened the bar and spent nearly all his time there feeling very inadequate but practising serving by sending mugs of water along the bar counter. Thus he gradually developed the extraordinary skill I have mentioned.

'About five months after the Kerrs left Oodnadatta a large droving team brought to the town a very big mob of cattle from north-west Queensland. No cattle had been bought to the South Australian rail head from that area before and the drovers were strangers to the town. To quench their thirst they went to the Railway Hotel. There they found a red-headed young man wearing a collarless shirt – Nellie could not starch his collars – who served beer in a way that none of them had ever seen before. They mentioned the barman's extraordinary skill to other drovers. Very surprised at what they heard, those drovers went to the Railway Hotel. The news spread like wildfire and Eustace had to telegraph for much larger supplies of beer.

'Even after Eustace engaged a laundress he did not wear a clerical collar or a coat in the bar. His earlier experience had convinced him that wearing clerical garb would depress the customers and send them away to another drinking place. The only priestly work he did was conduct a service and an occasional baptism on Sundays – the small congregation understood the need for Eustace to spend most of his time running the hotel and did not complain.

'However Eustace's mainly secular life was rudely interrupted when the Bishop's right hand man, the Archdeacon, arrived unexpectedly in Oodnadatta. This small, but rather bumptious prelate, was told by a member of the railway station staff where he would find the Reverend Eustace Burn. When the Archdeacon finally located Eustace in the crowded bar wearing no coat and a collarless shirt, serving beer to loudmouthed, blasphemous colonials who addressed the priest as 'Bluey', he ordered Eustace to return to Adelaide on the train that night. Eustace refused. The Archdeacon then said he would return to Adelaide himself that night and recommend to the Bishop that Eustace be unfrocked.

'Eustace sent an urgent message to Bill explaining the crisis which had arisen. Fortunately Dot's health had improved and Bill, after getting somebody to look after her, hurried back to Oodnadatta.

'When Eustace arrived in Adelaide he was taken to see the Bishop. His lordship gave Eustace a dressing down and told him the only way he could remain a priest was to go to Brisbane and become a member of the Papuan Missionary Service under the direction of the Bishop of Brisbane'.

•

Uncle Tom stopped speaking, looked at his watch and, as he jumped up, exclaimed 'Good God! I've got to get back to my ship'.

After taking hurried leave of us all he went off at a fast pace in the direction of the railway station.

His sudden departure left me disappointed, I still didn't know how on earth Uncle Eustace became a cannibal.

It was not until twenty-one years later, in 1946, when I went to England to attend an international conference, that I found out.

There was very little communication between the Burn part of the family and mine but I had heard that Uncle Eustace, during the 1930s, had become Master of the Newcastle-on-Tyne Charter House, a home for twelve Christian old men, established in the sixteenth century by a bequest from a prominent citizen. I wrote to Uncle and our correspondence led to my going to Newcastle for a week-end in October 1946.

The taxi from the Newcastle station put me down alongside a solid, wooden door in a high, thick, brick wall. On passing through I found myself in a large overgrown garden beyond which were the ruins of a substantial building. Half way between the door in the wall and the bombed-out building, a chimney topped with a Chinaman's hat rose about four feet out of the ground; smoke from it was drifting slowly towards me. The smoking chimney enabled me to find the entrance to the air raid shelter where my Uncle was living. It looked comfortable, with sleeping, working and living areas; a trek to the bombed house had to be made for major ablutions – a toilet and bathroom had survived the bombing.

Uncle Eustace did not look at all like his brother, he was of average height with a slight stoop, had reddish hair, thin on top and greying near the ears, his face was plain but surprisingly free of wrinkles for a man of seventy and his dark brown eyes sparkled when he smiled. His smile charmed me, and I noticed later seemed to charm everybody.

When I had settled in and we were drinking the first of Uncle's many brews of tea (made from what looked like tea dust and powdered milk and said by Uncle to be very good for the kidneys) we talked for a while about recent events in our own lives and those of our nearest kin but before long I got him to talk about his eleven years as a missionary in Papua. With considerable encouragement from me he continued to reminisce about those eleven years for a large part of the time I was with him. On the way back to London I jotted down a few notes. With the help of those notes I will try to give some impression of my Uncle's life as a missionary and an indication of what a patient, considerate and quietly humorous cannibal he was.

Uncle said that the Church of England established several missionary parishes in the north-east of Papua in the late 19th century but within a few years had difficulty in getting priests to serve there because that part of the country was very unhealthy for Europeans. Some of the first batch of priests died and others returned home shattered in health. As a stop gap South Sea Islanders (Kanakas), previously employed as cane cutters in Queensland, were sent to some parishes as Christian teachers and lay preachers.

When he reached Brisbane it was made clear to Uncle Eustace (not by the Bishop but by others with some knowledge of Papua) that the parish to which he was going to be sent had a most unhealthy climate and the greatest likelihood of inter-tribal fighting and cannibalism. These disabilities Uncle willingly accepted. However he was alarmed when just before he left Brisbane he was told that he would be responsible for a boarding school at the parish headquarters which had as pupils about thirty Papuan boys aged between six and fifteen. Having to supervise the teaching, clothing, feeding and caring for thirty wild, rowdy boys without specialised help – matron, housekeeper, laundress etc. – normally provided in a boarding school, remained a nagging worry to him throughout his long journey from Brisbane via Port Moresby (where he received instruction in the local language) to the parish headquarters near a village named Futin.

The day after he arrived at his headquarters Uncle went to look at Futin and was delighted with the appearance of the village with its quaint timber and bark houses scattered along a winding street on the edge of a tropical forest. However, he told me that he soon found visiting parishioners in those quaint houses was much less pleasurable than had been visits to parishioners in England and Oodnadatta. Every house in Futin was built on a wooden platform about seven or eight feet above the ground. The platform extended beyond the house and was reached by a steep ladder made of rough timber. The rungs in many of the ladders were unevenly spaced, notchy, very narrow or not horizontal. All members of a Papuan family were well acquainted with the peculiarities of the ladder giving access to their own home and even the very young and old went up and down without difficulty. But Uncle, who said he was an inept climber, nearly fell on several occasions when, high above the ground, he was trying to find and put his foot firmly on, one of the troublesome rungs. Also each time he managed to climb a ladder and enter a house he faced another problem. Every house consisted of only one room and for light and warmth (and the Papuans liked to be very warm) a fire was kept burning when any of the family were at home. There was no chimney and most of the smoke did not escape through the hole in the roof. Uncle was not used to a very smoky environment and his throat and mouth became very dry and his eyes sore and full of water. 'Not a physical condition conducive to cheerful social intercourse', my Uncle said.

About three weeks after he arrived at his Mission Headquarters Uncle went into Futin for the first time in the morning and found that only the older women – busy making cooking pots out of clay and cloth out of bark – were there. When told that the rest of the villagers were working in the gardens and shown a path leading to the gardens, Uncle decided to go and see how the villagers set about producing their ample supply of fruit and vegetables. However, before he had gone very far he met the villagers returning and was disturbed to see that, while each woman was staggering along carrying on her back a large string bag containing fruit and vegetables

311

and on top of it a big bundle of firewood, her husband was walking in front of her carrying only a native tomahawk. Uncle considered this was grossly unfair to the women but refrained from protesting because, he said, he quickly realized that it was the custom of the country and a native woman would no more want her husband to carry the food and wood than a woman in England would want her husband to wheel their child in a pram or hang out their washing on a clothes line.

Uncle had not been very long at his Mission Headquarters before he discovered a way of keeping in contact with each family in Futin without going into any of their houses. Every day towards dusk each family lit a fire in the street or under the house if it was raining and the women cooked the main meal of the day in large earthen pots. After the meal the members of the family remained together for a while around the fire chatting. Then the adults went up and down the street visiting neighbours while the children played. On two evenings every week (except when he was away visiting other parts of his parish) Uncle went into the village and joined one of the families in its after dinner chat.

Uncle said he was impressed with the cheerful, unhurried way both men and women went about their affairs throughout the day and the comfortable life – a good house and sufficient food and clothing for everyone – which their work produced. Breaks in the normal daily routine occurred on special occasions – weddings and similar celebrations – when everybody let off steam and danced and sang through most of the day and night.

Uncle surprised me by saying that when he arrived in Papua the villagers living on the coastal plain had enjoyed their easy-going, peaceful life for only about twelve years – since the colonial governments (first Queensland and then Australian) had put an end to the traditional inter-tribal fighting and cannibalism. Prior to the colonial governments establishing their control, the villages were fortresses, bare of trees and surrounded by high stockades with the only entrances through very low, narrow holes protected by heavy wooden doors. The villagers in those days were ever on the alert, in fear of their lives and could only work in their gardens protected by armed guards.

While he was in Papua, Uncle said, inter-tribal fighting still occurred in the mountainous areas and that a village called Kimba in his parish, which was at the foot of the mountains, was stockaded and its inhabitants lived in constant fear of raids from the wild tribesmen living in the mountains.

There were six South Sea Island teachers-cum lay preachers in Uncle's parish. After he had carefully checked the activities of the six he came to the conclusion that, although they were all earnest, well-intentioned men, five of them were severely handicapped by being practically illiterate. When he learned that the only schooling they had received was a few years at a church-run Kanaka night school – after working hard all day on Queensland sugar farms – he was not surprised. The sixth South Sea Islander (Jimmy) had spent several years at a primary school and could read and write quite well. He had only one important eccentricity. The proud owner of several guns, he spent most of his salary on ammunition and regularly fired his guns in the middle of the night to chase away evil spirits. Uncle found that Jimmy's gun firing was very popular with the inhabitants of the village in which he taught and preached. The Papuans apparently considered that it was more likely than his Sunday sermons to help them have a life free of malediction both before and after death.

However Jimmy's gun firing was not so highly regarded by my Uncle, especially as many evil spirits seemed to hang around when Uncle visited the village and, consequently, his sleep was constantly disturbed by Jimmy's efforts to chase them away.

The boarding school, the existence of which had worried Uncle Eustace, was next to his own house. Boys wanting to attend the school presented themselves at the age of five or six to Mark, the South Sea Island teacher and, as far as Uncle could ascertain, everyone was accepted even if mentally deficient. The boys left when they decided they had had enough schooling, usually between twelve and fifteen years of age.

The boys' house was a very large version of a typical village house. Around three walls of its very large room were two rows of broad shelves one above the other. These were the beds where the boys slept on native mats and kept their cooking pots and personal belongings. There was one door opening onto the platform. In common with the local custom the boys had a fire burning through the night. Twice during Uncle's first year in the mission the house was burnt down. The boys and the villagers were not unduly alarmed by the fires – a house burning down in the middle of the night was not uncommon and a new one was always constructed very quickly – but Uncle was alarmed, After bringing a lot of pressure to bear on the diocese headquarters he procured a blanket for each boy and a hurricane lamp as a night light and made the boys extinguish their fire before they went to bed.

The boys looked after their own clothing, hygiene, welfare and meals – two boys at a time, in rotation, preparing and cooking the meals. To Uncle's surprise (because the women always made the family meals) even the youngest school boys were competent cooks of a Papuan dinner. (However, despite detailed instructions from my Uncle, none of the boys working in his house could produce a drinkable cup of tea.)

Assisted by a missionary nurse, Ida Clark, who visited Futin for about a week every month, Uncle looked after the boys' (and also the villagers') illnesses and cuts and bruises at his 'first aid centre'.

The school day began when Mark knocked noisily on the door of the boys' home and shouted 'Gedd up' a number of times. There was never any response to that first summons or to several that followed. In between his spells of banging and shouting Mark stood looking towards the sea and puffing out smoke from his pipe. This sequence of events continued for about quarter of an hour. Then suddenly the door opened and the boys dragged themselves out onto the platform.

From sunrise until eight o'clock the boys worked in the mission area tending the gardens and repairing fencing and buildings. Between eight and nine they cleaned up their house, washed in the river, had breakfast and then talked or ran around outside their house.

At about nine o'clock each morning Mark stood at the school house door shouting repeatedly, 'Come 'ere!' Slowly, two or three at a time, the boys went into the school. But a small number always ignored the calls. After a while Mark would seize a stick and chase them. The rather corpulent Mark was no match for the boys who ran, turned, twisted and dodged behind trees until Mark gave up the chase, threw away his stick and then the runners and Mark went into the school.

School finished about mid-day, the boys had lunch, played games of their own devising, attended a short church service and then had their main meal. After the meal they talked either on their platform or around their fire before turning in.

Not long after he came to his mission parish Uncle sat at the back of the classroom while Mark was giving a lesson. The boys were being instructed in English, Pidgin-English and the local language. Mark had a beautiful, strong singing voice and whenever he was at a loss with a lesson he began a song in which the boys joined. Uncle was displeased to find that from time to time the boys talked to each other during the lesson. Uncle decided to help Mark stop this by showing him an example of what could be done.

At the end of the last lesson that day Uncle told Mark and the boys to remain in the classroom and he went through the Ten Commandments with them. As he had anticipated some of the boys talked and prominent among them was Winki, the oldest and biggest boy in the school. Uncle told them they could not expect to learn if they talked; they must give all their attention to the teacher. To impress that point, they were not to have free time that afternoon but were to move some large logs lying untidily in front of their house to the back of it. He called Winki to the front of the class and told him he would have to organise the work and make sure it was done properly.

While reading in his study in the afternoon Uncle heard the boys start the log shifting job. Soon they began to sing. The tune of the song was one he had heard sung in the village but the words seemed to be English. He went out onto the verandah to hear more clearly and watch the boys at work.

He found that a team would pick up a log and as soon as they started to walk with it, sing:

The priest he say
Somebody talkin'
Somebody talkin'
The priest he say
Somebody talkin'
Winki talkin'
Come 'ere.

The last line was sung very loudly and as it rang out all the boys jumped aside and the log fell onto the ground.

Winki was sitting with his back to the working party smoking a native pipe.

Uncle who smoked a pipe most of the time while I was with him, said that everyone in 'his' village (except the very small children) smoked, so did everyone in other villages in which mission staff lived. This 'harmless recreation' was encouraged by the church who always paid the villagers with tobacco for the food, materials, labour and other services they supplied – no money was used.

315

To smoke the tobacco the Papuans wrapped a small quantity in a leaf (or if it was available a bit of newspaper) and pushed it into a hollow piece of bamboo. Native pipes thus constructed were often passed around amongst a group of adults or children.

In a moment of generosity the diocese headquarters gave each of the villages a bell to summon the people to religious services. Uncle found these gifts were a mixed blessing. He mentioned his experience when, shortly after the bells were delivered, he went to the village in which Allen, a South Sea Islander, taught during the week and conducted a religious service on Sundays.

After breakfast on Sunday Uncle asked Allen when the church service would commence and was told ten o'clock. He then set off along the street to talk to the villagers. About nine thirty two vigorous young men, taking turns, began to ring the bell which was hung next to the school house where the religious service would be held. The bell ringers did not regard the bell as a musical instrument but as a means of creating an ear-piercing, clangorous sound. So great and incessant was the noise that Uncle had to give up talking and just walk up and down the street. At ten o'clock there was no sign of the church service starting. Uncle stopped at Allen's house where the teacher-cum-lay preacher was out on the platform enjoying a smoke with several of his Papuan friends. As Uncle told it, the conversation between him and Allen went something like this (with both men shouting above the noise of the bell):

Uncle: 'What time we have service?'

Allen (after some thought): 'Service by and by'.

Uncle: 'You said service at ten'.

Allen: 'Sometimes people come ten o'clock, sometimes they no come early'.

Uncle: 'Service just by and by?'

Allen (again after some thought): 'Service eleven o'clock'.

Uncle (hopefully): 'Bell stop ringing for a while?'

Allen (very brightly): 'No, bell ring all time'.

The last statement was greeted with much head nodding approval by Allen's Papuan friends.

Uncle resumed his walking up and down the village street.

•

Uncle told me that after he had been in the parish for about a year he had concluded that the affinity which obviously existed between the South Sea Islanders and the Papuans (which he did not want to disturb) was due, at least in part, to the South Sea Islanders' eccentric (by European standards) behaviour. That behaviour, Uncle said, appealed to the Papuans because they had a rather child-like approach to all matters not connected with their basic requirements for a comfortable life.

Having come to the conclusion that the South Sea Islanders' eccentricities helped rather than hindered the work of the mission, Uncle made no attempt to change the conduct of his aides.

A part of his life in Papua of which Uncle appeared to be justifiably proud was the good health he maintained for eleven years while a great many of his colleagues and other Europeans in the country had died or become seriously ill. He put down his success to rigidly sticking to a medical routine which protected him from malaria and to taking regular exercise in the form of a long walk every day on the beach near the village. When she was in Futin, he said, Ida Clark joined him in the beach walks.

With the mention of Ida Clark as a walking companion Uncle's tone became less matter-of-fact and he seemed to very fondly recall the pleasure he and Ida had got from watching the changes in the sky and the sea (which, he said, happened more frequently in the tropics than elsewhere), the enthusiasm with which they had discussed a wide range of mission and other matters and the wonderful feeling of freedom for a short time from their mission responsibilities that they had felt as they gleefully chased crabs, sea hoppers and other creatures living between the low and high water marks.

But after this brief reference to Ida he immediately reverted to his matter-of-fact tone to tell me about the difficulties of travelling within his parish and of communicating with people outside it. However, his short lapse into an affectionate recall left me curious to know how close was the relationship between he and Ida. (It was something that I found out when I met Uncle for a second time a few weeks later.)

Towards the end of my second day in Newcastle I mentioned that Uncle Tom had said he (Eustace) was a cannibal. Uncle laughed, then, after saying 'I won't deny it', went on to talk about cannibalism in Papua and his experience with it.

Uncle said the Papuans had plenty of fruit and vegetables but animal flesh was scarce – so much so that they ate any dog or pig that died and continued that custom after Uncle had explained the risk to their own health. All the older people in the parish had undoubtedly eaten human flesh. Some talked about it, saying that human flesh, which tasted like pig but had the advantage of not causing sickness which pig sometimes did, was the best meat.

It was in the village of Kimba that Uncle said he had become involved in cannibalism. Near the end of his first year in Papua the District Officer sent a message that there had been some fighting near Kimba and that he was going up to the village with a troop of armed police to 'sort out the problem'. He suggested that, as the village was in Uncle's parish, he might like to accompany him. Uncle, who had not been there, readily agreed. When they reached the village they were told that the inhabitants had been attacked in their gardens by wild men from up in the mountains. The 'wild men' had killed four of the villagers and carried away their bodies.

The District Officer went off with his policemen to find the culprits. Uncle remained in Kimba where he was made welcome by the villagers. He could not speak the local language but two men in the village spoke a little Duri – the *lingua franca* of that part of Papua.

A week later the District Officer and the police returned having found that the wild men had come from over the German New Guinea border and were therefore beyond the reach of the Papuan police force. Uncle went back to his parish headquarters with the District Officer.

Getting to Kimba was very difficult but Uncle did not want the parishioners living there to lose contact with the Mission and so ten months after his first visit he returned taking with him a Papuan young man who had graduated from the boarding school a few years earlier. Feeling very tired and hungry after five days of strenuous walking, they reached Kimba at dusk to find a great feast, interposed with singing and dancing, in full swing. When cordially invited, they joined in the feast and the celebrations but often during the night-long festivities dozed off. It wasn't until the next day that Uncle discovered what was being celebrated. Apparently two scouts from the village had seen a party of the wild men coming down from the mountains intent on attacking the villagers. The Kimba warriors had ambushed the wild men and killed three of them before the raiding party managed to break away and flee. The bodies of the three wild men were taken back to the village and they had formed part of the feast.

•

Before I left Newcastle Uncle and I arranged that Uncle would go to London a fortnight later and we would have lunch together.

When the day came, Uncle arrived at Church House (where the conference I was attending was being held) just before one o'clock and we immediately set off to find a restaurant. As Uncle said he knew the area well I asked him to decide where we should eat. It was a task he carried out very thoroughly, reading the menu exhibited outside and then going into each restaurant. At last he chose a small place called The Great Peter Restaurant. The two waitresses in the restaurant were obviously twins – both short, plump, dark-haired girls with the lovely pink cheeks and creamy skins commonly seen on English country girls.

When, after we sat down, I asked Uncle why he had chosen that restaurant, he said that the waitresses in The Great Peter looked more healthy and homely than those in the other restaurants. In London in 1946 very severe food rationing was in force and consequently Uncle's method was as good as any for the selection of a place to eat since the variety and quantity of food available in every restaurant and hotel was much the same.

Uncle's remarks about the waitresses led me to ask him whether there were any schools for girls in his parish.

He said there was a day school for girls at Futin when he arrived there and the teacher was a handsome South Sea Islander in his early thirties named Tommy. Fewer girls than boys offered themselves as pupils – probably because girls were required by their families to help in household duties and in the gardens. Whilst the girls were usually more diligent scholars than most of the boys, Uncle said their association with male teachers sometimes caused problems. He gave an example.

Tommy kept a fire burning in his house throughout the day and night and all the girls, except one, vied for Tommy's attention by collecting and delivering to him loads of firewood. The exception, a girl named Adin, during the last few years of her schooling frequently stayed behind when the classes ended and to talk to Tommy about the lessons. In Papua marriages were arranged by the parents of the boy and the girl and took place when the girl was thirteen or fourteen. At the age of fourteen Adin was married to a boy a few years older. Two years after the marriage Adin's husband died. Widows could choose any single man they fancied as a potential second husband. To indicate her choice the widow went to the man's home and

319

prepared a meal for him outside it. If the man ate the meal they became man and wife.

Adin, with her cooking pots and utensils, turned up outside Tommy's house and prepared a meal for him. Tommy fled and took refuge in Uncle's house. It soon became evident that everyone in the village was in favour of a marriage between Adin and Tommy and several showed their support by accompanying Adin each evening when she went to Tommy's house to cook a meal for him. Tommy moved most of his gear into Uncle's house and slept there every night.

Uncle found Tommy was a noisy sleeper, he both snored and talked in his sleep and these noises kept Uncle (a light sleeper) awake for most of the night. He therefore strongly supported Tommy's request to be transferred to another parish well away from Adin. The Vicar-General agreed to the transfer and Uncle was pleased when Tommy was replaced with a corpulent middle-aged, plain-looking South Sea Islander named Percy.

However Uncle became concerned when, a few months later, one of the girls made a habit of staying behind after the lessons to talk to Percy. She persisted with that practice until she was married at the age of fourteen to a young Papuan. Uncle kept a close watch on the health of the young man but had no cause for alarm; the young man remained in good shape throughout the rest of Uncle's time in Papua.

Before the lunch ended I asked Uncle whether he had kept in touch with Ida Clark after he left Papua. His reply saddened me. Ida and he had become engaged to be married in June 1910 but eight months later, while working in a village in another parish, she contracted fever and died within forty-eight hours.

After the lunch I walked with Uncle to the bus stop in Victoria Street. I had noticed that when we were looking for a place to eat Uncle smiled in his charming but unostentatious way at people we passed in the street and at members of the staff and customers near us in each restaurant we entered. His smile brought a pleasant smile to the face of everyone at whom he looked. When we were walking to the bus stop Uncle again smiled at the passers by and he got in return a pleasant smile even from the most sombre looking pedestrians.

When the bus came Uncle got a window seat and he waved to me as the bus drove off. That was the last I saw of him. He died suddenly soon after I returned to Australia.

www.ingramcontent.com/pod-product-compliance
Lightning Source LLC
Chambersburg PA
CBHW031105030726
47496CB00002BA/385